Titles by Gary Birken, M.D.

ERROR IN JUDGEMENT

FINAL DIAGNOSIS

PLAGUE

EMBOLUS

CODE 15

Morgan tried to calm the man. "I understand how upset you must be, but I promise you, your sons received expert medical care."

"My sons are dead, Dr. Connolly." Kaine's stony glare never shifted from Morgan's eyes. She didn't feel physically threatened, but his intimidating demeanor made her uneasy. It was obvious her words were falling on deaf ears.

Kaine dropped his hands to his sides. His voice never became louder but its added intensity left no possibility of misinterpretation. "I don't believe you did everything possible. Absent your excuses, the obvious conclusion is that you failed to save the lives of two healthy boys."

Without waiting for a response, Kaine walked past Morgan. When he got to the doorway he stopped. "If you think this is over, you're sadly mistaken. You have no idea who you're dealing with, and if I have anything to say about things, you and this hospital are going down."

CODE
15

GARY BIRKEN, M.D.

THE BERKLEY PUBLISHING GROUP
Published by the Penguin Group
Penguin Group (USA) Inc.
375 Hudson Street, New York, New York 10014, USA
Penguin Group (Canada), 90 Eglinton Avenue East, Suite 700, Toronto, Ontario M4P 2Y3, Canada
(a division of Pearson Penguin Canada Inc.)
Penguin Books Ltd., 80 Strand, London WC2R 0RL, England
Penguin Group Ireland, 25 St. Stephen's Green, Dublin 2, Ireland (a division of Penguin Books Ltd.)
Penguin Group (Australia), 250 Camberwell Road, Camberwell, Victoria 3124, Australia
(a division of Pearson Australia Group Pty. Ltd.)
Penguin Books India Pvt. Ltd., 11 Community Centre, Panchsheel Park, New Delhi—110 017, India
Penguin Group (NZ), 67 Apollo Drive, Rosedale, North Shore 0632, New Zealand
(a division of Pearson New Zealand Ltd.)
Penguin Books (South Africa) (Pty.) Ltd., 24 Sturdee Avenue, Rosebank, Johannesburg 2196,
South Africa

Penguin Books Ltd., Registered Offices: 80 Strand, London WC2R 0RL, England

This is a work of fiction. Names, characters, places, and incidents either are the product of the author's imagination or are used fictitiously, and any resemblance to actual persons, living or dead, business establishments, events, or locales is entirely coincidental. The publisher does not have any control over and does not assume any responsibility for author or third-party websites or their content.

CODE 15

A Jove Book / published by arrangement with the author

PRINTING HISTORY
Jove mass-market edition / December 2009

Copyright © 2009 by Gary Birken, M.D.
Cover design by MNStudios.
Interior text design by Kristin del Rosario.

ISBN: 978-0-515-14720-9

JOVE®
Jove Books are published by The Berkley Publishing Group,
a division of Penguin Group (USA) Inc.,
375 Hudson Street, New York, New York 10014.
JOVE® is a registered trademark of Penguin Group (USA) Inc.
The "J" design is a trademark of Penguin Group (USA) Inc.

PRINTED IN THE UNITED STATES OF AMERICA

10 9 8 7 6 5 4 3 2 1

To my parents

To err is human, to cover up is unforgivable, and to fail to learn is inexcusable.

SIR LIAM DONALDSON,
SPEAKING AT THE LAUNCH OF THE
WORLD ALLIANCE FOR PATIENT SAFETY IN
WASHINGTON, DC,
ON OCTOBER 27, 2004

DADE PRESBYTERIAN HOSPITAL

TO: All Officers, Department Chiefs, Chief Nursing
Officer.

FROM: Robert Allenby, C.E.O.

SUBJECT: CODE 15s

Listed below is a partial list of the types of
medical errors and adverse patient outcomes,
termed CODE 15s, which must be reported to the
state of Florida's Agency for Health Care Administration (AHCA) within fifteen days of their occurrence. Please be advised that *all* medical mistakes
that result in patient injury must be reported to
this office.

- Death
- Wrong surgical procedure
- Spinal damage
- Brain damage
- Surgery performed on the wrong patient
- Surgery performed on the wrong site/side
- Procedures to remove foreign objects remaining
  from surgical procedures
- Surgical repair of injuries or damage from a
  planned procedure
- Significant medication errors
- Failure to diagnose a life-threatening illness/
  injury

PART ONE

CHAPTER

1

DADE PRESBYTERIAN HOSPITAL
NORTH MIAMI, FLORIDA
MARCH 3, 2007

The port wine–colored rash that shrouded Andy Kaine's body was an undeniable omen of his impending death. Clad in a sterile green gown and wearing a protective plastic face mask, Dr. Morgan Connolly, chief of Emergency Medicine, moved to the head of the stretcher. She motioned to the paramedic who had just transported the critically ill young man to the hospital.

"What's the story on this kid?" she asked above the cacophony of numerous high-pitched alarms.

"He's a freshman at Florida International University. His girlfriend found him in his dorm room about forty-five minutes ago. He was completely unresponsive."

"What were his vital signs coming in?" Morgan asked.

"We had a lot of trouble getting a blood pressure. Maybe it was forty."

"What about a pulse?"

He shook his head. "We never felt one."

"When did you start CPR?"

"In his room. We also intubated him," he said, pointing to the plastic tube that they had placed through Andy's mouth and down into his windpipe.

Taking particular note of his ashen color and vaporous eyes, Morgan turned to Pam Devlin, the charge nurse. "His blood pressure's not registering on the monitor. See if you can get one manually."

"I just did," Pam answered. "It's thirty over zero."

From her new vantage point, Morgan studied the amorphous, punched-out lesions on Andy's torso. They each wept a blood-tinged straw-colored fluid and, as a group, seemed to be multiplying in front of her eyes. Morgan was quite familiar with the highly contagious strain of meningitis. It was one of the few diseases that instantly filled her with an all-encompassing feeling of doom and helplessness. Morgan took a step back.

Even though she knew a full-blown code blue was almost certainly an exercise in futility, she felt she had no choice.

"We're going to give this a shot. Continue the chest compressions." She then pointed to a plastic IV bag suspended from a metal pole. "Open up that saline all the way. Somebody get me a full loading dose of penicillin."

"He's crashing," Pam said, pointing at the flashing red display on the blood oxygen monitor that was in a freefall. "I can't get a blood pressure."

The respiratory therapist, who was standing next to Morgan, continued to squeeze the breathing bag. "I'm not getting much air in. His lungs must be filled with fluid."

Morgan eyes bolted to the cardiac monitor. It showed flatline. "Keep up the chest compressions and give him an amp of epinephrine."

"Giving it now," one of the other nurses answered as she injected the medication into Andy's IV.

"He's not responding," Morgan yelled. "Give him another amp."

"Going in now," the same nurse answered.

For the next half hour Morgan and the code blue team did everything possible to bring Andy back to life. But his face remained the color of chalk, and his eyes fell deeper into his skull, leaving his pupils widely dilated and hollow.

Finally, Morgan stepped back from the stretcher. The words of her mentor and professor of emergency medicine echoed in her mind with the same sobering effect as they had fourteen years ago when she was an intern: Any physician worth their salt will learn to recognize the difference between a resuscitation and a resurrection.

Morgan pulled off her gloves and noted the time.

"We're done here," she announced in a monotone. "Make the time of death ten past nine."

Morgan stepped away from the bedside and pulled off her sterile gown and mask. She tried, but she couldn't shift her eyes from Andy's lifeless face. Over the past ten years she had seen death come in many forms. But the loss of Andy Kaine and what was soon to follow would remain rooted in her memory for many years to come.

In a hush that inevitably follows the unexpected death of a young, healthy person, the nurses and other health-care providers steadily made their way out of the room.

Morgan stayed for a time, eventually finding a seat on a scuffed-up plastic chair. The fact that Andy's fate was almost surely sealed before the ambulance ever arrived was of little consolation.

Pam pulled up another chair and sat down beside her. "His girlfriend told the paramedics he was fine this morning. She saw him in the library studying for a marine biology exam."

"Dr. Connolly," came a hesitant voice from the doorway. "I know this is a lousy time but North Miami Rescue's on the phone. They're on scene of a bad car accident and want to speak with you stat about two injured kids."

Morgan filled her lungs and then let the breath slowly escape.

"What now?" she muttered before turning around and heading out of the room. When she reached the nursing station, the unit secretary handed her the red phone, which was used exclusively to communicate with the paramedics in the field.

"This is Dr. Connolly."

"This is North Miami Rescue, Doctor. We're on scene of a motor vehicle accident. We have two pediatric patients who were unrestrained backseat passengers. Their vehicle was broadsided on the driver's side. It took us twenty minutes to extricate them. We have them on backboards and would like to transport them to your facility."

"What are their vital signs?"

"Pulse and blood pressure both within normal limits."

"What's their neurological status?"

"The younger one's a little groggy. The older one seems okay. They're both able to respond to my questions."

"What are their ages?"

"Nine and seven."

"Are they having any trouble breathing?" she asked.

"Negative, but the nine-year-old is complaining of some chest pain."

"Anything else?"

"The seven-year-old is a little pale."

"Can you identify any major injuries?" she asked.

"Not at this time."

Knowing that paramedics tend to overreact when assessing injured children, Morgan said, "Both victims have normal vital signs and are breathing without difficulty. Is that correct?"

"That's affirmative."

"And both are alert and responding to your questions?" she asked.

"Yes, but we'd like to save some time by transporting them to Dade Presbyterian. We're less than ten minutes from your facility."

"Negative. We are not a state-designated pediatric trauma center. Both of your patients are stable. Transport them directly to Ryder Trauma Center per Dade County protocol."

"Will do. Thank you, Dr. Connolly."

Morgan replaced the phone and pushed back in her chair. She was just about to dictate a note documenting the events of Andy Kaine's death when Pam approached.

"You're not going to believe this," she said in a hurried voice. "The paramedics are bringing in Andy Kaine's roommate. He's already got the rash."

"How bad is he?"

"They said he's still breathing on his own but his vital signs were borderline."

"What's their ETA?"

"About five minutes."

"Are the parents here yet?"

"Patient Relations said that the mother is in the Far East on business. I'll check with them to see if the father got here yet."

"Let's use the trauma room," Morgan suggested.

"It's already set up." Pam turned and started to walk away. After a few steps, she stopped and turned around. "There's something else you should know. This kid's not just Andy Kaine's roommate. He's his brother."

Well aware of what she would soon be faced with, Morgan came to her feet. Fearing the worst, but seeking no explanations for the injustice or making any pleas for divine intervention, she simply walked toward the trauma room, ready to do her job.

CHAPTER

3

Waiting for any news regarding the condition of his sons, Mason Kaine, a muscular man with a jutting forehead that overhung narrowly spaced eyes, paced in front of the registration desk.

His apprehension mounting, he finally decided to find a seat among the countless others waiting restlessly for either medical attention or some news of their loved ones. Loosening his tie, he wondered why the hospital felt compelled to keep the emergency room's waiting room so oppressively hot. Normally he wasn't particularly sensitive to temperature, but the heat mingling with the foul scent of illness left his stomach in turmoil.

Ten minutes passed. His patience exhausted, he stood up and walked over to the same desk that he had already visited twice. He waited for the triage nurse, a frazzled-looking woman with washed-out and thinning silvery hair, to look up and acknowledge his presence.

"Excuse me," he began in a measured voice, trying to put aside the irritation on her face, "I'm still waiting for information regarding my sons."

"As I told you before, Dr. Connolly is very busy. She'll be out to speak to you as soon as she can. Now, if you'll just have a seat." Without waiting for a response, the nurse looked back down at the chart that she had been working on.

Kaine looked down at his watch. "But you told me that the doctor would be out to see me at least—"

She raised her eyes slowly. Stopping after every word, she said, "It's been a very busy night. We're asking all family members to bear with us and be as patient as possible." He watched as she craned her neck to see past him. He didn't have to turn around to know there was somebody behind him. The nurse, now wearing a scripted smile, said, "Dr. Connolly will be out as soon as she gets a free minute."

Before stepping aside, he looked over his shoulder. A pregnant woman seated in a wheelchair covered her abdomen with both hands. She tried, but the pain in her eyes was impossible for her to conceal. Begrudgingly, he moved aside. Seeing no other alternative, he returned to the long row of attached plastic chairs, sat down and placed his forearms flush on the armrests. He sighed in a way that betrayed his irritation. In addition to the dozens of people waiting to be seen, there were at least ten stretchers pushed against the wall holding patients who by all appearances had been abandoned. Directly across from him, a young mother with a fretful face pushed a blood-soaked hand towel against her screaming toddler's forehead. Next to her, a man with pasty skin wearing a tattered white T-shirt hacked uncontrollably.

A civil, spit-and-polish man by nature, Kaine was not one to become easily unglued. Looking around at the despair and hopelessness that surrounded him evoked little, if any, sympathy. He had always believed that when mankind crawled out of the caves, they were equal. What happened after that depended solely on the individual's skill and determination. Society was neither responsible nor made any guarantees. Compassion for the great unwashed, as he liked to call the less fortunate, was not an emotion he possessed.

Seeking any form of distraction, he turned and looked up at the fuzzy picture displayed on an undersized, wall-mounted television. After a minute or so he gazed back in the direction of the registration desk. He saw a young Asian man wearing green scrubs whispering to the nurse. When the man strolled back into the triage area, the nurse stood up and walked over.

"If you'll follow me to the consultation room, the doctor will be right out to see you."

Kaine stood up in silence. He followed directly behind the nurse, who escorted him to the small consultation room. The converted office was bare-walled and adorned only with a potted plant, a small upholstered couch and a wooden end table.

"Just have a seat," she suggested. "It shouldn't be too long."

The nurse then stepped outside. He watched her walk back to the registration area where she motioned to a woman in a thigh-length white coat with a stethoscope draped around her neck. When the woman approached the information desk, the nurse pointed in his direction. He was too far away to read her identification badge but he assumed it was Dr. Connolly.

She started toward him. He studied her carefully through the open door as she crossed the waiting area. It wasn't until she stood in the doorway that he could see the unmistakable look of doom in her eyes.

"Mr. Kaine, my name is Dr. Connolly." Morgan noticed the skin covering his forehead roll into fine parallel troughs.

"How are my sons doing?"

Morgan took a few steps closer before continuing, "Jason and Andy arrived about forty-five minutes apart. They were both suffering from advanced meningitis. Their vital signs were critically unstable." Kaine said nothing. He folded his arms and took a broad-based stance squarely in front of Morgan. She could feel his slate gray eyes transfixed on her like a powerful beacon. "The infection was far advanced and overwhelming. We began full cardiopulmonary resuscitation immediately. Unfortunately we were unable to—"

"Cardiopulmonary resuscitation? Excuse me, Doctor. Are you trying to tell me both my sons died?"

With no intention of doing so, Morgan averted her eyes for an instant. "I'm . . . I'm afraid so. I'm very sorry, Mr. Kaine. We did everything possible, but we were too late. Perhaps if they had gotten here sooner, we—"

"I'm confused, Dr. Connolly. When Andrew and Jason arrived in the emergency room, were they or were they not alive?" Morgan was instantly taken back by the lack of shock or disbelief in his voice.

"They were alive, but as I said they were in profound and irreversible septic shock."

"I understand, but I thought meningitis is curable with antibiotics."

"In most cases it is. But sometimes the disease has progressed too far and there's simply nothing we—"

"Did my sons receive antibiotics?"

"Of course," she answered.

"Were you aware that both Andrew and Jason received the meningitis vaccine?"

"I wasn't, but the present vaccine doesn't cover every possible strain of bacteria that can cause meningitis," she explained.

"And you're quite certain you gave every medication possible to reverse the shock?"

Morgan was accustomed to denial in family members who had lost a loved one, but Mason Kaine's behavior took on an odd and inappropriate note of resentment and antagonism she had never seen before.

"I assure you, Mr. Kaine. We—"

"My sons were perfect specimens. They were accomplished athletes. Neither of them was ever sick for more than a day or two in their entire lives. Now you tell me they're dead? With all due respect, Doctor, this makes no sense."

"Mr. Kaine, we're familiar with treating meningitis. Most of the time we're successful, but from time to time we run into a strain that . . ."

Kaine shook his head. His businesslike expression never changed. "I don't believe you," he announced one word at a time.

"I beg your pardon," she said with total exasperation.

"I'm an educated man, Doctor. My sons were alive when they arrived in your emergency room. With expert medical attention, they should have survived. I don't believe you're being truthful with me."

"I'm not sure I understand the implication of what you're saying, Mr. Kaine."

"There is no implication. I'm saying categorically that with proper medical care Jason and Andy should have survived."

He pressed his palms together, pulling his fingertips to his chin and then sending them out again until he was pointing directly at Morgan. "I'm saying you screwed up."

"With all due respect, I'm not sure you have the medical expertise or . . ." Morgan stopped in mid-sentence and said nothing further.

Kaine said, "I'm well aware that fatal hospital errors are an epidemic in this country."

Morgan took a few seconds to regroup. She quickly decided the last thing she was going to do was dignify his preposterous accusations by denying them or enter into a debate on medical mistakes.

"I understand how upset you must be, but I promise you, your sons received expert medical care."

"My sons are dead, Dr. Connolly, so I guess we'll never know the answer to that question." Kaine's stony glare never shifted from Morgan's eyes. She didn't feel physically threatened, but his intimidating demeanor made her uneasy. It was obvious her words were falling on deaf ears. Kaine dropped his hands to his sides. His voice never became louder but its added intensity left no possibility of misinterpretation. "I don't believe you did everything possible. Absent your excuses, the obvious conclusion is that you failed to save the lives of two healthy boys." Without waiting for a response, Kaine walked past Morgan. When he got to the doorway he stopped. "If you think this is over, you're sadly mistaken. You have no idea who you're dealing with, and if I have anything to say about things, you and this hospital are going down."

Morgan had the presence of mind to realize that it would be an exercise in futility to say anything further. Maintaining her silence, she watched Kaine thunder out of the emergency room. Finding herself somewhere between rattled and appalled, she fell into a small love seat. In view of Mr. Kaine's behavior, she had only one option available to her. She would report the matter to Arlen McMinn, the administrator on call. She had known Arlen long enough to know that his response would be to give Mr. Kaine some time to cool off and let Patient Relations handle the problem.

Trying her best not to think any further about Mason Kaine, Morgan closed her eyes and let her head fall back against the cushion.

"We need you in one right now, Dr. Connolly," came a harried voice from the doorway. Morgan started to her feet even before her eyes snapped open.

"What do we have?" she asked the nurse.

"A forty-year-old guy with severe chest pain and hypotension. We've called a cardiac alert."

Her mind darting off in a new direction, Morgan grabbed her stethoscope from around her neck and followed the nurse back into the main treatment area.

CHAPTER

5

FOURTEEN MONTHS LATER

Having just spent the last two hours organizing her lecture on patient safety for the residents teaching conference, Morgan Connolly strolled across the lobby of Dade Presbyterian Hospital.

Attractive in an exceptional way, Morgan's delicate facial bones, long, burnt reddish hair, and placid hazel eyes combined to bestow a classic beauty upon her. Waiting in front of the elevators, she fell victim to her incurable impatience and tapped the up button for the third time. Just as she did, a man with a stethoscope hanging around his neck walked up.

"Good morning, Dr. Connolly," he said.

Morgan turned and smiled politely at the gangly man, who, even though he stooped, towered over her.

"Dr. Hawkins. It's nice to see you again. How's retired life?"

"Well, I'd like to think of it as semiretired life. But even so, if I had any sense, I'd just quit completely and never set foot in this hospital again."

Morgan laughed, got up on her tiptoes, and then kissed him flush on his pointed cheekbone.

"A little work is good for your brain, Daddy," she said, looking into his warm eyes. "It'll keep the cobwebs to a minimum. There's just so much *Judge Judy* one man can watch."

"I thought I raised you not to be so judgmental," he said.

"You preaching to me about being judgmental is a little like Fagin expounding on the evils of pickpocketing." The elevator door opened and they both stepped on. "What are you doing in the hospital? I thought you only worked on Tuesdays and Thursdays."

"I heard you were giving today's teaching conference. I thought I'd attend. What's the topic?"

"Patient safety."

He sighed. "Let me guess. You're going to talk about avoidable patient errors."

"I'm the chairperson of the Patient Safety Committee, Daddy. What should I be talking about?"

"I know it's a timely and sexy topic, but remember what Groucho Marx said about his cigar."

"I'm not sure cigars and sick people in hospitals dying unnecessarily are analogous."

"I just think physicians are getting tired of hearing about medical mistakes."

"That's too bad, because there were ninety-eight thousand patient deaths in this country last year from preventable medical errors. I'm sorry our medical staff considers that boring. Physician arrogance and ambivalence continues to contribute to medical mishaps. If we don't change the culture of—"

He cleared his throat as if he were battling diphtheria and then tapped on his watch crystal. "There must be something wrong with my Timex. I thought your lecture didn't start for another ten minutes."

She grinned and shook her head. Ever since she was a teenager, he had been doing the same thing to her whenever she climbed onto a soapbox.

"What are your plans for the rest of the morning?" she asked him.

"I thought I'd go home and take a long nap."

"Sounds great," she said, patting him on the shoulder. "It will be good practice for the nursing home. Did you know that it's actually possible to get old without getting older?" she added, refusing to indulge his melancholy and mostly theatrical moods of late.

"The rumor mill says you're being considered for the Executive Committee."

"I thought you were no longer interested in hospital politics."

"I'm not, but I am interested in the professional accomplishments of my daughter."

"The answer to your question is yes, but it's not a big deal."

"Don't be so modest," he said, putting his arm around her shoulder. "You're making your old man proud. You seem to be the only one in the family making a difference around here anymore."

"Daddy, you're still a great orthopedic surgeon and the best chief of staff this hospital ever had."

"I appreciate the unbiased praise but that's all in the past." The doors opened on the seventh floor and they walked off in the direction of the conference center. "Are you still flying?" he asked.

"Every chance I get."

"Tell me at least you quit the aerobatic stuff."

"I've given it up temporarily."

With a curmudgeon's scowl he asked, "Why would a bright, educated, and sensible girl such as yourself want to turn tiny airplanes upside down?"

"Because I love it, and I need something more in my life besides this place."

"I thought that's why you got married."

She wagged her finger at him. "Daddy, we're not doing this now."

"Can't I even ask how you and Kevin are doing?"

"We're still separated and I'm not very hopeful things will work out. Okay?"

"I knew this would happen."

Smiling inwardly, she said, "It's probably because we didn't have that big church wedding you wanted."

"I simply don't understand why you two don't—"

Morgan put her hand to her father's lips. "You're not listening. We're not having this conversation now. One way or the other, Kevin and I will sort this out. We're both adults."

"I would say one of you is an adult. The other's a hormonal adolescent trapped in the body of a grown man." His brow creased as he added, "I always felt he intimidated you."

"I grew up with two older brothers who didn't exactly pamper me. I also survived a father who kept me on the tennis court until dark five nights a week, hoping to turn out the next Chris Evert."

"What's your point?" he inquired.

"Men don't intimidate me."

They strolled up to the entrance of the conference center. Before going in, Morgan turned and began straightening her father's bow tie.

"When are you going to snap out of this self-imposed funk?" she asked him. "Don't you think you've milked it for long enough?"

"Maybe if your mother were still with us, things would be better."

Morgan chuckled. "It's not as if Mom died or abandoned us, Daddy. You left her for your scrub nurse."

"That was a mistake that I now fully admit to."

"I'm sure you do, but it's a little late for that now. We all tried to warn you, but you wouldn't listen. You had already decided Amber was the answer to all your problems."

"She was a great nurse and for someone of her age, she had expansive knowledge."

"The only thing expansive about Amber was her boobs." Morgan finished fiddling with his bow tie and took a step back. "There, that's better."

"As long as you brought up the topic of your mother, how's she doing?"

"I didn't bring up the topic; you did. She married a brilliant, great-looking guy with more money than God who worships everything about her. She spends six months a year traveling the world. How do you think she's doing?"

"Someday she'll see through all that superficial stuff."

Morgan laughed again, opened the door to the conference center, and held it while her father walked through.

"How about dinner tomorrow night?" she asked. "I have something I want to tell you."

"Really? Who's buying?"

"It's your turn," she said firmly.

"In that case, I'll come over to your place and we'll order in Chinese. I have a coupon."

"And if it were my turn to pay?" she asked, following him down the center aisle.

"We'd be going to the Palm."

Morgan folded her arm around his waist and gave him a quick, but adoring, pinch. She then escorted him to an aisle seat before making her way to the front of the lecture hall. Catching herself in a quick grin, she wondered how he'd react when she told him over dinner tomorrow night that she was six weeks pregnant.

CHAPTER

6

Although he called himself Gideon, the man who limped into Dr. Allen Hawkins's office at five minutes to nine signed in as Stuart Artesian.

The name Gideon suited him well. The impulse to cast aside his God-given name and take the name of the angel had come to him in the form of a ghostly revelation six months earlier. Having no earthly need for the name bestowed upon him by his parents, he discarded it as easily as the individual who had borne it for the past forty years.

Even though he had now ascended to a higher purpose, he still thought about his old life. It had been one filled with backyard barbecues, homeowners meetings, and long days at the beach. It was a life he cherished, but one that had become nothing more than a collection of treasured memories. The realization that the only place he could relive those memories was in his mind was maddening. Thinking about the past often incited the terrible ringing in his ears that had been plaguing him for the last several months. Of late, he even considered consulting a physician, but he kept putting it off in the hopes the high-pitched humming would subside on its own.

Just as he was about to sign in, the frosted glass window in front of him wobbled open. A young lady wearing a floral shirt smiled. Her name badge read Judy.

"May I help you?" she asked.

"My name is Stuart Artesian. I have a nine-fifteen appointment with Dr. Hawkins."

Judy handed him a clipboard with a two-sided patient information sheet to fill out.

"Do you have your insurance referral with you?" she asked.

"I don't believe in health insurance. I'll be paying for the visit in cash."

Even though it was not a response she was accustomed to hearing, Judy simply smiled. "If you'll just fill out both sides of the form, Dr. Hawkins will be with you shortly."

Clipboard in hand, and with the assistance of a brandy smuggler–styled cane, Gideon hobbled across the waiting room and took a seat on a dark green upholstered couch. It had taken him two hours to prepare for his appointment with Dr. Hawkins. He had set his alarm for five to allow himself ample time to dye his hair, apply foam latex to his cheekbones, and affix a gray artificial mustache.

When he finished filling out the form, he reached into the inside pocket of his sports coat and removed a paperback book of advanced crossword puzzles. Over the past month he had completed most of them, leaving him only the last few to work on.

At that moment, Carrie Alexander, Dr. Hawkins's physician's assistant, stepped into the waiting room. "Mr. Artesian?" she asked, glancing around the room.

Gideon caught her attention by raising his cane. "I'm Stuart Artesian."

She took a few paces toward him. "We're ready for you."

Carrie escorted him down a long corridor and then into a nicely appointed examination room where she helped him onto a table. While he was getting settled, she read his patient information sheet.

"You mentioned you were referred to our practice by Dr. Connolly."

"That's right."

"Would that be Morgan Connolly?" she asked.

"Yes. She was the emergency room doctor who took care of my hand."

"Are you sure?"

With a smile he said, "I may be getting old and senile, young lady, but I can still remember the names of the doctors who treat me. I liked Dr. Connolly very much. When she told me she was referring me to her father and that she chaired the hospital's Patient Safety Committee, I was very comfortable."

"I'm sorry. I didn't mean to . . ."

"Don't you accept ER patients?"

"Of course," Carrie was careful to answer, still a little perplexed. She knew Dr. Connolly never referred patients from the emergency room to her father. She didn't know why exactly, but she was pretty sure it had something to do with hospital politics. Instead of trying to explain a difficult situation to Mr. Artesian, she moved on. "How did you hurt your hand?"

"It was stupid, really. I was in my garage trying to pull down some heavy boxes from an eight-foot shelf. I did okay with the first one, but I lost my grip on the second and it pinned my hand against the wall as it fell."

Carrie made notes as they spoke. "How long ago did this happen?"

He thought for a few moments. "I'd say about a month now."

"And is the pain is getting worse?"

"Definitely, and the swelling has never completely gone away," he answered, gently rubbing the back of his left hand.

"I noticed you walk with a cane."

"Oh that—it had nothing to do with the accident. I've had arthritis in my right hip for more years than I can remember. My family doctor told me I'll eventually need a hip replacement."

Before Carrie could ask her next question, the door opened.

"Mr. Artesian. I'm Dr. Hawkins."

They shook hands.

"Actually, it's Dr. Artesian."

"My apologies. Are you a physician?"

"No, but I was accepted to medical school. I decided to get my PhD in anthropology instead. I felt that teaching at a college level would be a more sensible life. I'm a full professor at the University of Miami."

"Do you live in Coral Gables?"

"Ever since I moved to Miami."

"What brings you all the way up here? There are a number of excellent orthopedic surgeons in South Miami," Hawkins inquired.

"I only see doctors who are on staff at Dade Presbyterian."

"Why's that?"

"I'm a thorough man, Doctor, and I've done my homework when it comes to patient safety and hospital mistakes. To put it bluntly, your medical staff's the best of a bad lot."

"What brought you to that conclusion?"

Gideon paused just long enough to move his cane a little closer. "Have you read the Institute of Medicine's report on medical errors?"

Being quite familiar with the landmark publication, Hawkins answered, "As a matter of fact, I have."

Gideon rolled on, "Then you must know that this country's hospitals are hopelessly unsafe. Do you realize that simply being admitted to a hospital is now the eighth leading cause of death in this country? It doesn't even matter what's wrong with you. In England, a patient has a one in three hundred chance of dying from a preventable medical error."

Hawkins rolled up a chair and sat down directly in front of his verbose patient. He then took his hand, turned it palm down, and began his examination. Hawkins was old school and had lived through a lot of changes in medicine. Overly familiar, opinionated patients were no longer an oddity in his practice.

"Does that hurt?" he asked, checking each finger and its range of motion.

"A little." Hawkins nodded and continued his examination. He hoped the brief silence meant his new patient had nothing further to say on the topic of patient safety. "I'll tell you something else," Gideon said, dashing Hawkins's hopes. "It's the patient's responsibility to make sure that he or she is safe. I wouldn't be admitted to any hospital unless I knew its Code Fifteen history."

"Code Fifteen history?"

"You seem surprised."

"It's not a term I hear patients use very often."

With a patronizing smirk, Gideon lowered his head and chuckled.

"Just because the medical profession wants to put a fancy name on its catastrophic errors doesn't mean the general public won't figure it out." Gideon glanced over at Carrie and then cleared his throat. "Excuse me, Dr. Hawkins," he began with a note of trepidation in his voice. "There's another matter of a more personal nature that I'd like to talk to you about."

Taking the less than subtle hint, she came to her feet and headed for the door. "I'll go check and see if the X-ray's ready. I'll see you over there, Mr. Artesian." Just before she closed the door she exchanged a bemused look with Dr. Hawkins regarding their self-important patient.

Gideon waited another minute before asking, "Do you love your daughter?"

"Excuse me?"

"The only reason I ask is because I loved my sons. I've been spending a lot of time these past months trying to figure out why your daughter decided to become a doctor. I mean, most people who make that choice have a conscience. They don't make callous mistakes and then deny responsibility for them."

Astonished more than angered by his patient's inflammatory comments, Hawkins stopped his examination and chanced a look. The supercilious grin had run from Gideon's face, leaving it pinched with rage.

His bewilderment soaring, Hawkins locked eyes with Gideon in a frigid silence.

CHAPTER

7

Before Hawkins could speak, Gideon's open hand shot past him like a hot piston.

Hawkins had no time to react before he felt the back of his collar being grabbed. At the same moment, he saw Gideon's opposite hand coming straight for his mouth. As if it were the next move in a precisely choreographed dance, Hawkins found himself being spun around with such extreme force, he felt as if he were made of papier-mâché.

With his back now slammed against Gideon's chest, his first instinct was to scream. But Gideon had already cupped his mouth shut with the palm of his hand. He tried anyway but all he could manage was a frantic series of muffled groans. Hawkins felt Gideon's forearm sliding down beneath his chin and onto his neck. Consumed with terror and now breathless, he was powerless to move under the death grip of Gideon's raw strength. Hawkins felt the man's arm tightening around his throat like a hungry constrictor. Still conscious, he could feel his windpipe being flattened.

Hawkins's field of vision contracted into an infinite blackness. The asphyxiation turned the whites of his eyes bloody from tiny arterial ruptures. His brain, exhausted of its vital supply of oxygen, began to swell. His pupils then rotated up in their vacant orbits and his facial muscles became flaccid.

Gideon was tempted to finish what he had come to do by

simply maintaining his stranglehold for another couple of minutes, but being a man of discipline, he decided to stick to his plan and resist the temptation to choke Hawkins to death. He released his grip, allowing the doctor's body to crumble to the floor. He observed the unconscious man for a few seconds to assure himself he was still breathing before reaching for his cane. Training his eyes on Hawkins's pallid face, he unscrewed the top and turned the hollow walking stick upside down. Using his index finger, he slid out a what appeared to be a simple apparatus consisting of a clear plastic tube attached to a large-bore medical needle. He uncapped the needle and set the device on the examination table.

Gideon stole a glance at his watch. He then reached into the inside pocket of his sports coat and removed a metal cylinder that was about the size of an ordinary flashlight. The device, which was sold under the name of Life Support, was a five-minute supply of emergency compressed air used by scuba divers. Gideon had considered a number of different ways to kill Allen Hawkins, but a massive collapse of his lung seemed the most fitting.

Completely focused on the task at hand, he attached the plastic tubing to the cylinder and then knelt down. Using his fingers to guide him, he located the space between Hawkins's ribs at the level of his right breast. Gripping the needle between his thumb and index finger, he easily slid it through the space and into Hawkins's chest cavity.

Confident in its position, he pushed the button on the Life Support system initiating an immediate blast of compressed air into Hawkins's chest cavity. The first effects were apparent within seconds. The high pressure created by the compressed air collapsed his lung like an accordion. As the pressure built further, it squeezed his heart against his chest wall, severely restricting its ability to pump blood. Hawkins's slow but effortless breathing instantly turned to a series of coarse grunts. His neck veins, engorged with oxygen-starved blood, appeared as if they would burst at any moment.

Gideon reached for his victim's hand. While the Life Support continued to empty its air with a barely audible hiss, he felt for the old man's pulse. It was threadlike, markedly irregular, and failing rapidly. Coming to his feet, he stared down at Hawkins. His face and lips were cobalt in color from the unremitting cyanosis. Gideon turned off the flow of air and pulled the needle out of Hawkins's chest. He then detached the plastic tubing from the Life Support and put it back in the cane. Next, he replaced the canister in his pocket. He checked his watch again. Two minutes and fifty seconds had elapsed from the time he had snatched Hawkins into his death grip.

Pleased with the ease of his plan's execution, Gideon reached into his pocket and pulled out a folded sheet of white paper. He looked around for a moment before setting it down on the countertop in plain view. Without so much as a backward glance, he picked up his cane and calmly strolled over to the door. Before reaching for the handle, he closed his eyes and used the next few seconds to force a horrid look of shock to his face. He drew a deep breath, flung the door open, and limped out into the hall. Looking around wildly, he spotted Carrie at the far end of the corridor.

"Dr. Hawkins collapsed," he screamed, while gesturing wildly at her. "I don't think he's breathing."

Carrie, with two other staff members right behind her, charged down the hall. They flew past him but stopped in the doorway for an instant before rushing in.

"Call nine-one-one," Carrie yelled.

"He was fine," Gideon insisted in a booming voice from the hallway, "and then, all of a sudden, he grabbed his left arm and fell to the ground."

When the pandemonium reached its crescendo, he moved off to the side. By this time, Carrie and the others were huddled around Hawkins, who was twisting and jerking from a major convulsion. Using the chaos of the moment, he made his way back down the corridor and then out to the waiting room. An unintelligible buzz filled the room from the anxious patients all craning their necks trying to figure out what the commotion was about. Acting as if nothing were amiss, Gideon walked out of Allen Hawkins's office and rode the elevator to the first floor.

Leaving the building through the main entrance, he climbed into his car and started for home.

Entering through the garage, he went directly to his bedroom and removed his disguise. When he was finished he went downstairs to the kitchen. Fancying himself a gourmet cook, he opened the refrigerator and took out a large bowl of eggs. Devoid of any remorse regarding the morning's events, he meticulously began preparation of a crabmeat omelet. Watching it cook, he became filled with a powerful sense of righteousness regarding his achievement.

At the same moment he savored the first bite of the omelet, the paramedics were racing the stricken doctor across the street to Dade Presbyterian's emergency room. He had no pulse or blood pressure and they were performing full CPR.

By the time Gideon had finished cleaning up the kitchen, Charles Barnes, the ER physician on duty, had already pronounced Dr. Allen Hawkins dead.

CHAPTER

8

From her terrace, seven stories above the Intracoastal Waterway, Morgan gazed down at the myriad of unhurried pleasure boats making their way up and down the man-made inland passageway.

Enjoying her first full day off in two weeks, she absently massaged her lower abdomen. When she looked down and realized what she was doing, it brought an immediate grin to her face. She imagined that most women facing the likelihood of a divorce wouldn't embrace the news they were pregnant. But Morgan felt that irrespective of what the future held for her, she was overjoyed at the prospect of being a mother.

After taking the last few sips of her cranberry juice, she stepped back from the railing and checked her watch. Annoyed at herself for losing track of the time and running the risk of being late for her first yoga class, she hurried back into her living room and grabbed her purse from a smoke glass coffee table. She was halfway to the front door when her pager went off. She glanced down at the digital display. It was the emergency room—the last place she wanted to hear from. After an aggravated groan, she picked up her cordless phone and dialed the number.

A man answered on the third ring. "This is Dr. Barnes."

Barnes was the vice chief of Emergency Medicine. He was

an accommodating and even-tempered man who had always been supportive of Morgan's agenda as the department chief.

"Hi, Charles, it's Morgan. Somebody paged me."

"I paged you. Are you in the hospital?" he asked in an unusually serious tone.

Fearing she was in peril of missing her yoga class, she said, "C'mon, Charles. This is my first day off in weeks. Whatever the catastrophe is, can't it wait until tomorrow?"

"I'm not calling about a departmental problem, Morgan."

With a measured amount of concern creeping into her voice, she asked, "You sound awful. What's going on?"

"I'm afraid it's your father."

"My father?" she grumbled with relief. "Don't tell me he yelled at one of the nurses again. I told him the next time he did that I wouldn't be able to save his—"

"Morgan, your father was attacked in his office a little while ago. The paramedics brought him straight here."

Her purse slipped from her hand. She fell into the couch. "Attacked?"

"At first I thought he had had a heart attack or stroke. But when I saw the marks on his throat . . ."

Morgan clamped down on the receiver, sending every muscle in her hand into spasm.

Desperately trying to maintain her composure, she asked, "Is . . . is he okay? Have the trauma surgeons seen him? It doesn't matter who's on call today, he'd want Katz or Fairland called."

After a difficult pause, Barnes said, "When he arrived, he was in full cardiac arrest. We . . . we tried to . . . I'm so sorry, Morgan. We tried everything. We just couldn't get him back."

With the finality of the words reverberating in her head, Morgan found herself helpless to move or speak. She heard what Charles had told her, but she couldn't fully process it.

Finally she uttered, "I . . . I don't—"

"May's our charge nurse today. She said she'd come get you."

A few more seconds passed. Feeling as if everything was

happening in slow motion, Morgan whispered, "No, I'd prefer to drive myself."

Her hand opened and the phone fell out. She glanced at her credenza where she had displayed a dozen or so framed photographs. Her favorite was the one of her father and her taken in Park City, Utah, on a skiing vacation.

Involuntarily, Morgan's eyes closed. The thought that Charles Barnes's phone call was some horrible mistake or awful nightmare from which she would soon awaken never entered her mind. As inconceivable as it was, she knew her father was gone. Having the presence of mind to slow her breathing, she waited a minute before reaching for her purse.

She hadn't taken more than a few steps when she suddenly felt light-headed. Stopping for a few moments, she steadied herself against a high-backed chair. When she felt her legs under her again, she took a few cautious paces toward the entranceway and summoned the elevator.

She exited the building and got into her car. It wasn't until she pulled away that the unthinkable reality of the situation finally got the better of her, leaving her frantically sobbing.

CHAPTER
9

It had been twelve hours since he had murdered Allen Hawkins.

Alone in his den, Gideon considered himself living proof that any rational man was capable of murder. He gazed over at the ornate grandfather clock that had taken him twelve months of painstaking work to restore. It was a hobby that most men would find tedious but one he embraced for just that reason.

He had never been a man prone to making capricious choices. In fact, he would defend forever that taking Hawkins's life was not a decision at all—it was a moral imperative. He imagined that there were unenlightened individuals who might consider his actions unthinkable, but it made no difference. Irrespective of what the future held for him, he would never feel the need to explain himself to anybody—especially anyone who didn't cling to the same moral ideology as he did. He was quite comfortable in his own skin, required nobody's approbation, and had no qualms about remaining an unsung hero.

Heavy in thought, he reached forward and flipped on a small brass lamp that sat on the corner of his desk. If he had a single regret in life, it was that he hadn't, in fact, fulfilled his enduring passion of entering the world of academia. Only in the university environment would he have been recognized as a true luminary and given the opportunity to share his wisdom with young, impressionable minds. It would have been a more noble life than his present one, and one that would have pleased his mother.

He lightly rubbed his ears. The incessant ringing showed no signs of easing off. He again pledged to himself that he wouldn't allow the inexplicable annoyance to affect him in any way. Looking down at a white legal pad, he studied the list of names he had carefully printed months earlier. He moved forward in his chair, picked up a black fountain pen, and drew a single line through the second name on the list. After a momentary pause, he drew another line identical to the first. And then, as if his hand were being guided by a mind of its own, he ran the bold nib back and forth through the name. Only when it had become indecipherable, did he stop and slip the pen back into its granite base.

Feeling the fatigue of the day and with nothing further to do, he turned off his tarnished brass desk lamp, stood up from his desk, and headed for the door. After crossing an expansive foyer, he climbed a spiral wooden staircase that led to the master bedroom. The only light in the room shone from a wall-mounted flat-screen television. The volume had been muted by the woman who lay asleep in the wood-carved canopied bed. After studying her face for a minute, he crept silently to within a few feet of her.

She was not the woman he had fallen in love with, and it was only when he closed his eyes that he could remember her saintly face. He wanted to kiss her on her forehead but he knew it would be a futile gesture. He picked up the remote control from her night table and turned off the television. Finally, he walked over to the opposite side of the bed, got undressed, and quietly slipped under the covers. In the darkness, he could feel the regular cadence of her breathing.

He closed his eyes for a time, but sleep evaded him. His

mind focused on the next name on his list. He knew Morgan
Connolly's death alone would never be sufficient atonement
for her role in the death of his sons. He would therefore see to
it that before she was ushered off to hell, she would suffer so
unbearably that she would envy the dead.

PART TWO

CHAPTER

10

It had been two weeks since her father's funeral, and it was Morgan's first day back in the office.

The first week following his death had been the worst. Fortunately, she had many friends who had lost a parent, and they were all anxious to offer her words of encouragement. A few days earlier she realized two important facts. The first being that she would always miss her father dearly; and the second being it was time to get back to work.

Sitting at her desk trying to catch up on a long list of administrative responsibilities, Morgan barely heard the three quick raps on her door. When she finally looked up, she saw Benjamin Docherty standing in her doorway. As usual, he was casually dressed. Just the sight of him brought an easy smile to her face.

"Come in," she said, gesturing him forward. "What are you doing here? I thought you had retired from medicine."

"I'm just here for a visit," he said taking the chair across from her. He turned it to the side, allowing him the extra room he needed to stretch out his lanky legs. "I just wanted to make sure you were doing okay."

"I think I'll miss him for a long time, but I feel okay and I think I'm ready to get back to work."

"About five years ago, my parents both died unexpectedly within a few months of each other. I don't think you ever get completely over it."

"I've been meaning to call and thank you," she said.

Looking a little perplexed, he asked, "Thank me for what?"

"For being such a great friend through the worst few weeks of my life." Ben's normally tanned face instantly reddened.

Three years older than she, Ben had the same agile build as Kevin but his facial features were softer and more contoured. Before he gave up the practice of internal medicine to open a flight school, he and Morgan had shared in the care of dozens of patients and had served on several hospital committees together. They agreed on most issues and had a similar problem-solving style, but it was their mutual passion for flying that was the cornerstone of their friendship. Morgan had never thought of Ben as a complicated man. He was a die-hard bachelor, and although he claimed he simply hadn't found the love of his life, Morgan suspected he suffered from the same commitment phobia that plagued most single male doctors. She didn't find many men physically attractive, but Ben was a noteworthy exception.

Morgan asked, "No lessons today?"

"Actually, I have one this afternoon. He's a nervous eighth-grade English teacher who combines no instinct for flying with closing his eyes on every takeoff and landing."

"Sounds like an interesting way to fly an airplane."

"It's been a little scary for the both of us."

She laughed. "I guess you should have thought of that before you gave up that booming practice you had."

"I'll take a hundred nervous flying students over an office full of hypochondriacs any day of the week."

"What happened to your driving passion to save mankind?" she asked.

"Let's just say that the day-to-day practice of internal medicine didn't turn out to be as advertised in med school and residency. "

"So you have no regrets about getting out?" she prodded.

"None," he assured her. "If you had any sense, you'd get

out too. Just say the word and I'll make you a partner in my flight school."

Morgan smiled. "I'm not exactly in a position to retire. Of the two of us, I'm not the one who sold their medical software company for fifteen million dollars."

"I thought the sale price was confidential."

"Not according to the *Miami Herald*."

Stroking his two-day stubble, Ben said, "I don't think I remember that article."

"Sure you do. It was the one where they referred to you as Dade County's most eligible bachelor. As I recall, you crowed about it for a month." She closed the file she had been reviewing. "Do you mind if I ask you something?"

"Go ahead," he told her.

"Why would somebody who already had a degree in bio-medical engineering, a master's in business administration from Wharton, and their own computer software company even apply to medical school?"

With a light shrug of his shoulders, he answered, "I don't know. It just seemed like a good idea at the time." He reached forward, plucked a mint from a crystal candy dish, and un-wrapped it. "Have the police come up with anything?"

"Not really."

"It's only been a couple of weeks."

"Actually, two weeks is considered a long time in a murder investigation, especially if you don't have a single decent lead."

He grinned. "When did you become an expert on murder investigations?"

"It's a new millennium, Ben. There's a world of informa-tion on the Internet."

"When was the last time you spoke to the police?"

"I called the lead detective on the case a couple of days ago. He was very polite but . . ."

"Polite's nice," Ben said, taking note that her face was cast in frustration, "but what you need is information. He must have said something."

"Not really. He mostly tap-danced around things. The police have a strict policy that prohibits them from discussing a lot of the details of a criminal investigation with anybody—especially family members. I didn't get the feeling he's too optimistic about making an arrest in the foreseeable future."

"Did you discuss the autopsy results with him? I'm not a detective, but causing somebody to die of a collapsed lung can't be the type of thing they see every day."

"He didn't say anything about that but he still thinks the murderer knew my father. He's guessing he was a disgruntled patient or family member who went off the deep end. The problem is that nobody who works in my father's office has been able to come up with a single patient who comes close to fitting the profile." Morgan paused just long enough to push her chair a little closer to her desk. "When you consider that my father took care of thousands of people in his career, it makes the prospect of finding his murderer gloomy at best."

"Why would the police look at his entire career? If anybody was furious enough at their doctor to murder him, I would suspect they would act sooner rather than later."

"I would have no way of knowing that."

"What's the detective's name?"

"Wolfe."

"You could try speaking to somebody higher up in the department," Ben suggested.

"If I go over his head, he's going to find out about it, which will only make things worse. I suspect he already has me labeled as a grief-stricken relative who is overly involved in the investigation. The other problem is that he and his partner are obviously overworked. He reminds me every time we talk that my father's murder is not the only investigation he's working on." Morgan pulled the legal pad closer. Mindlessly drawing overlapping circles. "I can't let this thing go just because the police are overworked. I am going to go over to my father's office. I want to speak to his office manager and anybody else who was there that day."

Looking at her askance, he said, "If I didn't know better, I'd say you're launching your own investigation."

"Call it what you want, Ben. I need answers."

He uncrossed his ankles and pulled his legs in. "I know you're frustrated. And I would never tell you I understand how you feel or what you should do . . . but—"

"But what?"

"I just think you might want to give this a little more thought before you go charging headlong into something that might create real problems for you."

"Listen, Ben. I can't sit back, do nothing, and pretend none of this ever happened. My father didn't raise me to sit in the back of the bus."

"I'm not telling you to abandon the issue. I'm only suggesting you tap on the brakes a little. Even if you're not thrilled with the progress of the investigation so far, you might want to consider giving the police a little more time."

"I'm not sure more time will make a difference."

"You're also going to have to consider the possibility that the man who murdered your father may be impossible to find. In spite of what the police think, he may be an untreated schizophrenic who had no connection at all to your father."

In a shared silence, Morgan came to her feet and then walked around behind her chair.

Her voice was calm but echoed with resolve. "Sane or psychotic, I despise him. I couldn't care less if he's completely normal or if his soul is so full of demons he can barely breathe." She placed her hands on top of the chair. "I'm going to do everything in my power to make sure he doesn't get away with what he did to my father." Ben was just about to make another plea for restraint when Morgan held her hand up. "If you're going to suggest I take a knee on this thing, you're wasting your time."

Ben had known Morgan long enough to realize that trying to dissuade her from doing anything she had made up her mind about would be like trying to sink a battleship with a flyswatter. After a few seconds of thought, his gaze returned to Morgan.

Her face had suddenly turned the color of chalk.

"For God's sake, Morgan. You look like a ghost. Are you okay?" He stood up and walked around to her side of her desk. "I'm sorry if I said anything to upset you, but I was only trying to—"

With her chin pressed against her chest, she held up her hand to silence him. Speaking between quick breaths, she said, "Unfortunately, this has nothing to do with our conversation. I'll be okay. It's been happening a lot lately."

Morgan yanked open the top drawer of her desk and snatched a packet of saltines. Tearing off the wrapper, she popped one in her mouth. While she chomped away at it, she grabbed for an open can of warm Coke that was sitting on her desk. She took two long swallows. When she put the can down, she looked up at Ben. His lips were sealed together in an obvious attempt to conceal a smile.

"Coke and crackers," he said. "That's an interesting mid-morning snack."

She waited until she swallowed the second cracker and said, "I was going to tell you."

"That's great news. How far along are you?"

"About eight weeks."

"Tell Kevin I said congrats."

"If I ever see him again, I will," she answered, seeing no reason to play cat-and-mouse games with him regarding the shambles of her marriage. She gulped down more of the Coke. The nausea started to pass. She inhaled deeply and let the breath slip out gradually.

"I'm sorry, Morgan. I didn't mean to pry—"

"You're not prying. Actually, I assumed you knew."

"I guess I've had an inkling for the last few months. When I didn't see Kevin at the funeral . . . well, I kind of guessed things weren't going so well. What does he think about you being pregnant?"

"I haven't told him yet." Morgan looked directly at Ben. "Please keep this between you and me for a while. The only other person I've told is Jenny Silverman. The last thing I need right now is to be the latest grist for Dade Presbyterian's gossip mill."

"She's an excellent obstetrician."

"And a good friend."

"Your color's coming back," he said, pointing to her face. He returned to his chair. "I guess these things can get pretty complicated in a—"

"There's nothing complicated about it. Kevin's been drowning in a sea of self-pity for a long time. When my capacity for understanding began to wither, he found a more sympathetic and much younger emotional buoy to hang on to."

"Is there any chance of working things out?"

"I don't think so."

"What about counseling?"

"Kevin doesn't believe in it."

"You could go alone."

"I did."

"And?"

"It's like getting on a seesaw by yourself. It's tough to make much progress," she explained, tossing the wrapper from the crackers into the trash. "Let's not talk about Kevin anymore. It may bring back my nausea."

Ben grinned. "Are you going to stop flying?"

"Not a chance."

"Good," he said. "How about Saturday?"

"What time?"

"How does one sound?"

"I'll be there."

Just before he reached the door, he said, "Look, Morgan. I'm hardly an expert on relationships but if you need somebody to talk to . . . I mean, all you have to do is pick up the phone."

"I appreciate the offer, Ben."

"Congrats again," he said, heading for the door. "I'll give you a call later."

Ben followed a short corridor to the back stairwell. He yanked open the door and started down three flights of gray concrete stairs. He thought about Kevin and the two times he had approached him to invest in one of his wild enterprises. Being savvy enough to recognize blue smoke and shady business ethics when he saw them, Ben had politely passed both times. The experience had left him wondering how Morgan could be married to such an unprincipled individual. He never discussed his negative impression of Kevin with her, but he suspected she knew how he felt.

Reaching the ground floor, he pushed open the heavy metal door that accessed the street. Ben considered himself an introspective man who was well aware of his shortcomings. Being dishonest with himself wasn't one of them. He couldn't deny that a part of him felt true remorse for the emotional trauma Morgan would face going through a divorce. But a larger, perhaps more selfish, part was gladdened by the prospect of Morgan being single. He never denied his romantic feelings for her, but he always played by the rules and kept them in check.

Walking along the side of the hospital to the crosswalk, he gazed skyward. It was a perfect day for flying. When the light changed, he started across the street. Was it not for his well-developed sense of self-restraint, he would have surely smiled from ear to ear.

CHAPTER
11

At ten minutes past seven in the morning, a deeply sedated Tony Wallace was wheeled into operating room number three.

A native Floridian, the talented reporter for the Fort Lauderdale *Sun-Sentinel* had spent his career moving from one assignment to the next at a pace that reflected how many unpaid bills lay stacked upon his desk. Fifty-nine years of age and forty pounds overweight, Wallace had been smoking two packs of Camels a day since he had enlisted in the navy a week after his eighteenth birthday.

In spite of his ill-advised lifestyle and laissez-faire attitude toward his health, he had never had a serious problem until two years ago when he began having chest pain. After an extensive evaluation and a lengthy trial of controlling his coronary artery disease with medications, his family doctor referred him to Dr. Kirby McBride for surgical evaluation. After several meetings, Wallace decided to proceed with the bypass procedure.

Thirty minutes after his patient had been placed on the operating table, Dr. McBride, scalpel in hand, was ready to begin. The only thing delaying him from making an incision was the go-ahead from the anesthesiologist, Mike Quintana.

After checking his equipment and measuring Wallace's vital signs one last time, Quintana looked up and said, "We're good to go."

In the next instant, McBride made a deep incision directly down the middle of Tony's chest. He then used a special air-powered high-speed saw to divide his breastbone and expose his heart. The final step before going on bypass was to place the large plastic tubing into the heart and the aorta, the largest artery in the body.

When McBride was finished, he looked over at Todd Kettering, the chief pump technician.

"Are we ready?" he asked him.

Todd gave him the thumbs-up and answered, "You're good to go, Boss."

McBride, short in stature but long on confidence, looked over the top of the anesthesia screen at Quintana.

"Go ahead and give him the heparin. Let me know when he's fully anticoagulated."

"Ten thousand units going in," Quintana answered as he pushed five cc's of the heparin into the IV tubing.

A minute passed. Dr. McBride looked over his shoulder at Todd. "Can we go on bypass?"

"The ACT's greater than four-eighty. The patient's fully anticoagulated. We can go on whenever you're ready," Todd assured him.

"What's the heparin for?" one of three medical students standing behind Todd whispered.

Continuing to check his systems and without looking at her, he asked. "What happens to your blood if you cut your finger?"

"It bleeds," she responded.

"Forever?"

"No. Until it clots."

"Exactly," Todd said. "This heart and lung bypass machine that you're looking at is just like a giant water pump that makes a fountain work. What do you think would happen to our imaginary fountain if we were pumping hundreds of gallons of water and, all of a sudden, that water turned to ice?"

"I guess the pump would jam and the fountain would stop."

"That's right. And the same is true here. If Mr. Wallace's

blood should clot, we wouldn't be able to circulate it. That's why we give heparin. It thins out the blood and prevents it from clotting."

Dr. McBride said, "What do you say, Todd? If today's lecture on heparin's over, I'd like to get on with this operation."

Todd had known McBride for years and was well aware that his sarcastic sense of humor was harmless.

"We're ready," he answered.

"Here we go," McBride said, releasing the large clamps on the tubing. The result was to immediately allow the blood to flow from Tony Wallace's heart, through the tubing, and into the pump where it would receive oxygen before being returned to his body.

"We're up to speed on the flow," Todd said.

"Go ahead and give the cardioplegia," McBride told Quintana, who then injected a highly concentrated solution of ice-cold potassium into Tony's bloodstream. The effect was to bring his heart to a complete standstill.

"Why do they have to stop the heart?" the student asked Todd.

"Because it's delicate work trying to sew the grafts in. It would be impossible to do with the heart pounding away."

With his magnifying glasses in place, McBride began sewing in the three separate vein grafts that would bridge Tony's blocked arteries. Forty-five minutes after he had placed the first stitch, he tied the final suture.

"I'm done here. Let's give him a couple of units of blood and start re-warming."

The process generally took a few minutes and would be the necessary last step before Quintana and McBride would work together to start Tony's heart beating on its own again.

It was at this point that McBride felt comfortable enough to step back from the table and relax for a few minutes.

"Have you started the nitroglycerine drip yet?" he asked Quintana.

"Just hanging it now," he answered.

With his arms crossed in front of him, McBride closed his eyes and took a few deep breaths. His mind drifted to the Mediterranean cruise he and his wife were scheduled to take next month. It was a vacation he felt he deserved and one that his wife insisted he desperately needed.

McBride opened his eyes and glanced down at the operative field.

"Shit," he yelled. "I've got huge blood clots in the pericardial well. What the hell's going on, Todd?"

Todd's voice and manner were equally distressed.

"I don't know, Boss, but I got the same thing here in the tubing. This guy's making clots like crazy. The whole God damn pump's clotting off."

McBride's eyes flashed back to Quintana. "You said you gave the heparin."

"I did," he insisted, scanning the monitors and checking his IV lines. "This shouldn't be happening."

"We gotta get this guy off bypass right now," McBride shouted at Todd, knowing that was the one small chance Tony Wallace had of surviving. "He'll need to go back on as soon as you've changed all the tubing."

"I'm already working on it," Todd answered.

"He's too cold," McBride said, pounding his fists together. "His heart will never start on its own. We've probably already stroked him out by showering his brain with clots. I'm clamping the tubing. I'll massage the heart until you get the circuit changed and we can go back on bypass."

McBride and Quintana exchanged a desperate glance. McBride knew they were both thinking the same thing; Tony Wallace's chances of making it out of the operating room were rapidly approaching zero. "Give him another bolus of heparin right now," McBride said.

Quintana held up an empty syringe. "It's already in."

Cradling Tony's lifeless heart in both of his hands, McBride continued to squeeze the flaccid organ once every second.

"There's no blood in the damn heart. It's all clots. Does he have a blood pressure?" McBride asked.

"Of course not. The guy's blood has turned to cement," Quintana answered with equal frustration. "You need blood that circulates to have a pressure."

"God damn it, Todd. How much more time do you need?"

"I'm changing the circuit as fast as I can, but it'll take another four or five minutes."

Kirby McBride felt his own heart racing. Todd might as well have told him he needed seven or eight hours because it wasn't going to make a particle of difference. With sweat pouring down the back of his neck, McBride took a deep breath and continued squeezing the motionless heart.

Another five minutes passed. He looked over at Todd who was still working feverishly to replace the tubing. Finally, he gazed up toward the ceiling as if he were somehow seeking divine intervention. Without anybody having to say anything, the bedlam in the operating room changed to an eerie silence.

The heparin hadn't worked. All of Tony Wallace's blood had clotted.

McBride turned his eyes toward Quintana and asked in a defeated voice, "Is it possible that he accidentally got the protamine too soon?"

"C'mon, Kirby. I'm not a rookie, for God's sake. We never reverse the heparin until the patient's off the pump."

"I'm . . . I'm sorry, Mike. I had to ask."

McBride had done almost four thousand open-heart cases in his career and he had seen every mishap, complication, and disaster known to cardiac surgery. He was both knowledgeable and experienced on the subject of operating room calamities. Most of all, he knew the difference between a fixable complication and an irretrievable catastrophe. A heart and lung machine clotting off in the middle of a pump run was a clear example of the latter. He knew the moment he saw the first blood clot that irrespective of what he did, Tony Wallace's fate had already been sealed.

McBride stood silently in front of his patient, his eyes trained on the operating table.

Finally, he cleared his throat and announced, "We're stopping. Please note the time."

He looked over the top of the sterile drapes at Mike Quintana, who nodded and said, "I agree."

McBride pulled off his gown and gloves and tossed them into a large bin. Walking toward the door, he knew the details of what had just happened would spread through the hospital like a brush fire in a high wind. He heaved a breath of despair and wondered how he'd tell the people waiting for news of Mr. Wallace's operation that he had been killed by an inexcusable surgical debacle.

CHAPTER

12

The moment Morgan Connolly walked into the waiting room of her father's office, her mind was showered with painful images of his funeral.

Hundreds of Allen Hawkins's friends, colleagues, and patients had crowded into the cathedral that he devotedly attended every Sunday to offer their respects to a much-loved man and a revered member of the community. Although it was the most difficult thing Morgan had ever done, she delivered a tender eulogy to the man who had always been her hero.

"Hi," Annalisa Gregory said, snapping Morgan out of her dreamlike state. Annalisa had been her father's office manager for the past ten years. Nobody knew Allen Hawkins's professional side better or admired him more than she did. "How are you?"

"Things are starting to get back to normal," Morgan answered.

Annalisa took her by the arm. "I was so happy you called. Let's go back to my office. We can talk there." Annalisa directed Morgan to a small love seat and then pulled up a chair and sat down directly across from her. They talked for a few minutes about the impact of her father's death on the office and how different things were now. Although there were two other orthopedic surgeons in the practice, they were all business with respect to both their patients and the staff.

"You mentioned on the phone that there was something specific you wanted to talk to me about."

Relieved that Annalisa had been the one to broach the topic, Morgan said, "I have some questions about what happened the day my father died."

Annalisa looked circumspect. "Are you sure you want to talk about this, Morgan?"

"I'm sure."

"Okay. I'll answer whatever I can."

"Can you tell me what you remember from the moment you knew something was wrong?"

"I was in my office when I heard all the commotion in the hall. I came running out and went straight to the exam room. We did CPR until the paramedics arrived."

"According to the police, the man identified himself as Stuart Artesian," Morgan said.

"That's right."

"Do you remember seeing him when he left the office?"

Annalisa shook her head. "The hallway was packed and the place was in chaos. I didn't meet him when he signed in, and he wasn't in the examination room when I got there." She shook her head. "You might want to speak with Carrie. She did the initial evaluation."

"If she's available, I'd really appreciate it."

"No problem," Annalisa said, picking up the phone and paging Carrie overhead. She had barely set the phone down when a young lady with short, reddish blond hair and a coppery complexion appeared at the door. Annalisa gestured her to come in. "Dr. Connolly would like to talk with you about the day her father was attacked. Do you have a few minutes?"

"Of course," she said, stepping into the office. Annalisa pointed to one of the two chairs in front of her desk. Carrie sat down.

Morgan had known Carrie Ahern since the day she had come to work for her father. She was two months shy of her nineteenth birthday at the time. It was largely because of

Allen Hawkins's encouragement that Carrie had completed her undergraduate education and then went on to become a certified physician's assistant.

"Annalisa mentioned to me that you did the initial evaluation on Artesian," Morgan began. "What do you remember about him?"

"He was a little strange, but it wasn't like there were a bunch of alarms going off in my head."

"What do you mean by strange?" Morgan asked her.

"He was way too familiar for a first-timer," Carrie explained, pushing a few strands of hair from her forehead. "A lot of patients are talkative on their first visit, but it's usually because they're nervous. He seemed totally relaxed and he acted like he was some kind of expert on hospitals and doctors. He kept trying to impress your father with everything he knew about patient safety and Code Fifteens." Carrie moved forward in her chair a couple of inches. "He said he knew you, Dr. Connolly."

Annalisa and Morgan exchanged a curious look.

"Did he mention my name specifically?"

Carrie nodded. "He said you saw him in the emergency room, and that you had referred him to your father for further treatment of his hand."

"Wait a minute. Are you saying he knew I was Dr. Hawkins's daughter?"

"He absolutely knew. I remember because it surprised me."

Morgan gazed over at Annalisa for a second time. "This doesn't make any sense," she insisted. "I don't tell patients who my father is, and I would never refer a patient to him. The other orthopedic surgeons on ER call would have a meltdown if they thought I was showing favoritism." Morgan stood up. She walked over to Annalisa's desk and sat down on the corner. "Did he say anything else about me?"

"He knew you were chief of the Emergency Department and the chairperson of the Patient Safety Committee."

"How in the world would he know that?" Morgan asked, without really expecting a response. "Why did you leave the exam room? Normally, you wouldn't do that."

"He told your father he had a personal health problem that he wanted to talk to him about. He didn't actually ask me to leave but I took the hint."

"Do you remember anything else he said?" Morgan inquired.

Carrie's eyes narrowed in thought. "It wasn't anything he said, but there was definitely something else weird about him."

"What do you mean?"

"He didn't look right."

"What do you mean?" Annalisa asked.

"I'm in the gym six days a week. People's faces can sometimes fool you but it's different with their bodies. For an old guy hobbling around on a cane, he looked to be in pretty good shape."

Carrie's observations came as no surprise to Morgan. The police had already told her that based on the violent nature of the crime, they assumed Artesian was a younger man who had disguised his appearance.

"Anything else?" Morgan asked.

Carrie paused briefly and then added, "Only that he needed a good orthodontist."

Morgan barely heard the overhead page requesting Carrie to come to the X-ray room. When she saw Carrie glance over at Annalisa, she pushed herself off the desk. She walked over to Carrie and extended her hand. "Thanks a lot. You've been a big help."

"I'm very sorry about your father, Dr. Connolly. He did a lot for me over the years. I lost my dad last year."

Morgan thanked her again and walked her to the door. She waited for Carrie to disappear down the hall before closing the door.

"Do you think she told the police all that?" she asked Annalisa.

"She must have. They interviewed her for almost an hour."

Morgan shook her head. "I don't remember treating anybody recently with a hand injury who might fit Artesian's description."

"That's because you probably didn't."

"Excuse me?"

"Whoever this guy was—he lied about everything. I went over his patient information form with the police in detail. It was like reading a fairy tale. After we were done, one of the detectives called the medical records department over at the hospital to see if Artesian had ever been a patient. They said they had no record of anybody by that name ever being seen in the emergency room."

"He might have used a different name," Morgan pointed out.

"I guess that's possible."

"I'm going to pull up my patient encounters by diagnostic code. It will show me all the hand injuries I've treated in the last year."

"What do you think about Artesian claiming to have known you?"

"I had no idea," Morgan said, pressing her palms and fingertips together. "But I'm not surprised. The police are pretty strict about sharing information about their investigations."

"Did they tell you about the note?" she asked in a hesitant voice.

A look of bewilderment flashed across Morgan's face. "What note?"

"He left a note, Morgan. Artesian left a note," she repeated, stopping after each word.

"He put it on the counter. I didn't notice it until right after the paramedics took your father over to the hospital. I gave it to the police."

"Did you read it?"

She nodded. "Normally, my memory's not that good, but I

guess this is the kind of thing you never forget. It said, *Hell is truth denied. Comes now the penance for the third of three.* He signed it *Gideon.*"

"The third of three? What's that supposed to mean? Three what?" Morgan asked, thinking to herself that whoever Stuart Artesian, or Gideon, as he called himself, really was, his plan to kill her father was very well orchestrated. Having spoken with both Carrie and Annalisa, Morgan didn't feel there was any reason to talk with any of the other staff.

"Thanks for all your help."

Annalisa met Morgan in the middle of the office and gave her a long hug. "Bill and I want to have you over for dinner."

"As soon as things calm down," Morgan promised, realizing that Annalisa's invitation didn't include Kevin and that she must have heard about their separation. Morgan was relieved Annalisa had the courtesy to spare her a barrage of questions about it.

They walked together through the lobby. "I'll call you about dinner," Morgan told her again when they reached the door.

Heavy in thought regarding the note Gideon had left, Morgan barely remembered leaving her father's building and walking to her car. Before pulling out, she put the Thunderbird's top down. With the warmth of the sun blanketing her shoulders, she thought about everything Carrie had said.

The question that continued to plague her was, why had he made it a point to inform Carrie that he knew she was Allen Hawkins's daughter? He had to have known Carrie would tell the police. And why would he leave that cryptic note? As disturbed as she suspected Gideon was, she was convinced he was a man with an unambiguous agenda and a very specific method to his insanity. It didn't take a criminologist to see he was inviting the police to engage in some twisted mind game with him.

Morgan looked in her rearview mirror and slowly backed out of her parking space. As much as it frightened her to consider the possibility, she had to wonder if Gideon's strange preoccupation with her meant that she too was part of his ruthless obsession.

CHAPTER
13

When Gideon spotted Jimmy's Place, a well-known family restaurant in North Miami, he put on his directional signal and turned into the parking lot.

Before he got out of his car, he checked the time. If her schedule hadn't changed, Faith Russo would be working lunch. Gideon hadn't come across Faith by pure happenstance. To the contrary, he had invested a considerable amount of time and energy searching for just the right woman.

Once he had decided on Faith, he spent several weeks carefully cultivating his relationship with her. When he walked through the front door, the first thing he noticed was that the usual lunch-hour chaos was winding down. On the line, one of the short-order cooks was tossing a salad while the other stood in front of the grill tending to a sizzling burger.

Gideon finally spotted Faith at the far end of the three-sided counter taking an order. He bypassed a few empty tables and took a seat at the end of the counter. As soon as Faith saw him, she smiled and waved. At the age of twenty-six, Faith Russo was possessed with a trusting nature and a tranquil disposition. She had a rail-thin figure, generous eyebrows, and a slightly upturned nose. From the beginning, Gideon saw her as a street-smart survivor, always looking for a shortcut to a better life. In spite of a deadbeat for an ex-husband and a few lackluster boyfriends, Faith was steadfast in her optimism that she would one day meet the right man who would rescue her from the day-to-day drudgery that had become the mainstay of her life.

Filling a brown mug with coffee, she walked over and set it down in front of him.

Knowing Gideon only as Steve, she said, "You're a little late today. What'll you have?"

"How about tuna and tomato on whole wheat toast? Eighty-six the lettuce."

She grinned and shook her head. "I don't know why I even ask."

"What do you mean?"

"You always order the same thing," she said with a flirtatious giggle.

"Once you've found what you like, there's no reason to keep experimenting," Gideon said, stroking the back of her hand. "How are those kids of yours?"

"They're a handful, but I love 'em to pieces."

"Do you think you'll have any more?"

She chuckled as she scribbled his order down. "For the right guy, maybe."

"Really?"

She waved the check in the air. "Let me go put this in. I'll be right back. You look tired."

"I've been working pretty hard lately."

Gideon watched her walk over to the line and clip the check to a rotating rack. She looked back at him every few seconds. Ignoring her other customers, she strolled back and began wiping down the counter.

"What is it that you do again?"

"I'm a health-care consultant," Gideon told her. "I advise hospitals how to improve their patient satisfaction."

"What do you mean by patient satisfaction?" she asked, topping off his coffee.

"Hospitals want to make sure their patients are happy with the care they receive."

"Why? What choice do they have? It's not exactly like going to Disney."

"That's just the point. People do have a choice. Nowadays, hospitals are no different than all those car dealerships down Seventh Avenue," he said, pointing toward the large window. "They both compete for your business in a big way."

"So why do these hospitals need you?"

"My company evaluates patient satisfaction and then provides the hospital with key information on how to improve it."

"Which hospital do you work for?" she asked.

"Several, but Dade Presbyterian's my biggest client."

"You're up, Faith," came a voice from the line. She glanced over, saw that her order was ready, and went to pick it up.

"How do you find out if the patients are happy or not?" she asked, putting his plate down in front of him.

"Lots of ways but mostly by interviews and surveys." He took the first bite of his sandwich and reached for his a napkin. "If you don't mind me asking, how much do you make as a waitress?"

"On a busy day, I can make a hundred in tips."

"For the way you guys work, that doesn't sound like much."

"It's not bad compared to some of the other jobs out there. It's not like I'm a brain surgeon or a real-estate tycoon."

She picked up the saltshaker, wiped it clean with a damp rag, and then replaced it on the counter.

"You seem pretty good with people to me."

"I never thought about it too much, but I guess I am," she said with a light shrug.

"Supposing I told you that you could make a thousand dollars for a few hours of work? What would you say?"

She snickered, looking at him as if he was being more mischievous than offensive.

"I'd say why pay for something you could get for free?"

"I'm talking about a business proposition."

"You're serious?"

He held up three fingers. "Scout's honor."

"What would I have to do?"

"It's simple. We'd prep you first and then send you into Dade Presbyterian's emergency room where you'd pretend to be a patient. Afterward, we'd ask you a bunch of questions about how you were treated."

Her eyes narrowed. "All I have to do is go to the emergency room, fake like I'm sick, and then tell you about it."

He nodded.

"And for that I get a thousand bucks?"

"Pretty much. I'd have to prep you first. But in a nutshell, that's it."

"What do I do if the doctor orders medications for me or wants to give me some kind of a treatment?" she asked.

"We try to create scenarios where that doesn't happen, but even if it does, I'll teach you how to talk your way out of it. What do you say?"

"Are you kidding? Of course, I'll do it."

"Good. Give me your phone number. I'll give you a call in a few days."

Faith tore off one of her checks, wrote her phone number on the back, and handed it to him.

"It almost sounds too good to be true," she said with a sudden look of hesitancy. "There's no way I can get in trouble for this, is there?"

"Of course not. The hospital administration is paying us to do this," he assured her. "And this could be just the beginning. Some people we've hired have done so well that we've used them at other hospitals. We've even sent a few of them out of state and paid all their expenses plus their fee."

"This is a godsend. Those stinkers of mine all need new clothes," she said.

"How far do you live from Dade Presbyterian?"

"About twenty minutes, I guess."

"That's perfect. We like to do these at night so all you'll need is a babysitter and we're in business."

Faith was now beaming as she extended her hand. "I really appreciate this, Steve."

"Are you kidding? You're the one who's helping me." Gideon took the last bite of his sandwich and stood up. "Let's hope this is the start of something really special."

Faith blushed.

"There's just one thing," he said, pretending to look around with concern. "I'd really appreciate it if you wouldn't discuss this with anybody."

"How come?"

"When people hear about something like this, they all want to get in on the act. The last thing I need with my schedule is to be flooded by a million requests for jobs."

"Not a problem," she said, raising her finger to her lips.

Gideon handed her a twenty-dollar bill. "I'll speak to you in a couple of days."

"Sounds great. I'll be right back with your change."

"Keep it," he said. "Get something for the kids."

"You're so nice," she told him. She then looked in the direction of the cash register where the manager was busy with a customer. Gideon was just about to stand up when she quickly leaned over and kissed him softly on the cheek.

Walking toward the front door, he was pleased with how easily he had been able to bring Faith into the fold. He harbored some remorse about using her as a pawn. But her involvement in his affairs would be brief, and it would give an otherwise inconsequential person the opportunity to serve a much higher purpose.

CHAPTER
14

Apart from performing an occasional FAA flight physical, Ben Docherty was firm in his decision never to return to the day-to-day grind of practicing medicine.

Having just completed an examination of a radiologist who had recently decided to return to flying after a twenty-year layoff, he stopped at the CB Discount Pharmacy to pick up the morning newspaper. The establishment, which was located directly across the street from Dade Presbyterian, had been there almost as long as the hospital and was one of the few independent drugstores to have survived the invasion of the national chains.

Making his way past the usual swarm of people waiting impatiently for their prescriptions to be filled, Ben worked his way toward the main counter. He was just about to reach for the *Miami Herald* when he saw Morgan standing in front of the cashier.

From behind her he said, "Do you want me to call the phone company for you?" he asked. "I think your voice mail is on the fritz."

Recognizing his voice immediately, she shook her head, turned, and said, "I got home late. I was going to return your call but then I remembered about calling you past nine o'clock."

"What are you talking about?"

"C'mon, Ben. Every time I call you much past nine, I wake you up. It's like calling a nursing home."

Guilty as charged and seeing no reason to try to debate the point, Ben moved on. "Did you go over to your father's office?"

"I went yesterday."

"And?"

"It was sad. I guess I miss him more than I thought."

"It's only been few weeks. Give yourself a little time," he told her. "Did you get a chance to speak with anybody?"

Morgan stepped up to the cashier and paid for her hodge-podge of candy and sundries.

"I have to meet with the first-year residents in about twenty minutes. Walk me over to the library and I'll tell you about it."

Ben nodded and pointed toward the exit. Morgan put her change in her purse and they started for the hospital.

"I spoke to the office manager and his physician's assistant. Her name's Carrie. I think you may have met her at the office Christmas party."

"The name's familiar."

"Do you remember I told you that the man who killed my father signed in under the name of Stuart Artesian? "

Ben nodded.

"It seems he left this mysterious note neatly folded on the countertop. It read: *Hell is truth denied. Comes now the penance for the third of three.* He signed it *Gideon*."

"Does that mean anything to you?"

"That's all I've been thinking about since yesterday," she said, shaking her head. "I can't come up with a thing." The light turned green and they quick-walked across the street. They continued under an ivy-covered walkway until reaching a revolving glass door that accessed the main lobby of the hospital. While they walked, Morgan filled Ben in on everything else she had learned from talking to Carrie and Annalisa.

"The police never said a word to you about any of this?" Ben asked.

"Remember what I told you about how they conduct their investigations. They don't share information with anybody. I'm getting pretty frustrated."

"I still think you have to give them more time. It's not as if you have a lot of other options."

"I'm trying to be patient, Ben, but there are a lot of things about my father's death that don't make sense. If this guy, Gideon, were simply a disgruntled patient, he could have murdered my father in a lot simpler way. Why did he go to such extreme lengths? Why would he leave that cryptic note . . . and why would he take the time to kill my father by filling his chest cavity with air and collapsing his lung?"

"I don't know if there's an answer to that. The problem is you're trying to logically account for the actions of someone who is almost certainly irrational."

"I don't know how to measure his insanity, but he's definitely methodical."

They walked down a long hallway adorned with a series of bronze plaques recognizing the past chiefs of staff of the hospital. With five minutes to spare, they reached the library. Once inside, they made their way to a small glass-fronted study room and sat down at a racetrack-shaped conference table.

"I had breakfast in the doctors' dining room today," Ben began. "Everybody was taking about some disastrous open-heart operation. Did you hear about it?"

"I chair the Patient Safety Committee. Of course I heard about it. I was probably the first one they called."

"Who was the surgeon?" Ben asked.

"McBride."

"He's a good technician. What went wrong?"

"We don't know yet. I spent most of yesterday afternoon with him and everybody on the cardiac team." She stopped and filled her lungs with a deep breath. "We can't figure it out. The operative record is clean. From all appearances, it was an uneventful case—no mistakes."

"Until the pump clotted off, you mean. Are you going to report it as a Code Fifteen?"

"Ben, a cardiac bypass pump clotted off in the middle of an open-heart operation and the patient died. Are we going to report it?" she asked rhetorically. "We'll be lucky if the Agency for Health Care Administration doesn't make this case their poster child for Code Fifteens."

"Have you started a root cause analysis?" he asked.

"The committee's meeting tomorrow to get it rolling. I'm sure it will be a long, drawn-out process. This case was bad enough, but coming on the heels of our last Code Fifteen, which also involved a Cardiac Care Center patient . . . well, I'm sure you can imagine everybody's a little edgy to say the least."

"Bob Allenby must be ready to kill himself."

"He is the CEO of the hospital," Morgan said. "The Cardiac Care Center was his baby. Up until a couple of months ago we never had a Code Fifteen involving a heart patient. Now we've got two and they're both bad ones."

"What was the other one?"

"It was a pacemaker case involving a young woman. It happened a few weeks ago. It was a totally routine procedure until about eight hours after surgery. For no apparent reason, she suddenly developed a disturbance in her cardiac rhythm. They couldn't get her heart rate below two hundred. She eventually had a full cardiac arrest. They worked on her for almost an hour but couldn't get her back."

"That sounds like ventricular tachycardia. What caused it?"

"I wish we knew. We reviewed every aspect of the case. It was probably the most thorough and exhaustive root cause analysis I've ever been involved with. We still haven't come up with a thing," Morgan said with a long sigh. "They made me the chairperson of the committee for a reason. I'm supposed to be an expert on patient errors. I don't feel like I'm doing my job very well. I know there's an answer to all of this, but for some reason I'm just not seeing it."

"Then take it to the next level. Try treating it as if it were a complicated aviation accident."

Morgan's eyebrows arched in question. "Which means what exactly?"

"Dismiss your assumptions and expand the possibilities. I'd start by talking to everybody involved again, but this time look beyond the obvious."

Morgan looked at him as if he'd been reading her diary. "It's funny you should say that. I called Dana McGinley yesterday. She was the CCU nurse assigned to Miss Greene. I'm supposed to meet with her later today. She was interviewed by Arnie Miller from Neurology but I never spoke to her personally."

"If you don't mind me saying so, you seem pretty discouraged."

Before Morgan could respond, three young women dressed in pale blue surgical scrubs burst through the doors in laughter. When they saw Morgan and Ben, a sudden sense of decorum came over them.

"Whoever's doing the first case presentation, get it ready. I'll be right back," Morgan told them as she and Ben stood up. They walked back to the library's entrance.

"Have you heard from Kevin?" he asked.

"Not a word."

From her unconcerned manner and tone, he assumed she wasn't crestfallen about it. For the past couple of days, he couldn't help from wondering if Morgan had already started dating. He wanted to ask her to dinner but the fear of embarrassing himself kept him tongue-tied. He couldn't imagine anything more humiliating than allowing Morgan to know he was romantically interested in her only to find out that she considered him like another older brother instead of a love interest. He knew how friendly she was with her obstetrician, Jenny Silverman. He was also familiar from personal experience with Jenny's incurable compulsion to fix up every unattached woman she knew.

"What are you thinking about?" Morgan asked him. "Your lips are moving."

"Excuse me?"

She laughed. "Where are you?"

"I . . . I was thinking about work. I'm having a problem with one of my planes," he answered without hesitation.

Morgan looked at him as if he were growing a second head right in front of her eyes.

"One of your planes has a problem. That's your dilemma?"

"Uh-huh."

With circumspect eyes she asked, "Have you thought about asking one of your fifteen mechanics to have a look at it?"

He nodded slowly. "That's a good idea," he said, without a single illusion of how ridiculous he was sounding.

"Give me a call later. I want to talk to you a little bit more about what Carrie told me."

"What time?"

"I'm going to meet with Dana around five. It shouldn't take more than an hour."

"I'll call you at around six."

"I have a better idea. Why don't you take me to dinner? We can talk then." She turned and started back for the meeting room. "I'm in the mood for Italian. Pick a place. I'll speak with you later."

"Sounds good," Ben said, trying not to sound like he had just won the lottery and wondering how Morgan could sound so blasé about them going out for the first time.

So much for trying to gather the nerve to ask her out, he thought as he headed back toward the hospital's main lobby. It wasn't until he reached the street that the self-satisfied smirk finally left his face.

CHAPTER 15

At five p.m., Morgan pulled into the parking lot of Donovan's Grill.

The newly opened sports bar was a favorite among the Dade Presbyterian nurses. As soon as Morgan walked into the restaurant she spotted Dana McGinley sitting at one of the booths that surrounded a granite-topped rectangular bar. Above each of the booths, the wood-paneled walls were bedecked with a wide variety of sports memorabilia.

"This is a lot better than meeting in the hospital," Morgan said as she slid into the booth.

"I was just thinking the same thing. Maybe you can use your influence and persuade administration to schedule all of our meetings here," Dana suggested.

Before taking the position of assistant nurse manager of the Cardiac Care Center, Dana had been a tried and true emergency room nurse. She and Morgan had worked numerous backbreaking shifts together and had emerged from the ordeal as good friends. Barely five feet tall and with no airs or graces, Dana remained a trim one hundred pounds irrespective of how many calories a day she consumed.

"I'm sorry I'm late," Morgan said. "I was reviewing a case for a hospital in Illinois. I guess I lost track of the time."

"Why would a hospital in Illinois send you a case to review?"

"They had a serious patient error and wanted me to make some suggestions how to change their system to avoid the same thing from ever happening again."

"What kind of a case?"

"It involved a twenty-year-old motorcyclist who sustained a major head injury. The hospital followed their usual protocol and pronounced him brain-dead. He had designated himself as an organ donor, so they called the transplant harvest team from the university hospital. The trouble was when the transplant team was preparing the kid to remove his organs, he coughed."

"Coughed? How can you be brain-dead and cough?"

"That's just the point; you can't. He was in a bad coma but very much alive. The organ harvest was obviously canceled and five weeks later the kid walked out of the hospital."

"Are you kidding?"

"I wish I were."

"So now what do you do?"

"I'll write the hospital a diplomatic letter suggesting changes in their protocol for pronouncing people brain-dead."

"That's quite a story," Dana said, signaling an approaching server. She then reached across the table and covered Morgan's hand with her own. "How are you doing?" she asked.

"It's been a rough few weeks. Getting back to work has helped a lot."

A young man wearing a red apron and a white shirt strolled up to the table. "What can I get for you ladies?" he asked, placing a napkin in front of each of them.

"I'll have a sour apple martini," Dana said.

"A Coke for me."

"A Coke? What happened to the queen of the margarita?"

"I've kind of lost my taste for margaritas," Morgan said.

Dana smiled at her knowingly. "A temporary situation, I hope. Maybe about nine months."

"I just found out a couple of weeks ago. I'm not keeping it

a secret, but I haven't exactly scheduled a baby shower at the Ritz either."

"Congratulations," Dana said, reaching across the table and squeezing her hands. "When are you due?"

"Late October."

"That's terrific news. I'm really happy for you." Morgan and Dana spent the next fifteen minutes catching up on the latest hospital gossip. Dana was already working on her second martini when she asked, "When were you going to tell me about Kevin?"

Morgan sighed. "How did you know?"

"Discretion's not one of Kevin's strong suits. A bunch of the nurses have seen him out." She reached across the table and took Morgan's hand. "We've been friends a long time, and I'm not trying to poke my nose into your affairs, but if you need someone to talk to, call me." She smiled painfully and added, "It's not as if half of us haven't been through the same thing."

Morgan spoke to Dana for a few minutes about the divorce but when the time was right, she broached the topic of the Code 15 and Alison Greene's death.

"I know you've already spoken to Dr. Walters, but as the chair of the Patient Safety Committee, I wanted to talk to you myself."

"Sure."

"Do you remember what Miss Greene's condition was when you admitted her?"

"She was rock stable."

"When did she start to crash?"

"It was about six hours after I got her from the recovery room. Her heart rate suddenly jumped from seventy to three hundred."

"Then what?"

"She dumped her blood pressure. That's when we called the code blue and began CPR. Dr. Balbuenas was on the floor and he came running. He's one of the sharpest docs we have, but he couldn't do anything to restore a normal heart rhythm."

"The medical record said you coded her for about thirty minutes before you finally gave up."

"That sounds about right."

"The committee has been over every aspect of her care—every blood test, X-ray, and medication she received, and we don't have the first clue what the hell went wrong. Do you have any ideas?"

"I've seen a lot of patients develop heart rhythm problems," she said, shaking her head. "There's almost always a reason."

"Except in this case."

"I wish I could help, Morgan, but I have no idea why she went into ventricular tachycardia or why we couldn't get her out of it."

"Were there any other nurses besides you taking care of her?"

"I took a dinner break but I don't remember who I signed out to."

Remembering Ben's advice regarding looking beyond the obvious, she asked, "Forget about the medicine part of this thing for a second. Did anything unusual or unexpected happen?"

Dana held up her glass while she pondered the question. "The cross," she answered.

"What cross?"

"After her parents left, she had another visitor. He said he was a friend. He was pretty talkative. He must have told me three times he was a professor at Broward College. I was a little surprised because he looked more like a jock than a professor."

Nodding from the memory as she put her glass down, Dana said, "Right before he was about to leave, he put a cross around her neck."

"What's so unusual about that?"

"In the first place he wasn't a family member, and in the

second, he didn't ask if it was okay. Most people would have. He just put it on, said good night, and left."

"I still don't see what—"

"Later on, when she coded and we started CPR, I removed it so it wouldn't interfere with the chest compressions. When Balbuenas called off the code and we started to clean up, I put it back on. When her parents came in to see her and make the funeral arrangements they saw the cross and flipped out."

"Why?"

"Because they're Jewish," Dana said with a painful frown. "It was on her admission facesheet but I had no reason to check. They were livid. They demanded to know how the hospital could have made such a thoughtless mistake."

"What did you tell them?"

"I told them the truth and immediately apologized."

"Did they calm down?"

"A little. They wanted to know the man's name so I checked the visitor's log and got it for them."

Dana reached for her purse. She opened it and pushed her hand all the way to the bottom. After a few seconds of digging around, she pulled out a white envelope. She tore open one end and spilled a silver cross into her opposite hand.

"You saved it?" Morgan asked.

"I was going to report the whole mess to the nursing supervisor and give her the cross, but I guess with all the commotion, I forgot." She handed the cross to Morgan and then pointed at the envelope. I wrote the guy's name down right there. He signed in as I. Ogden. The parents told me they had no idea who he was."

"Besides being a little talkative, do you remember anything else about him?"

"Not really." Her mouth creased into a subtle grin.

"What?" Morgan asked.

"He had a big gap between his front teeth. The reason I remember is because he reminded me of the first guy I dated in college."

Morgan held up the cross. Watching it twirl slowly on its delicate chain, it struck her as quite simple and inexpensive. The incident was certainly an unfortunate one, but of little importance with respect to the Code 15. She assumed Mr. Ogden was simply a good-intentioned friend who didn't know Miss Greene was Jewish.

She set the cross down next to her cell phone.

"When are you working again?" Morgan asked.

"Not until the end of the week. I'm looking forward to the time off." Dana pointed at Morgan's empty glass. "How about another Coke?"

"I'd love to, but I kind of have a date."

"What does that mean exactly—kind of have a date?"

"It's just dinner."

"Who are you going with? Do I know him?"

"I'm not sure if—"

Dana grabbed Morgan by the wrists. Her eyes widened. "Don't tell me you're going out with Ben Docherty."

Morgan averted her eyes. "Why would you think that?"

"You are," she said.

"I didn't say that."

"You didn't have to. I knew it. Before he retired, everybody knew he had a major thing for you."

"That's ridiculous."

"I think I speak for every single woman in Broward and Dade County when I say if you take Ben Docherty off the most eligible list, we're going to come after you with a noose."

Morgan laughed. "I'd better get going."

"Call me later. I want to hear every tawdry detail."

"Thanks for your help."

Morgan reached for the check.

"Let's split it," Dana was quick to insist.

"No way. This was hospital business. I'm sure Bob Allenby will be overjoyed to pick up the tab." Morgan reached for the cross to return it to Dana. A puzzled look came to her face when she realized it was stuck to the metal casing of her cell phone. She pushed her thumb against it with increasing force until it finally slid off. Befuddled for the moment, she held up the cross to study it. "That's weird."

"What is?" Dana asked.

"This cross is magnetized." Morgan put it back on the phone and then slid it off again. "It's pretty strong for such a small thing."

"I've never seen anything like that."

"Do you mind if I hold on to this for a while?" Morgan asked.

"Go ahead," Dana told her, sliding out of the booth. "I'm going to make a little stop before I leave. Call me."

"Thanks again."

Morgan held the cross up, studying it intently. There was something perplexing about it but she couldn't quite figure out what. She put the cross against her cell phone again and slid it off. Deep in thought, she didn't notice the man who walked past her on his way back to the bar. If she had, she might have noticed he had gapped front teeth and that his eyes were fixed on the crucifix. After another minute or so, Morgan stood up and headed across the restaurant.

Taking his seat at the end of the bar, Gideon clenched his fist in frustration. Even without her uniform, he had recognized Dana McGinley as the nurse who had taken care of Alison Greene. He'd been sloppy; a mistake he had compounded by underestimating Dr. Connolly's persistence. After taking a minute to collect himself, he decided his oversight, while unforgivable, would not prove to be a fatal error. He glanced toward the front of the restaurant just as Morgan walked out. He dropped a ten-dollar bill on the bar and stood up.

By the time he reached the sidewalk, Morgan was getting into her car. He considered following her but decided to resist the temptation. Instead, he strolled off in the opposite direction. He was in no position to take any chances or speculate about anything. He had to assume Dr. Connolly now knew that Alison Greene was wearing the cross the night she died and that it was magnetized. The question was whether she'd be able to attach any significance to what most doctors would consider two unrelated facts.

For the moment he felt cautiously optimistic and saw no reason to alter his plans. But he would proceed with even a greater degree of care—fully aware that at any time, Dr. Morgan Connolly could figure out exactly how he had killed Alison Greene.

CHAPTER

16

After racking his brain for most of the afternoon trying to decide where to take Morgan for dinner, Ben finally decided on Pizzola's, a small neighborhood Italian restaurant close to the ocean.

They had been seated for about ten minutes when their waiter, a portly man with a meager salt-and-pepper goatee, brought over the bottle of Chianti Rufina Ben had ordered. Contrary to his earlier concerns, Ben was completely at ease. He held up the basket-bottle wine, waiting for Morgan's approval. She pointed about one-third of the way up her glass. With the delicate aroma of simmering garlic drifting across the restaurant, Ben filled her glass to the level she requested.

"The food here is great here. I hope you'll be able to enjoy it," he teased, pointing to her stomach and then half filling his own glass.

"That's usually a morning thing but I appreciate your concern," she said with a mock laugh, reaching for the menu. "Actually, I'm famished. Everything looks great."

The waiter returned and after listening to the specials, Ben ordered the stuffed tilapia, while Morgan selected a pasta dish with a spicy arrabiata sauce.

"Were you able to track down your mother?" he inquired.

"I finally caught up to her in Saint Petersburg. I left a message at her hotel. She called me back a few hours ago."

"It seems like you're speaking to her more often lately."

"We've always been close. It doesn't seem to matter how often we talk, but I think we've both been trying a little harder since my father died."

"What does she think about you being pregnant?"

"She's ecstatic about the idea. She's already got the nursery in her house planned out."

For the next hour and a half, they enjoyed their food, laughed, and talked nonstop about flying, traveling, and a host of other innocuous topics. There was no discussion of Code 15s, police investigations, or hospital politics.

While they were waiting for the cappuccinos they had ordered, Morgan asked, "How come you haven't asked me about my meeting with Dana?"

"You seemed to be enjoying dinner. I assumed if you wanted to talk about it, you'd bring it up."

Morgan waited until the waiter had placed the cups in front of them.

"Actually, I wouldn't mind getting your input."

"In that case, go ahead," he told her.

"From a medical standpoint, it was pretty much as I told you. The only strange thing was that immediately before she arrested, she had a visitor. He signed in as I. Ogden. Dana said he was a professor at Broward College. Right before he left, he put a cross around her neck."

"What's so strange about that?"

"Nothing except Miss Greene happened to be Jewish. It caused a major problem when her parents came in to make the funeral arrangements and saw the cross."

"I agree that's an unusual thing to happen, but the explanation seems obvious enough. Whoever this visitor was, his heart was in the right place. He just didn't know she was Jewish."

"I guess that's possible."

"You don't sound convinced."

"Dana was going to give the cross to the nurse in charge,

but she forgot. When we met she remembered it was at the bottom of her purse. After I looked at it, I put it down. It stuck to my cell phone like it had been painted with superglue. I could barely slide it off."

"You mean it was magnetized," Ben said, suddenly noticing the remarkable change in her expression and the fatigue in her eyes. Before Morgan could say anything more, he added, "You look worn out. Why don't we talk more about this tomorrow?"

Morgan acknowledged his suggestion with a half smile and a nod.

During the short ride back to her condominium, Ben purposely kept the conversation light. When he pulled up to the circular driveway, the doorman stepped out and opened the door for Morgan. Ben got out and walked her to the elevator.

"Thanks for taking me to dinner," she said, leaning forward and giving him a kiss on the cheek.

When the elevator doors rolled open, he reached for her hands, gave them a quick squeeze, and said, "I'll call you tomorrow."

Instead of taking I-95, he decided to drive down A1A. His home was on Bal Harbor about a twenty-minute ride from Morgan's condominium. Lumbering along behind a white panel truck, he thought about the evening and how well it had gone.It was nice for once not having to deal with the usual painful nonsense that accompanied a first date.

As he pulled out and sped past the truck, he grinned inwardly. For the first time, he had more than just an inkling that Morgan's interest in him might be more than platonic.

CHAPTER
17

DAY FIVE

There were few things in the world that Morgan loved more than Limerick, her nine-month-old Irish Red and White Setter.

Walking him at sunrise on the Hollywood Broadwalk, a two-mile-long beachfront walkway, had become an inviolate part of her schedule. Lined by a diverse group of shops, boutiques, and cafés, the Broadwalk attracted a steady stream of walkers, skateboarders, and joggers.

Morgan had been strolling for about ten minutes when Limerick suddenly began wagging his tail wildly and yanking her forward. It took only one glimpse to understand why he was so overjoyed. With his signature grin covering his face, Kevin walked up. He caught Limerick's front paws as he jumped up and petted his head. At the moment, Kevin was the last person she wanted to see.

"I love this guy," he said. He turned his gaze toward Morgan and added, "I haven't heard from you in a while. How's it going?"

"How did you know I'd be here?" she asked.

"You may be a complicated woman, but you're a creature of habit and as predictable as the tides." Kevin took Limerick's leash and they started walking. Morgan said nothing. "Things are looking great," he began with his usual inflated optimism.

In spite of his incurable vanity, Kevin had recently attained his fortieth birthday with a minimum of emotional damage. A self-proclaimed real-estate entrepreneur with a great gift of gab, he was always in search of that life-defining deal that would make him a player. Unfortunately, he was a man who wanted all of life's privileges but without any of the responsibilities.

It was his promise of greatness, sapphire eyes, and pale blond hair that had originally drawn Morgan to him. An avid distance runner with the muscular legs to prove it, Kevin generally avoided the pit bull approach in his dealings with people, opting instead for more subtle methods. They had met while she was at Tampa General Hospital as an emergency medicine resident. He was a graduate student at the time in international business and there was an instant attraction and undeniable chemistry between them. They soon agreed upon an exclusive relationship and were married a year later.

"What are you doing here?" she asked him as two teenage in-line skaters flew by.

"Can't a guy pay his wife a visit?"

Seeing nothing innocent in his question, she snickered. "In case you've forgotten, we've been separated for the past six months."

"I thought we agreed to work on things."

"Work things out? Apart from a few dinners out and what they stupidly led to, I've barely heard from you in weeks."

"You're right, but in my defense, I've been working like a one-armed paperhanger on a new project. I don't want to jump the gun but it looks like this one's going to be huge. I'm only targeting seven-figure investors, but if you're interested, you might want to dip your toe in the shallow end."

"Thanks, but I think I've dipped my toe for the last time." Morgan looked at him as if he were trying to sell her five times more life insurance than she needed. "Let me see," she began slowly. "It's baseball season, isn't it?"

An all-too-familiar look came to his face. "Baseball season? What's that got to do with anything?"

"I seem to remember that Major League Baseball is your preferred sport to bet on."

"C'mon, Morgan. I told you. I'm all done with that." He held his hand over his heart, a sure sign to Morgan that he was lying.

"Save the crap for the customers, Kevin. It demeans both of us. How much do you owe?"

After a few seconds, his manufactured look of surprise changed to one of concession. He dropped his head.

"I sometimes forget how sharp you are."

"Don't work me. Just tell me how much you owe."

With a short sigh, his saccharine grin evaporated. "Eight thousand will give me some wiggle room."

"Wiggle room? That sounds more like a zip code. I hope you're kidding."

"I wish I were," he muttered.

Morgan looked past him in silence. She then pointed to the railing. He followed her over.

"I'm sorry for your trouble, Kevin, but I'm not bailing you out this time."

"I'm not asking for a handout, baby. I just need a bridge loan until this deal hits. As soon as it does, I'll pay you back every nickel plus interest. This time it's a sure thing. I wouldn't be asking you if it weren't."

She shook her head. "Don't call me 'baby.' And the answer is no. I'm not bailing you out this time."

Kevin squatted and petted Limerick again. He couldn't look at her at first.

"These are serious people, Morgan," he said without raising his eyes. "They won't think twice about coming after me."

Whatever contempt and disdain she harbored for Kevin paled in comparison to the desperation in his voice and the humiliation in his eyes when he finally did look up at her.

Gazing out at the four-footers rolling up to the beach, she said, "I'll send you a check for two thousand. That's all I can afford. You'll have to find the rest on your own."

"I . . . I don't know what—"

"What happened to Gamblers Anonymous? Did you ever go?" she asked, wondering what had become of the man she'd married.

"The last thing I need is a bunch of losers telling me how to run my life. Just because I've been a little unlucky lately doesn't mean I have a gambling problem."

"Losers?" she said more to herself than Kevin. Convinced that any further attempts to persuade him to deal with his addiction would be futile, she stood silent.

He leaned back against the railing. "This new deal requires that I go on an extended business trip."

"Is this extended trip solo or is Kim going with you?"

"Kim?"

She raised her hand. "Don't even bother, Kevin. I knew about her before you moved out. I was going to ask you to give her up until I realized you were too old to grow a conscience. Is this trip really about business or are you running?"

"Running? From what?"

"Me, our marriage, Kim, the bookies. You tell me."

"I'm not running from anybody, Morgan. I told you. It's a business trip." Unable to maintain eye contact with her, he looked away. "I should get going."

"I've seen a lawyer," she stated flatly.

With a halfhearted grin, he handed the leash to Morgan. There was no surprise or anger in his voice. Only defeat. "I'm sorry I've disappointed you. I guess it just got too hard trying to keep up with a superstar wife." He started to walk north but then turned back around. "I'm sorry about your father. I really tried to make the funeral, but I was right in the middle of a—"

"Don't worry about it."

He nodded. "Thanks for the money. Remember, it's just a loan. I'll call you when I get settled." He shoved his hands into the front pockets of his cargo pants. But instead of starting back down the Broadwalk, he just stood there.

"Is there something else?" Morgan asked.

"When do you think you might be able to . . ."

"I'll send you the check today."

Morgan reached down and stroked the top of Limerick's head. Watching Kevin walk away, she wondered what could have possessed her to think he would be able to deal with her being pregnant? Starting back toward her condominium, she thought about the first time she'd met him. He was larger than life—ready to take on the world and any challenge it tossed in his path. How could such a bright, energetic, and creative man with an absolute limitless future have become so totally lost? She couldn't help but wonder if she was in any way responsible for his failure.

It was an unsettling feeling, but the man she'd just spoken to was as unknown to her as any random face in the crowd. Morgan believed in the institution of marriage, but she was also a realist. If there had been a faint glimmer of saving their marriage, it was now gone. And for the first time since they had separated, the thought of divorcing Kevin was more liberating than anything else. The realization didn't leave her despondent, nor did she feel a sense of tragedy. To the contrary, it was as if a huge burden had been lifted from her.

CHAPTER 18

Morgan stared down at the check she had just written to Kevin.

Even though it had been a couple of hours since their meeting, her mind-set regarding the fate of their marriage was unchanged. Putting the check in the envelope, she made herself an irrevocable promise it would be the last one she'd ever send. When she was finished addressing it, she tossed it in her outgoing box, gathered up the stack of monthly patient complaints, and headed across the hall to the emergency department's conference room. Of all of her administrative responsibilities, evaluating and responding to patient complaints was her least favorite. The majority were from disgruntled patients who cited lengthy wait times, indifferent ER personnel, and dissatisfaction with the doctor's treatment plan.

Irrespective of how frivolous they were, the administration required that all department chiefs respond to each and every complaint on a timely basis. The era of patient satisfaction, or the Ritz-Carlton approach as the doctors called it, had finally arrived at Dade Presbyterian Hospital. Morgan's usual response was to write a sincere letter of apology, which seemed to do the trick most of the time.

Before reading the first letter, she reached for her lukewarm can of Coke. Her queasiness had become less frequent, but she still wasn't ready to face the day without her soda and a stack of saltines within easy reach. Morgan picked up the letter, but before she read the first word the door opened about halfway. Kendra Slater, her secretary, poked her head in. Morgan noticed she was wearing an ornate silver crucifix around her neck.

"Don't forget about your nine thirty meeting with the nurses," Kendra told her. "Elena from Urgent Care has already called me twice to confirm."

"I won't forget."

"I'll remind you again in a half hour anyway."

"You're getting a little obsessive, Kendra."

"Lucky for you," she said, closing the door.

Forgetting about the stack of correspondence in front of her, Morgan's mind shifted to her meeting with Dana and the magnetized cross. As much as she tried to convince herself the cross was unrelated to the Code 15, she remained plagued by the strange event. She still wondered why Alison Greene's visitor left the cross in the first place. If he knew her well enough to visit her in the hospital, wasn't it likely he knew she was Jewish?

Morgan's eyes suddenly widened. Shaking her head in disbelief, she couldn't believe it had taken her this long to connect the dots. Without stopping to gather up the patient complaints, Morgan marched out of the conference room and went straight to her office. Without stopping to check a new stack of messages on her already cluttered desk, she opened the top drawer and grabbed the cross Dana had given her.

Speeding past Kendra, she said, "I'll be tied up for a little while. Don't page me unless it's urgent."

CHAPTER
19

With eleven hundred physicians on staff at Dade Presbyterian Hospital, the designated area for doctor parking in the eight-story garage was necessarily large.

Wearing a blue blazer with a stethoscope sticking out of the waist pocket, Gideon stood at the far end of the lot gazing over the tops of the parked cars. Although he was familiar with Morgan Connolly's teal-colored Thunderbird, it still took him ten minutes of walking up and down the rows until he spotted it parked between two towering SUVs.

Clenched in his hand was the GPS tracking device he had purchased earlier that day from a security store in North Miami. The gentleman who waited on him was quite accommodating, taking considerable time to explain exactly where to place the device and how to monitor the vehicle's exact whereabouts twenty-four hours a day from his laptop computer.

He approached Morgan's car from the front. He then took a few seconds to casually look around to make sure his actions would go unnoticed. He was just about to kneel down and attach the GPS device behind the bumper when his eye caught Morgan's open flight case sitting on the front passenger seat. Popping out of the top of the case in clear view was a brown thermos. Gideon stared at it for a few seconds before a generous smile swept across his face. Inspiration comes in many forms, he thought to himself, and that included dumb luck.

By no means ready to kill Morgan Connolly, he now had a very simple way of causing her an untold amount of personal terror. He kneeled down and stuck the homing device in place. Still grinning, he stood up, took one final look around, and then walked away.

20

With the crucifix clenched firmly in her fist, Morgan exited the elevator on the tenth floor.

Directly across from where she stood was the cardiac electrophysiology lab and the office of its director, Dr. Mira Ramon. Morgan walked through the registration area and then into the lab. In spite of its expansive size, the facility was still crowded with monitors, examination tables, and a multitude of sophisticated diagnostic instruments. Morgan looked toward the back of the lab. Seeing that Mira's door was wide open, she marched straight back to her office. Before she could tap on the door, Mira looked up, smiled, and waved her in. Morgan had known Mira since coming to Dade Presbyterian and they had always gotten along well.

Mira's office was hardly a showplace. Except for a painting of Victoria Falls, the walls were bare. There was one short bookcase behind her aging wooden desk but most of its shelves had nothing more on them than a skinny layer of dust. If there was a saving grace, it was the perfectly arranged bunch of bright yellow daisies in a crystal vase that she had placed on her credenza.

Mira closed the patient file she was reviewing. She slid her tiny reading glasses down her nose until they sat perched on the tip.

"It's so nice to see you, Morgan," she said with a sympathetic smile, coming out from behind her desk. She took Morgan's hands in hers. "How are you doing?"

"I'm doing okay."

"It was a beautiful service. Your father was certainly beloved."

"Thank you."

Mira sat down on the corner of her desk. She pointed to two empty mugs. "I'm making some tea. Would you like some?"

"No, thank you."

When Morgan didn't say anything further, Mira folded her arms across her chest and said, "If you don't mind me saying so, you look like a lady with something on her mind."

"I need a favor."

"How can I help you?"

"I could really use a quick education on pacemakers."

"Why the sudden interest in pacemakers?" Mira asked.

"It involves a recent Code Fifteen that the Patient Safety Committee is reviewing."

"I assume you mean the one involving the pacemaker insertion—not the open-heart case."

"How much do you know about the case?"

Mira stirred her tea, the spoon tapping against the inside of the mug. "I know the basics. Her death was hardly a secret."

"I spoke to the physician who represents the pacemaker company. He assured me that it couldn't have been a pacemaker problem."

Mira snickered and then took another bite of her Danish. "Now there's an objective opinion if I've ever heard one."

"You obviously disagree."

"The woman underwent placement of a pacemaker and died several hours later. I don't think you can make a categorical statement that it's impossible there could have been something wrong with the device. There's always a reason why patients go into V-tach. Who ran the code?"

"Will Balbuenas," Morgan answered. "He and I have been

over the chart so many times we could probably recite it by heart."

"What were the patient's potassium and other electrolyte levels?" Mira asked.

"All normal."

"What about her medication doses? Did you check them?"

"Ten times," Morgan answered. "Everything was right on the money."

"Did she have a heart attack? That can cause cardiac irritability and lead to V-tach."

"We ruled that out. Her EKG and cardiac enzymes were normal."

"Did her blood oxygen level drop right before the V-tach started?" Mira inquired.

"Not according to the nurse who took care of her."

Mira tapped her fingertips together. "I haven't reviewed the chart but it sounds to me like you've eliminated all the usual causes of V-tach."

Morgan reached into the pocket of her white coat, pulled out the cross, and held it up.

A puzzled grin fell upon Mira's face. "I appreciate the gesture, but I was hoping to help you without resorting to divine guidance."

They shared a quick laugh.

"Miss Greene was wearing this when she arrested," Morgan said.

"Are you suggesting that being religious might make one more likely to develop a fatal arrhythmia?"

"Not as a rule, but maybe in this case it did." Morgan placed the cross on the base of Mira's desk lamp. "The cross is a strong magnet. I remember reading somewhere that magnets are used to adjust pacemaker settings."

"A pacemaker can be programmed in a few different ways," Mira explained. "Normally, it's set in what's called an

EP mode, which means it only fires when it senses a problem with the patient's heart rate."

"What kind of a problem?" Morgan asked.

"If the person's heartbeat falls below a preset rate, the pacemaker kicks in and speeds it back up."

"So the pacemaker would be kind of a backup."

"In a manner of a speaking."

"So why would you ever have to change the settings?" Morgan asked.

"If the patient's cardiac condition changes, we might have to reprogram the pacemaker. You have to remember that these things are surgically implanted. Altering the settings would mean we'd have to reoperate on all these people. That's why the manufacturers and bioengineers came up with the idea of using magnets to change the settings."

Morgan pointed at the cross. "Is it possible that if a magnet was close enough to Alison Greene's pacemaker, it could have changed the settings?"

"It's possible," Mira answered.

"Could that lead to a problem?"

"Absolutely. If this woman's heart was beating normally, and for some reason the pacemaker started firing, it could have drastically upset the normal electrical currents of her heart. The heart's wired very efficiently, but it's also exquisitely sensitive. If a pacemaker was improperly set and fired at the wrong time of the cardiac cycle, it could upset the conduction system and cause a type of V-tach that would have been extremely difficult to reverse."

"So it is possible," Morgan whispered.

"In the absence of another plausible explanation, I would say it's quite possible."

"This is unbelievable," Morgan muttered to herself as she slid the cross from the lamp. "I wonder how somebody would have gone about magnetizing it?"

"I doubt anybody magnetized it," Mira informed her.

"I beg your pardon."

"It was probably manufactured that way." Mira reached for the cross and held it up. "I've seen these before in alternative health catalogues. They're made by companies that sell products related to magnetic therapy."

"What in God's name is magnetic therapy?" Morgan asked.

"The theory is that a magnet creates an electrical field that has profound healing properties. Supposedly, it's a very safe way to treat a myriad of aches and pains."

"You can't be serious," Morgan said.

"I'm very serious. In fact, one of their hottest-selling products is a magnetic mattress. I guess it's kind of a heal-while-you-sleep approach to perpetual wellness. It may all be a bunch of bologna, but it's probably harmless."

After a short sigh, Morgan said, "Not in Alison Greene's case. Thanks, you've been a huge help."

"Anytime. Good luck."

Instead of returning to her office, Morgan took the elevator down to the first floor. Stepping out into the lobby, she couldn't shake the lingering feeling that she was overlooking something that was so obvious a child would see it. She stopped at the information desk and smiled at a high school volunteer who was helping with visitor identification passes. Morgan reached for the physician's phone and tapped in Ben's number.

Much to her surprise, she didn't get his voice mail.

"Are we still on for tomorrow?" she asked.

"Absolutely. I'll meet you at your hangar at three." After a momentary pause, he asked, "Are you okay?"

"Sure. Why do you ask?"

"Because you already called me this morning to confirm."

Realizing Ben was right and having no reasonable explanation for the repeat call, Morgan simply said, "I guess I forgot. I'll see you out there."

Morgan hung up the phone and turned around. Leaning

back against the information desk, she quickly became lost in thought about her conversation with Mira. It was only the husky voice of a man inquiring about visiting hours that brought her back from her dreamlike state. Morgan smiled to herself and then started for the exit. A few feet from the revolving glass doors, she noticed a fine but readily apparent tremor of her hands. Trying to ignore the outward sign of anxiety, she continued through the doors and out onto the sidewalk.

Walking through a mist-like sprinkle from a single rain cloud, Morgan made her way toward the parking garage. Although she never questioned her ability or determination to remain emotionally functional, she couldn't deny her level of anxiety was starting to soar. Not knowing how the events of the next few weeks would play out was nerve-racking. She never held herself up to be a spiritual person, but if she didn't know better, she would swear that some higher authority was determined to test her resolve.

She looked up to see the cloud floating off to the east. She thought about her father and how much she missed him. Thinking about their inviolate ritual of going out for Sunday morning breakfast and talking about everything from hospital politics to professional basketball brought a smile to her face. There were many things that saddened her about his death. But more than anything, the realization that he wouldn't be there to share in the joy of her baby's birth was the most painful.

CHAPTER
21

DAY SIX

Staring at the monitor, Dr. Jenny Silverman passed the rectangular-shaped ultrasound probe across Morgan's lower abdomen for a final time before concluding her examination. When she was finished studying the last image, she picked up a folded white towel from the countertop and wiped the ultrasound jelly from Morgan's tummy. Jenny had one of the busiest obstetrical practices in the county but had never allowed her demanding schedule to damper her boundless enthusiasm and devotion to her patients.

"You were pretty accurate with your estimation," Jenny said, helping Morgan to a sitting position. "I'd say you're about two and a half months pregnant."

Morgan dangled her legs over the side of the table. "Did everything look okay on the ultrasound?"

"Perfect," Jenny answered. Morgan nodded briefly and then tossed her a flicker of a smile. She said nothing as Jenny rolled the ultrasound machine to the other side of the room.

"What's going on with you and Kevin? Has anything changed since the last time we talked?"

"I've decided to file for divorce. I guess it finally sunk into my thick skull that Kevin's never going to change."

"This is not the same Morgan Connolly I spoke to last month. You sound a lot different."

"I feel a lot different."

"What about a social life?" Jenny asked.

"I'm not worried about that right now."

A coy smile came to her face. "Really? I heard you went out with Ben Docherty."

"How did you find out about that?"

"You guys shouldn't have picked such a popular Italian restaurant," she said with a wink.

"It was just dinner."

"Who have you been talking to about all this?" Jenny inquired.

"I've interviewed a few attorneys but—"

"I wasn't talking about a lawyer. I was asking if you've seen a therapist."

Morgan shook her head.

Jenny continued, "I know you have a lot of friends, but sometimes it's better to get the input of a professional."

"I guess I haven't thought seriously about . . . about talking—"

"If you need the name of somebody, just let me know."

"Thanks."

"What do your mom and brothers think about all this?"

"My mother's been supportive, but she's got her own life. It's kind of the same with my brothers. We're close when it comes to certain things, but not about our personal lives. Anyway, they both live overseas and we don't get to see each other that often."

"Let's go out for dinner this week."

"I'd love that."

"I'll check my on-call schedule and give you a call," she said, shutting down the ultrasound machine. "We have a GNO scheduled this month. It's been a while since you've been to one. You should come."

GNO, as Jenny always refered to it, was an acronym for girls' night out. She had organized the group of young professional women about two years ago. Every few months they got together for dinner. Most of the early evening was spent trying new wines, complaining about their jobs, and bemoaning their relationships. But as the night progressed and the wine took hold, the conversation generally shifted to the more humorous side of their lives.

"Why don't you e-mail me the information," Morgan suggested. "I'll do my best to make it."

Jenny took her by the arm and escorted her out of the examination room and then down a broad, royal blue–carpeted corridor. When they reached the door that led to the waiting room, she gave Morgan a hug.

"Make sure you stop on your way out to make an appointment. I want to see you in four weeks."

"I'll do it," Morgan promised.

"Good . . . and don't forget about girls' night out. I'm not taking no for an answer. Call me if you have any cramps, bleeding, or any other problems."

After thanking Jenny again, Morgan left the office and rode the elevator to the lobby. She checked the time. She was running late for a meeting with the blood bank and she was still planning on going flying with Ben in the afternoon. Oblivious to her surroundings, she quick-walked toward the exit.

A stocky man seated on a tan leather sofa and wearing a blue denim shirt worked at his laptop. Having excellent peripheral vision, Gideon watched as Morgan disappeared into the parking lot. He then took a few moments to shut down his computer and snap the screen closed. When he finished, he slid it into a black leather computer case, stood up, and headed for the door.

CHAPTER

22

Morgan arrived at North Perry Airport at five minutes to three. The airfield, located in West Hollywood, was the busiest general aviation facility in Broward County and the one Ben had selected to open his flight school.

Morgan pulled up behind her hangar, a glorified prefab garage in desperate need of a fresh coat of paint, parked on a dusty patch of barren ground, and stepped out of her car. When she hoisted the door and saw the sun reflect off the propeller of her red, white, and blue Cirrus, her mood was immediately elevated. A born aviator, Morgan first experienced the ecstasy of flight as a freshman in college. Once bitten by the flying bug, she flew every chance she got. Six months after her first flight, she earned her private pilot's license. By the time she finished her internship, she was an instrument-rated instructor with a multi-engine certificate.

Morgan made her way around the airplane to the far end of the hangar where she kept a gas-powered dolly. After securing it to the nose wheel, she gave the rope a quick tug, bringing the dolly's two-horsepower engine to life. She then flipped the dolly into gear and guided the plane out of the hangar onto the tarmac.

Before beginning the preflight, she opened the passenger side door and tossed her leather flight case and thermos of coffee on the backseat. Just as she stepped down off of the wing, she saw Ben pull up in his twenty-year-old black Porsche coupe. The car, which Morgan suspected he treasured more than life itself, looked as beautiful now as the day his father had driven it out of the showroom.

"Looks like we have a perfect day for flying," he yelled as he maneuvered his way out of the car.

Joining her in front of the left wing, Ben slipped on his sunglasses. Morgan ran her hand over the leading edge of the wing and asked, "Where do you want to go?"

"Your call."

"Why don't we head out over the Everglades and then circle back over Key Biscayne?" she suggested.

"Are you sure? There's a bunch of thunderstorms to the west."

She looked at him sideways and then smiled. "Would that be according to your trick knee? Because I just checked with flight services and there isn't any weather between here and Naples." She shook her head. "You act like I'm one of your students. Since you opened that flight school you've become intolerable."

"I just want to make sure the person I'm flying with is on her toes."

"If my memory serves me correctly, I believe I got my instructor's ticket before you did." They walked around to the back of the wing. Ben tested one of the ailerons by carefully raising and lowering it.

"Anything new with the pacemaker case?"

"I went to see Mira Ramon this morning. I wanted to talk to her about the cross."

"How come?"

"I remembered that magnets are sometimes used as a means to change pacemaker settings. I wanted to ask her if she thought it was possible that the cross could have altered Alison Greene's pacemaker and caused the ventricular tachycardia."

Ben nodded a couple of times. "Interesting idea. What did she say?"

"She felt in the absence of another reasonable explanation, it was quite possible. So I called the pacemaker manufacturer to get their opinion."

"Let me guess," he said with a chuckle. "They said it was an impossibility."

"The rep I spoke to didn't categorically deny it could happen, but he was quick to point out that they had never received a single report of such a malfunction."

"I've spent a lot of time with biotech executives. Admitting liability for their products is not exactly their strong suit." Ben knelt down like a catcher and inspected the landing gear. "Have the police come up with anything regarding the note Gideon left?"

"If they have, they haven't shared the information with me."

"What about the Tony Wallace case? Have you made any progress figuring out what went wrong?"

"None."

Ben stopped fussing with the landing gear and watched as Morgan looked overhead for a few seconds. The disappointment in her face couldn't have been more apparent. She knelt down next to him and began examining the landing gear.

"I just did that," he said patiently.

Slapping her hands together to shake off the dirt from the tire, she said, "Now, we've done it twice."

Morgan stood back up. Ben followed.

"Did you speak to Bob Allenby about—"

"I have an idea," Morgan announced, bringing her index finger up to her lips. "Let's forget all this hospital stuff and go flying."

"Sounds like a good idea. Whose turn is it in the left seat?"

"Yours." Morgan pointed to her lower belly. "If this kid's going to fly solo by the time she hits her first birthday, I want to get her up flying as soon as possible."

Ben grinned and then without giving it a second thought, gave Morgan a huge hug. Standing there in silence, the impulse to kiss her swept over him. But even as awkward as he was when it came to affairs of the heart, he knew the timing was wrong.

A few more seconds passed and he stepped back. "Let's get going."

Morgan followed Ben into the plane and settled into the right seat. After putting his headphones on, he looked out the window to make sure the area around the plane was clear. He then started the engine and taxied out to the active runway. When he received clearance from the tower, he took one final look around, pushed the throttle forward, and started his takeoff roll.

With very little encouragement from Ben, the Cirrus lifted off of the runway. Climbing out to the west, they crossed Broward County, cleared Route 27, and then headed out over the Everglades. It was a cloudless day, and from twenty-five hundred feet, the endless waves of saw grass loomed over the dull earth tones of the wetlands.

Morgan unscrewed the cap of her thermos and poured herself half a cup of coffee. For the next hour, they talked about many things, but not a single word was uttered about Code 15s, her father's death, or hospital politics. When he made a gentle bank over Key Biscayne, Ben, who was an avid tennis player, pointed out the nationally renowned tennis center.

"If you'll give up the controls, I'll take us in," she told him.

"Even though you own this little beauty, I'm not sure you can fly a plane as demanding as this one."

She laughed. "I could fly the box it came in. Just sit back and observe."

Concentrating on her flight instruments, Morgan descended through some broken clouds and entered the landing pattern at North Perry. A few minutes later she set the plane down on the centerline and taxied back to the hangar.

Ben walked Morgan to her car.

"Have you given any further thought to taking on a few students?" he asked her. "You have an instructor's rating. It seems like a shame not to use it."

"I'd like to . . . it's just that I have so much going on right now. Why don't you ask me again in a few months?"

"The offer's always there. Let me know if you change your mind."

Morgan got into her car and started the engine. "Call me later."

Thinking about Ben the entire time, she followed the perimeter road toward the airport exit. Perhaps it was because she had given herself permission to move on, but whatever the reason, her romantic feelings for him were soaring. At the moment, other than her pregnancy, it seemed as if Ben Docherty was the only bright spot in her otherwise disastrous life.

CHAPTER

23

Morgan wasn't more than a mile from the airport when her cell phone rang.

"I just thought of something," Ben said. "I was wondering if you had spoken to Dana McGinley again?"

"Not since we met for drinks. Why?"

"It may be just a coincidence but you mentioned that the man who left the cross told Dana he was a professor at Broward College."

"That's what she said," Morgan stated, reaching forward and turning the volume down on her radio. "What difference does it make?"

"I was just thinking that we're seeing a more learned group of murderers these days."

Morgan shook her head. "What are you talking about, Ben?"

"You also told me the man who attacked your father told Carrie that he taught at the University of Miami. I just thought it was a bit coincidental that both of these guys were college professors. It's not exactly the profession that conjures up an image of a homicidal lunatic." Morgan didn't answer immediately. Her mind flashed back to her conversations with Dana and Carrie. "Are you still there?" Ben asked after a few more moments of dead silence.

"I'm here. I was just thinking about what you said."

"Maybe it's nothing. I just thought it was a little strange. I'll call you later."

Morgan tossed the phone down on the passenger seat. Thinking about the two men, it didn't take her long to remember that Dana had described the man who visited Alison Greene as husky. Carrie had said that the man who killed her father was athletic in appearance. Two men with no apparent relationship: both with noticeably good physiques and both claimed to be college professors. Morgan rolled to a stop behind a city bus puffing a thick gray exhaust. Prodding her memory even harder, she then recalled Dana mentioning that the man had a gap between his two front teeth. At the time, she had dismissed the coincidence immediately, but she now recalled Carrie saying something about Gideon's teeth as well.

The light changed. Morgan slowly accelerated. Squinting from the rays of a bright orange sun low in the western sky, she flipped her visor down. Her mind remained fixed on the two men. With a mounting sense of uneasiness, she cautioned herself not to jump to any unsubstantiated conclusions. But after another few minutes passed, Morgan knew she couldn't dismiss her suspicions without knowing for sure—especially since the answer to her question was a single phone call away.

CHAPTER
24

With each ring, Morgan tapped the steering wheel with increasing impatience. She was just about to hang up and redial when Annalisa answered.

"Orthopedic Partners of South Florida. May I help you?"

"Hi, Annalisa. It's Morgan."

"How are you?"

"I'm fine. I was wondering if Carrie was working today?"

"She sure is."

"Do you think I could speak to her for a sec?"

"Of course. Hold on. I'll connect you to her portable," Annalisa said. "You sound upset. Are you sure you're okay?"

"Everything's fine, but something's come up and I have to ask her a quick question."

"No problem."

After a few moments passed, Morgan again found herself tapping the steering wheel. The elevator music was beginning to grate on her nerves. Finally, Carrie picked up the phone.

"Hi, Dr. Connolly."

"I'm sorry to interrupt you, but I wanted to ask you about something you said the other day."

"Sure," came Carrie's immediate response.

"I seem to recall you mentioning something about the man who attacked my father having something wrong with his teeth."

"I said he needed a good orthodontist."

"You mean his teeth were crooked?"

"Not exactly. He had a big gap between the two front ones."

Morgan inhaled sharply. Without realizing it, her grip on the phone suddenly tightened.

"You're sure?" Morgan asked.

"Positive."

Morgan swallowed hard. "Thanks a lot, Carrie. I didn't mean to bother you. I'll speak with you soon."

She flipped her phone closed and tossed it on the passenger seat. As far-fetched as it seemed, Morgan couldn't dismiss the possibility that Alison Greene and her father were the victims of the same man. If her suspicion was correct, it begged a vexing question: What possible connection could there be between a young woman who needed a pacemaker and a semi-retired orthopedic surgeon that would provoke someone to want to kill them both?

CHAPTER
25

From the sidewalk, Morgan stared up at the four-story North Miami Police Headquarters.

With mounting trepidation, her decision to speak with Detective Wolfe didn't seem as irrevocable as it had twenty-four hours earlier. In spite of Ben's words of encouragement, she was pessimistic regarding the chances of Wolfe embracing her theory that there was a connection between the death of her father and Alison Greene.

Still teetering on canceling her appointment, Morgan continued to stare at the building.

"Sometimes you just have to hold your nose and jump," she whispered to herself with a half grin, realizing that's what her father would say if he were standing next to her.

She walked through the main entrance and into the lobby. After checking the directory, Morgan climbed the three flights of stairs and followed a short hall to the homicide division. A little winded from the effort, she stopped for a minute to catch her breath. Jenny Silverman's constant reminders to continue to exercise reverberated in her mind. When her breath returned, she continued down the hall until she reached the homicide division. Gathering the last bit of courage she needed, Morgan opened the door.

Sitting behind a desk, a young woman with puffy cheeks

and thick glasses stared at her computer screen. After a few moments, she looked up.

"May I help you?"

"My name's Morgan Connolly. I have an appointment with Detective Wolfe."

The woman picked up her phone and tapped in a four-digit extension. "There's a Ms. Connolly here to see you." She nodded twice as she listened. She then hung up the phone and gestured to a wooden bench a few feet away. As her head disappeared back behind her monitor she added, "Detective Wolfe will be right out."

"Thank you."

Morgan walked over and found a seat on the far end of the bench. She looked around hoping to spot a magazine, but there weren't any. Sitting there, she contemplated the best way of pitching her case to Wolfe. Before she could get very far, she saw him approaching. His hair looked longer and more disheveled than she remembered. He was carrying a single manila file folder in one hand and a foam cup in the other. He needed a shave.

"It's nice to see you again, Doctor."

She stood up. "I appreciate your taking the time to see me."

Morgan followed him to his office. He took a seat behind his desk and invited her to take the chair across from him. The window edges were grimy and his desktop looked as if he hadn't opened his mail or read a memo in months. A half-eaten Danish sat atop a scuffed-up leather briefcase. The few certificates that hung on the wall appeared as if they had been placed by somebody with no sense of symmetry.

"Can I get you something to drink?" he asked.

"I'm fine, thank you."

"How can I help you?"

"We haven't spoken in a while. I understand the details of your investigation are confidential, but I was still hoping you could give me a general idea of how things are going."

Wolfe flicked some crumbs from his shirtsleeve. "We're working on the leads we have and trying to develop new ones. I'd say we're making progress, but it's slow."

"Have you found any of my father's old patients who might have wanted to harm him?"

"As you told me, he was much adored by his patients."

"So your answer is no."

"I'm afraid it's going to be a long process, Dr. Connolly. We've interviewed everybody who was in the waiting room that day. We're also reviewing the video of the parking lot hoping to see this guy getting in or out of his car."

"I assume that hasn't led anywhere either?" Morgan asked, wondering how long it could possibly take to review an hour's worth of surveillance tape.

"Not so far."

Taking every precaution to sound reasonably concerned but not inappropriately meddlesome, Morgan said, "I'm not sure it means anything, but there's something I'd like to make you aware of."

Wolfe pressed his palms together and gestured for her to continue.

"I'm the chairperson of Dade Presbyterian's Patient Safety Committee. One of our roles is to review all cases that involve a medical error. Recently, we had a young woman in our Cardiac Care Center die for no apparent reason. I can't go into the details, but suffice it to say they were extremely bizarre. Just prior to her death, she had a visitor. The man was very athletic in appearance, had a gap between his two front teeth, and claimed to be a professor at Broward College." Morgan paused for a moment to gather her thoughts and try to translate the expression on Wolfe's face. It was neither condescending nor indifferent, but she felt a sudden sense of urgency to get to the point. "The reason I mention this is that I spoke to my father's physician assistant a few days ago. She told me that the man who attacked my father also claimed to be a college professor. As I'm sure you recall he—"

"He was well built and had a gap between his two front teeth."

Morgan nodded.

A perplexed look came to Wolfe's face. "But this patient you referred to . . . this young woman. She died as the result of a medical mistake. Your father was murdered. I'm not sure I see the connection."

Morgan said nothing.

Wolfe swiveled in his chair. A few more seconds passed. When the light went on, his voice filled with skepticism. "Dr. Connolly. I hope you're not trying to tell me that this woman who died unexpectedly was actually murdered . . . and that you suspect the man who killed your father was responsible."

Holding back a sigh, Morgan counted to three before responding. "I'm simply making an observation. Both men were athletic-looking. They each had a gap between their teeth and they both claimed to be college professors. That seems pretty coincidental to me."

"I agree. That's a bit of a coincidence but—"

"Look, Detective. My committee has looked at this case dozens of times. We've spoken to everybody involved and gone over every aspect in detail. The bottom line is we have absolutely no clue why this woman died."

"Which hardly constitutes a case of murder."

"But don't you think that—"

"Dr. Connolly," he began slowly with a raised hand. "Unfortunately, the fact that you can't explain her death doesn't mean somebody killed her. I'm not a doctor, but I would venture to say that it's not unheard of for a patient to die for no apparent reason. Is it the hospital's official position that this woman's death may not have been the result of natural causes?"

Morgan averted her eyes. "No."

"I assume you've already checked to see if she had ever been a patient in your father's practice?"

"There's no record of her," she confessed.

Wolfe pushed some files aside and then reached for a blank piece of computer paper.

"Does the hospital keep the names of the patients' visitors?"

"The cardiac ICU does. He signed in as I. Ogden. I went on Broward College's website. There's no such professor listed."

Wolfe picked up his pen again. "Well, the University of Miami doesn't have anybody on their faculty by the name of Stuart Artesian either."

"I can understand why Artesian lied. Why would Ogden?"

"I don't have the first clue. But if I've learned anything in twenty years on the job, it's that people lie for more reasons than you can count." Wolfe ran the back of his hand across his brow. "Look, Doctor, I'll do what I can to check out this guy, Ogden. Unfortunately, there are probably thousands of athletic men in South Florida with gapped teeth who have a penchant for lying."

Thankful for any assistance, Morgan said, "I appreciate your help."

"You mentioned there was a committee involved in investigating this case."

She nodded.

"I assume it's made up of doctors."

"Largely," Morgan said.

With circumspect eyes, he inquired, "Are you the only one who feels this woman may not have died from natural causes?"

Regretting ever setting foot in his office, Morgan answered, "I would say that I'm the only one who's considered the possibility."

"I think you know what I'm going to say," he told her, tossing the pen onto a brown blotter. "It's not within the purview of this office to routinely investigate the deaths of hospital patients. We would only get involved if the hospital contacted us and made a formal report to the state."

Morgan stood up. "I felt I should bring the information to your attention. I guess you'll have to decide what to do with it." She watched Wolfe's barrel chest fill with a profound breath. "Thank you for taking the time to meet with me."

"Dr. Connolly, please understand that a police investigation is based on statistical likelihoods and probability. I give you my word we're doing everything humanly possible to find the man responsible for your father's death."

Feeling handled and seeing no reason to be coy, Morgan asked, "I'm not a police officer, but I have a strange feeling you haven't heard the end of Gideon."

"Gideon?"

"I know about the note."

"How come that doesn't surprise me?" Wolfe came out from behind his desk and walked Morgan back to the reception area. "Please try to remember that we have a lot of investigations going on and I do have significant manpower restraints. If we come up with anything, I promise I'll call you."

Morgan left the building with no regrets. Her fears of feeling foolish or embarrassed were more imagined than real. She had no illusions that Wolfe would do anything more than a cursory investigation of Ogden, but that was more than she had an hour ago. After allowing a slow moving line of cars to pass, Morgan quick-walked across the street. She then headed into the public parking lot.

She knew Ben would be anxious to hear how her meeting had gone. She glanced down at her watch. It was almost ten. Before getting into her car, she rechecked her schedule on her PDA. She had no other commitments until a two o'clock conference with the nurses. Instead of calling him, she decided to take a ride out to his flight school and catch him between lessons.

CHAPTER

26

"Please tell me you're kidding," Robin St. Clair, director of Dade Presbyterian Hospital's operating room, groaned into the phone.

The last thing she wanted to hear on one of the busiest mornings she could remember in months was that Morgan Connolly wanted to do another review of the Tony Wallace case.

"It will only take a half hour," Morgan assured her.

"That's what you told me last time and we wound up—"

"I promise. Thirty minutes."

"Please, Morgan. Not today. I have ninety cases on the schedule. Besides, we've already done this twice."

"I swear. This will be the last time."

Robin had always been the consummate team player. It was probably the single most important reason she had risen so quickly in the operating room administrative hierarchy.

"What time?" she asked with a groan.

"It's eight now. How about nine?"

"I'll set you up in the conference room."

"Can you possibly see if Todd Kettering's available?" Morgan asked.

"He just finished an emergency case. I'll tell him you want him there."

"I'm sorry about this, Robin, but I've got Bob Allenby and

everybody else in administration breathing down my neck about this case."

Robin paused. "You're on the hospital's executive committee, Aren't you?"

"All the department chiefs are."

"Good. Just remember us when the operating room budget comes up for approval."

Morgan said, "I'll enthusiastically vote yes on everything. If I have anything to say about it, you'll have the best-equipped OR in the state."

"I'll remember you said that," came Robin's dubious response. "I'll see you at nine."

chapter 27

Morgan arrived in the operating room a few minutes early.

Robin walked in a few minutes later. In one short hour, she had converted the teaching center and conference room into a staging area for the Tony Wallace case. In the middle of the room, a long folding table was stacked high with medical devices, supplies, and surgical instruments. Lined up against the far wall sat three cardboard cartons, also filled to the brim with drugs and other medical supplies that had been used in the case. Morgan walked up to the table.

"Where do you want to start?" Robin asked.

Morgan picked up the photocopy of Tony's medical record and thumbed through it until she found a copy of the operative note.

After reading it through, she said, "Let's just concentrate on the last few minutes leading up to the pump clotting off. I want to go over those events in their exact chronological sequence just the way they happened the morning of surgery." She looked toward the door. "Is Todd going to join us? I really need him."

"I spoke to him about twenty-five minutes ago. He was just checking the circuit on one of the pumps. He said he'd be over as soon as he finished."

"Good. There was something I wanted to ask you," she said to Robin.

"Sure."

"Did anybody report anything out of the ordinary from the night shift?"

"For instance?" Robin asked, tilting her head slightly to one side.

"Did you receive any reports of any unauthorized persons in the operating room?"

"Absolutely not."

"Were there any new staff assigned to the Wallace case?" Morgan asked.

"No. Dr. McBride had his regular team."

Morgan flipped to the anesthesiologist's handwritten record of the case. She skipped down until she got to the medication section and marked the page.

"Okay, let's get started," she said, scanning the cartons until she found the one containing the medications. She opened the top and looked inside. "I assume all the meds are still in here?"

"Nothing's been touched. Everything's just the way we left it last time we did this—and the time before."

"Good," Morgan responded, unruffled by Robin's sarcasm. She began by removing the medication bottles and lining them up on the table. There were exactly fourteen. Just as she was completing her inventory, Todd, dressed in undersized rumpled scrubs, walked in.

"Is it just me or is anybody else having déjà vu?"

Morgan was the first to reply. "Thanks for coming. I appreciate your forbearance."

Todd rubbed his chubby hands together. "Let the games begin."

"When did you first notice the clots?" she asked him.

"After the grafts had been sewn in and we were rewarming."

"Tell me specifically how that's done."

"We simply bring the temperature up on the circulating

blood. If we can't get the patient's temp back to at least ninety-seven degrees, it's hard to get their heart started again."

"And I assume Mr. Wallace's temp was coming up okay."

"It was."

"Fine. What do you do next?"

"Nothing. Once the heart is warm, it generally starts beating on its own. After that, if everything looks good, we take the patient off bypass."

"How long does the whole process take?"

"About twenty-five minutes."

Morgan walked back over to the table. "Okay. Let's concentrate on what happened from the time you started the rewarming process until the pump clotted off. What exactly were you doing?"

"I was checking the circuit and talking to the medical student."

"Who was the first to notice there was a problem?"

"Dr. McBride. He saw clots in the pericardial well and let me know. When I checked the circuit, I had the same thing."

"What did you do?"

"I started changing the circuit tubing as fast as I could."

"What was Dr. McBride doing?"

"You mean besides having a heart attack of his own?"

"C'mon, Todd," Robin interjected. "We need straight answers or we'll never get through this."

"Sorry. There really wasn't too much he could do other than squeeze the heart and hope we could get the whole circuit changed."

Morgan studied the medication flow sheet. "Exactly what time does your record show that you started re-warming?"

Todd looked down at his own record and then ran his finger down the left margin. "At nine forty-five."

"I want to concentrate on something we kind of glossed over the first two times. What was Dr. Quintana doing while you were re-warming?"

"Checking vital signs and giving whatever meds are required."

"From what I can tell, the only drug Mr. Wallace received once re-warming was started was nitroglycerine. The infusion began at nine forty-eight."

"That sounds right. The nitroglycerine drip decreases the amount of work the heart has to do and helps recovery. Anesthesia routinely gives it when we start re-warming."

"Did you give any meds?" she asked.

"Nope."

"The nitroglycerine drip? Do you know when the pharmacy sent it over?" she inquired, picking up the five-hundred-cc bag of saline that contained the nitroglycerine in solution.

"It wasn't sent over by the pharmacy."

She looked up. "What do you mean?"

"Dr. Quintana made the drip himself."

"Why?"

"It's routine. All of the anesthesiologists make up their own drips. They feel it's safer."

"When do they do that?" Morgan asked.

"It's usually when they're setting up for the case."

"Could the medical student have accidentally done anything to the pump that might have caused it to clot off?"

"Not a chance," Todd insisted. "It's a firm policy that students aren't permitted to do anything except observe."

"Was that the first time she'd worked with you?"

"No. She'd been with me for a couple of weeks," he answered with a puzzled look on his face.

Morgan put the IV bag down. "According to the record the first clots were noted at nine fifty. That would have been five minutes after the re-warming process was started, and about two minutes after the nitroglycerine drip was hung."

"That sounds about right."

"Assuming this wasn't some kind of pump malfunction, what else could have caused the problem?" Morgan asked.

"The only other possibility would be that the heparin wore off and Mr. Wallace started making clots again."

"But I thought you monitor the patient's state of anticoagulation during the pump run and give as much heparin as necessary to prevent clot formation."

"We do."

"And?"

"Mr. Wallace had an ACT at nine thirty-five that showed he was very adequately anticoagulated. There's no way his blood could have made a clot. He did not require any additional heparin."

"But that was fifteen minutes before the clots were first noted. Could the heparin have worn off that quickly?" she asked.

"Not a chance."

"But normally you don't wait for the heparin to wear off before you come off of bypass," Morgan said.

"No. When the patient's ready to come off, we give protamine, which immediately reverses and neutralizes the heparin."

"Which would mean the patient would be able to make clots again."

"Instantly," Todd said.

Morgan raised her eyes from the IV bag and looked squarely at Todd. "So if it wasn't a pump problem and Mr. Wallace had plenty of heparin on board—what the hell happened?"

Throwing his arms up in the air, he said, "It's kind of like I've been saying all along. There is no explanation."

Morgan reached for the two bottles of protamine and held them up.

Todd shook his finger at her. "No way. I know what you're thinking and you can forget it."

"Really?' Morgan answered.

"The protamine was the first thing Dr. McBride and Dr. Quintana checked." Todd walked over and pointed to the bottles in Morgan's hand. "These were the only two bottles in the room, and as you can plainly see their metal seals are unbroken. There's no way the patient accidentally got any protamine."

"How can you be so sure?" Morgan calmly asked.

"With all due respect, Dr. Connolly. I just told you the vials were never touched. You can see for yourself the seals are unbroken."

"I guess we still don't know—"

"I don't know why the pump clotted off, but it wasn't because Mr. Wallace mistakenly got a premature dose of protamine." Todd crossed his arms. "I don't want to appear arrogant, but we do this every day, which makes us incapable of making a mistake of the magnitude your suggesting."

Morgan smiled at him courteously, thinking to herself that it was Todd's overconfident attitude that frequently set the stage for tragic medical mistakes.

Morgan said, "About six months ago a relatively healthy woman ran out of her blood pressure medication. She couldn't find an open pharmacy so she went to her local emergency room because she was starting to feel a little light-headed from her pressure going up."

Todd said, "Are you trying to make a point or did this really—?"

"Really happen? The hospital's right here in Miami. May I finish, please?"

"Sorry."

Morgan went on, "The doctor prescribed eight milligrams of the blood pressure med to be given intravenously. The nurse misread the order and thought he wanted eight hundred milligrams. She then proceeded to go to nine different locations in the hospital in order to gather up the twenty-six vials of the medication necessary to prepare the dose. At no time did it cross her mind that this was a little out of the ordinary. She then tried to put this massive overdose in a liter bag of saline, but because it wouldn't fit she hooked a second liter bag onto the first. When she finished preparing this lethal injection, she then opened up the IV and walked away to attend to another patient."

"And the end of the story is that the patient died," Todd said.

"Yes, she did. But the reason I'm telling you this is because there were no systems in place to prevent this catastrophe. The machines that dispensed the drug weren't computer linked so they couldn't block her from taking twenty-six vials of the same medication within thirty minutes. None of her colleagues checked the dose. Nobody was suspicious about this strange-looking double IV bag she jury-rigged. What I'm trying to say is that the culture of safety in that hospital was inadequate to prevent an overworked and fatigued nurse from making a fatal mistake."

Todd shrugged. "I understand that people die of medical errors. I just think the whole thing is way overstated."

"Really? Do you know how many patients in this country were injured or died last year because of medication errors?"

Todd rolled his eyes. "I'd be guessing. Maybe a few thousand."

Morgan walked across the room, stopping a few feet in front of Todd. "Try one-point-five million—so don't tell me we're incapable of making a medication error. The only thing we're incapable of is losing our arrogance. Maybe when we do, we'll cut down on medical mistakes and have a safer environment for our patients."

During the uncomfortable silence that ensued, Morgan replaced the medications in the carton box. She then closed the lid but left the IV bag containing the nitroglycerine on the table.

"I guess we'll just have to keep trying to figure out what went wrong." Without making eye contact, she added, "Thanks, Todd. I appreciate your help."

Todd started for the door. Before he stepped into the hall he said, "You might as well give up, Dr. Connolly. We're never going to figure out what went wrong."

"He seems a little annoyed," Morgan told Robin.

"This case has generated a lot of speculation and innu-endo. If it was a pump problem, Todd's ultimately responsible. He's understandably defensive."

"It would help if we'd stop blaming people and start blam-ing our antiquated systems," Morgan stated, picking up the nitroglycerine drip. "Do you mind if I borrow this?"

"Borrow it?" Robin asked with vaulted eyebrows.

"Let's just say it's official business of the Patient Safety Committee. I'll bring it back as soon as I can."

Robin looked at Morgan as if she were proposing homi-cide. "I'm going to recheck these boxes in forty-eight hours. I kind of like this job. Try not to get me fired."

"Your job is safe. Thanks for your help."

Morgan was rapidly becoming convinced that everybody involved in the Tony Wallace case was as pessimistic as Todd was regarding the chances of ever figuring out what had caused the pump catastrophe. The strange irony was that as long as they remained convinced his death had been nothing more than an unfortunate medical error, they were probably right.

Morgan left the operating room and headed straight for Dade Presbyterian's laboratory. She glanced down at the ni-troglycerine drip she held in her hand. She knew it was a long shot, but she still held out hope that very shortly, she would have indisputable proof that Tony Wallace's death was not the result of some bizarre or unavoidable medical error.

CHAPTER

28

.

With the nitroglycerine drip in hand, Morgan strolled into Dade Presbyterian's main laboratory.

Surrounded by a flurry of activity, she spotted Dr. John Ackerman tinkering with a sophisticated-looking piece of laboratory equipment. Ackerman had been the director of Laboratory Services at Dade Presbyterian for the past ten years. Good-natured at heart, he was, at times, annoyingly glib and especially masterful at making a long story longer. His sappy sense of humor frequently sent even his closest friends scurrying for cover. But in spite of his minor peculiarities, he was an instinctive pathologist with an encyclopedic fund of medical knowledge.

"John?" Morgan asked, walking up behind him.

He glanced over his shoulder, massaged his scaly forehead with his fingertips, and then smiled.

"Well, well. Dr. Morgan Connolly. It's not often I get paid a visit from our chief of Emergency Medicine. What can I do for you?"

She shook his extended hand, noticing his new crop of hair plugs, which did little to improve his appearance.

"I'm actually here in my capacity as a member of the Patient Safety Committee."

He came to attention and saluted. "In that case I'll be especially cooperative. Have a seat."

"I have a couple of questions about one of our Code Fifteen cases."

"What's the patient's name?"

"Tony Wallace."

"The clotted cardiac bypass pump?"

"That's the one."

"I'm all ears."

"Would you happen to know if there's any specific test or assay available that can detect the presence of protamine in an IV solution?"

His answer was immediate. "To my knowledge, there's no assay for protamine either in the blood or an IV solution."

"Are you sure?" Morgan asked, feeling whatever glimmer of hope she had fading.

"I'm quite certain there's no specific test commercially available."

"Well," she said with a short sigh. "I appreciate the information."

"You seem disappointed," he said. He then pointed at the IV bag. "What do you have there?"

"It's a nitroglycerine drip. I was hoping you could tell me if there was any protamine in here, but I guess I was wasting—"

"Wasting your time? I don't think so."

Morgan's eyes narrowed. "John, didn't you just tell me that you couldn't—"

He held up a finger. "You asked me if there was any test available that would directly measure protamine in solution, and I told you there wasn't," he answered, taking the IV bag from her and studying it from every conceivable angle. "Sometimes there are mysterious ways of figuring things out without the help of some multibillion-dollar drug company."

Fighting to stay patient and indulge John's unusual sense of humor, Morgan pressed her palms together. Before she spoke, she raised them to her face as if she were praying. "John, I just need to know if, by any means available to you, you can tell me if there's protamine in this IV solution."

"Absolutely. It's not a problem."

Morgan took a step closer. "How?"

"By indirect means."

"Would you mind explaining that to me?"

"All we have to do is find a willing volunteer, draw a tube of blood from that brave individual, and then add some heparin to it."

"I'm listening. Go on."

"You would agree the heparin will anticoagulate the blood. It won't be able to make any clots."

"I agree."

"We can even prove it's anticoagulated the same way the cardiac surgeons do before they put a patient on bypass by doing an ACT test on it."

"Then what?"she asked.

"Once we've proven the ACT is abnormally high," he said, tapping the IV bag, "we simply add a little of this IV solution you've brought to the blood-heparin mixture and do the ACT test again." He paused briefly. "Do you see?"

Morgan's look of bewilderment quickly faded and became frozen as a smile. "If there's protamine in the bag, then the ACT test should neutralize the heparin and the second ACT should return to normal."

"Bingo. But if there's nothing in here except nitroglycerine, then—"

"Then the ACT should remain high because the heparin won't be neutralized or reversed."

"You got it," he said, pointing right at her.

"When can we try this?" Morgan asked.

He smiled annoyingly. "As soon as you roll up your sleeve."

Morgan frowned. She hated being stuck with needles. She looked at Ackerman, who was still smirking. After a few seconds, she blew out a long breath and rolled up her sleeve.

CHAPTER

29

Even before the tech slid the needle into Morgan's vein, she cringed with anticipation.

"Your jaw muscles are tighter than a banjo string," Ackerman said. "If I had known it was going to be this traumatic for you, I would have volunteered myself."

Before Morgan could answer, she felt the hot pinch of the needle penetrating her skin.

"We're almost done, Dr. Connolly," the tech said, exchanging an amused look with Ackerman. As soon as he had filled the red-top tube with ten cc's of Morgan's blood, he handed it to Ackerman.

"I'll get started on this. As soon as you've recovered from your little ordeal, you can join me over there by that little blue ACT machine."

By the time the tech had made sure there was no bleeding from the puncture site and had placed a Band-Aid on Morgan's arm, Ackerman was already adding the heparin to the tube of Morgan's blood. He flipped the tube over several times to make sure the drug was well mixed. He then removed a small amount and introduced it into the ACT machine. It took only about thirty seconds for the result to appear on the digital display. It read six hundred fifty.

"Okay," he said to Morgan. "The normal ACT should be about a hundred so we've successfully anticoagulated your blood. You wouldn't be able to make a clot now if your life depended on it."

Next, Ackerman reached for the IV bag containing the nitroglycerine drip. Using a small needle and syringe he removed five cc's of the solution and injected it into the tube that contained Morgan's blood and the heparin. Once he had thoroughly mixed the contents, he held it up in the air and tapped the tube several times.

"What are you looking for?" she asked.

He gave a light shrug. "I don't know, but in every old doctor movie I've ever seen on TV, the brilliant pathologist always holds the tube up, studies it intently, and then taps it a few times."

Morgan rolled her eyes but said nothing. She watched as Ackerman withdrew a small amount of blood from the tube and introduced it into the ACT machine. Morgan stood with her arms crossed staring at the blank digital display.

When the number ninety flashed up, her eyes remained locked on the display. Finally, she looked over at him. He was now stone-faced.

"No doubt about it," he said. "There has to be protamine in the nitroglycerine drip."

"The question is, how did it get there?" Morgan asked in just above a whisper. "John," she began slowly, "I'm not sure what I'm going to do with this information yet, but it's absolutely imperative that you don't discuss this with anybody. I'm sure I don't have to tell you that is an extremely delicate matter."

"I understand," he said in a manner that left no doubt in her mind that he would respect her wishes.

"Can you find someplace safe for that tube of blood?"

"I know just where to put it," he assured her. Morgan could feel his eyes probing her. "If you need me, just let me know."

"Thanks, John."

As she started away, he said. "Your father and I were good friends, Morgan. He was an exceptional physician and an extremely insightful man. If he were here, I'm sure he'd tell you to proceed with extreme caution."

Ben had just finished teaching a one-hour introductory course in instrument flying when his secretary, Lisa, motioned for him to pick up the phone.

"Who is it?" he asked from across the large classroom he had recently added to his school. Lisa had worked for Ben since the day he opened his medical practice and had come with him when he changed careers. She was indispensable, but not one to embrace a strict professional office environment.

With a saccharine smile, she wagged her finger at him and in a singsong voice said, "It's Dr. Connolly. You'd better hurry."

Ben pointed at her and then feigned slitting her throat. She covered her face and pretended to shudder in fear.

He picked up the phone. "Hi."

"I just met with John Ackerman. We analyzed the nitroglycerine drip used in the Tony Wallace case. Somebody put a massive dose of protamine in it. I suspect it was intentional."

Ben sat down in one of the folding canvas-backed chairs in the front row. "Slow down a sec. What makes you so sure it wasn't accidental?"

"The only person who makes up the drip is the anesthesiologist, and that was Mike Quintana. I've spoken to Mike on three separate occasions about the case. He's positive every med he gave and every drip he prepared was fine."

"Mike's a meticulous physician, but he's also a human being . . . and, if my memory serves me correctly, you're the one who's always saying human beings make mistakes. I just don't see how you can categorically reject the possibility that Mike made an error."

"Because for each open-heart case the pharmacy sends the anesthesiologist two vials of protamine. I've examined both of them. They were untouched as the day they were shipped from the factory."

"I assume Mike made this drip the morning of surgery."

"Uh-huh."

"Then explain one thing to me. How would anybody, in the middle of a busy open-heart operating room, be able to add protamine to a drip without being seen?"

"They wouldn't. But if somebody had snuck into the OR a few hours before the operation . . . say three in the morning when the suite was closed, he could have drained the nitro-glycerine bottle and substituted protamine. That way when Mike made up the drip, he would have thought he was adding nitroglycerine to the IV solution when he was really adding protamine."

"That sounds a little far-fetched, Morgan."

"But it's possible," she insisted. "Weren't you the one who told me to open my mind and treat this investigation as if it were an aviation inquiry?"

"But why would somebody do that? What would be their motive?"

It was a question Morgan expected him to ask. "I don't know," she told him. "Not yet, anyway."

"Aren't you suppose to meet with Bob Allenby today?"

"I'm on my way now."

"Are you also going to tell him what you just told me?"

"Bob's looking for answers. It's my job to provide them."

"I'm sure Bob's looking for answers, but I think he's look-ing for medical explanations. Once you tell him you suspect that we've had two Code Fifteens caused by criminal acts . . .

well, that's going to be a tough bell to un-ring. We talked about the fire, aim, ready approach to things."

"I appreciate your concern but I don't see what choice I have. I'm obligated to tell him."

"I'll remember you said that." Ben stopped for a few moments. He then said, "Listen, I'm flying up to Vero Beach late this afternoon to pick up some parts for one of my planes. Why don't you come with me? We can talk about your meeting with Bob. "

"I'll go if I can fly."

"One way," he told her firmly.

"What time?"

"Meet me on the flight line at four."

"I'll be there."

Ben came to his feet slowly and walked over to a small table. He tapped the power button on his laptop. Waiting for it to boot up, his mind became preoccupied with Morgan and her meeting Bob Allenby. If he concluded that Morgan was a grief-stricken, stressed-out physician who wasn't thinking rationally, things could go south for her pretty fast. Ben was sure the first thing Bob would do after Morgan left his office would be to call John Ackerman to confirm her story. But what hadn't occurred to Morgan was that Bob might assume it was Morgan who had tampered with the drip to give credibility to her conspiracy theories.

Morgan stepped off the elevator on the eighth floor and strolled down a long hallway until she reached the corporate offices of Constahealth, Dade Presbyterian's parent organization.

She was just about to walk into Bob Allenby's outer office when her cell phone rang. She checked the caller ID. When she saw it was Kevin, she cringed. She doubted whether he was calling simply to say hello but after listening to the phone ring a couple of more times, she decided to take his call.

"Hello."

"I got your check and just wanted to call and say thanks."

Knowing Kevin rarely thanked her for anything, she said, "If you're calling to ask me for more money, you can just—"

"Take it easy, Morgan. I'm not calling about money. I told you. In a few months I'll be swimming in the stuff. And don't think for a second I'm not going to give you your fair share. We're still married and the law says everything's fifty-fifty."

Fully understanding his cryptic message, Morgan shook her head.

"It's nice to see you've become so conversant in Florida divorce law. Look, Kevin, I'm running late for a meeting, so unless there's something else . . ."

"Did I remember to mention to you before I left that I'm a couple of months behind on my Mercedes payment?"

"C'mon, Kevin. I can't believe you didn't—"

"Relax, Morgan. If they call you, just tell them we're separated and that you don't know where I am."

"That's a great idea except for one minor detail. The lease is in both of our names."

"Just put them off until I get back."

"And ruin my credit? I don't think so. I pay my bills. Have a great trip."

"Don't be so melodramatic, Morgan. Try to be a little supportive for a change. Maybe we'd still be living together if I hadn't become exhausted trying to live up to your expectations."

All too familiar with Kevin's canned speeches and lame explanations, Morgan flipped her phone closed. Determined not to let his financial irresponsibility ruin her day, she put her phone back in her purse.

She continued down the hall and pushed open the large glass door leading to Bob Allenby's office. Julia, his secretary, was one of the few people in his employ who didn't quake at the mere mention of his name.

"Go ahead in. He's waiting for you," she told Morgan with a quick wave.

"What kind of mood is he in?"

She looked up from her desk. "Well, it's still pretty early, but I haven't heard any screaming or the sound of shattering glass coming from his office."

"That's something," she said, with a quick laugh.

Morgan knocked on the door, waited a few seconds, and then stepped into Allenby's dark wood-paneled office. She saw him on the other side of the room, gazing out of his window.

"Come over here and share this incredible view of Port Everglades with me."

Morgan crossed the room, taking up a position beside him. Bob was a square-jawed man with brick-like shoulders that he oftentimes joked were necessary to support the weight of the hospital. The chronic puffiness under his closely spaced eyes made him appear older than his fifty-one years.

She gazed out the huge window. It was a clear day and

the deep-water harbor with its massive concrete docks loaded high with cargo bins and tumultuous activity was, as Bob so aptly put it, an incredible sight.

"How've you been?" he asked.

"Fine. I should have called and thanked you for coming to the funeral."

"Your dad and I were very good friends. We accomplished a lot of great things for Presby together." He looked over at her. "Have the police come up with anything?"

"Not really."

"Let's have a seat," he suggested, gesturing toward a small mahogany conference table with four leather chairs around it. Morgan waited to see where he was going to sit and then took the chair across from him. The pressure of being the chief executive officer of Dade Presbyterian for the last fifteen years had taken its toll on him in the form of two stomach ulcers and a blood pressure that would have already given most people a stroke. "I wanted to talk to you about these two unfortunate cases from the Cardiac Care Center. The buzz in the hospital is that you figured out what happened."

"The buzz?"

"It's a hospital," he said with a casual shrug. "Word gets around—even to the CEO's office."

Morgan wasn't surprised that Bob knew something was up. She had been as discreet and diplomatic as possible regarding her inquiries, but as he just implied, hospitals are notorious for their rumor networks.

After an inward sigh, she said, "I believe I know what happened, but I don't think you're going to like it."

He regarded her politely. "I appreciate your cautious approach, but I'm running out of time. We have two unexplained and rather serious Code Fifteens. If we don't come up with some answers pretty soon, we'll have every inspector from the Agency for Health Care Administration down here with pitchforks and lanterns. If you think you know what happened, I'd like to hear about it."

Running out of wiggle room, Morgan said, "As bizarre as this may sound, it looks like Alison Greene died of a cardiac arrest caused by a magnetized cross."

Allenby cupped his chin and then stroked his thick mustache. "I'm not a doctor, so I'm unaware of how a magnetized cross could harm anybody."

"Magnets can affect pacemakers in many ways. They can even cause a fatal heart arrhythmia. I checked with Mira Ramos and she agrees."

"And Mr. Wallace?"

"He received a medication that made the pump clot off."

"You can't be serious."

Morgan took her time to explain what had occurred to Tony Wallace in layman's terms. When she finished, Bob rubbed his chin and asked, "How could we have made such a colossal series of mistakes?"

"That's what I'm trying to tell you, Bob. I'm not sure we can assume these two deaths were unintentional patient errors."

Bob's gaze intensified. Finally and in an unexpectedly calm tone, he said, "What are you trying to say, Morgan?"

"I think there's a strong possibility that somebody intentionally tampered with the nitroglycerine bottle and that Miss Greene's visitor intentionally placed a magnetized cross around her neck knowing it would cause a problem."

His tone became patronizing. "Surely, there have to be other, more rational, explanations."

"I've spent a lot of time on these cases, Bob. If anybody can come up with one, I'm all ears."

Bob's complexion took on a scarlet hue. "Do you have any idea what you're suggesting?"

Morgan found herself at a delicate juncture. Raising the possibility the Code 15s were intentionally caused and actually proposing it were quite different. She understood Bob's astonishment. The Cardiac Care Center had been his brainchild, a project he had shepherded from its inception to the ribbon cutting. The result was the most comprehensive and profitable state-of-the-art heart surgery program in south Florida. To Bob's credit, his vision had proven to be a booming success.

Morgan said, "I think you're going to have to strongly consider that these two patients didn't die accidentally."

With a dumbfounded look on his face, Bob spread his fingers and placed his palms flat on the conference table.

He cleared his throat twice and then said, "If I report to the Agency for Health Care Administration that there's a deranged lunatic loose at Dade Presbyterian who's killing our heart patients, they'll shut down the Cardiac Care Center faster than a New York minute. As soon as they've done that, they'll probably insist we all admit ourselves to the psych hospital. Do you have any idea of the types of sweeping disciplinary powers AHCA has when it comes to dealing with Code Fifteens?"

"Of course I do."

"If what you're saying should ever become public, the damage to this hospital would be irreparable. It's like when somebody gets accused of molesting a child. The accusation's as bad as the deed. Guilt or innocence doesn't really matter."

"With all due respect, Bob, don't you think it—"

"Hear me out," he interrupted. "I've listened to everything you've said very carefully, and I truly believe you've done an incredible job figuring out how Mr. Wallace and Miss Greene died. But that doesn't mean they were murdered. Doesn't it make more sense that their deaths, while tragic, were unintentional medical mishaps?"

"I don't believe so. What I do believe is that our first responsibility is to the safety of our patients."

"I'm well aware of our responsibilities. What I'm saying is, just because we don't know exactly how these Code Fifteens occurred doesn't mean we should go off the deep end and come up with some preposterous explanation that could potentially destroy the Cardiac Care Center."

"I've spent a lot of time looking at these cases. All I can tell you is that at the moment, it's the only explanation that makes any sense."

Bob leaned back in his chair. His tone became much calmer. His next question came as no surprise. "Have you discussed your suspicions with anybody else?" Before she could answer, he injected, "I hope you haven't spoken to the police about this, Morgan."

She did her best to look appalled. "Give me some credit, for goodness sake," she told him, wanting to cross her fingers behind her back.

He stood up and walked back over to his desk. He picked up a stack of pink phone messages and began nonchalantly leafing through them. When he was finished, he folded them in his hand and then casually strolled back toward the conference table.

"Have you received any grief counseling since your father passed away?"

Although she was frustrated, Morgan smiled. "No, Bob. Do you think I need some?"

"I think you'd agree that all of us could use a little help from time to time."

"My father's death and my state of mind have nothing to do with my conclusions regarding these Code Fifteens."

"All I'm saying is that with the demands of running the emergency department and the Patient Safety Committee coupled with losing your father, well . . . you've been under a lot of stress lately. Maybe you came back to work too soon."

Morgan was resolute not to show any outward signs of becoming unglued.

"I'm fine, Bob. The problem isn't my emotional well-being. The problem is finding out what really happened to these two patients."

"It seems to me you've already done that."

"I think you know what I mean."

"There's no way I'm reporting these two deaths to the state as some type of criminal act," Bob said categorically.

"Excuse me," Morgan said.

"It seems obvious that Mr. Wallace was the unfortunate victim of a bizarre but inadvertent medication error. We've seen these types of mistakes before."

"And Miss Greene?"

"How could the nurse have known that the cross was magnetized or that it could result in a serious pacemaker problem? I'm sure her visitor meant no harm. The entire thing was just a peculiar sequence of events that led to a horrible tragedy."

Morgan waited a few seconds before asking, "Do you really think the Agency for Health Care Administration is going to believe that?"

"I think they're more likely to believe a rational explanation involving systems failures than some outrageous explanation that shifts blame to some imaginary homicidal lunatic."

"But you must know that—"

"The only thing I know is that you and your committee diligently performed a comprehensive root cause analysis for each of these cases and now have rational explanations to explain what happened." He slapped his hands together and added, "The rest is up to the investigators from AHCA. If they raise the issue of criminal activity . . . well, I guess we'll have to deal with it. But we're certainly not going to plant that seed in their suspicious heads."

"You just can't leave it at that, Bob."

He shrugged and stood up. "Well, I'll tell you what. I just did." He walked her toward his door. "I'd like you to write your reports in a calm, rational, and professional manner. I also need an action plan that I can show the AHCA team, which outlines how these problems will never happen again." He paused for a moment before going on. "What I don't need is a screenplay for Steven Spielberg's next movie."

"You may regret this, Bob."

"I'm prepared to take that chance. Just call me when the committee's report is ready so I can have legal review it."

Seeing the futility in pursuing the conversation any further, Morgan said, "I'll call you when we have something."

"Good. I'll look forward to reading it," he told her, escorting her to his outer office.

Morgan walked past Julia's desk. A casual glance behind her was all she needed to confirm her suspicion that Bob was standing in his doorway watching her. To her dismay, the meeting had gone pretty much as Ben had warned her it might. The one saving grace was that she now knew that irrespective of what the facts of the Code 15s were, Bob Allenby would fight tooth and nail before allowing Dade Presbyterian to be the main attraction in some embarrassing media circus.

CHAPTER

32

The sunset flight back from Vero Beach had been a beautiful one.

After taxiing Ben's Mooney Ovation back to his flight school, Morgan shut down the engine and slipped off her headset. From the right seat, Ben pushed open the door and climbed out onto the wing. Once he was on the tarmac, he turned to help Morgan down.

"That was a perfect hour of flying," he told her, taking her hand and making sure she stepped down without incident.

"Except for your approach. You were at least a hundred feet high."

He rubbed his chin. "I sometimes forget which one of us owns a flight school."

"I have those same feelings myself every time we fly together."

After a short grumble under his breath, he said, "Mike will tie her down. Let's go inside."

Walking toward the school, they continued to review each aspect of the flight. Once inside, they went straight into Ben's office where Morgan fell into a burgundy leather chair that sat below a constellation of wall-mounted aircraft prints. Ben's entire facility was appointed considerably nicer than any flight school she had ever been in. Between its vast size, high-end aviation artwork, and luxurious furniture, Morgan felt as if she were sitting in the private office of the Boeing Company's CEO.

"You haven't mentioned a word about your meeting with Bob."

"I was waiting for the right time."

"I assume that meant things didn't go too well."

"That's not entirely true," she said.

"What did you tell him?"

"Precisely what I told you," she answered, knowing Ben would give her the I *told you so* speech.

"What was his response?"

"He made it abundantly clear that the hospital's official report to AHCA would identify the causes of deaths but would include nothing that suggested criminal behavior may have played a role." With a minor frown, she added, "Before I could raise an objection, the conversation shifted to my grieving process and how it was affecting my professional judgment and performance."

Morgan felt a cramp in her left calf. She rubbed the back of her leg for a few seconds before standing up and walking around.

"I could speak to Chuck Bingham."

"The chairman of the hospital board?" she asked, not really surprised that Ben was traveling in those circles. "I didn't know you guys were pals."

"Let's just say we've had a long-standing business relationship."

"I appreciate the offer, but what good would it do?"

"Chuck might feel that Bob's a little out of line on this one. You're the chairperson of the committee assigned to investigate Code Fifteens. This is a medical investigation. Bob can't cover things up or style the inquiry to suit the hospital's agenda, especially when it's an issue of patient safety. Bob may not agree with your findings, but I don't think he can summarily dismiss them without further investigation. I think Chuck might agree with me."

"If you speak to Chuck, he'll go straight to Bob, who will then say that I'm a stressed-out practitioner with a Hollywood imagination. Even if Bingham is open-minded, he's going to give Bob the benefit of the doubt. The other downside is that now you've involved yourself in this mess."

"Which I couldn't care less about. I'm not beholden to anybody at Presby."

"I appreciate you trying to help, but Bob will assume I put you up to it. There's no telling what he might do."

"It's your call. But if you change your mind, the offer stands."

"Thanks, but I think the way to approach this is to come up with irrefutable proof of what really happened. That's the only way to compel Bob to be honest with the AHCA investigators. I also suspect it's the only way we'll ever find out who killed my father."

"It sounds like you're giving up on Detective Wolfe."

"I'm not giving up, exactly; I'm just not totally relying on him."

Morgan's less-than-veiled implication was clear. In spite of his advice, she had no intention of giving up on her own investigation. He wouldn't abandon his efforts to persuade her to tread carefully, but for the moment, lecturing her again about the disastrous effects her amateur inquiry might have upon her career seemed hopeless.

CHAPTER
33

At eleven thirty p.m. on Friday night, Faith Russo strolled up to the registration desk of Dade Presbyterian Hospital's emergency room.

Even though the man she knew as Steve had spent the better part of an hour prepping her, she was still more nervous than she thought she'd be.

After giving the nurse some basic information, she was told they would call her as soon as possible. She was then directed to the waiting area. In spite of her trepidation, the registration process had gone well. Her confidence strengthened, Faith took the first empty seat she saw.

Some of the people waiting to be seen paced the floor, while others had fallen asleep in their chairs. An elderly woman with a pained expression on her face pressed an icepack against her shoulder while she rocked back and forth in her seat. Every few seconds she moaned softly and shook her head.

Faith spotted a magazine on the empty seat next to her and picked it up.

She was thumbing through it for the third time when she heard her name called. As Steve had instructed, she checked her watch. It had been just under an hour since she registered.

With a noticeable limp, which she had rehearsed coming across the parking lot, she made her way over to the triage area. A nurse wearing a floral shirt greeted her and then asked her to describe the circumstances of her knee injury. Faith took her time and recounted the events of her fictional bicycle fall. When the nurse was finished entering the information on her chart, she motioned to one of the orderlies, who grabbed a wheelchair and strolled over.

The young man helped Faith into the chair and then took her straight back to examination room number seventeen, which was one of three orthopedic rooms. He wished her good luck and slid the glass door closed behind him. She had been waiting only for a few minutes when a second nurse walked in. Faith guessed she was about her own age.

"Miss Russo?" she asked with a pleasant smile.

"Yes."

"My name's Denise. I'll be the nurse taking care of you. How's your knee feeling?" she asked, walking over and taking a closer look.

"It still hurts quite a bit."

"Your chart said you were bike riding," Denise said, picking up the chart.

"I'm afraid so. I guess I could have used a few more lessons before going for the land speed record."

"I ride all the time and I fell twice last week." Denise then took Faith's blood pressure and checked her pulse. When she was finished, she said, "The doctor should be here in a minute."

"I hate to ask you this, but . . . do you have a female physician on duty tonight?"

"Dr. Connolly's on. She's also the chief of the department. She's great. You'll love her." Denise grinned before adding, "I think she's also a bike rider."

"I know it's a silly request—I mean, asking for a woman doctor—but I think I'd be more comfortable."

"It's not a problem. A lot of women do it." Denise then whispered, "To tell you the truth, I feel the same way."

Faith had no idea why Steve had made such a big point about telling her to request a woman doctor. She just assumed it was part of the survey. When Denise walked out of the room, Faith checked her watch.

Six minutes later, the glass door slid open.

"Miss Russo?" Morgan asked holding out her hand. "I'm Dr. Connolly."

"It's nice to meet you," Faith answered, shaking her hand.

"Tell me about your fall."

"It was kind of stupid. I was taking a bike ride earlier this evening and fell." She flexed her leg and rubbed her knee.

"Did you hit your head or injure any other part of your body?"

"No, just my knee."

"Let's have a look," Morgan said, putting the chart on the counter.

"Sure."

Morgan moved to the exam table and gently extended Faith's right leg. There was no swelling or bruising of her knee. When Morgan finished her exams she said, "It really doesn't look too bad. I think you were pretty lucky."

"That's good news."

Morgan spent the next few minutes questioning Faith regarding her general health and the details of the accident. When she was finished, she pulled her stethoscope from around her neck and listened to Faith's hearth and lungs. She then checked her other leg, her arms, and completed her exam by feeling Faith's belly.

"How's your tummy feel?"

"Fine."

When Morgan was finished she stepped back and sat down on a small chair.

"Well, I don't see any swelling of the knee and it's not too tender to movement. It's probably just a mild sprain. But just to be on the safe side, I think we should get an X-ray."

Anticipating Morgan's suggestion, Faith inquired, "Do you think that's really necessary?"

"I'd hate to miss something," Morgan answered.

"I just found out I'm pregnant, Dr. Connolly, and if you think it's just a mild sprain, I'd rather skip the X-ray."

"Have you had any vaginal bleeding or cramps since the fall?"

"No. Everything's fine."

"Who's your obstetrician?"

Faith's mind went blank. "I feel so stupid," she said. "I just can't think of his name right now."

"It's not important. We can cover your abdomen with a lead apron. There will be absolutely no risk to the baby."

Faith paused for a moment, pretending to think about Morgan's suggestion. "I appreciate your concern, but I'm just not comfortable, Dr. Connolly."

"I understand. I'll have the nurse fix you up with a knee brace. I'll come back after it's on to give you your discharge instructions."

"Thanks," she told Morgan, sitting up and moving to the end of the bed.

Faith was especially careful to make mental notes of everything that occurred. She liked Dr. Connolly, finding her attentive and caring. Overall, she was quite pleased with the care she'd received. Impressing Steve was very important to her. She wanted to make sure the report she gave him was detailed and accurate.

A few minutes later, Denise returned with a knee brace and showed Faith how to put it on. Just as she finished securing the last Velcro strap, Morgan came back in.

"Thanks," Faith said.

"No problem," Denise told her. "We Olympic cyclists have to stick together." She walked over to the other side of the exam room and returned with a clipboard. "I just need you to sign here. As soon as Dr. Connolly is finished, you're out of here."

Morgan walked over to the examination table and checked the placement of the knee brace.

"How does it feel?"

"Pretty good," Faith answered, counting the minutes until she could get it off.

Morgan finished writing the prescription and tore it off the pad. "Here's something for pain. I also wrote the name of an orthopedic surgeon you can call if the pain doesn't go away in a couple of days. If the knee starts to swell in the next twenty-four hours, you can put some ice on it." Morgan looked up and added, "You're sure about the X-ray?"

Faith leaned forward and rubbed her knee.

"It's feeling much better now, Dr. Connolly. But if it's not better in a few days, I'll have the X-ray done. I promise."

Morgan extended her hand, shook Faith's, and then headed for the door.

"Call us if you need anything," Morgan said as she walked out of the room and headed in the direction of the nursing station.

With several patients with minor complaints still to be seen, she crossed her fingers and prayed the Dade County knife and gun club would remain quiet for the rest of her shift.

Under normal circumstances, the nature of Faith Russo's ER visit was so routine that once Morgan had moved on to her next patient, it would become one of thousands of forgettable cases. But as Morgan popped the top of her soda and took the first sip, she had no way of knowing that nothing could be further from the truth.

With her knee brace securely in place, Faith limped out of the emergency room.

Strolling past a new parking garage under construction, she had to admit she was quite proud of herself. For someone who had never been a professional mole, she had pulled it off like a seasoned veteran. She hoped that Steve would share her enthusiasm.

She made her way down a narrow tree-lined street that ended at a gravel field, which the hospital was using as a temporary parking lot. When she had first arrived, the lot was almost filled, forcing her to park her aging Toyota Camry at the far end. Now, it was practically empty, and the thought of walking across the entire field filled her with trepidation.

Reaching down, she released the straps of the knee brace and pulled it off. There was a large metal Dumpster a few feet away. Without giving it a second thought, she tossed the annoying brace over the rim and into the container. Before starting out, she took a careful look around. When she saw nobody, she clutched her purse as if it were a diplomatic pouch and marched directly down the middle of the lot.

The area was scantily lit by two portable light towers, which were powered by a loud gasoline-driven generator. It was not until she reached the halfway point that Faith realized the farther she went, the darker it became. Her eyes darting back and forth, she made it a point not to drift off of the parking lot's centerline. When she finally spotted her car, she heaved a breath of relief. Approaching the driver's side door, Faith reached into her purse for her keys. It was at that moment she heard the footsteps. Her eyes shot up. About thirty feet away, she could easily make out the silhouette of a man. Given his rapid pace and the direction from which he was coming, it was obvious he had spotted her. As frightened as she was, she never took her eyes off of him. A few seconds passed, and she could see he was stocky and that he was wearing a baseball cap.

With her heart coming out of her chest, she continued to fumble for her keys. The crackle of the gravel under the man's feet grew louder with each step he took. Fighting off the panic, she pounded her memory to recall anything of the rape awareness class that she had taken with some of the other waitresses.

She shook her purse fiercely, hoping the sound of the jingling keys would guide her hand. The man was now close enough that the dim splashes of light reflected off of his face. At that instant he smiled and waved. Placing her hand to her heart, she dropped her head and took a huge breath.

"Steve, you scared me to death. What are you doing here?" she asked.

"Waiting for you," he answered.

She giggled. "Do you have any idea what time it is?"

"I told you we'd talk after you left the emergency room."

"I didn't think you meant in the middle of the night."

He pointed in the direction of the emergency room.

"Do you see that big hospital over there? They're paying my company a fortune for the information that's now in that pretty little head of yours. I'm not about to let you sleep on it and forget even the slightest detail."

"I was going to make notes as soon as I got home. Faith looked around and pretended to shiver. "Doesn't this place give you the creeps?"

Gideon shrugged. "I played rugby in college, competed in ten triathlons, and can bench twice my weight. Anybody who feels like messing with me is welcome to try."

As opposed to most everything else he had ever told Faith, his assurances of his physical prowess and combative skills were quite true.

She leaned her head to the side. Hoping he had more on his mind than just business and gaining in confidence, she whispered, "I'll make a deal with you."

"Really?" he asked. "What kind of a deal?"

"I'll do the interview now if you take me out for a drink afterward."

He stroked her arm. "That sounds like an offer I'd be a fool to turn down. What time do you have to be home?"

She looked down at his hand. "I guess that depends. My babysitter's great about staying over."

Concealing his contempt for her promiscuous behavior, Gideon smiled and pointed to her car.

"Why don't we dispense with our business? Then we can go have that drink to celebrate your first assignment as a covert hospital appraiser."

Faith got in on the driver's side, tossed her purse on the backseat, and waited for Gideon to climb in opposite her. He pushed his seat all the way back and pulled out a small notebook and a fountain pen. He then adjusted the rearview mirror, fiddling with it for a few seconds until he got it just right. Faith wondered why, but not enough to ask him.

She turned on the engine and let the air conditioner run. When she looked up, she saw him glancing out of her window. She turned, took a look as well but saw nothing.

"Let's get started," he said. "How did it go?"

"Fine. The registration process went well, and I saw a very nice doctor."

"Good. What did you tell him was wrong with you?"

"Him was a her. Remember? You told me to request a woman doctor."

He pointed at her and winked. "That's right. I did. You have a good memory. Did you mention anything about your tummy?"

"You told me to tell the triage nurse that it hurt but not to mention it to the doctor."

"Good, and what was the physician's name?"

"Dr. Connolly."

"Did she do a complete examination?"

"Yes."

"You're sure? She checked every part of you and not just your knee?"

"She was very thorough."

"How about blood tests?"

"She said I didn't need any."

"What about an X-ray?" he asked.

"She wanted to do one, but I told her I was pregnant and that I'd rather not."

"Good. Did she give you a hard time?" he inquired, pretending to make notes as she spoke.

"She wasn't thrilled about it, but she didn't make a thing about it either. She just made me promise to come back if I still had pain in a few days."

Faith noticed that he seemed a little distracted even though he kept asking her very specific questions. She was also baffled as to why he kept looking around. Finally, when he had asked his last question, he closed his notebook and smiled at her.

"I think that about takes care of everything. You did a great job. I'm sure we'll have more work for you in the future."

"Are you serious?" she asked with delight.

"You'll have a check for one thousand dollars within the week. I'll bring it to the restaurant. Now how about that drink?"

Faith noticed that he was easing toward her and that his eyes were all over her. Hoping he was getting ready to kiss her, she stared into his eyes and leaned closer. His left arm moved across the top of her seat and found its way onto the back of her neck. He began to gently massage her. The only sound that filtered into the car was the droning of the generators.

"That feels great," Faith said, closing her eyes. "Have you ever thought about changing professions?"

After a few seconds, when Gideon didn't answer, she opened her eyes and turned her head. At first she was confused by his wildly piercing eyes. But when he seized her hair and drew it into his fist, she gasped. Her first and only scream came when he snapped her head back.

Overcome with terror, she shot her hand out, desperately looking for the door handle. With her hand still flailing, she suddenly felt his palm cup her chin. Using her fingernails to claw his cheeks, she thrashed back and forth trying to free herself from his death grip. But with one powerful jerk, Gideon spun Faith around and then snatched her over the console until her back was pressed tightly against his chest.

From his position behind her, he was able to easily slip her into an inescapable stranglehold that compressed both of her carotid arteries and windpipe. With no blood flow to her brain, she quickly wilted in his arms. From the bleak darkness of her mind, a cluster of dazzling multicolored lights darted past her like a laser show. Sadly, the brilliant flashes lasted only a few seconds. They were the last conscious image of her life.

Lying in his arms, Faith's chest moved easily with each breath.

Gideon could have snapped her neck like a dry twig, but that was not his plan. To the contrary, he needed her alive; at least for the next hour or so. Realizing she would soon be recovering consciousness, he pushed her back into the driver's seat. Her head bobbed a couple of times before it flopped against the window. Grabbing her by her shoulders, he spun her torso toward him.

With his eyes fixed on her upper abdomen, he made a fist and then slowly drew it to the level of his ear. He felt every particle of strength in his body gather in the fist. And then, with explosive force, he drove it deep into the soft tissues of her abdominal wall. The blow struck her just below the left rib cage. The dull thud it made was only a small measure of its devastating power. Faith never moved, nor did she utter a sound. After a slow half breath, Gideon again drew back his hand. Letting it explode, the accuracy of his second blow mirrored the first.

Satisfied he had shattered her spleen and that she was at this very moment bleeding massively, he removed a clean white washcloth from his pocket and wiped down everything he had touched. He then flipped on the small courtesy light under the visor and leaned over toward Faith. He wasn't surprised to see she was still breathing, but her effort was labored and shallow.

Gideon glanced down at his watch. He then waited for exactly three minutes before reaching over and placing his fingertips on her wrist. Her pulse was racing and threadlike, confirming his suspicion that she was already in shock from uncontrolled internal bleeding. Her face, usually animated and ruby, was drained of any color.

As if he had just finished a routine errand, Gideon got out of the car and left the parking lot the same way he'd come in. On his way home, his thoughts were of Faith. Although she was innocuous and unoriginal, she was a pleasant enough person. And while her death was unfortunate, it was essential.

Sitting in his den, Gideon waved a crystal snifter containing a fifty-year-old cognac under his nose.

He leaned back in his leather club chair and gazed across the room at the ornate antique grandfather clock that stood in the corner. The unbearable ringing in his ears had finally decreased to a tolerable level. When it had been exactly thirty minutes since he had left Faith to bleed to death, he opened the bottom drawer of his desk, pulled out a cell phone, and tapped in a number. It rang four times.

"Emergency room."

Gideon cleared his throat. "I'm sorry to disturb you, but I was just leaving the hospital and noticed a woman getting into her car in the parking lot. It was a small red Toyota. The reason I'm calling is because she looked pretty wobbly. I probably should have stopped or called right away but . . . well, I had just come from seeing my wife and I was a little—"

"That's okay," Matt Petrakis, the unit secretary, said. "Where exactly was this again?"

"In that dirt parking lot across the street from the emergency room—down at the far end."

"I'll let security know. Thanks for calling."

"You're welcome," Gideon said.

Having a pretty good idea of what was about to unfold in Dade Presbyterian's ER, Gideon couldn't help but grin. With nothing

"What do we have?" Morgan asked, craning her neck to see above the crowd of nurses and other ER personnel feverishly working on a young woman.

"We're not exactly sure," answered Justine as she cut the woman's pant leg from ankle to thigh. "This one's a little bizarre. Security found her in her car a few minutes ago. She still had her hospital identification band on." Justine paused for a moment and looked up. "It's Faith Russo. The woman we just discharged with the knee injury."

Moving toward the bed, Morgan could feel her throat clamping down. "The one who fell off her bike?"

Justine nodded.

Morgan took a long look at the woman's face. "This is impossible," she muttered. "It was a minor fall."

"That may be, but at the moment she has no pulse or blood pressure. Security called the paramedics. They began CPR as soon as they got to her."

It was only her years of training and experience that allowed Morgan to dismiss the shock and bewilderment of the moment and get on with the business of saving Faith Russo's life.

The assistant head nurse had already started an IV and was now placing a series of heart monitor leads on her chest. A respiratory therapist held a plastic mask that was attached to a black bag over her nose and mouth. With each squeeze of the bag, he forced one oxygen-enriched breath after another into Faith's lungs.

Without looking up, Morgan yelled, "Forget masking her. Let's get a tube in her right now—and keep up the chest compressions." She turned back to the respiratory therapist. "We'll need a ventilator set up right now. Get some help if you need to."

"We have one ready to go," she answered.

Morgan reached across Faith's chest and stripped off her blanket. Her eyes froze in disbelief at her swollen abdomen. Morgan didn't have to review a long list of diagnostic possibilities. She knew exactly what she was dealing with.

"This woman's bleeding internally. Get the general surgery resident down here right now," she said, spreading her hands out wide on Faith's belly. "We need another IV. When it's in, start another liter bolus of Ringer's solution. As soon as you have it, give her two units of O-negative blood. I also need ultrasound in here stat."

"I'll get the blood," came a voice from the back of the room.

Morgan examined Faith's abdomen carefully. "There's no entrance wound," she announced. "There's a small bruise right under the rib cage. This has to be blunt trauma," she added, thinking to herself that the mark wasn't there when she first examined Faith. She turned to Justine. "This woman probably needs to go to the operating room. Where the hell are the surgeons?"

"They're on their way," the unit secretary yelled from the doorway.

Justine said, "I think they'll all be in the OR with that guy who got crunched on his motorcycle."

Morgan grabbed a metal scope from the red crash cart. The cart was present in all critical care areas and was stocked with every conceivable device and medication that might be required for a code blue. She flipped the blade of the scope open, locking it into place. She then opened Faith's mouth and slid the blade toward the back. The light on the end of the scope helped Morgan see her vocal cords.

Without moving her eyes, Morgan held her hand out. "Give me a seven tube." As soon as she had it in her hand, she slid the tip of the clear plastic tube between Faith's vocal cords and down into her windpipe. "We're in," she announced. "Start bagging her. How about that blood?"

"We're hanging it now. We still can't get a blood pressure," Justine announced.

"Give her an amp of epinephrine and two of bicarb. And somebody mix up a dopamine drip," Morgan ordered. She looked up at the monitor—still no vital signs.

Camille Olson, the chief resident in surgery, charged into the room. She was dressed in scrubs with a mask tied around her neck.

"Somebody talk to me," she said, moving immediately to the head of the bed next to Morgan.

Justine answered, "This is a thirty-year-old woman who we saw about an hour ago. She had fallen from her bike. All she had was a mild knee sprain."

Camille looked at Justine sideways. "How did we go from a mild knee sprain to an abdomen like this?"

Morgan hesitated. "Her abdomen was fine when I discharged her."

Camille didn't look up. Morgan knew she wouldn't criticize the care the patient had received in front of the ER staff.

"Maybe she underestimated how hard she fell," Camille offered, performing her own examination of Faith's abdomen.

"When she left here she was fine," Morgan insisted, as she continued to order medications and run the code blue.

"What do you think happened?"

"I have no idea. All I know is security found her in her car with no pulse or blood pressure and called the paramedics." Morgan pointed at the cardiac monitor. "She came in flatline and that's the way she's stayed."

Camille took a step back. "How long have you been coding her?"

"About fifteen minutes," Justine answered.

"What about taking her to the OR?" Morgan asked.

Camille looked at her with surprise. "She has no vital
signs. What am I going to do for her in the OR? It'll be a
warm autopsy."

Morgan knew Camille was right but she was desperate.

Cass Drury, who had been the night ultrasound tech at
Dade Presbyterian for years, pushed her portable ultrasound
machine into the room.

"We want to see the abdomen," Morgan said.

Cass selected one of the ultrasound probes and placed it just
under Faith's breastbone and began scanning her abdomen.
After no more than a few seconds, she pointed to the monitor.
"This looks bad. Her whole belly's filled with blood."

Camille said, "She must have a bad liver or spleen injury—
maybe both." She moved closer to Morgan. Speaking in just
above a hush, she said, "I'm only the chief resident, Morgan.
You're the attending, so it's your call, but I don't think we
have anything to offer her. We're too late."

"We can't give up that easily," Morgan insisted. "The
woman's barely in her thirties, for God's sake." She turned
to the nurse who was doing the chest compressions. "Don't
stop the CPR."

Camille stole a second glance at Justine, who urged her on
by nodding a few times.

"Okay," Camille said. "Let's give this one more shot."

Under Morgan's and Camille's direction, the entire team
worked at a frenzied pace for the next twenty minutes doing
everything possible to resuscitate Faith. But in spite of their
Herculean effort, her heart never beat once. The blood loss
had been too massive and the state of shock irreversible.

Finally, Camille stepped back from the table. She said
nothing. Justine came around to the other side of the stretcher
where Morgan was standing. She placed her hand on Mor-

gan's forearm and whispered, "She's gone. It's your call when we stop."

When Morgan didn't answer, Camille said, "We've been coding her for thirty-five minutes with absolutely no response. Her pupils are fixed and dilated. From a surgical standpoint there's no reason to continue."

With the futility of the situation finally obvious, Morgan scanned the defeated faces of the staff who had shared in the struggle to save Faith Russo's life.

In a clear but shaky voice, Morgan said, "We're finished here. Somebody please note the time."

An eerie hush filled the room as everybody except Morgan and Justine filed out. Morgan walked over to the opposite side of the room and sat down. The stark realization of Faith Russo's death took hold of her with a sickening sense of guilt and desperation. Her eyes never moved as she sat there without the first clue of how she could have missed such a devastating injury.

Picking up empty medication boxes from the floor, Justine stopped for a moment and looked over at Morgan. "Are you okay?"

"I . . . I don't know. I'm the chief of the department. I'm the one everybody expects to set the standard for excellence in patient care."

"Are you suggesting you did something wrong? It was a routine minor orthopedic injury. Her vital signs were fine. There was no reason to suspect she—"

"I should have ordered an abdominal ultrasound."

"For a sprained knee? Be reasonable, Morgan. There's not a physician in this department who would have done that."

Morgan pressed her palms and fingers together. "She told me that the only thing that bothered her was her knee. I examined her abdomen anyway. It was fine."

Justine cleared her throat. "The triage nurse said she mentioned that she did have a small amount of abdominal pain. She included it in her triage note."

Morgan reached for the chart. "I saw the note. That's why I specifically asked her about her abdomen."

"Let's just get through the shift," Justine suggested. "I'm sure there will be an autopsy. We'll know more after it's done."

"I don't need an autopsy to confirm the obvious. The woman fell from her bike, ruptured her spleen, and I missed it. It's as simple as that."

"Nothing's as simple as that."

"I'm responsible. We'll have to report this to the state as a Code Fifteen," Morgan said, feeling emotionally drained. "That poor woman. She told me she was a single mom with three kids. She had no other family. What in God's name is going to happen to those children?"

"We have a great team of social workers. I'm sure they'll take care of everything. You didn't do anything wrong," Justine assured her again. Morgan barely heard Justine's words. Her mind was reeling, trying to understand how she could have made such a huge mistake. Finally, she stood up and made her way back to the nursing station. On the brink of tears, she struggled to collect herself.

Morgan took a measured look around the emergency room. Everybody around her, including those who had just helped in trying to save Faith Russo's life, was already busy at work attending to new patients. It was as if it was just another busy Friday night and nothing out of the ordinary had happened. The strange irony was that Morgan had been guilty of the same type of unemotional response herself many times in the past. But tonight was infinitely different. The feeling of being directly responsible for another human being's death had shaken her to the core.

CHAPTER

38

At nine a.m. Monday morning, Morgan walked through the gleaming metal doors that accessed Dade Presbyterian's morgue.

It had been a long, wearisome weekend. She had spent most of Saturday wallowing in guilt, self-doubt, and remorse. Ben had gone out of town and although she had spoken to him a few times, she decided to wait until he returned to tell him what happened. As soon as he landed on Sunday, he came to her apartment bearing Thai takeout for dinner.

At first, Morgan had difficulty sharing her dismay with him regarding what had happened. As she expected, Ben was supportive and insightful. He reminded her that no physician was immune to poor patient outcomes. He also pointed out that missed diagnoses and errors in treatment were inevitable, especially if one chose to be an emergency room doctor. The only way to get back on track was to be introspective about what had occurred, lick your wounds, and show up for your next shift. Ben's pep talk was sufficient to renew her confidence, raise her spirits, and make her more comfortable about the prospect of getting back to work. Equally important was that she was now questioning not only the events surrounding Faith's death but her own accountability as well.

Typical of most hospitals, Dade Presbyterian's morgue was a dreary, featureless room with cement block walls, gray countertops, and a scuffed linoleum floor. Directly in the middle of the room, bolted to the floor, was a long stainless-steel table. The table was brightly illuminated by two overhead surgical lamps.

Morgan walked across the room and grabbed one of the white plastic bunny suits from the top of a large stack. Holding it in front of her, she stepped into its legs, pulled it up over her shoulders and zipped it up the front all the way to her neck. When she entered the autopsy room, the chief of Pathology, Everett Canfield, was putting on his gloves.

Canfield was a chronically cranky man who had lost his smile more years ago than anybody could remember. With shaggy eyebrows and crusty skin, he ran the pathology department with no imagination. Morgan wasn't alone in her belief that the only thing saving his job was his twenty-five years of service and his close personal friendship with Bob Allenby. Influential in hospital politics, he was one of the few members of the medical staff that Morgan had locked horns with on more than one occasion. Based on their history, she assumed he didn't hold her in high esteem.

She watched in silence as he stepped up to the table. His only acknowledgment of her presence was a fleeting glance and a cursory nod. His assistant handed him a scalpel and with one steady stroke, he made an incision from the top of Faith's breastbone all the way down past her umbilicus. For all his pomposity, Canfield was an adept and experienced pathologist.

While joking with his technician, he divided the muscle layers of Faith's abdominal wall.

"Okay, let's have a look," he said, using a scissors to incise the last thin layer that separated him from Faith's abdominal cavity. The instant he opened it, there was a huge gush of old, dark blood. Based on the ultrasound findings from the emergency room, Morgan was hardly surprised.

"Let me have the suction," he told the technician. He then plunged the plastic sucker deep into Faith's abdomen and removed the remaining blood. Most of it was liquid, but some of it was in the form of huge clots, too large for the sucker. Shaking his head, he reached his cupped hand into her abdominal cavity and began scooping them out.

"Every drop of blood she has is in her abdomen," the tech said. "She never had a chance."

Canfield never looked up. "It's no wonder she's dead," he stated in a condescending voice. When there was no more blood, he slid his double-gloved hand to the upper right part of the abdomen. "The liver's fine—no cracks, lacerations, or contusions." He then moved to the left side, reached up toward the diaphragm and curled his fingers around her spleen. He pulled it gently forward so he could examine it.

"How does it look?" Morgan asked trying to peer over his shoulder.

"Like an elephant sat on it. It's shattered into a dozen pieces. This is undoubtedly the cause of death."

"Are you positive?" Morgan asked.

With raised eyebrows, he answered, "I doubt she was born this way. Obviously, this woman sustained a major blunt force to her abdomen and bled to death from a pulverized spleen. This is not exactly the brain-breaker case of the month."

Morgan took a step back and folded her arms. She doubted whether Canfield had read Faith's entire medical record.

"This woman was seen twice the night she died," Morgan told him. "The first time she came in she complained of knee pain. Her pulse and blood pressure were normal, and her abdomen was completely normal. We checked her out thoroughly and discharged her. Less than an hour later, she returned in cardiac arrest with an abdomen full of blood. How do your findings explain that?"

"Do you really want me to answer that?"

"I wouldn't have asked if I didn't," she said, undaunted by his insulting innuendo.

"Denial and ego aside—you missed her ruptured spleen the first time you saw her."

"I don't think so," Morgan insisted, pointing to the spleen. "She told us her bike accident occurred hours earlier. Anybody who had sustained an injury like that would have bled to death within minutes."

"I'm an educated man, Dr. Connolly. I call them as I see them. I don't rely on tea leaves, crystal balls, or a Ouija board. If I'm standing under a bridge and I hear hoofbeats, I think of horses, not zebras."

"What's your point?"

"There is no point. I'm simply saying I can't say with complete accuracy how long it will take somebody with a crushed spleen to bleed to death. What I can say with certainty is that I've been around a long time, and I've seen plenty of overconfident young physicians show up in my morgue and deny the obvious—even though it's staring them right in the face." He reached for a larger scissors. "As painful as this is for you, Doctor, the woman died of an undiagnosed ruptured spleen."

"With all due respect, you weren't in the ER when they brought her in. If you had been, your opinion might—"

"My opinion would be the same." He then added nonchalantly, "Don't be too hard on yourself. The ability to objectively assess your patient outcomes takes some physicians years to acquire."

The tech snickered, which further infuriated her. Looking at Canfield's smug face, Morgan wondered what in the world made him think he knew anything about treating patients. The only patients he ever dealt with were already dead.

Seeing no reason to debate the issue with him, Morgan unzipped her bunny suit and headed for the exit. She was almost to the door when something suddenly occurred to her. She turned around.

"Was she pregnant?"

Canfield shifted his attention to the pelvic organs for a moment, examined the uterus, and said, "It doesn't appear so." He looked up with an inquisitive expression. "What the hell difference would it make if she were pregnant or not?"

"I was just curious. I appreciate you allowing me to attend the autopsy, Dr. Canfield. I'll look forward to reading your report as soon as it's dictated."

"You'll get the second copy. I had a call from Bob Allenby earlier. He's first in line. Evidently, you're not the only one who's quite eager to see my report."

Feeling her anger swell even further, Morgan gave serious consideration to telling Canfield what she thought of his offensive disposition. Instead, she simply shook her head, turned back around, and again started back for the exit. Just as she was about to go through the door, she heard Canfield and his assistant trying to muffle their laughter.

CHAPTER
39

Still fuming over the way she'd been treated by Canfield, Morgan sat by herself in the doctor's dining room nursing a cup of jasmine tea.

She looked up for just long enough to see Ben making his way toward her table with a tray heaped high with food. He set his tray down and took the seat across from her. Morgan looked at her own tray, which contained only a modest fruit plate.

"How can you eat so much?" she asked.

He plucked a napkin from a metal dispenser and spread it on his lap. "And good morning to you, Dr. Connolly."

"Sorry. Good morning."

"How are you feeling?"

"Mentally or physically?"

He shrugged. "Take your choice."

"Let's see. I'm only vomiting every other morning now. My clothes are all starting to get tight and, even though I know it's too early, I think somebody kicked me last night."

"All good things," Ben said, spreading a mound of grape jelly on his toasted bagel. "I assume you went to the autopsy."

"I just came from there. "

"Who did it?"

"That jerk, Canfield." Morgan watched as Ben stirred the

third packet of sugar into his coffee. When he reached for the fourth, she snatched it from his hand. "I'll tell you what. Let's give your pancreas a break this morning."

"Now there's the Morgan Connolly I know and love. What did the autopsy show?"

"A belly full of blood and a fractured spleen," she said with a quick shake of her head.

"You sound surprised. I thought that's what you were expecting."

"I guess a small part of me was praying for something else."

"C'mon, Morgan. ER medicine's a tough specialty. It's easy to miss things."

"That's just the point. I don't think I missed anything."

He looked across the table at her with circumspect eyes, dabbed the corner of his mouth, and said, "That's not what you've been saying all weekend."

"I know."

"Isn't it possible the diagnosis wasn't obvious the first time you saw her? I'm not a trauma surgeon but I seem to recall that injuries to the spleen can sometimes be tricky to detect."

"The subtle ones maybe, but not the massive type that killed this woman. I saw her spleen this morning. It was shattered beyond recognition. There's no way she could have had a bike accident in the middle of the afternoon and then sauntered into our emergency room at eleven o'clock looking like a rose. She never would have lived that long."

"If you're not disputing Canfield's findings regarding the cause of death, then the only possible explanation for this woman's death is that her injury occurred soon after you discharged her."

"Which is precisely what I think happened. I've been thinking about this case nonstop since you left last night. I'm starting to realize that there are a lot of inconsistencies regarding what happened."

"For instance?" Ben asked.

"For one, she told me she didn't want an X-ray because she was pregnant. I asked Canfield to check. She wasn't pregnant."

"Did you do a pregnancy test on her?"

"The second time."

"And?"

"It was negative." Morgan said.

"Maybe she wasn't sure about being pregnant. The other possibility is she was simply wrong."

Morgan shook her head. "She was definite about it. She told me she'd already had her first visit with an obstetrician."

"So she was lying. There are dozens of reasons why she might have lied to avoid an X-ray."

"Give me one."

"Maybe she was phobic about radiation or just in a hurry to get out of the ER." Ben removed his glasses and set them down next to his tray. "I guess the question is: What difference does it make if she was pregnant or not—or what her reasons were for not wanting an X-ray?"

Morgan pushed her tray forward, giving her just enough room to rest her hands on the table. She leaned in. "About forty-five minutes after I discharged her, the unit secretary received a call from a man. He said he saw a woman in our parking lot wobbling as she got into her car. He then asked the secretary to call security and inform them."

"I assume this turned out to be your patient."

Morgan nodded.

Ben massaged the bridge of his nose and then replaced his glasses. "Well, if she was bleeding internally and going into shock, it's quite possible she could have been unsteady."

"But when she left the emergency room, she was fine. Does it seem reasonable that in the time it took her to get from the ER to her car, she bled into a shock from an injury that occurred twelve hours earlier?"

Ben waited for a group of nurses to walk by and said, "Were there physical signs at the autopsy indicating a severe blow to the abdomen?"

"Canfield made note of a bruise on her abdomen under her left rib cage. I saw the same thing when the paramedics brought her in."

"How can you be so certain it wasn't there the first time you examined her?"

"Because I checked her belly thoroughly. There were no bruises of any kind on her abdominal wall. I even made a note of it on the chart."

Ben regarded her intently for a few seconds before asking, "Was there evidence of a sexual assault?"

"None."

"Since I'm sure you spoke with them, what did security say? Did they think she was robbed?"

"The guard who found her said she was slumped over the steering wheel. He found her purse undisturbed on the backseat." Morgan checked Ben's eyes for a reaction. From the look on his face, she suspected he knew where she was headed. "When a woman drives alone, she puts her purse on the seat next to her—not in the back. If her purse was on the backseat, I'd bet anything there was somebody sitting next to her."

"Every square inch of the hospital's under video surveillance. Why don't you ask security to see if there's anything on their tapes?"

"I thought of that. Unfortunately, the ER lot's a temporary one. Apart from a golf-cart patrol every couple of hours, there is no other surveillance. The other interesting thing is when they brought her in she wasn't wearing her knee brace. One of the guards found it hanging over the top of the Dumpster."

"Maybe she found it uncomfortable."

"Or maybe she never needed it in the first place," Morgan said. She then leaned over her tray and said in just above a whisper, "I don't believe this woman ever fell off a bicycle. I don't believe she suffered any injury at all that day. I think she was faking the whole thing and had some other reason for coming in that night."

"For instance."

Morgan held up both hands. "I don't have the first damn idea why she would put on a charade like that."

Ben's focus changed when he noticed Morgan's face was the color of chalk. "Are you okay? You look terrible."

She covered her mouth with her fingers. "I may have spoken too soon about the morning sickness."

"Do you want to—"

"I'll be fine in a minute," she assured him. "This case will definitely have to be reported to the state as a Code Fifteen. As the treating physician, I'm going to be right in the middle of an AHCA investigation."

"I wouldn't worry about that," Ben said. "You have an exemplary record. This woman's death, while tragic, is an incident, not a pattern."

She tossed Ben a cautionary look. "I'm not sure AHCA will view things quite as charitably as you are. Canfield's autopsy report will be an important part of their inquiry. If the state concludes that I missed the diagnosis and negligently discharged Faith Russo from the emergency room, they will consider this case a wrongful and preventable death." Morgan shook her head slowly. Ben could see she was struggling not to lose her composure. "Faith Russo was a young, healthy woman with three children. There's no predicting what disciplinary action they could take against me."

Ben said, "You're looking at the absolute worst scenario." The words were barely out of his mouth when Morgan grabbed her tray, pushed her chair back in, and stood up.

"I'll give you a call later," she said. "Are we on for dinner?"

"Sure. You pick the place."

Ben watched her leave the cafeteria. What concerned him the most was that he knew Morgan was right about AHCA. They would almost certainly open an inquiry into the Faith Russo case, and it was equally probable she would fall under intense scrutiny.

Even if Morgan were exonerated, the investigative process

alone would be an embarrassing nightmare that would haunt her for months. Trying to cope with such an investigation would be tough enough under normal circumstances—trying to do it in the early part of a pregnancy would be a daunting challenge.

CHAPTER

40

DAY FOURTEEN

From his wooden deck and under a warm sun, Gideon sat on his white slat-back rocking chair, gazing at his garden.

Absently, he spun his Rubik's Cube in one hand. Normally, he'd be engrossed in aligning the multicolored squares—a feat he could now do in just under four minutes. His skill level didn't make him tournament ready, but it was, nevertheless, an impressive achievement that had taken him a year of steady practice to attain.

With each passing day, his fear that Morgan Connolly had figured out how Alison Greene died grew stronger. He was well aware that trying to confirm his suspicions could place him at considerable risk. But after spending many hours contemplating his limited options, he decided an attempt was worth the risk. His plan was well conceived and well rehearsed. Setting the cube down on a small wooden table, he stopped rocking, reached for his cell phone, and tapped in the number of the Cardiac Care Center.

"CCC. This is Jean. May I help you?"

"This is Mr. Tillinghouse in Patient Relations. May I speak with Dana McGinley please?" he asked.

"Please hold."

Dana, who had been called in at five a.m. on her day off to take care of a young woman suffering from a postpartum blood clot to her lungs, was just finishing up her morning charting when she saw the unit secretary motion for her to pick up the phone. With a puff of exasperation, she put down her laptop and reached for the phone.

"This is Dana."

"Miss McGinley. My name's Hugh Tillinghouse. I work in Patient Relations. We've recently been asked to look into the Alison Greene case and I was hoping you might be—"

"I was expecting to hear from you."

"I beg your pardon."

"I assume you're calling me because her parents have made a formal complaint about the cross."

"They expressed some concerns. I'm not sure I'd call it a complaint," Gideon answered, hoping Dana would take him where he wanted to go. "I've spoken to them a couple of times. I told them I would get back to them after speaking with you."

"I'm a conscientious nurse, Mr. Tillinghouse, but I generally don't check to see what religion my patient happens to be. I feel terribly about what happened, but I think the parents' gripe is a little misdirected. They should be talking to Mr. Ogden. He's the one who placed it around her neck."

"I can assure you that nobody in administration feels you did anything wrong. However, the hospital does feel it would go a long way to soothe the parents' pain if we could offer them an explanation of what happened. Being a Code Fifteen, I know it's a sensitive case. Because of her role on the Patient Safety Committee, I spoke with Dr. Connolly. I told her I'd be calling you. She mentioned to me that you two have already discussed the case in some detail."

"We met last week. That's when I assured her that it was Mr. Ogden who put the cross around Alison's neck."

"Did you mention that to the parents?"

"I did, but they didn't know him."

"You're quite certain Miss Greene wasn't wearing the cross when she came from the recovery room?"

"I'm positive. I didn't have any idea it was magnetized until I met with Dr. Connolly. She was the one who discovered it."

Gideon felt the hollow of his stomach suddenly wince in spasm. His worst fear realized, he asked, "Do you know how we might be able to contact Mr. Ogden? I was hoping I could convince him to call the Greenes."

"I'm sorry. I don't."

Gideon deliberately sighed loud enough for Dana to hear him.

"You might be able to find him by contacting Broward College. He said he was a professor there."

"Did he mention what department he was in?"

"Not that I recall."

"I'll try to check it out," he said.

"If I see him again, I'll tell him to give you a call."

Taken back by her comment, Gideon asked, "See him again?"

"It doesn't happen very often, but every now and then one of our visitors will come back to visit somebody else or they just want to talk to one of us about something."

Trying to keep the pretense going, Gideon said, "But you only saw Mr. Ogden once. You probably wouldn't even recognize him."

"I think I would," she said immediately. "He had a very distinctive look about him. He also had a big gap between his front teeth."

Gideon resisted the sudden impulse to smash the phone against the nearest rock. Summoning every drop of restraint he had, and taking caution to speak in a normal voice, he said, "I know how busy you must be so I won't take up any more of your time. Thank you for your help. By the way, please remember that Mr. Allenby considers this case to be of an extremely sensitive nature. I'm sure you understand."

"Patient confidentiality," she said. "I know the drill."

Dana hung up the phone and started back toward her patient's room. Being an ICU nurse, she had been involved in many situations involving unhappy family members where patient relations had intervened. Mr. Tillinghouse's call was one of many similar calls she had received since coming to work at Dade Presbyterian. It wasn't one she was likely to give any further thought to.

GIDEON went inside and made his way upstairs to his bedroom. He set his cell phone down on an exquisitely crafted baroque dresser. Gazing at his image in an antique gold-framed mirror, he parted his lips and studied his front teeth. He thought about all the times he had considered having the space closed. He had even seen a highly touted dentist who specialized in cosmetic problems but had never made the follow-up appointment to have the bonding procedure done.

Still staring into the mirror, Gideon used his index finger to explore the gap between his teeth. With an ever-growing appreciation of Morgan Connolly's intelligence and compulsive nature, he reached for his cell phone. There was no doubt in his mind that she had gotten an excellent description of him from both Dana McGinley and her father's physician assistant.

With a half smile, he scrolled through his phone book. When he reached Dr. David Areca, the dentist whom he had seen in consultation, he dialed the number.

CHAPTER
41

DAY FIFTEEN

Sitting at the nursing station, Morgan finished writing an antibiotic prescription for a teenager with a sinus infection.

It was still early in the day and the patients hadn't started flooding the emergency room as yet. She was studying a chest X-ray when her pager went off. It was her office. She picked up the nearest phone.

"Mr. Allenby would like to see you," Kendra told her in an uncharacteristically formal voice.

"Is he standing right in front of you?" Morgan asked.

"Yes, I believe so."

"Great," she muttered. "Put him on."

"Good morning, Morgan. I was hoping we could have a chat."

"I'm in the ER, but things are pretty quiet. Can we talk over here?" she asked, wondering how he had acquired such an uncanny sense of bad timing.

"That would be fine. I'll be right over."

Morgan replaced the phone and looked over at the chart rack. Fortunately, there were no new patients to be seen.

"I'll be back in a few minutes," she told the charge nurse.

As soon as Morgan walked out of the department, she saw Bob approaching. From the somber look on his face, there was little doubt in her mind regarding the purpose of his call.

"I'm sorry to interrupt but it's rather important." He pointed across the hall. "Why don't we talk in the library?"

"Fine," she answered, thinking to herself that calling the small converted office with one recycled table and one hand-me-down bookcase a library was the euphemism of the month.

Morgan unlocked the door, waited for Bob to walk in, and then followed him inside. They sat down at the table. He pressed his palms together and then lightly tapped his fingertips.

"We have a problem, Morgan. I received a call from AHCA about an hour ago. As I feared they might, they're sending a team down from Tallahassee to do an on-site investigation of our recent Code Fifteens. Not only do they want to look at the Tony Wallace and Alison Greene cases, they also want to see everything we have on Faith Russo."

"That doesn't make any sense. It hasn't even been two weeks since Miss Russo's death. I spoke with Blair Clarke in risk management a couple of days ago. Our formal reports to AHCA haven't even been sent out yet."

"I understand that."

"So why are they sending an investigating team down?" she asked.

"Because they can."

"I beg your pardon?"

"AHCA is under no obligation to wait for the hospital's final report prior to pursuing an investigation." He paused briefly. "Look, Morgan. You're focusing on the wrong thing. AHCA's coming. Trying to understand the method to their madness isn't important. At the moment, we have a tough but manageable problem on our hands. My fear is that if we don't handle this thing just right, it could snowball into a major catastrophe."

"What do you suggest?" she asked, already beginning to silently cringe in anticipation of his answer.

"We have to show the state that Dade Presbyterian Hospital delivers excellent and consistent health care, and that these patient errors were nothing more than unfortunate aberrations."

"Unfortunate aberrations?"

"Exactly. We have to persuade them that we fully understand what went wrong and that we're actively revising our patient care protocols and instituting measures to avoid a repeat occurrence." Bob fiddled with the Windsor knot of his tie. "We've got one swing at the green here and we'd better not shank it."

Hardly surprised by Bob's action plan, Morgan asked, "When are they coming down?"

"They said they'd let us know in a few days, but I suspect it will be sooner rather than later." Bob stopped talking just long enough to clear his throat. "There's one other matter we should discuss. You were the treating physician in the Faith Russo case. You're also the chairperson of our Patient Safety Committee. I think AHCA would view that as a clear conflict of interest."

"I agree. In fact, the same thing occurred to me and I decided to limit my involvement to the Tony Wallace and Alison Greene cases."

The relief Morgan expected to see in Bob's face was conspicuously absent.

"That may not be enough," he said with an obvious note of reluctance. "I think the smart move is for you to step down as the committee chair."

"Step down? Why in the world would I—?"

"It would be temporary, Morgan—just until we get past this mess."

Morgan pushed back in her chair. She then interlaced her fingers and said, "I hope this doesn't have anything to do with our talk the other day about my level of stress, because if that's the case, I think you're—"

"Morgan, this is a time for putting our personal agendas aside for the good of the hospital."

"But you're not giving me the—"

He raised his hand. "I've already discussed the matter with the board and they agree with me. I assured them you would understand and do the right thing."

With Bob having made up his mind, and with the backing of the hospital board, Morgan knew it was pointless to pursue the discussion. To borrow from his endless supply of corny sports metaphors, she was being expected to take one for the team.

"It appears I have no choice."

"I think in time you'll see this is the most sensible approach to our problem. I'll give Sal Hutchinson a call. He's been vice chair for a year. He should be able to handle things for a while. I'll tell him to get in touch with you so that you can bring him up to speed on things."

Morgan pushed her chair back and stood up. Allenby didn't follow.

"That only leaves the matter of how we handle the Faith Russo case," he said.

Morgan's entire body rattled with frustration. "I thought we just decided that I was stepping down until the investigation was complete."

"I'm afraid it's not that simple. In view of Dr. Canfield's autopsy findings, we obviously have a problem."

Morgan retook her seat. "What kind of a problem?" she asked, growing weary of his tap dance.

"I've asked Eileen Hale to go over the specifics with you."

"Eileen's our director of Medical Affairs. Why would you like me to speak with her?"

"Because your involvement is a medical staff issue, I think it's more appropriate if you two hashed things out. Just give her a call sometime today."

"With all due respect, Bob, this is absurd."

"You've been going through a lot lately. It's hard to lose somebody who—"

"Bob, I loved my father dearly and I think about him every

day. But that doesn't make me a nonfunctional physician or human being. Losing a parent is something we all face. I'm fine."

"I understand you're pregnant and that you're also having significant marital problems."

"Which are hardly original occurrences around here. My personal life in no way impacts on my ability to do my job."

Bob's kindly smile was devoid of any sincerity.

"You're an important member of our medical staff. We're trying to help. Once all this unpleasant business with AHCA's behind us, we can get back to business as usual." He stood up and started for the door. "We'll talk again in a few days."

Bob's quick departure left Morgan staring across the room. If there had been anything made of glass within arm's reach, she would have smashed it against the wall.

"What a joke," she whispered, fighting to control her exasperation at Bob's phony Dutch uncle approach.

Feeling she was nearing the end of her rope, Morgan reminded herself she had most of her shift to complete. Doing everything in her power to temporarily stick her conversation with Bob in some far recess of her mind, she stood up and headed back to the emergency room.

CHAPTER
42

At four p.m., Morgan signed out her patients to the oncoming physician and went straight to her office.

She sat down at her desk and reached for the tall stack of phone messages that always awaited her at the end of the day. Leafing through them absently, her mind switched to the phone call she was about to make to Eileen Hale. It was one of those moments when she needed her father's perceptive advice. Ever since she declared her intention to study medicine, his compassionate and incisive guidance had always played an important role in her professional decision-making. Morgan found herself smiling as she thought about his unique way of sorting through the irrelevancies of a difficult problem to focus on its salient parts. Perhaps more than anything, she missed their special friendship.

Morgan tossed the messages back on her desk. After another few minutes, she picked up the phone and dialed Eileen's extension. Eileen and Morgan had attended medical school together at the University of Florida. Following graduation, Eileen went to California for her residency while Morgan headed south to Tampa. They became reacquainted when they began working at Dade Presbyterian. Having a similar work ethic and approach to the practice of medicine, they had always gotten along well.

"Office of the director of Medical Affairs."

"This is Dr. Connolly for Dr. Hale. I believe she's expecting my call."

"She's on another call but she told me to interrupt her if you called. Hold on, please." After a minute, Eileen's secretary came back on. "I'll connect you now."

"Hi, Morgan. Is it true about you being pregnant?"

Morgan had to smile. "It's true."

"When are you due?"

"The beginning of October."

"Congrats."

"Thanks."

"So how are you?"

"I guess that depends on how this conversation goes."

After a deafening silence, Eileen said, "Bob asked me to get in touch with you. He has some concerns about these recent Code Fifteens."

"I gathered as much when I spoke to him."

"I'm not going to sugarcoat it. Canfield called Bob right after the autopsy. He insisted you blew it. He said you missed a diagnosis any third-year medical student could have made. I don't have to tell you that Bob puts a lot of faith in Canfield's opinions."

"That may be part of the problem."

"Bob feels as if the recent stress in your life may be clouding your professional judgment."

Promising herself she wouldn't become unhinged, she said, "I wasn't aware Bob was a trained psychiatrist."

"When you're the CEO of a huge hospital, you don't need to be. He told me that he had had a long talk with you about the Code Fifteens and that instead of conducting a rational investigation, you had gone off on some absurd witch hunt."

"I'm not sure I would agree with his assessment. Bob's looking for easy explanations. Unfortunately, they're not there. I informed him of certain possibilities I felt he should be aware of. I wouldn't call it a witch hunt; I would call it doing my job. Unfortunately, Bob felt these alternative explanations could damage the hospital's reputation and instructed me not to pursue them. What's worse, he's using my involvement in the Faith Russo case to make sure I have no contact with AHCA regarding the other Code Fifteens."

"You may be a hundred percent correct. But the problem is that your disagreement with Bob could lead to major problems for you. As I'm sure you know, he has certain discretionary powers regarding patient safety; especially how it applies to physician competency and behavior. He doesn't need me or anybody else to advise and consent."

"I thought I had certain rights as a member of this medical staff."

"You do. And you're more than welcome to exercise them. That's assuming you want to get into a full-blown battle with the hospital over this thing."

"What are you suggesting?" Morgan asked.

"Sometimes it's smarter just to choose a less complicated path."

"In other words, I should ignore my principles and cave in."

"I'm not telling you what to do. I'm simply suggesting you focus on what's important and resist the temptation to move to center stage and demand justice at the top of your lungs."

"We've known each other a long time and I appreciate the advice, but I have a nagging suspicion that you have your marching orders from Bob and that we haven't discussed them as yet."

"Bob's instructed me that the hospital has to take some type of action. I'd like to do that without leaving a paper trail. The state's funny about what needs to go into and what can be omitted from a physician's permanent file, especially as it pertains to corrective actions."

Morgan didn't need a map and a flashlight to see where this conversation was headed.

"What are my options, Eileen?"

"I suggest you voluntarily submit to a couple of sessions of psychological counseling. It's no big deal and it will almost certainly get you out of the trap."

As objectionable as Eileen's suggestion was, Morgan was politically astute enough to know she would ultimately lose if she went head-to-head with Bob and the administration.

To confirm her suspicions, she asked, "And if I refuse?"

"Bob will insist that the matter be turned over to the Quality Assurance Committee. If your colleagues on the committee agree with him and label you an impaired physician, they can require you to undergo psychological counseling as an absolute condition to remain on the medical staff. Unfortunately, once it's on that level, we're obligated to notify the state."

Morgan looked up at the ceiling. "It doesn't seem like I have much of a choice."

"I can't tell you what to do, but in my opinion, the smart move is to agree to go to short-term counseling."

"You know," Morgan began in a subdued tone, "Bob's been around a long time. He's as masterful as anybody at maneuvering around state investigating committees. Counting Faith Russo, he has three Code Fifteens to answer for."

"What's your point?"

"He knows the most important thing a hospital can do is demonstrate that they've taken aggressive corrective action in rectifying the problem that caused the patient error. It would certainly look good to AHCA's investigating team if the incompetent and stressed out ER physician who took care of Miss Russo had already been counseled and had agreed to get into therapy."

"I'll deny ever having said this, but I think we both know that the hospital will always come first in these types of unpleasant situations. Ultimately, physicians are always expendable."

"Which, in this case, makes me the sacrificial lamb."

"I wouldn't get too philosophical about things. All you have to do is handle the problem correctly and things will get back to normal."

It didn't take a clap of thunder and a flash of lightning for Morgan to realize that Eileen was right. Undergoing a couple of sessions of counseling wouldn't kill her. And at the moment it seemed like the only way to protect her position in the hospital.

"Is it my choice of therapist, or do you have somebody in mind you'd like me to see?" Morgan asked.

"Do you know Will Johnson?"

"No."

"He's a psychiatrist with a special interest in stress-related syndromes in physicians. We've sent a number of physicians to him and have gotten great feedback."

"He sounds like a real peach. I can hardly wait."

Eileen laughed. "Well, at least you haven't lost your sense of humor."

"How do you suggest I keep this confidential? The last thing I need is for every physician on staff to know I'm in obligatory counseling."

"That won't be a problem. Will's practice is entirely outpatient. He's not on staff. His office is a guesthouse on his property, and he's very discreet regarding his schedule. You won't run into anybody."

"How many times do I have to go?" Morgan asked.

"That's up to him. But in the past, he's signed off on some people after three or four sessions."

"Terrific."

"I'm sorry about all this, Morgan. I'll let Will know you're going to call. I'll e-mail you his number. Call me as soon as you've seen him. Good luck."

For the next fifteen minutes, Morgan sat at her desk thinking about her conversation with Eileen. She considered herself to be as savvy as any physician regarding hospital politics. She didn't need a banner plane to inform her it would be foolish to fight this battle. Morgan was convinced she could complete the sessions without abandoning her efforts to find out who was responsible for the Code 15s. It might be Bob Allenby's agenda to whitewash the real causes of the Code 15s and deceive the AHCA, but it would never be hers.

Her life at the moment was hardly the one she had bargained for. In spite of what she had just told Eileen Hale, she had no intention of cowering in a corner and watching everything she had ever achieved as a physician spiral down the drain. She was determined to take whatever measures were necessary to deal with her problems but she would do so with an abundance of caution. That would mean taking Ben's advice regarding flying under the radar. The one fortunate thing was she knew exactly where to begin.

CHAPTER
43

Morgan had been over Faith Russo's medical record often enough to remember that she had listed a restaurant called Jimmy's Place as her employer.

After sitting in the restaurant's parking lot for a few minutes bolstering her courage, Morgan finally got out of her car and went inside. It was lunchtime. Just beyond the counter, two frenzied cooks manned a large grill with an overhanging mirror. From a row of searing hamburgers, grease spattered into the air. The noxious scent left Morgan a tad queasy.

Morgan spotted an empty table toward the back. Before it disappeared, she made her way over and sat down. It didn't take long for a frumpy-appearing waitress wearing elastic support hose and a hairnet to duckwalk over with a glass of water and a silverware setup.

"My name's Mattie," she said pulling out her order book. "What are you having?"

"I'll have a waffle with maple syrup," Morgan answered.

"To drink?"

"Coffee, please."

"Got it," Mattie said, chomping away on piece of bubble gum while she finished writing the order.

"Would you mind if I asked you a personal question?" Morgan inquired.

Mattie lifted her eyes. She hesitated for a moment and then said, "Do we know each other?"

"My name's Meg Reid. Faith Russo was my cousin. Did you know her?"

"We only have eight waitresses working here. We all knew her."

"I came down to Florida to help get her affairs in order. There seem to be a lot of unanswered questions about what happened at Dade Presbyterian that night. I've spoken to some folks at the hospital, but I'm getting the runaround."

Mattie slipped her order pad into her pocket. "What did you want to ask me?"

"How well did you know Faith?"

"We worked a lot of shifts together. We'd talk from time to time but I never saw her outside of the restaurant." Mattie pointed across the restaurant to a woman counting out change in front of the cash register. "Amelia probably knew her best. She's managing today."

Morgan looked in the direction Mattie was gesturing. "Do you think she would mind talking to me?"

Mattie shrugged. "All I can do is ask her."

"Thank you."

Morgan watched Mattie stroll over to the cash register and tap Amelia on the shoulder. She spoke to her briefly. Amelia nodded a few times as she ran a credit card through the machine. She then finished giving the last customer in line their change, slammed the register drawer shut, and started toward the table.

Stocky with an upturned nose and a puffy face, Amelia Carranza had fled her native Cuba under the cover of darkness twelve years earlier. She was barely eighteen the night her raft washed up on the Fort Lauderdale beach. The only job she had ever had was at Jimmy's. Barely speaking English, she started as a dishwasher. Plugging away day and night, she eventually became a waitress and then an assistant manager.

"Mattie said you wanted to speak with me."

"I'm Faith Russo's cousin. I was hoping you could answer some questions."

"Faith never mentioned you."

"We aren't particularly close now, but when I heard what happened, I felt obligated to come down and help with the kids."

"Mattie said you had some questions."

"There seems to be a lot of confusion regarding the events surrounding her death. The hospital is saying one thing and the police are saying something else. Faith and I were pretty close growing up and I'd like to know the truth."

"All I heard was that she had some kind of an accident and bled to death."

"I'm afraid it was a little more complicated than that. I've spent a lot of time talking to the police and the people at the hospital. The only thing they agree on is that she had a very severe injury that caused her to bleed to death. What's unclear is how it happened."

Amelia pulled out a chair and sat down. "I'm not sure I'll be able to help, but I'll try," she said in a sympathetic voice.

"I have some suspicions that Faith's injury didn't happened accidentally. I think she may have been attacked. I'm trying to find out what she did that day. Mattie said you two were friendly. I was hoping you might know."

"I saw Faith that night, right before she went out. I took my kids over there to play with hers."

"Did she mention if she had been injured earlier that day?"

Amelia shook her head. "She didn't say anything."

"How did she look?"

"Fine. She had a new hairdo and was practically dancing around the living room." Amelia paused, allowing an affectionate smile to cross her face. "That was the most excited I'd ever seen her. When I asked her where she was going she told me she had a business meeting."

"A business meeting?"

"I asked her, who the hell schedules a business meeting

on a Friday night?" Amelia waited while Mattie set Morgan's waffle down in front of her. "I figured there had to be a guy mixed up in this thing somewhere."

"When Faith went to the emergency room, she told the nurses she'd fallen off her bicycle earlier that day and had twisted her knee."

"Her bicycle?" Amelia asked, unable to contain a dubious giggle.

"She told the nurse she rode all the time for exercise."

"Let me tell you something. I don't know how much money you make or where you live, but people like Faith and me don't have time for bike riding, spinning classes, or long, lazy afternoons at the spa. Between raising our kids alone and working here sixty hours a week, there isn't too much time for the high life."

"You mentioned before that you thought Faith might have been seeing somebody. Could she have been with him that night?"

"All I know is that she spent the whole day shopping with her kids. I couldn't believe all the stuff she bought. It was way more than she could afford. She told me she put it all on her credit card." Before Morgan could ask another question Amelia motioned to one of the waitresses on the floor. "Tell Mike lunch is on me today and that I'm glad he decided to become a cop." The waitress walked over with the check; Amelia signed it and then turned her attention back to Morgan. "There was a guy who started coming in about three months ago. His name was Steve. At first, I'd only see him once a week or so, but then it seemed like he was in here for lunch almost every day. He always wanted to be seated at Faith's station. It never made sense."

"What do you mean?" Morgan asked.

"This guy was the whole package. Good-looking, well dressed, and obviously loaded. Like I said, it didn't make sense. Guys like that aren't interested in working girls with three kids who are lucky if they clear five hundred a week."

"Do you think this guy was the one Faith was supposed to have the business meeting with the night she died?"

"I guess it's possible."

"Has he been back in the restaurant since Faith died?"

Tilting her head to one side, Amelia looked past Morgan. Her expression became pensive. "I hadn't thought about it until now, but I haven't seen him."

"I have to ask you something that may sound a little strange. Do you happen to remember if this guy had a gap between his front teeth?"

Amelia shrugged her shoulders. "I never noticed. Why would you ask that?"

"It doesn't really matter," Morgan said, looking down at her watch and then coming to her feet. "I should let you get back to work. You've been a great help." Morgan reached into her purse, pulled out a small notepad, and wrote down her cell phone number. She handed it to Amelia. "If you think of anything else that might help, please give me a call."

Happy that the charade was over, Morgan left a tip on the table and then headed to the front to pay her check.

CHAPTER

44

It was four in the afternoon when Morgan pulled up to her hangar.

Anxious to get in the air, she grabbed her black flight case off of the backseat and got out of the car. Although she enjoyed flying with others, going up solo was a uniquely different experience and one she enjoyed equally as much.

Once Morgan had rolled the Cirrus out, she began her preflight check. She was about half finished when her cell phone rang. Recognizing the number, she had a sudden overwhelming urge to toss the phone into a nearby ditch. Instead, she took a deep breath and then dialed her office. Kendra answered.

"Dr. Connolly's office."

"It's me, Kendra."

"Sorry to bug you but Dr. Docherty's flight school just called. They asked if you could stop over there before you take off. He wants to see you about something."

"Thanks," Morgan said, relieved that the message didn't involve an urgent problem requiring her to go back to the hospital. She had no idea what Ben wanted, but as much as she tried to deny it, she welcomed the opportunity to see him. Morgan finished checking her fuel and then walked over to her car.

From two hundred yards away, Gideon slowly lowered his binoculars. Aviation buffs were common around the airport, which made him unconcerned about being observed.

The moment Morgan pulled away, he stepped away from his car. The only thing separating him from Morgan's plane was a dry, dusty field with its occasional patch of brown, sun-scorched grass. Pushing his hands into the pockets of his tan golf jacket, he started across the field.

As he got closer to the plane, Gideon gazed around to assure himself that nobody was in the immediate area. He then climbed up on the wing and opened the passenger side door. As he'd hoped, Morgan's flight case was sitting on the seat. The same thermos he'd seen in her car that day was in plain sight lying on top of her charts. He reached over and felt it. It was warm. He then unscrewed the top.

Reaching into his pocket, he pulled out a small glass vial that was half filled with a clear liquid. Having taken extraordinary care to be precise in his calculations, he held up the practically tasteless medication and studied the level of the drug in the bottle. Anything less than a single cup of coffee should leave Morgan impaired but still capable of flying, which was precisely his intent. Killing her now would not only be far too easy, it would be inadequate. There would be plenty of time later to arrange for Morgan Connolly's death in the weeks to come. Today his only interest was to provide the good doctor with the most frightening experience of her life.

Satisfied that everything was in order, he carefully unscrewed the cap. As he had anticipated, the thermos was filled to the top. Making sure his hand was steady, he emptied the drug into the thermos. He then returned the container to exactly where he had found it.

After a final look around, Gideon stepped out on the wing, climbed down, and headed back across the field.

CHAPTER

45

Having just been informed by Ben's secretary that he was giving a lesson, and that he hadn't left a message for her, Morgan returned to her car.

More than a little miffed, she called her office to see what the misunderstanding had been.

"What was the message?" she asked Kendra for the second time.

"Exactly what I just told you. The guy told me to tell you that Dr. Docherty wanted to talk to you before you took off."

"Did he leave a name?"

"No, but he made sure to repeat the message twice," Kendra insisted.

Rather than lose any more flying time trying to understand the mix-up, Morgan told Kendra she'd call her later.

Twenty minutes later Morgan cleared the end of the runway 9-Left. Continuing her gentle climb to the west, she set her GPS for Naples. At eighteen hundred feet, she started out over the eastern Everglades. Glancing down, she watched the russet wetlands pass easily under her wings. Off to the north, a caravan of perfectly spaced eighteen-wheelers rolled across Alligator Alley.

When her altimeter indicated she was at forty-five hundred feet, Morgan gently tipped the nose down and leveled off. It was a warm day and the thermals coming off the wetlands created a mild chop. Reaching into her flight case, she pulled out her thermos of coffee and poured herself three-quarters of a cup. Raising the plastic cup to her lips, she took a few short swallows.

Morgan rechecked her heading. She was just about to take another sip when the nose of the plane abruptly dropped. At the same instant, the Cirrus pitched hard to the right. Morgan recovered quickly from the unexpected turbulence, returning the plane to level flight. She immediately checked her instruments. Everything seemed to be okay. The only adverse effect of the unanticipated turbulence was that her cup was now empty and the coffee was soaking into the cloth upholstery of the seat next to her.

With the plane now steady and level in smooth air, Morgan rechecked her engine instruments to make sure everything was functioning normally. Satisfied that everything was okay, she estimated she would be over Naples in forty minutes.

At first, the disturbance in Morgan's vision was so subtle that it escaped her attention. When she finally realized she was squinting to read the instruments, her immediate thought was she needed a new prescription for her contacts. But when another minute passed and she suddenly felt light-headed, her level of concern for both her safety and that of her baby's abruptly heightened. She considered whether her blood sugar had dropped. The possibility left her wanting to kick herself for forgetting to bring along a snack.

Straining to keep her eyes open reminded Morgan of the occasional highway hypnosis she had fallen victim to on a long trip. She fought the stupor by forcing her eyes open and slamming herself bolt upright in her chair. Nobody knew better than she that most of the flying community considered physician pilots as too cavalier when it came to safety. The stereotype had always bothered her, but she used it as a constant reminder to be an ultraconservative flyer who emphasized safety above everything.

Without any deliberation, she banked the plane to the right

until she completed a one-hundred-and-eighty-degree turn, putting her on a direct course back to the North Perry Airport. Reaching overhead, she adjusted the vent to blow directly at her. The steady stream of air rushing over her face did little to allay the stupor and nausea.

She reached for the microphone.

"This is Cirrus One-Niner-Five-Tango-Foxtrot. I'm twenty-five miles west of the airport. I'm experiencing extreme vertigo. I'm at forty-five hundred feet and requesting a straight-in approach."

North Perry tower's response was immediate. "Cirrus-One-Niner-Five-Tango-Foxtrot. You're cleared for a straight-in approach."

Morgan replaced the microphone. She found by holding her head steady and locking her eyes on the horizon, she could partially control the dizziness. Fighting off the terror that gripped every part of her, she started a slow descent.

CHAPTER

46

As he always did when he was giving a lesson, Ben monitored the tower's frequency.

When he heard Morgan's urgent transmission, he was helping a nervous student on his first landing. Ben took control of the airplane, aborted the landing, and then called the tower to inform them that he would assist by escorting the pilot in.

Morgan's radio crackled, "Cirrus One-Niner-Five. What's your present status?"

She recognized Ben's voice immediately. She reached for her microphone.

"I . . . I'm experiencing considerable vertigo and double vision."

While climbing to two thousand feet, Ben completed a tight turn until he was heading due west. "Okay, Morgan. Are you able to give me your position?"

Morgan lowered her eyes from the horizon. Struggling to pick up any visual clues from the indistinct ground structures, she finally recognized Route 27, which marked the eastern extent of the Everglades.

She keyed her microphone. "I'm a mile or so west of Twenty-seven."

"Can you make out your altitude?" he asked.

Squinting and moving her head back and forth to see the

altimeter, she answered, "I think I'm at eighteen hundred feet."

"I'm five miles east of you. I'm going to line up on your right wing and bring you in. I should have a visual in a couple of minutes. You'll be fine. Just hold your head steady, stay calm, and concentrate on your flying. We'll get you home."

"I'm getting worse, Ben. I . . . I can barely read my instruments," she answered in a cracked and frightened voice.

"I've got you," he said. "Don't change your course. You're due west of the airport and lined up fine. We'll have you down in a couple of minutes."

When she looked out of her window she could make out the shadowy silhouette of Ben's blue-and-white Cessna moving in off of her wing. She guessed he was about three hundred feet away.

"Okay, Morgan. The tower has cleared all the traffic and authorized a straight-in approach. I'm going to take you all the way in."

Morgan looked over the top of the Cirrus's silver prop. Every few seconds she stole a glance out of her window to make sure she was still on Ben's wing.

"Can you see the runway?" Ben asked. "It's dead ahead."

It took her only a few seconds to find it but it looked more like a slithering serpent than three thousand feet of straight asphalt.

"I . . . I see it," she told him.

"Great. We're about five miles out. You're a little high, Morgan. Ease her down at about three hundred feet. If you have trouble seeing your instruments, just focus on my right wingtip. "Is your vision any better?"

"It's still very fuzzy," she answered, struggling to sound unruffled.

From the mounting spasm in the small muscles of her hands, she knew her grip on the controls was too tight. Forcing herself to relax, she eased the yoke forward coaxing the plane to again descend.

"That's perfect," Ben said. "Your flight path's perfect. That's I-75 right below us. You're doing great, Morgan. Don't bother communicating with me unless you have to. Just concentrate on your flying."

Leaning forward over the controls, she stared out over the nose of the aircraft. Among a myriad of small buildings and other objects that flowed into each other in a kaleidoscope of indistinguishable shapes, Morgan was able to make out the trailer park that was just to the north of the airport. She had made this same approach hundreds of times before and knew every landmark.

"Just stay with me," Ben said. "We're only a couple of miles from the field. You're lined up fine. Let's drop down a little more."

Morgan tried to nudge the controls forward but this time she pushed too hard, sending the nose of the aircraft plunging.

"Ease her back up," Ben said in a calm voice. "You're doing fine. You should be able to see the numbers."

Slowing her breathing and fighting off the nausea, Morgan pulled back on the controls.

"I see them."

"Good. You're a little fast, Morgan. Ease off on your power. Bring her down to about eight hundred feet." Morgan forced her eyes open, fastening them on the 9L painted on the end of the runway. "You're drifting a little left, Morgan. Bring her back a little."

She nudged the plane back to the right. She glanced out the window just long enough to make sure she was still lined up on Ben's wingtip. Along with the pounding vibration of the engine, she could feel her wingtips drifting up and down. Her instinct told her she was less than a minute from touchdown. All at once, everything she had ever learned about landing an airplane flooded her mind. Although she could hear Ben's transmissions, his voice had become surreal, as if all this was happening in a fantasy.

Morgan fought to stay lined up on the middle of the run-

way, but it seemed to pitch from side to side as if she were trying to land on an aircraft carrier in rough seas. She swallowed
hard. The adrenaline pumped into her bloodstream, whipping
her heart furiously.

She eased back on her controls.

"You're right on the money, Morgan. Just keep it on the
centerline."

Morgan watched as the ground rushed up at her faster than
she anticipated. Her corrections were clumsy and unschooled,
forcing the airplane to slip treacherously to the right.

"C'mon," she screamed, pulling the Cirrus back on course.
"Have you forgotten how to land an airplane, for God's sake?
You're greasing it. Pull the nose up. You're coming in too
high. Right rudder. Use some flaps."

The runway streaked by. Fighting off the panic that now
had her in a death hold, Morgan pulled the plane's nose up,
putting the Cirrus into a controlled stall. More and more of
the runway continued to race past. She pulled the throttle all
the way back, praying she'd touch down with enough runway
to roll to a safe stop.

The plane continued to fall until, finally, the landing gear
slammed against the runway. But the rough touchdown sent
the right wing soaring and Morgan careening into the door.
Fighting to keep control as the plane hurtled down the runway
on one wheel, Morgan finally forced the wing down, allowing
both wheels to grab the runway.

Even though she was now on the ground, she had come
in much too fast. Refusing to lose the battle now, Morgan
quickly gained control of the plane and brought it back to the
centerline. Whatever glimmer of relief she felt was quickly
extinguished as she saw the end of the runway charging at her.
Having no other choice, she crunched down on the brakes,
sending the plane into an oblique skid. For the first time,
Morgan's eyes slammed shut. But instead of the plane doing
a ground loop as she had intended, it came to a rapid stop on
the last turnoff.

Slowly opening her eyes, Morgan shut down the engine. Then, consumed by an overpowering feeling of relief, she leaned forward across the controls and dropped her head. Forcing herself to take one slow breath after another, her only thoughts were for her baby.

It was only a matter of seconds before she heard knocking at the passenger-side door. She looked up at the anxious men in paramedic uniforms staring at her. She leaned over and flipped up the lock.

The two men helped her out of the plane and onto a stretcher. After they made sure she was strapped in securely, they wheeled her to a waiting ambulance.

CHAPTER
47

Ben touched down five minutes after Morgan, taxied over to his flight school, and quickly got into his car.

When he pulled up to her hangar, he saw her sitting on the side of the stretcher flanked by the two paramedics. Both men had their arms folded. He got out of his car and started toward them.

"I'm feeling a lot better," he heard her reassure them. "I'm an emergency room physician. I think I'd know if I needed to go to a hospital."

By this time, Ben was just a few steps away. Morgan looked up. Her face was drained of blood. Supporting herself like a tripod, she sat with her arms locked out with her hands grasping the handles of the stretcher

"Dr. Connolly, we're just trying to—"

"I appreciate your concern," she told the skeptical paramedic, "but I'm fine now."

Ben pointed to her tummy. "The next time you and junior decide to go flying without a copilot, you might want to bring along a Hershey Bar."

Morgan reached for Ben's hands and gripped them tightly. Turning her head all the way to the side and looking at him through eyes that were starting to swell with tears, she said, "Thanks for getting me down."

"You're a great pilot. You got yourself down."

"Please tell these guys that I don't need to go to the hospital," she said with pleading eyes. "I'm already feeling a hundred percent better."

Ben turned to the paramedics. "I'm Dr. Docherty. How's she doing?"

The more senior of the two answered. "Her vital signs are fine, but she's still pretty unsteady. We gave her an IV bolus of glucose and then checked her blood sugar."

"What was it?" he asked.

"One-twenty," Morgan piped in before either of the paramedics could answer. "I'm feeling fine and I'm going home. I don't need to go to the hospital."

Morgan glared at Ben, leaving little doubt in his mind as to her feelings regarding a visit to the emergency room.

"She seems like she's getting better, and I don't think we can change her mind about letting us take her to the ER."

"I could have told you that fifteen minutes ago and saved you guys a lot of time," he said, covering a smile with his hand and then snugging his aviator sunglasses a little higher on the bridge of his nose. "I'll tell you what. I'll hang out with Dr. Connolly and keep an eye on her. If she's not a hundred percent in the next half hour or so, I'll transport her to the hospital myself. How's that?"

After exchanging a dubious look with his partner, the first paramedic said, "Okay, Doc."

They then helped Morgan down from the stretcher and over to Ben's car. She managed to get in with only a small amount of assistance. They drove over to Morgan's hangar, got out, and sat down on two vinyl lawn chairs that were on borrowed time. The wind had picked up a little and there was a large cluster of thunderheads gathering to the west.

Ben leaned forward, picked up a handful of stones, and tossed them one at a time in the direction of a rusted-out oil drum that was now a makeshift garbage can.

"Maybe we should give Jenny Silverman a call," he suggested. "She might want you to come in for some blood work and an ultrasound."

"I'll call her when I get home. I really think the whole thing was caused by low blood sugar. I'm a lot better since I got the sugar."

"Or maybe you're just getting the flu," he suggested.

"I hadn't thought of that." She paused for a moment before going on, "Did I thank you for getting me down?"

"I think so."

"I guess I'll have to talk with the FAA," she said.

"You'll have to fill out a report. With your record, I don't think it will be a big deal."

A defeated look crossed her face. Morgan had told Ben about the letter from AHCA the same day she'd received it.

"I guess I'm getting kind of used to being investigated by governmental agencies."

"Take it easy on yourself," he said, sensing his advice had fallen well short of the mark. "Let's just call your recent bad luck inconsequential missteps in the great trek of life," he added.

"I'm not in the mood, Ben."

"Sorry," he said, coming to his feet. "C'mon, I'll take you home. I'll come back later with one of my guys and get your car." He extended his hand. "Do you think you can walk?"

"Aren't you forgetting something?"

"I don't think so," he responded, helping her out of the chair.

"What about my airplane?"

Ben pointed across the airfield at Morgan's plane, which was moving slowly toward them on the taxiway.

"I called Mike. He'll hangar it for you. It's pretty hot out here, Morgan. Let's get going."

Seeing she was still a little wobbly, Ben held on to her arm.

She asked, "Did you call my office and leave a message

for me to come over to your school and see you before I took off?"

"No."

"Will you do me a favor and see if any of your instructors or office staff did?"

"Sure," Ben said, gesturing toward his car.

"Let's wait a couple of minutes. I want to get my flight bag out of the plane."

"I'll bring it to you later when I drop your car off," he offered, noticing that the color in her face was slowly returning.

"I'd rather wait for it. There's something in there that I need."

"What could be so important in your flight bag?"

"Why do you need to ask so many questions?"

"Sorry. I think it's a great idea to wait for your flight bag."

Ben helped Morgan back into the chair. They watched in silence as Mike taxied her plane up to the hangar.

GIDEON took a few steps away from his car. Standing beside a freshly painted chain-link fence, he watched a silver banner plane swoop down, tail hook a long white streamer advertising a new Fort Lauderdale café, and then begin a lumbering climb to the east. Being a man who prided himself on meticulous attention to detail, he was overjoyed with his triumph. Having monitored every tower and plane-to-plane transmission, he knew her flight had unfolded exactly as he had hoped. He slipped the binoculars back into their brown leather case. Now that he was sure she had returned unscathed, the prospect of inflicting even greater emotional pain on her before she died pleased him to no end.

Instead of basking in his triumph, Gideon climbed back into his car and started for the airport exit. Following behind a group of careless cyclists, he closed the distance to no more than a few feet from a small woman who trailed the pack.

Waiting for her to turn around and discover her peril, he wondered if Dr. Connolly had the deductive powers to figure out that her sudden illness at twenty-five hundred feet might not have occurred by pure chance. If she were able to connect the dots, it would certainly make the game more interesting.

His patience running thin, Gideon edged even closer to the cyclist and then blasted his horn.

CHAPTER 48

DAY TWENTY

It had been three days since Morgan's near-fatal flight.

At Ben's insistence, she had gone to see Jenny Silverman the next morning. After doing a complete examination and performing an ultrasound, Jenny assured her that everything was fine and that she could expect to be the mother of a very healthy baby. She also told her to take a few days off. Ben had stopped over all three nights with dinner and had kept her company until she was ready to go to sleep. The last night, he slept on her couch. Adding to Morgan's sense of relief, but not coming as a surprise, she suffered no further from the strange symptoms that had almost cost her her life.

When she walked into her outer office, Kendra handed her a stack of mail.

"How are you feeling?" she asked.

"Great," Morgan responded, shuffling through the letters.

"You got a certified letter this morning. I put it on your desk."

"Thanks," Morgan said as she walked into her office.

She went directly over to her desk and picked up the letter. It was from the Agency for Health Care Administration. Reaching for a silver letter opener, she carefully sliced the envelope open and removed the single sheet of stationery. Morgan unfolded the letter, read it twice, and then tossed it back on the desk. As she feared, she was being notified that she was part of an investigation examining the care rendered to Faith Russo.

Feeling the beginnings of a headache, she massaged the sides of her forehead. Even though the letter came as no surprise, she still felt as if somebody had plunged a knife into her heart. Picking up the letter again, she reread the paragraph that informed her she could either respond to the allegations in writing or set up an appointment to speak with the case investigator. There was no question in her mind she would opt for the face-to-face meeting.

Pondering the shambles of her life, Morgan raised her eyes and gazed over at her diplomas and certificates.

"Dr. Hale's on line one for you," came Kendra's voice over the intercom.

"Thanks," she said, reaching for the phone.

"Hi, Morgan. I just wanted to let you know that I called Will Johnson. I explained to him what's going on. He's expecting a call from you."

"I guess that means Bob hasn't softened his position on me undergoing counseling."

"I'm afraid not."

Hardly surprised, Morgan asked, "Do you have his number?"

Eileen read Will's number to her twice.

"I'll call him as soon as we get off."

"You sound a little down. Is everything okay?" Eileen inquired.

"Except for my professional life being in a free fall, everything's fine."

"Have a little faith. Meet with Will a couple of times and I'm sure things will turn out fine. Just try and keep an open mind."

"I'll try," she assured Eileen with a sigh.

"Good. Call me after your first session."

Morgan thanked Eileen and promised to keep her in the

loop. Still feeling the full effects of humiliation regarding what lay in front of her, Morgan switched lines and dialed Will's number.

A man answered after two rings. "Hello."

"Is this the office of Dr. Johnson?" Morgan asked, wondering if she had dialed the wrong number.

"It is."

"My name is Dr. Morgan Connolly. I'm calling to make an appointment."

"This is Will, Morgan."

"I . . . I'm sorry. I assumed . . . I mean I thought I was talking to your medical assistant."

"I like to answer my phone. If I can't get to it, my voice mail picks up."

"If this is a bad time I'll be happy to call back later."

"Now's fine."

"I'd like to arrange some time to meet with you."

"When would be a good time for you? Eileen told me your schedule's pretty tight."

Taken aback by how accommodating Will was, she answered, "I can always change my schedule, so anytime that's good for you, works for me."

"In that case, how does the end of the week sound? I'm taking my wife and kids sailing Friday but if you could come over in the late afternoon—say at around four."

"That will be fine," she told him, thinking to herself that the sooner she got started with this thing, the sooner she'd be finished.

"I'm in Davie. I use my guesthouse as an office." Morgan used the same piece of paper to write down the directions to his home. "Park in my driveway and then follow the footpath between the house and the garage to the back. You can't miss it."

"I assume Eileen mentioned that the administration is insisting that I speak with you. I agreed, but I'm probably doing it for all the wrong reasons."

"Maybe that's a good place for us to start. I'll see you Friday."

Wanting to kick herself for making such a dumb comment, Morgan said good-bye and hung up the phone. "Round one to the psychiatrist," she muttered, shaking her head.

CHAPTER 49

As soon as she hung up the phone, Morgan reached for her can of Coke.

Swiveling her chair around, she looked at a photograph on the top shelf of her bookcase of her father and her at a Florida Panthers hockey game. She still thought about him frequently, but the reality of being without him was becoming easier to accept with each passing day. Her eyes drifted down to the lower shelves of the bookcase. Every text she had purchased since her first day of medical school was in mint condition and arranged by subject.

Morgan reached for a notepad and a pen. Mindlessly at first, she began doodling—a habit she had picked up in high school whenever she was in the throes of a tough problem. After she had filled the top of the page with tiny squares, triangles, and other senseless symbols, she wrote down every word of the note Gideon had left in her father's office. Studying the words individually, she drew a box around certain groupings. Retracing the lines over and over again, her eyes became transfixed on the phrase *the third of three*. It was still the part of Gideon's cryptic note that intrigued her the most.

"Three what?" she muttered before filling her lungs fully. "Three mistakes? Three operations? Three family members?" Nothing seemed to make any sense. On the last line of the page, she printed the numeral 3. She then wrote a second 3 next to the first, but the number thirty-three didn't seem important. Morgan then reprinted the numbers, this time spacing them apart. After considering the number for a few seconds, she absently drew an oblique slash between the two digits. Before she raised the pen from the pad, her eyes widened.

"It's too obvious," she whispered, tapping away on her blotter with the tip of the pen. But she couldn't force herself to dismiss the notion purely because of its simplicity. "The third of three could be a date—it could simply mean the third of March." Although the date struck a familiar chord, she couldn't attach a specific significance to it. Morgan reached for the phone and dialed the private line of her father's office.

Annalisa answered.

"Hi, Annalisa, it's Morgan. I wonder if you could check on something for me?"

"Sure."

"How far back do you keep records of my father's schedule?"

"I'd say about five years. Ever since we computerized the office."

"If I were interested in a specific date, could you tell me what his schedule was for that day?"

Morgan anticipated the hesitancy in Annalisa's voice. "I guess so . . . but—"

Not wanting to field a salvo of questions, she said, "It's important. I'd really appreciate your help."

"What's the date?"

"March third."

Annalisa laughed, leaving Morgan a trifle bewildered. "I don't need a computer to check that date, Morgan. Your father was out of town just like he always is the first week of March."

Morgan's confusion vanished. "His time-share in Costa Rica. I can't believe I didn't remember."

"It would have taken a nuclear war for him to have missed it," Annalisa said with obvious affection. "There wasn't any room left in his office for all those pictures of him fishing."

Morgan exhaled. "Thanks for your help, Annalisa."

"When are we getting together for dinner?"

"My schedule's been horrible, but I'll call you. I promise."

Morgan replaced her phone on the cradle. She thought about her father's yearly trip to the same plush resort on the west coast of Costa Rica. About eight years ago, he and his four friends had decided to make it a father-daughter event and she had gone along. Even though she had always despised fishing, it had turned out to be a terrific week and one that she had always cherished. Because they were all lifelong friends, Morgan knew the men her father traveled with quite well.

Thinking about the day her father was killed, she spun her chair a half turn to her right. Her mind then focused on Gideon's curious preoccupation with her. Morgan pushed her chair up to her computer and rolled out the keyboard. She woke up the machine and then signed on to the hospital's secure intranet. The first thing she did was bring up the emergency room physician's shift schedule for March. She checked it twice. She hadn't worked on the second or the third.

Admitting it was a shot in the dark, Morgan checked the schedule again—only this time for March of the previous year. The schedule flashed up. Crossing her arms in front of her, she sat back in her chair—her eyes glued on the monitor. She had worked the evening shift on the third. For some reason, the date nagged at her.

All at once, she was filled with an uneasy feeling. A few moments later, an unnerving chill flashed through her.

"Oh my God," she whispered.

She quickly switched screens to her patient encounter log. The record indicated every patient she had treated during that shift. Scrolling down through the alphabetized list, she stopped midway through. Her eyes locked on the screen, reading the names of Jason and Andrew Kaine over and over again. The stark image of one of the most painful and upsetting experiences she had known as a doctor leapt into her mind with the same precise clarity as if had happened an hour ago.

For months afterward, every time she treated a young man with a fever and a rash, her blood ran cold. But at the moment, the deaths of Andy and Jason were not the only thing plaguing her. The vivid recollection of her conversation with Mason Kaine and what followed filled her mind. It was two days later when she was called by one of the assistant administrators. He had received several calls from Kaine threatening everything from a formal complaint to the state to going on television. The administrator assured Morgan the problem would be handled by the Risk Management department and the director of Patient Relations. When several weeks went by and Morgan had heard nothing further, she assumed Mason Kaine had come to his senses and realized she was not responsible for the deaths of his sons.

Now, eighteen months later, she suspected she was wrong. The more she thought about Gideon's note, the more she warned herself not to jump to any conclusions. It was possible that *the third of three* had nothing to do with March third, and that Jason and Andy's deaths on that day was a pure coincidence. But as much as she tried to convince herself, she couldn't dismiss the notion that Mason Kaine had never given up the ghost and that he could quite possibly be the one who murdered her father.

CHAPTER
50

Ben and Morgan exited the back of her building and headed for the pool area.

"I still can't believe Bob's forcing me to speak with a psychiatrist."

"He's trying to cover his ass. I would advise you to do the same."

"You make it sound so simple."

"That's because it is."

"Easy for you to say."

They walked over to a couple of slatted chaise chairs and sat down. It was a mild afternoon with a sparse breeze coming off of the ocean.

"Something tells me you didn't call me over here to discuss Bob's insistence that you see a psychiatrist."

"I think I figured out what Gideon meant by 'the third of three.'"

"Interesting," he said, slipping on his sunglasses. "I'm all ears."

For the next few minutes, Morgan gave Ben an account of everything that had happened the night she took care of Andy and Jason Kaine, especially mentioning her strange encounter with Mason Kaine.

"The man insisted on knowing every detail of the care his sons received. He even asked me what antibiotics I had given them. For a while, he tried to act unemotional and business-like, but it was obvious his anger was mounting. I tried to make him understand his sons had a deadly disease and there was nothing more I could have done to save them. That's when he started to get angry. The harder I tried to make him under-stand, the angrier he got. Finally he stormed out of the ER—but not before threatening to take me and the hospital down."

"Those were his exact words?"

"Verbatim. It's not the kind of thing you forget."

"Was that the end of it?" Ben asked.

"Hardly. I reported the incident to the administrator on call, who referred it to the hospital attorney and Patient Relations. Over the next couple of months, Kaine called the hospital repeatedly trying to set up a meeting with Bob Allenby. His request came with a list of demands. Not only did he insist on a public apology, he also wanted me dismissed from the medical staff for gross negligence."

"Did he sue?"

"No. The hospital continued to placate him from arm's length. Eventually, he stopped calling."

"It sounds like he cooled off and decided to get on with his life."

"Or maybe he became so overwhelmingly frustrated that he cracked and decided to look for justice in a different way."

"That doesn't make any sense. He had no gripe with your father," Ben pointed out.

"Not directly, anyway."

Ben paused for a few moments. He cupped his chin be-tween his thumb and fingers as he spoke. "So you're suggest-ing Mason Kaine is Gideon and that he killed your father to get even with you."

"Before you dismiss the idea as ridiculous, just think about something for a second. I don't have any children. If Kaine wanted me to feel the same devastating emotional trauma he had suffered from the loss of his sons . . . well, it's possible he would have gone after my father instead of me."

"What are you basing this theory on?"

"The science of psychiatry. It's a well-described phenomenon that an overpowering and unremitting grief reaction can drive an otherwise normal person to act in a bizarre manner."

"You're not just talking about boys behaving badly—you're talking about homicidal insanity," Ben said.

"Just hear me out. We know that Kaine was consumed with anger over the deaths of his sons. He hits a stone wall looking for retribution from a hospital administration that's doing nothing more than politely appeasing him. Becoming more enraged, and with no resolution to the conflict, he has a psychotic breakdown and decides to take matters into his own hands, which—"

"Which led him to believe that he was some kind of modern-day avenging archangel?"

"Maybe that's why he signed the note *Gideon*," Morgan suggested.

"I think Gideon was just a regular angel."

"I'm being serious, Ben."

"There's just one hole in your theory. Do you remember telling me you suspected there was a connection between your father's death and the Code Fifteens?"

She agreed with a nod.

"Assuming you're right—why would Gideon . . . or Kaine . . . a man who hated you so much that he killed your father, feel the need to murder innocent cardiac patients? What would be his motive? Why would he want to sabotage an open-heart operation? Even if he could pull it off, which is highly unlikely, why would he do that?"

"You're asking me to explain the actions of a deranged individual. I can't do that . . . not yet, anyway." Morgan's intense gaze suddenly drifted down. "And, by the way, I don't think it would be as hard as you think."

"What wouldn't be?"

"Tampering with the open-heart medications. Have you ever been in the heart surgery suite at three in the morning?"

"Not lately. But it sounds like you have."

"It's empty and pitch-black. I did a hypothetical walk-through."

"When was this?" he asked.

She glared at him. "What difference does that make?"

"What were you going to offer up as an excuse if you got caught?"

"I didn't have a plan B. What you should be asking me is what I found out."

"What?" he inquired with a noisy sigh.

"That it would be no big deal for somebody dressed in OR scrubs, especially if they had a hospital ID, to inconspicuously find his or her way back into the cardiac surgery suite, fill the nitroglycerine bottles with protamine, and sneak out again. The whole thing would take about three and a half minutes."

Rather than debating the plausibility of Morgan's hypothesis any further, Ben decided to try a different approach.

"You mentioned to me that Bob Allenby and the hospital board are really feeling the heat from AHCA regarding the Code Fifteens."

"That would be an understatement," she said.

"I'm just wondering what the board's reaction would be if they learned that their chief of Emergency Medicine told AHCA's investigative team that her father's death and the recent rash of Code Fifteens were being intentionally perpetrated by a psychotic killer who called himself Gideon?"

"Your point being that I should do the politically correct thing and roll over and play dead."

"I'm not saying you should abandon the problem. I'm simply suggesting you tap on the brakes a little. You have your career to think of."

"Give me a little credit for having some political instinct. As long as I stay outside of the hospital, I'm sure I'll be okay."

"What's that supposed to mean exactly?"

"I was thinking about going to see Jason and Andy's mother. I know where she works."

"In the first place, she probably won't speak to you. In the second, even if she does, she'll tell Kaine and get him all fired up again," Ben countered.

"I don't think so. They're divorced."

"How would you know that?"

"It's public information."

"So now you're spending your days in the courthouse going through divorce records?"

"Of course not. I had somebody do it for me."

"Have you talked to Detective Wolfe about all this?"

"I called him yesterday. He listened politely and told me he'd look into things and get back to me."

"You don't sound convinced."

"No comment," she told him.

"It's obvious you've made up your mind. Just be careful," Ben warned. "If there's anything I can do to help you . . ."

"I appreciate the offer."

"On a lighter note," he began. "There's a special production at the Broward Center next week. It's called *Fifty Years of Broadway.* I know how much you love Broadway musicals so I thought you might like to go."

She looked at him with affection. "I'm shocked. I had no idea you were a patron of the arts."

"I'm not a graduate of the Paris Conservatory, but I enjoy a good musical from time to time."

"Really?" she asked.

"Absolutely."

"Name one."

Sporting an easy smile, Ben answered, "I loved *Inherit the Wind.*"

"No doubt one of the great Broadway musicals of all time."

"Are you in or not?" he asked, getting up and extending his hand.

"Totally in," she told him.

"C'mon. I'll walk you back to the elevator. I have to get back to the airport."

It took a few seconds for Morgan's grin to fade. Ben was certainly putting on the full-court press. She thought about how quickly their relationship was changing. It was exciting, but she had known more than one couple who had wonderful platonic relationships capsized forever by allowing romance in. There was no reason to be unnecessarily pessimistic but at the same time she would remain cautiously positive about her burgeoning relationship with Ben.

CHAPTER
51

Before submitting the coffee from her near-fatal flight for chemical analysis, Morgan made sure to locate a private laboratory that didn't do business with Dade Presbyterian.

She was familiar with these types of labs, which catered largely to local physicians and smaller businesses that drug tested their employees. After a number of phone calls, she finally settled on a small facility in west Hialeah. For the first time since purchasing her Thunderbird, she was relieved that the salesman had convinced her to buy the navigational system. Without it, she never would have found the tiny lab, which was sandwiched between a chiropractor's office and a delicatessen.

A three-note chime sounded when Morgan pushed open the front door. Standing behind the counter, a chunky man with a solitary eyebrow looked up from his morning newspaper.

"Can I help you?" he asked. His nametag read Gordon Bowen.

"I'd like to drop off this specimen for evaluation," Morgan answered, handing him the plastic container.

With an indifferent look on his face, Bowen held it up to the light. After studying it from every conceivable angle, he removed the cap and took three quick sniffs from a safe distance. Following an indiscernible grumble, he replaced the cap and placed the container on the counter.

"I'm sorry, missy, but I've only been doing laboratory analysis for twenty years so you're going to have to help me with this one a little."

"Help you?" Morgan asked.

He pointed to the container. "What bodily fluid might this be, because if I didn't know better, I'd say it was stale coffee."

"It is stale coffee."

After a fleeting look, he asked, "What am I testing this for—more caffeine than the manufacturer claims should be in there?"

"I'd like you to run a complete toxicology panel on it."

He picked up the container again.

"Let me guess. You're on the outs with your boyfriend and you want to know if he's trying to poison you."

"Does my reason really matter?"

"Listen, missy. We're not here to—"

"It's doctor. You may call me doctor."

"Excuse me," he said mockingly, raising his hands. "Just so I have this right; you're requesting that we analyze your morning cappuccino for lethal substances. Is that correct, Doctor?"

"You got it. When will you have the results?" Morgan asked, seeing no reason to enter into a battle of the wits with somebody who was obviously unarmed.

Bowen pushed an order pad across the counter.

"If you'll just fill this out, we should have the results early next week."

Feeling Bowen's eyes all over her, Morgan quickly filled out the forms and headed for the door.

The ride back to her high-rise seemed to go by much faster than the trip down.

Once inside her condominium, Morgan leafed quickly through her mail and then went into her living room. Through a bay window, she gazed north along A1A. On the opposite side of the street, a large American flag atop a bank building waved outstretched in a sturdy ocean wind.

Morgan walked over to a leather recliner her father had given her for Christmas. She sat down and hoisted her legs up on the footrest. She wasn't positive, but for the first time her ankles seemed a little swollen to her. Even without the lab's official report, she was convinced that the coffee would contain some type of tranquilizer. The mysterious phone call she received from Ben's flight school no longer seemed so mysterious. Luring her away from her plane for a few minutes was all the time somebody would have needed to drug her coffee.

The dilemma now facing her was what to do if her suspicions regarding the coffee proved to be correct. Reporting the information to the police or Eileen Hale would almost certainly backfire. They both doubted her mental stability and would probably assume she had tampered with the coffee herself to prove her conspiracy theory wasn't a figment of her imagination.

Morgan closed her eyes. She wasn't prone to midday naps but when she felt herself becoming heavy-eyed, she surrendered and allowed herself to drift off to sleep.

CHAPTER
52

Located in Coral Springs, the Argosy Travel Agency was tucked away in a small but fashionable strip mall.

Standing in the agency's entranceway, Morgan gazed at a large grouping of extravagantly framed serigraphs of exotic destinations that adorned the light beige walls. She felt invisible among the dozen or so preoccupied agents who sat behind identical desks fiercely pecking away at their keyboards.

After a couple of minutes, and with no apparent hope of being helped, Morgan strolled over to an elderly woman at a small desk who appeared less frenzied than her colleagues.

"Excuse me," Morgan began. "I'm looking for Adele Kaine."

The woman removed her reading glasses from the tip of her skeletal nose and let them drop on their eyeglass cord. With an exaggerated effort, she rotated her chair around and peered down the long central aisle.

She gestured toward the back of the office and in a scratchy voice said, "That's her at the second-to-last desk on the right."

"Thanks."

Adele was talking into a headset but looked up immediately when Morgan approached her desk. She covered the mouthpiece and whispered, "I'll be off in a sec. Have a seat."

From the multitude of files, brochures, and pamphlets scattered across her desk, it looked as if her work area had been decimated by a major windstorm. Smartly dressed and sporting a French manicure, Adele wore a pricey diamond-and-ruby tennis bracelet but no rings. From the soft and wrinkle-free appearance of her face, Morgan surmised she had availed herself of a good plastic surgeon.

"How can I help you?"

"My name's Morgan Connolly," she said, extending her hand.

"Have you used our agency before?"

"Never."

"What type of trip are you planning?"

"Actually, I'm not here about a vacation. I work at Dade Presbyterian. I'm an emergency room physician."

Adele's pleasant smile faded into a circumspect stare. "I remember your name, now. You took care of my sons the night they died."

Morgan nodded. She had spent considerable time rehearsing for this moment, but now all of her preparation seemed woefully inadequate. In spite of her effort to appear calm, she suspected Adele sensed her apprehension. Dismissing the idea of being aloof any longer, she said, "I apologize for not calling first, but it's rather important that I speak with you."

"I'm a little confused, Dr. Connolly. My sons died well over a year ago. Why would you come see me now?"

"Because I need your help." Morgan answered.

"I don't think I understand."

She then took an unhurried breath before explaining her predicament to Adele. "I'm being harassed. I have reason to believe you may know the man responsible."

Adele set her pen down.

"I know what happened between you and my ex-husband the night my boys died. My question is, if you think you're being harassed, why aren't you talking to the police?"

Morgan was a little taken back by Adele's candor but still wanted to proceed as gingerly as possible.

"I have spoken with them. Let's just say I'm having difficulty convincing them of my concerns."

"I'm sorry, Doctor, but I still don't understand what I can do to help you."

Fearing Ben had been right and that she had made the trip in vain, Morgan said, "Ms. Kaine, it took every drop of courage I have to come here today. I wouldn't be here unless I was feeling a little desperate."

After an uncomfortable few seconds of silence, Adele reached down, opened the bottom drawer of her desk, and pulled out her purse. "Why don't you call me Adele?" she said, sliding the drawer shut and coming to her feet. "There's a coffee shop a few stores down. We can talk there."

Encouraged, but with guarded optimism, Morgan followed Adele out of the travel agency and toward the coffee shop.

There was no line and they each ordered a coffee. Adele reached into her purse and pulled out her wallet.

"My treat," Morgan said, placing a ten-dollar bill down on the counter.

"Thanks. Do you want to sit inside or out?" Adele asked.

Morgan looked around the coffee shop and said, "Out."

It was a dreary spring morning, but with the promise of the sun burning off the ash-colored clouds that filled the western sky. Morgan followed Adele past several empty tables, eventually sitting down toward the end of the sidewalk.

Adele wasted no time with pleasantries. "Was there something specific you wanted to ask me?"

"I guess the first thing I'd like to know is if you have any idea if your ex-husband's still living in South Florida?"

"I'm not sure. I've only seen Mason once in the last five years or so, and that was at the funeral. We didn't speak. In fact, we made sure to stay on opposite sides of the church. But to answer your question, I think he probably still lives in the area. I ran into one of his old golf buddies a few months ago. His name's Charlie Shaiman. He leases high-end cars. Mason's name barely came up, but Charlie mentioned he had gotten him a car recently." Adele took a hard look at Morgan.

"How sure are you that Mason's the one who's been harassing you?"

Morgan took the first sip of her coffee. "I'm not sure. At the moment I'd call it an educated guess."

"So you came here today hoping I could explain his atrocious behavior to you." Morgan nodded. "The answer's simple," Adele said with a relaxed shrug. "It's because he was born that way."

"I beg your pardon?"

"Mason was born with two giant chips on his shoulder." Adele reached into her purse and took out a pack of cigarettes and a disposable lighter. She stopped for a moment, held up the pack, and asked, "Do you mind?" Morgan gestured to go ahead. "What you witnessed was Mason Kaine being Mason Kaine. It's probably the main reason I divorced him, although the list of other reasons is endless." Adele took two quick puffs of the cigarette and then promptly crushed it out in a plastic ashtray. "It's the only way I can quit," she explained before going on. "My ex-husband's a selfish, insensitive, and hopelessly spiteful human being. His reaction to anything that went wrong in his life was to assume that somebody was to blame for it. Once he convinced himself of that, he would then go after that person like a pit bull."

"Did you have any reason to think that your sons received poor care?"

"I come from a family of doctors. My father was an anesthesiologist in Broward County for over thirty years. He had just retired. He spoke to one of his colleagues at Dade Presbyterian. He took a look at the chart and assured him that nothing more could have been done to save Jason and Andy." Adele picked up her cup but stopped before it reached her lips. "My father was right about Mason."

"What do you mean?"

"He told me that Mason was the type of man who looked in the mirror every morning and saw a ten. The problem was, everybody else saw a two."

An hour earlier Morgan hadn't a clue if Adele Kaine would even speak to her. Now, questions were popping into her head faster than she could ask them. Even allowing for ex-spouse bashing with its usual embellishment, Morgan suspected that Adele was painting an accurate picture.

"Do you happen to know where he works?" Morgan inquired.

Adele laughed. "Mason work? I don't think so. Mason was a trust-fund baby. He would never dirty his hands with anything as bourgeois as a real job. The problem was that he fancied himself as some high-powered entrepreneur and venture capitalist. Unfortunately, his track record putting deals together fell well short of his overinflated opinion of himself. In a way, it's a shame."

"Why?" Morgan asked.

"Because for all his faults, the guy's brilliant. He would get interested in some obscure topic and then devour everything that had ever been written about it until he was an expert. I remember for about six months he did nothing except build antique trains. When he got bored with that he decided to get a PhD in music theory. The trouble was, nothing kept his interest." Adele shook her head. "What a waste of God-given talent." The sun finally showed itself and Adele reached into her purse for her sunglasses. "Why don't you ask me what's really on your mind? Why don't you ask me if I think Mason's capable of harassing you?"

"Do you?"

"Without a doubt. As soon as I filed for divorce, he put a team of private investigators on me around the clock. I hoped things would get better as time passed but they got worse. I would come out in the morning and find my tires slashed or my car keyed. My credit cards would get mysteriously canceled and all kinds of salespeople would call. It was obvious what was going on. Finally, my lawyer got a restraining order against him. Even with the judge's order, I was scared to death."

"It's hard to believe you ever went through with the . . . the . . ."

"With the marriage?" she asked flatly. "Mason was born with the gift of gab. He could talk his way in or out of anything." Her voice suddenly switched to a regretful monotone. "I guess I thought I was in love. It took me a while, but I eventually figured out I'd made the worst mistake of my life. Hopefully, I've gotten a little wiser with age." Adele sat silently, watching as a young mother pushing a twin stroller walked by. "Do you have any children?" she asked Morgan.

"I'm pregnant with my first."

"Congratulations," she said with a painful smile.

"I'm sorry, Adele. I didn't mean to . . ."

Adele pulled a tissue from her purse. "I was a mess after my boys died but I'm better now." She forced a smile. "It's amazing what a year of therapy can do for you."

"Do you mind if I ask you one last thing?" Morgan asked.

Adele nodded.

"As I mentioned, I only spoke to your ex-husband briefly that night. I was a little preoccupied with his behavior, so I wasn't exactly concentrating on his appearance. I have reason to believe the man who has been stalking me has a gap between his front teeth."

"Mason's teeth were fine," she said shaking her head slowly. "But a couple of years ago, I remember hearing he was hurt pretty badly playing rugby. They took him straight from the field to the hospital and into surgery. He broke a couple of facial bones and knocked out several teeth."

"But from what you've told me, your ex-husband's a man of means. I'm sure he would have undergone reconstructive dental work."

"You would think, but very little of what Mason did was either predictable or made sense."

"Did he ever mention the name Gideon?" Morgan asked.

Adele shook her head. "Not that I remember."

Morgan extended her hand across the table. "I should let

you get back to work. You've been very helpful. I can't thank you enough."

They stood up together and headed back to the travel agency. Adele reached into her purse and handed Morgan her business card.

"I know we hardly know each other, so you'll forgive me if I say that you seem a little frightened. My cell phone number's on the card. Call me anytime if you want to talk. We probably have more in common than either of us knows."

Morgan reached for the card and smiled. "I may take you up on that. Thanks again."

"I hope things work out for you."

Morgan waited for Adele to go back inside before heading back to her car. She slid in behind the wheel and started the engine. Before backing out of her parking place, she thought about Mason Kaine's rugby accident. She suspected Ben would call it a long shot, but it was certainly possible that Mason Kaine could have been left with a gap between his teeth that he chose not to repair. There was another possibility that was even more far-fetched, but the thought of it made her shudder.

Perhaps it was nothing more than her intuition, but something kept telling her she was one step closer to proving who had murdered her father.

CHAPTER
54

After attending Jenny Silverman's girls' night out, Morgan headed south on the Florida Turnpike.

If she hadn't promised Jenny she would go, she probably would have found an excuse and stayed home. To her surprise, however, she had thoroughly enjoyed the evening and had no regrets about attending. She didn't know how, but for three hours she managed to tuck the shambles of her life away in some remote crevice of her mind.

Absentmindedly, she drifted toward the left, but the sudden blast of an eighteen-wheeler sent her swerving back into her own lane. After a labored breath, she threw the peeved trucker an apologetic wave.

Her cell phone rang.

"I'm sorry I couldn't call earlier," Ben said. "My meeting just broke up. I'm on my way back to the airport. How was girls' night out?"

"I had a good time. I'm glad I went."

"Good. Did you speak with Adele Kaine this afternoon?"

"I did."

"And?"

"It was a very enlightening conversation, to say the least. And contrary to your gut feeling, she was a fountain of information."

"I'm a little surprised."

"I was too, at first. But once I found out how much she

detests her ex-husband, I understood. I think she actually welcomed this or any other opportunity to bash him."

"Is she still in touch with him?"

"She's only seen him once in the last few years."

"Does she share his opinion regarding the care her sons received?"

"Not at all."

"What did she tell you about him?"

"Kaine fits the profile to a T of somebody who might be capable of psychotic behavior if stressed enough."

"What are you basing that on?"

"Everything I've read about abnormal stress reactions."

"Did you ask her about his teeth?"

"While she was married to him, his teeth were normal. But she told me he was an avid rugby player. A couple of years ago, he got kicked in the face. Evidently, the trauma to his mouth and facial bones was pretty significant. She didn't know a lot of the details but she had heard he needed emergency surgery. I assume that would have included extensive dental reconstruction that might require some kind of bonding process to close any spaces."

"Not to state the obvious," Ben said, "but that would leave him without a gap, not with one."

"Assuming he went through all that dental work."

"Does he have any money?"

"He's loaded," she said.

"So why wouldn't he have had his teeth reconstructed?"

"I don't know. Maybe he decided it was too much of a hassle and there are worse things than going through life with a gap between your teeth. Or maybe he did have them repaired and then had the bonding removed."

Ben's eyes narrowed. "I beg your pardon?"

"According to the police, the man who killed my father went to extreme means to disguise himself. If Kaine was the one responsible and he had already decided there would be other victims . . . well, maybe he had the bonding removed."

Ben cleared his throat. "That's pretty far out there, Morgan."

"Maybe," she said. "I guess what I need is a recent picture of the guy. I've been on the Internet trying to track down anything I can about him. There's no property in his name that I can find. He obviously has an unlisted phone number. I'm not even sure he still lives in the area."

"You could get a private eye involved," Ben suggested. "They might even be able to get a photograph."

"I thought about that, but I didn't know where to begin to find someone."

"I can take care of it," he said. "One of my longtime students owns her own agency. E-mail me everything you know about Kaine and I'll give her a call. If she can't figure out where he is and get a picture of him, nobody can."

"Thanks a lot."

"Are you going to call Detective Wolfe about all this?" he asked.

"If I do, I suspect he'll listen politely and then tell me he'll get back to me. And since I'm still waiting for him to get back to me on a number of other things, why bother?"

"I thought you might say that," he told her. "Look, I'm just pulling into the airport. It's only about a thirty-minute flight back down to Hollywood. I want to talk to you more about this. I'll call you as soon as I land."

"Just come over. I'd rather talk in person."

"Fine," Ben said. "Listen, we worked right through dinner. Do you have anything to eat?"

"I have three-day-old baked ziti and a half-eaten apple crumb cake. Take your choice."

"As tempting as that sounds, I'll just pick something up on my way over."

"Call me when you get here."

Morgan set her phone down and within a few seconds was again deep in thought. If she assumed it was Kaine who had orchestrated both her father's murder and the Code 15s, the assumption begged a key question, which she had no answer for. What was the common link between these individuals? What could her father, Faith Russo, and possibly even Tony Wallace all have in common that infuriated Kaine enough to take their lives?

Morgan had no rosy illusions about her situation. More than anything, if there were a way out of this predicament . . . if there was any hope of vindicating herself, she needed to know more about Mason Kaine—much more.

CHAPTER
55

DAY TWENTY-THREE

The past twelve hours had been one of the more grueling shifts Morgan could remember.

She had treated everything from an embedded splinter in a five-year-old's foot to an insulin overdose in a brittle diabetic. The only saving grace was that she'd been so totally immersed in caring for her patients that she hadn't once thought about her father's death or the Code 15s. With her morning sickness subsiding, her only problem approaching her second trimester was feeling more tired than usual.

After finishing her charting, Morgan signed out to the night-shift physician, gathered her things together, and left the emergency room. Crossing the lobby, the only thing on her mind was getting home and falling into her recliner. Morgan was within steps of the exit when she noticed Bob Allenby coming toward her. Their eyes met simultaneously, making it impossible for her to pretend she hadn't seen him. Bob was the first to wave.

Burying an exasperated sigh, Morgan smiled and waited for him at the revolving glass doors. Watching him approach, she couldn't help but notice an uncharacteristic swagger in his step.

"Are you on your way to the parking garage?" he asked.

She nodded.

"Good, I'll walk you to your car."

They kept the conversation light as they made their way

beneath a canopied breezeway and past the valet parking. Morgan noted immediately that Bob's demeanor was particularly upbeat. She knew the team from AHCA had been in the hospital for the past two days.

Morgan was debating the wisdom of bringing up the topic when he said, "The folks from AHCA finished up. We had the exit interview about an hour ago."

"How did we do?" she asked as they emerged from under the canopy.

"They weren't very happy, but fortunately we were able to convince them that the Code Fifteens resulted from a combination of unavoidable events and system breakdowns."

"That's great news. I guess congratulations are in order," Morgan said, concealing her dismay that AHCA had decided against undertaking a more thorough investigation.

"It may be a little early for an end-zone celebration. We've still got our work cut out for us. AHCA's giving us six weeks to submit a detailed action plan itemizing specific safety nets that we'll implement to prevent similar errors from ever happening again."

"Your staff obviously did a great job."

"I haven't slept in three nights wondering if they'd close down the Cardiac Care Center. All I can say is, thank God, they didn't."

The last car passed and they started across the street.

"Did the investigation team say anything specific regarding the Faith Russo case?" Morgan inquired.

Bob covered a dry cough with the side of his fist. "They completed a detailed study of the case."

"And?"

"They found no fault or deficiencies in Miss Russo's care from the hospital's standpoint."

Hardly surprised, Morgan said, "I assume their vindication doesn't include the physicians involved."

"They didn't say specifically, but I would assume it doesn't."

"I guess we both have a pretty good idea who they're going to hang for this case."

"Don't be so paranoid, Morgan. AHCA's a responsible government agency. They're not in the business of conducting witch hunts."

"Responsible government agency?" she asked in a cynical voice. "A couple of weeks ago you referred to them as the second coming of the gestapo."

"I think you're taking what I said out of context."

"You also called them an unpredictable bunch of squirrels. Am I taking that out of context too?"

They walked up to the glass-enclosed elevator that ran along the outside wall of the parking garage.

"My opinion of AHCA's not the issue. My advice to you is to stay focused on what's important and try not overreact."

"With all due respect, Bob, it's not your neck that's centered on the chopping block." Morgan slapped the up button repeatedly. "I'm being investigated by the state medical board. That's not exactly the same as appearing in front of Judge Judy."

"All I'm saying is that if you handle things correctly, you'll be fine."

"That's what everybody keeps telling me, but they're not facing disciplinary action. They act as if this is some minor setback and that I have absolutely nothing to worry about."

"I didn't say you don't have a problem. I'm just trying to point out you simply keep—"

"It sounds to me like—"

Bob held his hand up. "Let me finish. You're a bright and politically savvy woman. I would expect someone of your insight to know which battles to fight and which ones to back away from."

"It's easy for everybody to—"

Bob raised his hand for the second time. Struggling to remain silent, Morgan stared at the digital display atop the elevator frame. The doors rumbled open and they stepped on.

"I'll echo what Eileen told you. You've got your whole

career in front of you. If the folks at AHCA think you're being cooperative and forthright, you'll probably just wind up with a letter of guidance."

"Just a letter of guidance?" she asked, wondering if his response would be so cavalier if an official Florida agency sent him a letter pointing out his incompetence.

"It's a slap on the wrist, Morgan—a two-minute penalty. It doesn't even count as a black mark against you. They're just telling you that they feel you could have handled the case better. It's not personal."

"All that means is that it's not personal to them. To me it doesn't get any more personal than this. They're playing with my life and everything I've worked for."

With a discouraged face, he said, "They're just doing their job."

"They weren't in the emergency room the night Faith Russo came in."

"Unfortunately, Florida law doesn't require them to be."

The elevator slowed to a stop at the fourth floor. Morgan stepped off first. Bob stopped and smiled at a chatty gaggle of nurses who strolled by.

"Listen, Morgan. Don't let a misplaced ego cloud your usual good judgment. The fact is you did miss the diagnosis."

"You mean according to Everett Canfield."

"He's the pathologist of record."

"Unfortunately," she said.

"What is that supposed to mean?"

"Nothing," she said, having no interest in elaborating on her disdain for Canfield.

"You're letting this thing get the best of you. The AHCA investigators know that doctors are human and even the best ones make mistakes—especially when they work in busy emergency rooms."

"I don't have a God complex. I'm well aware that I'm not infallible, but in the case of Faith Russo, I didn't make a mistake."

"All evidence points to the contrary according to the autopsy findings. It's a pretty damning report. You might want to consider that before you start spouting off to AHCA about murder conspiracies." Bob stopped long enough to take a quick look around. "Where are you parked?"

"Right over there," she answered, pointing down the nearest row of cars.

"I hope you realize that if AHCA decides you're emotionally unstable and labels you an impaired physician . . . well, a letter of guidance will seem like an hour of sixth-grade detention compared to what they'll probably do."

Morgan took the time to choose her words carefully. "I'm not going to self-destruct, Bob. I know how to play the game. I know you think I've become a grief-stricken paranoid, but give me a little credit for having some common sense."

He finally smiled. "I never doubted it for a moment. Now, as soon as this Faith Russo affair is wrapped up, give me a call. We need to talk about getting things back to normal." He started to walk away. "We still feel you're an important part of Dade Presbyterian's future."

"I appreciate that."

Instead of getting into her car, Morgan looked out over the concrete wall at the brightly lit emergency room entrance. A pair of ambulances, with their backing-up alarms filling the night, backed into the receiving bay.

In spite of his reassurances, Morgan harbored serious doubts whether Bob Allenby or any member of the hospital's board of directors would ever again consider her a key member of the medical staff.

CHAPTER

56

DAY TWENTY-FOUR

There were probably several ways Jack Casto could have made his living, but being a thug came naturally to him, and it never occurred to him to try his hand at anything else.

Casto was a bullnecked, hulking man of thirty-five who prided himself on never allowing his emotions to interfere with his work. A native of Miami, he had no particular knowledge or training in the martial arts or any other combative science, relying instead on his monstrous size to do his talking for him.

The moment Morgan pulled out of the doctor's parking lot, Casto, driving a rented white Taurus, fell in behind her. After following her for three miles, she turned down a narrow palm-lined street and then into the parking lot that served a small cluster of stores. The largest one, which was flanked by a Cuban café and a hair salon, was a high-volume dry cleaner.

Casto watched her park and then took a space at the far end of the lot. When he saw her disappear into the dry cleaner, he stepped out of his car, opened his second pack of cigarettes of the day, and packed them hard against his palm.

Five minutes passed before Morgan emerged from the store with her cleaning slung over her shoulder. Taking a lengthy final drag, he flipped the butt between the grids of a rusted-out sewer grate and started across the lot.

He reached Morgan as she was about to lay her cleaning across the passenger seat.

"Excuse me, Dr. Connolly. I wonder if I might have a word with you."

Morgan stopped and studied Casto's face for a few moments.

"I'm sorry. I can't seem to place—"

"We've never met, Doctor. I was hoping to speak with you briefly about your husband." Morgan pulled the tethered hangars around to the front and held her dry cleaning folded over her arms. "Let me get those for you," he offered, taking the hangars from Morgan before she could protest.

"I was hoping you might help me locate Kevin."

"Are you a friend of his?"

"Let's just say I represent a group of businessmen who are interested in getting in touch with him."

"Businessmen?" Morgan asked with a pretty good idea of why the man holding her dry cleaning was looking for Kevin.

"He's out of town," she said directly. "I don't know where he is or how to reach him."

Jack looked away for a moment, smiled as if somebody was trying to lure him into a shell game, and then shifted his gaze back to Morgan. His grin faded.

"You'll have to excuse me for saying this, Doctor, but it's a little hard for me to believe that your husband's out of town and you have no way of contacting him?"

Seeing no reason to offer a lengthy explanation to the polite stranger, Morgan said, "I'm sorry. I can't help you."

She reached for her dry cleaning. Casto made no effort to hand it over to her.

"Dr. Connolly, your husband made some bad business decisions and now he owes my associates a great deal of money. If you help me collect on this bad debt, things will be a lot easier for everybody involved."

In mounting desperation, Morgan looked around hoping to

spot somebody who might help her. There was nobody. Standing in the middle of a parking lot in broad daylight should have offered her some sense of security, but her unchecked fear continued to soar. The only thing working in her favor was a combination of her better judgment and instinct—both of which were crying out not to make a scene.

"How much money does he owe you?"

Casto coaxed his wraparound sunglasses higher on his nose. "Ninety thousand dollars."

"My God," she muttered.

"The men I represent are anxious to recover their money as quickly and as painlessly as possible. So I ask you again, Doctor, do you know where I might find your husband?"

Her options narrowing, Morgan said, "All I know is that he's out of town. Kevin and I are separated. We barely speak to each other. He has a new cell phone and I don't know the number." She again reached for her dry cleaning. "Now if you don't mind, I'd like to—"

Jack passed Morgan her clothes, but as he did he curled his squat fingers around her wrist. His grip was strong but not painful.

"Dr. Connolly, your deadbeat husband's into us for ninety large, and it sounds like we're not the only ones he's run out on. I think we both know he's nothing but a degenerate gambler. You'd be doing us both a big favor if you'd just tell me where he is."

"I've already told you. I don't know where he is or how to reach him."

Casto sighed, released his grip, and handed Morgan her dry cleaning. He took a step back.

"I like your style, Doc, but feisty can get old after a while. My boss is a civil guy, but it would be a big mistake to confuse his courtesy with weakness." He then added, "If I can't find your husband, I'll be back to talk to you again." He started to turn and walk away but stopped in mid-step. "By the way, I wouldn't mention our little conversation to the police or anybody else." He then tapped the brim of his Florida Marlins cap and, without as much as a backward glance, walked away.

Until she saw his car pull out of the parking lot, Morgan didn't move. Her mouth was as dry as cotton and her fingers were still quivering. After another minute or so, she climbed into her car. The man had left no ambiguity regarding the measures he would take to recover the money Kevin owed. Morgan put the key in the ignition and started the Thunderbird's engine. Driving home, she barely took her eyes off of the rearview mirror. When she was sure he wasn't following her, her fear quickly became overwhelmed by anger. She reached into her purse, yanked out her phone, and dialed Kevin's number.

CHAPTER

57

DAY TWENTY-FIVE

Following Will Johnson's instructions, Morgan followed a broad flagstone path past his two-story Georgian-style home until she reached the backyard.

She estimated Will's property to be at least two acres, making it a distinct departure from South Florida's usual monotonous, zero-lot-line parcels. When she passed the garage, she saw the white guesthouse that Will used as his office. It was a cozy, palm-shaded building with a red Spanish-tile roof.

Taped to an urn-shaped brass doorknocker was a note from Will requesting she go inside, make herself comfortable, and that he would join her shortly. After a twinge of hesitation, she opened the door and stepped inside. From the foyer, Morgan gazed into the smartly decorated living room. Especially impressive were the silk-paneled window treatments and the large red area rug that lay in front of a long leather couch.

Morgan closed the door and then strolled across the teak floor and sat down on the couch. The most striking thing about the room was that there was nothing that even remotely resembled a physician's office. Conspicuously absent was a desk, a computer station, or any medical charts. What struck her as even more peculiar was the absence of any framed medical diplomas, degrees, or certificates on the walls.

Morgan heard the door open. She glanced at her watch and started to come to her feet.

"Don't get up," Will said from a distance. Dressed in jeans and a gray sweater vest over a white T-shirt, he held a large container of coffee in each hand. He stopped next to her and handed her one.

"I'm sorry I'm a little late. I can't start a session without Mudslide coffee."

"Mudslide?"

"Try it. It's incredible. I'm addicted to the stuff."

Morgan set the container down on an end table. "As much as I'd love to drink this, I'm pregnant. My limit's one a day and I'm already into next month."

"Congratulations," he said with chuckle.

"You have a beautiful family," Morgan said, pointing to a large studio photograph of his wife and children mounted above the fireplace.

"They're great. I don't know what I'd do without them."

Unable to shake the uneasy feeling of her first therapy session, Morgan kept her eyes glued on the wall. Next to the family portrait, there was a grouping of photos of Will rock climbing.

"Do you climb?" he asked her.

"I've done some inside climbing. Nothing like that," she said, pointing at the photos.

"Which club?"

Ignoring the tempting aroma of the coffee that was begging her to reach over and take a sip, she said, "The one in Fort Lauderdale." Morgan looked at the photos again. "Do you really free climb?"

"In my younger, more high-spirited days. Now I use a rig. What do you like to do when you're not running the emergency room?"

"I fly."

He looked up with a smile. "How long have you been a pilot?"

"Since college."

"How often do you go?"

"A couple of times a week. I keep my plane at North Perry."

"I envy you. It's something I've always wanted to try."

"I have my instructor's rating. If you feel like it sometime, I'll take you up for an introductory lesson."

"If my wife says okay, I just might take you up on that."

Will sat down in a deep leather chair that faced Morgan. He popped off the lid of his coffee with his tapered fingers and took three quick sips before setting it down.

"If you don't mind my asking, how did you become the hospital's designated therapist to the doctors?"

"I volunteered," he answered.

"That sounds too simple for Dade Presbyterian."

"As it turns out, very few therapists are interested in doing this kind of work. Most hospitals have a hell of a time finding doctors who are willing to work with other doctors."

"How did you get interested in this type of therapy?"

"I started out by seeing a few physicians. One referral led to the next and from then on it kind of took on a life of its own. In less than a year, I was seeing doctors exclusively. When I decided to officially limit my practice to working with physicians, I went to see Eileen Hale."

"I assume she was receptive," Morgan said.

"It was kind of like walking in to the Salvation Army and offering to ring a bell and collect money at Christmas time." Morgan chuckled. "Eileen started sending me physicians right away." Will used a remote to lower the classical music filling the room. "Did you have any trouble finding the place?" he asked.

"Your directions were perfect."

"Good. Tell me about yourself," he said in a relaxed voice.

"Just like that?"

"Just like that," he answered.

With some subtle coaxing from Will, Morgan spent the next hour talking about her childhood, her marriage, and her role as the director of the emergency room. Will had an obvious knack for putting people at ease, which made it easier for her to talk. She found him to be bright and unpretentious. She assumed he went into psychiatry because he tended to see the best in people.

Will finished making a few notes, capped his pen, and looked up.

"Tell me about how you're coping with the death of your father."

His request was direct but didn't put Morgan off.

"I don't have many heroes. It was hard to lose him."

After a few less probing questions, he asked, "Do you think losing your father has affected your work?"

"I still think about him often, and I'd be lying if I said I didn't miss him. But I realize that losing a parent is a reality. It's something we all go through."

"So you're saying . . ."

"I'm saying that I'm going through a grieving process— but I'm handling it. So my answer to your question is no, I don't think his death is affecting my work."

"Eileen told me about a problematic case you recently had in the ER. I believe the patient's name was . . ." Will stopped and began flipping through his pad.

"Her name was Faith Russo."

"Do you have any idea why Bob Allenby is concerned that your care might have been impaired by stress?"

Morgan simply shrugged. "I guess you'd have to ask Bob."

"He's not here."

"In that case, I'd tell you to consider the source."

"Which means what exactly?" he asked with an arched brow.

"I'm not sure I'm comfortable saying anything further."

"That's fine. We can talk about whatever—"

Morgan felt obligated to explain her answer. "When we first spoke, you told me you would need my permission to speak with Eileen Hale regarding our sessions."

"There's something you should understand, and maybe I should have clarified it before we began. Nothing we talk about in this room will ever leave this room. My job is to offer an opinion as to whether the recent stress in your life is impairing your performance as a doctor. I don't have to divulge the specifics of what we discuss to do that."

Hoping she hadn't offended him, she said, "I didn't mean to imply that you would violate my—"

"I'm not a referee, Morgan, nor do I have any interest in hospital politics, Code Fifteens, or what makes Bob Allenby nervous. I'm bound by the same code of ethics you are."

Feeling a minor wave of nausea, which she attributed to both the moment and her pregnancy, Morgan stood up and walked around to the back of the couch.

"Are you okay?" he asked.

"Could I trouble you to make it a little cooler in here?"

"Sure," he said, coming to his feet and walking over to the thermostat.

"Bob Allenby's an experienced and highly effective hospital administrator. You don't get that way unless you're politically savvy. Bob's problem is that he's prone to tripping over his job."

"I'm not sure I understand what you mean by that."

"Suffice it to say, his vision's sometimes impaired by corporate blinders."

"Is that what's going on in the Faith Russo case?"

"In my opinion, yes. I don't think Bob's interested in finding out what really happened that night. The truth might be embarrassing or damaging to Dade Presbyterian. The corporation will always come first. Patient care issues, including patient safety, will get elbowed if he perceives them to be a threat to the hospital. Faith's death came on the heels of two Code Fifteens that involved patients in our Cardiac Care Center. Both patients died as a direct result of catastrophic errors. Bob's approach to the root cause analysis was to find scapegoats and quick explanations to satisfy the

AHCA investigation team. He had no interest in discovering the truth."

"I assume you shared your concerns with Bob directly."

"I did, and I think we both know that's why I'm here today. He told me my conclusions regarding the Code Fifteens were, at a minimum, far-fetched, and at the most, irrational."

"Eileen Hale said that you suggested the Code Fifteens may have been intentionally orchestrated by somebody."

"Leaving emotion and politics out of it, and objectively examining the facts, it seems like a distinct possibility."

"But don't most medical mishaps have a logical explanation? The medical literature's full of case reports about bizarre coincidences and mistakes that have led to devastating patient injuries."

"But those are the exceptions. More than eighty percent of medical mistakes are the result of easily identifiable human negligence, not bad luck. There are no simple explanations to account for a whopping dose of protamine winding up in a nitroglycerine bottle—or for a magnetized cross to mysteriously find its way around the neck of a Jewish patient with a newly placed pacemaker." Will looked down for a few seconds to make some notes. After a brief silence, she said with dismay, "You have the same disbelieving look on your face that Bob had when I told him what I had discovered."

"Is it important to you that I be convinced?"

"Yes," she answered, without knowing why.

"I know the basics about the Faith Russo case, but I'd like to get your impression of what happened."

"The entire thing was a setup to make me look incompetent. There was no way that woman had a lethal injury to her spleen the first time I saw her."

"Why would somebody want to set you up?"

"Because this individual believes I committed malpractice in the care of his family."

"So, you know who this person is."

"His name's Mason Kaine." Morgan realized she was

sounding more paranoid with each answer, but she had come this far and her lines of retreat were for all intents and purposes nonexistent. She spent the next few minutes telling Will everything she suspected about Kaine.

Will set his pad down on a small glass table next to his chair.

"I guess the concern of the hospital is that this conspiracy theory of yours is distracting you from your work—or worse, making you an unsafe physician."

"That's totally absurd. Physicians lose parents and grieve just like anybody else. That doesn't mean we turn into paranoid, nonfunctioning doctors."

"But in Bob's—"

"Bob's dealings with me have been ethically unconscionable. I've never been treated so unfairly in my life."

Will didn't respond immediately. Morgan knew he was giving her time to compose herself.

"Hypothetically, what would you do if it turned out that Bob was right and you were wrong about how these patient errors occurred?"

"I'd be in his office the same day to apologize. But if I'm right about what's going on at Dade Presbyterian, more innocent patients are going to die—a lot more."

Staring at Will's solemn face, Morgan realized her tone and vehemence were flirting with inappropriate.

Will looked at his watch.

"We've been talking for almost two hours. I think that's enough for one day."

After taking a few moments, Morgan inquired, "Would I be out of line to ask you for some feedback?"

"I don't think so. An unraveling marriage, your father's death, and the pressure of running an emergency room and the Patient Safety Committee. I think that entitles you to feel a little downcast." Before Morgan could press Will for more specific information, he said, "I think we should talk again. Are you available next Monday afternoon, say around three?"

Morgan leisurely came to her feet. Intent on not sounding discouraged, she said, "I'll check my schedule, but I'm pretty sure I can. I'll call you tomorrow to confirm."

Will walked with Morgan to the front door and then back down the flagstone path to her car.

"I know things look pretty gloomy right now, and at the risk of this sounding a little trite and corny—these things do generally work themselves out."

With her lips pressed together, she managed a brief smile. "After they work themselves out, who do I see about getting my reputation back?"

"I wish I could answer that, Morgan."

"You think I'm out of my mind, don't you?"

"I hope so," he answered. "Because if you're not, there's an insanely dangerous man out there somewhere."

PART THREE

CHAPTER
58

After three years of backbreaking studies at the University of Florida, Michael Allenby remained unconvinced that he was cut out to be an electrical engineer.

With midterms onrushing like Colorado rapids, Michael had been hitting the books ten hours a day. His only hedge against the stress of exams was his inviolate five-mile run he took every night at exactly ten p.m.

The small college town of Gainesville had been a major change from the urban upscale neighborhood and private school environment of south Florida that he had been raised in. The strange irony was that he preferred the more bucolic setting of northern Florida and had been recently toying with the idea of pursuing a career in academics instead of trying to claw his way to the top in the private sector.

Studying at the kitchen table, Michael looked up from his electromagnetics text at a wall-mounted clock that hung over the refrigerator. It was five minutes to ten. Michael removed his reading glasses and flipped the book closed. Andi Crittenden, the young lady he had been living with for the past two years, was asleep on their couch. He got up from the table and quietly went into the only bedroom to put on his sweats and sneakers.

Right before he slipped out of their third-story apartment, he checked Andi one last time and put on his Gators cap.

Michael spent a couple of minutes in the parking lot stretching out. He looked overhead at a crescent moon playing peekaboo with a skeletal sheet of clouds. It was unseasonably cool, which he viewed as a godsend as it would make his mini-marathon less demanding. Michael hadn't changed his route in several months. The five-mile course took him through the quiet side streets of Gainesville in a gradual loop. What he liked most about it was that it kept him well away from the main campus with its abundant temptations.

When he was finished stretching, he zipped up his sweat top, ran in place for a few seconds, and then took off. Once he was out of the parking lot, he turned north along Archer Road until he reached the entrance to one of the city's oldest neighborhoods. As he always did, he ran along the left side of the road so he could watch the oncoming traffic. He had been running about fifteen minutes when he reached a narrowly inclined hill. The hill was approximately a quarter of a mile and lined by tall spruce trees.

Inhaling deeply, he charged up the hill. Once he reached the top, he slowed his pace and started down. Jogging lazily, he did everything possible not to think about electrical engineering or his exams. Instead, he continued without a care, thinking about Andi and their upcoming spring break cruise to the western Caribbean.

He watched as two cars passed him. The first flashed its brights, which Michael acknowledged with an appreciative wave. As an experienced nighttime jogger, he knew the greatest hazard to him was the careless motorist. He was about two hundred yards from the bottom when he spotted another car just starting up the hill. As he sometimes did, he glanced over his shoulder. There were no cars coming from the opposite direction. When the oncoming car was about a hundred yards away, he suddenly heard the late-model sedan's engine gun. He assumed it was a high school kid experimenting with his father's car. Keeping a careful eye out, Michael immediately moved as far left as he was able without tumbling into the sewer ditch that bordered the road.

The car rapidly accelerated but it never wavered from its lane. In the next instant, the car's high beams came on, but instead of a flash, they remained on, forcing Michael to shield his eyes from the piercing light. It took only a few seconds more for the car to close the distance between them. With the sedan still traveling in its lane, Michael assumed they would pass each other without incident. But it was exactly at that moment, just when his apprehension was fading, that the car suddenly made a violent swerve to the right. Even though the glare of the onrushing lights obscured his vision, Michael could still make out the outline of the sedan barreling down on him.

His bloodstream surged with adrenaline.

Drawing on nothing more than instinct, he dove to his left. His reaction time was near instantaneous. Three feet off the ground, with his arms outstretched in a headlong dive, he sailed toward the ditch. He prayed once he was airborne, the out-of-control car would blow past him. Unfortunately, his prayer went unanswered. There was no screeching of breaks. The first and only sound he heard was the explosive thud of three tons of high-speed steel tearing through the lower half of his body. The incredible force of the collision sent his entire body into a wild flat spin, catapulting him another five feet into the air before tossing him facedown in the ditch.

Fortunately, he didn't strike his head, and within a few seconds, Michael opened his eyes. The pain tore at him as if somebody had buried a pair of axes deep into his thighs. Hot blood from his shattered pelvic bones and mangled soft tissues gushed out, soaking his pants. Forcing himself to take the pain, he slowly picked up his chin and looked up the hill.

The car had pulled over about twenty yards away. Straining to focus, he saw nobody, but he could hear the engine running. A few seconds passed, and the car door slowly swung open. Its interior light cast a shadowy glow that was sufficient for Michael to see the silhouette of a hulking man emerge from the car. His relief was instantaneous but fleeting. Instead of running toward him, the man stood beside his car, gazing up the hill.

Assuming the man didn't see him, Michael yelled out, "I'm in the ditch. Help me." The man didn't move, but Michael knew he heard his cries for help.

"Please help me," he screamed again between labored breaths.

But the man didn't take a single step. In stead, he climbed back into his car and slowly pulled away. Michael closed his eyes and allowed his head to drop to the soggy muck. He knew the man would not return. After a few deep breaths, he reached down to see if by a miracle his cell phone case was still clipped to his sweatpants. It was gone.

The mounting terror of not being found consumed him.

About two minutes passed before the first car approached. It was heading down the hill and Michael waited until the last possible moment before waving and calling out to it. He screamed as loud as he ever had but the car never slowed. A half dozen other vehicles passed by in the next twenty minutes, but none heard his pleas for help. Fearing for his life, he closed his eyes and prayed.

Just when he thought he would lose consciousness, he heard the first bark of the dog. His eyes snapped open. The sound of distant footsteps became steadily louder. On the ground in front of him, the bright beam of a flashlight appeared.

Two coeds walking a golden retriever climbed down into the ditch.

"My God," the one holding the leash said.

"We're calling nine-one-one," the other one told him. "We're nursing students. We're going to stay with you until the ambulance comes."

In a pained, shaking voice, he said, "Somebody hit me. He stopped, but then he took off."

"Don't worry about that now," she said, kneeling down next to him. She then reached for his hand and felt for his pulse.

"Thank you," was all he could manage.

Five minutes later the air was filled with the wailing siren of an approaching ambulance. Seconds later, with its orange-and-red strobe lights flashing, the rescue van came into view at the top of the hill. The girls jumped up, moved to the shoulder of the road, and flagged it down. Two paramedics jumped out, opened the back doors of the vehicle, and wheeled over a collapsible stretcher. The more senior one took Michael's vital signs and then started an IV. As soon as it was securely taped into place and his legs were splinted, the two men carefully transferred him onto the stretcher and loaded him into the ambulance. As they were trained, their time on scene was as brief as possible.

Ten minutes later, they rolled Michael Allenby into the main receiving bay at the Shands Hospital Trauma Center.

CHAPTER 59

DAY TWENTY-NINE

After a twenty-minute drive from the hospital, Ben and Morgan pulled into the parking of the Broward County offices of the Agency for Health Care Administration.

"The most important thing is to keep your cool," he told her as they got out of his car and headed for the entrance. "I know a couple of doctors who have gone through this. Just explain to the investigator in a calm and logical manner exactly what happened. Be careful not to come across as an arrogant doctor with a God complex. The last thing you want him to think is that you view yourself as someone incapable of making a mistake."

"I got it, Ben. You've told me all of this ten times. Have a little confidence," she said, getting the feeling he was more nervous than she was.

"You'll be fine. Just as long as you remember to—"

"To leave my attitude at the door. I know."

"I think you're ready. I'll wait for you right here," he said, pointing to the only couch in the lobby.

Ben gave her a quick hug, kissed her, and gave her the thumbs-up. "It's just like the first time you soloed."

Morgan rode the elevator up to the fourth floor. After identifying herself to an indifferent receptionist, she was escorted into a small office. Devoid of any windows, the unadorned room contained only a metal desk, two straight-backed chairs, and an empty bookcase. Except for a few haphazardly placed color photographs of minor Florida officials, the walls were bare.

Using the time to bolster her confidence, Morgan went over her plan. As Ben had suggested, she would confidently but calmly defend her care of Faith Russo. Irrespective of how the interview progressed, she would not allow herself to become unglued. A few more minutes passed and Morgan was left with nothing to do except look at the photographs on the wall. Finally, after what seemed like hours, the door opened and a middle-aged man in dire need of a haircut strolled into the office. As if he were the only one in the room, he settled in behind the desk, took out a handkerchief and wiped his nose. He then reached into his briefcase and pulled out a large manila file.

"My name's Matthew Cochran," he announced as if he were running for office and then handed her one of his business cards. Before saying anything more, he arranged the contents of the folder into two neat stacks. "The purpose of this meeting is to offer you the opportunity to respond to the complaint made against you regarding your treatment of Faith Russo. After our meeting, I'll prepare a report and submit it to the board of medicine. Let me make it perfectly clear that I have no role in their deliberations or decisions." He wiped his nose for a second time. "Do you have any questions before we begin?"

Morgan found his dispassionate monotone reminiscent of a tired waiter's recital of the Saturday-night dinner specials for the twentieth time. She was tempted to tell him that although he might find these proceedings to be a matter of routine, they were humiliating and disconcerting to her. But with Ben's advice still echoing in her mind, she said instead, "I have no questions."

He picked the top paper from the first stack.

"I have a brief description of the Code Fifteen along with the complaint, which I'm sure you know was anonymous. I'd like to get your side of things from the first moment you met Miss Russo." He then raised his eyes to meet hers for the first time since he had paraded into the office.

Anxious to plead her case, Morgan moved to the front of her chair and laid her forearms on the armrests. For the next twenty minutes she went through every aspect of Faith's treatment in methodical detail. Ever careful to avoid sounding like a defensive physician struggling to explain away a poor patient outcome, she conducted herself in a professional manner and confined her comments to the medical facts of the case.

When she finished, Cochran took a minute or so to complete his notes.

"I want to make sure I'm clear on something. Is it your opinion that Miss Russo did not have a ruptured spleen the first time you saw her?"

"That's correct."

"Would you please explain to me again how you reached that conclusion?"

"There was absolutely no physical or laboratory evidence that any of her abdominal organs had been injured in any way. As you can see from the medical record, I carefully documented my findings before discharging her."

Morgan watched while he again pored over the ER record.

He asked, "Would I be fair in reporting to the board that you reviewed the triage nurse's note before examining Miss Russo?"

"I reviewed it in detail." Morgan knew he was referring to the nurse's notation that Faith had complained of vague abdominal pain. Before Cochran could question her on the point, she went on to add, "In fact, it was because of the admitting nurse's entry that I repeated Miss Russo's abdominal examination. When I found nothing abnormal, I again asked her if she had sustained an injury to any part of her abdomen. She told me she hadn't."

Cochran slid his reading glasses off and set them down on the desk. He appeared puzzled. It was the first hint Morgan had that tucked away in some small fissure of his robotic brain, he was listening to her.

"I'd like to include something in my report that indicates why you believe Miss Russo was hurt after she left the emergency room. Is there anything in the police or paramedic's reports that would substantiate your theory?"

"I'm afraid not," Morgan answered with a sudden loss of resolve.

Cochran replaced his glasses, interlaced his fingers, and set his hands on the desk.

"Dr. Connolly, I've been an AHCA investigator for twenty years. If I've learned anything it's that these cases rarely come down to what a physician thinks or theorizes. The only thing that matters is what he or she can prove."

"I wasn't with Miss Russo when she left the emergency room, so there's no way I can prove that's when her injury occurred. All I can tell you is that it's the only explanation that makes sense."

"Is there anything else you would like me to include in my report?"

She shook her head. "Not that I can think of at the moment."

Cochran returned Morgan's file to his briefcase.

"I'm truly sorry this happened to you. I'm a registered nurse by training. I worked in a busy emergency room for five years, so I have a pretty good idea of the crazy things that can go wrong." He paused for a few seconds while he checked to make sure his briefcase was locked. "I'm not supposed to say this, but I hope things go your way."

With a note of desperation in her voice, Morgan asked, "Is there anything else I can do?"

"The board meets in two weeks. Your case is one of the last ones on their agenda. From what I see here, all they'll have to base a decision on is your statement and the medical records. You're going to have to convince them that Faith Russo was injured after you saw her the first time."

Morgan looked squarely at him. "I'm not a police officer, Mr. Cochran, and two weeks doesn't give me much time."

"I understand, but anything that would refute Dr. Canfield's autopsy report and his . . . his editorial comments would greatly help your case."

"Editorial comments?"

"He included a letter that accused you of being under great personal stress. He suggested that it might be the cause of your faulty medical judgment."

Morgan wanted to scream.

"Can he do that?"

"It may not be considered proper procedure, but there's no law against it."

"I thought his job was to offer an objective opinion regarding Faith Russo's cause of death. He's a pathologist, not a psychiatrist. He has no right to make unfounded and unqualified statements regarding my emotional state."

"You're preaching to the choir, Dr. Connolly."

"Why would the board even look at such a letter?"

"Normally they wouldn't. But coming from Dr. Canfield . . . well, they probably will. He's one of the board's most respected consultants. They've asked him to offer opinions on several cases over the years. They hold him in very high regard."

"Great," Morgan said, crossing her arms and pushing back in her chair. "What's the point in even defending myself?"

"As I mentioned before, it's impossible to predict what the board will do. In addition to being the key caregiver in a particularly bad Code Fifteen case, you have a highly respected pathologist who's claiming you're responsible for it. If you want to help yourself, find something of substance in your defense that the board won't be able to ignore."

"What I need is more time. Will they give me a postponement if I request one?"

"Not without a compelling reason," he said, coming to his feet. Morgan remained seated.

"You have my card. If you should have any questions, please call me."

"Thank you," Morgan told him with a polite but faint smile.

After Cochran left, Morgan sat in the office pondering her ever-worsening predicament. Entangled in a Gordian knot of uncertainty, one fact seemed clear: she had to find Mason Kaine. Ben was right. For all she knew Kaine could have moved out of Florida a year ago. It would be pointless to try to enlist the help of the police department, but based on her conversation with Adele Kaine, she didn't think she needed to.

After another minute or so, Morgan stood up and left the room. She was not a woman prone to paranoid ideations. But as she made her way down the hall, she'd swear the entire machinery of Florida's medical authority was conspiring against her.

CHAPTER

60

Gideon knelt down on the shallow incline of his multitiered rock garden.

Scrutinizing his work, he was at last satisfied that the spacing and alignment of the purple and white impatiens were perfect. Pushing himself to his feet, he brushed the crusted dirt from his jeans. He then made his way down an azalea-lined gravel trail until he arrived back at his house. He climbed the four steps leading to a wooden deck and then walked over to the railing.

From the middle of his shoulder blades, a razor-sharp pain climbed upward and then over his neck before sinking into the depths of the base of his skull. Determined to ignore the stress-induced pain, he gazed out over his beautifully landscaped property.

Subconsciously, his grip on the railing tightened until the last drop of blood was squeezed from his hands. The news that AHCA had failed to impose any significant sanctions on Dade Presbyterian had quickly disseminated through the hospital. When word reached him, he was infuriated. At a minimum, he had expected the inspection team to require the hospital to pay a substantial fine and to order a temporary suspension of the cardiac program pending an in-depth review of its safety record.

The flames of Gideon's anger were further fanned by the

knowledge that, in the absence of significant penalties from AHCA, the Code 15s wouldn't receive any media attention. From the beginning, he had counted heavily upon television and the newspapers crucifying Dade Presbyterian hospital for their unsafe practices.

Irrespective of what had happened to this point, he couldn't allow AHCA's spineless dereliction of duty to weaken his resolve. Righteousness would always be on his side. This time, he vowed to himself, he would leave nothing to chance. He would create a Code 15 of such staggering proportions that the media would have a field day with it. A public outcry would result that would echo all the way to Tallahassee. AHCA would have no choice but to return to Dade Presbyterian and do what they should have done the first time.

His determination renewed, Gideon released his grip on the railing and went into his house. Entering the sunroom through a set of white French doors, he strolled over to a wicker love seat that overlooked his garden. A large ceiling fan cast a welcomed stream of cool air across his face and neck. He closed his eyes. His breathing slowed and soon became deeper.

His last thought before falling asleep was that he would not allow Morgan Connolly to do anything more to interfere with his plans. To his dismay, he would have to change his tactics. He could no longer afford to indulge himself by tormenting her. It was time to arrange for her death. He owed at least that much to his sons.

CHAPTER
61

Morgan's second session with Will Johnson was even more free-flowing and productive than the first.

They spent most of the time discussing her interview with AHCA, her conversation with Adele Kaine, and the other events that had transpired since they had last spoken. At no time was Will judgmental or did he make her feel as if her concerns were irrational or groundless. Most important, she was confident that nothing they talked about would leave his office.

"We still have a few minutes left," he told Morgan, flipping his notepad back to the first page. "Is there anything else you'd like to talk about?"

Having a captive expert in human behavior sitting directly across from her was an opportunity too appealing for Morgan to pass up.

"Anything?"

He nodded.

"I know you spend most of your day trying to talk people off of the ledge. I'd like to discuss something a little different."

"I'll try and shift gears," he said, sporting a cautious grin.

"I'd like to know what type of person might become irrational as the result of a severe grief reaction?"

He picked up his container of coffee and took the last swallow.

"What you're asking for is a personality profile of an individual who might be predisposed to such a psychotic breakdown."

"Exactly."

He flipped a few pages back in his notes.

"This wouldn't have anything to do with Mason Kaine, would it?"

"Let's just say we're two physicians discussing an interesting psychiatric case."

"Fine. Any standard psychiatric textbook would say that the type of breakdown you're describing is rare. On the other hand, there are numerous case reports in our scientific journals suggesting it's a more common phenomenon than we once believed, and that it doesn't necessarily mean the individual is psychotic."

"Is there a particular personality type that would be more prone to an extreme grief reaction?" she asked.

"Inflexible, highly structured individuals. Somebody who was confident in his or her convictions and didn't require the moral input or approval from those around them. Other characteristics might include aversions to change and problems with anger management."

"How about unappeasable and unwilling to negotiate?" Morgan inquired.

"Absolutely."

"Would this individual enjoy setting others up for failure in order to aggrandize themselves?"

Will chuckled. "I see you've already done some reading on the topic. Coals to Newcastle bringing me into this conversation."

"How prone would such a person be to committing a violent act?"

"That's hard to say. But anybody could become violent if subjected to enough frustration from an unresolved conflict, especially if they felt that one of their loved ones had been unfairly victimized. Throw revenge into the mix and violence would become much more likely."

"I'm glad I didn't become a shrink," she said, coming to her feet.

"I think we should get together again."

"I had a feeling you might say that."

"Is coming here really that bad?" he asked.

"No, as long as there's an end in sight."

Will stood up. "I think we're getting close," he told her, walking her to the front door and then down the driveway. "I'll check my calendar and give you a call."

Morgan climbed into her car. Still hoping to keep her sessions with Will as confidential as possible, she said, "Call me on my cell phone. It's a lot easier than trying to get me through my office."

"No problem," he assured her, closing the car door.

Morgan weaved her way easily through the noontime traffic. She thought about nothing except what Will had told her about irrational grief reactions. From what little she knew of Mason Kaine, he fit the profile. But unsubstantiated theories and conjecture wouldn't be enough for the police, Dade Presbyterian Hospital, or the state of Florida. With the AHCA investigator's words of warning echoing in her mind, Morgan feared her time would run out before she could gather the information that would exonerate her with the board of medicine.

But what terrified her even more was that if she couldn't learn more about Mason Kaine—if she couldn't crawl into his warped mind—she wouldn't be able to stop him. Tangled within a confusing mesh of unanswered questions, there were two certainties. The first being that left to his own devices, Kaine would kill again, and the second being Dade Presbyterian hadn't seen the end of their Code 15 problem.

CHAPTER

62

Located in downtown Fort Lauderdale, the Broward Center for the Performing Arts was a modernistic architectural achievement that was kept solvent by its many philanthropic supporters.

As soon as the curtain came down on the first act, Morgan and Ben strolled out to the lobby.

"The entire cast is incredible," she told him above the buzz of the equally enthusiastic patrons congregated around the concession area. "How do you like it?"

"I'm enjoying it."

"Really? Because I thought I caught you nodding off during the *Chorus Line* number."

"No way," he insisted.

Before she could tease him any further, Morgan felt her pager vibrate. The unexpected page and what it might bring sent her upbeat mood into a tailspin.

With a pained frown, she checked the message. "It's the ER."

"I thought you were off."

"I'm never off," she moaned, clearing the message. "It must be important. I'd better call in. I'm going to go over by the window so I can hear better."

"Do you want anything?"

"Get me a big chocolate bar," came Morgan's immediate response.

Ben looked at her sideways. "Really?"

"Is there a problem?"

"No. I . . . I was just thinking about that huge chocolate soufflé you had for dessert. On the way out of the restaurant, the waiter told me he'd never seen anybody eat an entire one by themselves."

"Then he's obviously never waited on a pregnant woman. If you disapprove of my cravings, I'll be happy to get my own Snickers."

"That won't be necessary," he answered, lifting his hands in total surrender.

Morgan walked over to a thirty-foot floor-to-ceiling window that overlooked the theater's main entrance. She removed her cell phone from her purse and tapped in the number.

"Emergency room. This is Dr. Pierre."

"Hi, Amy. It's Morgan. What's up?"

"I'm sorry to bug you, but we just had a mock, unannounced disaster drill. We thought we might need you, but we got through it okay. Everybody did a great job."

"What was the scenario?"

"Fifty kids trapped in an overturned bus."

"That's pretty creative," Morgan said, after allowing a huge breath of relief to slowly escape her lungs. "How did you handle the triage?"

"We transferred most of them to the pediatric trauma center at Ryder. Anybody critical or over the age of fourteen we kept here."

"Sounds fine to me. Why don't we get everybody together for lunch tomorrow? We can go over the drill in detail."

"I'll organize it, but we'd rather hear about your date."

Morgan allowed herself a short laugh. "Is anything personal or sacred in that place?"

"Not if you want to go to the theater with south Florida's most eligible bachelor."

She smiled. "I appreciate your interest in my personal life, but you might mention to the gang that the only item on the agenda will be the disaster drill. I'll see you tomorrow."

As Morgan made her way back across the lobby, she caught sight of Ben talking to a slender woman who looked vaguely familiar. After a minute or so, he shook her hand and walked back over.

"Everything okay in the ER?" he asked, handing her the candy.

"It was nothing. Who were you talking to?" Morgan asked with no reluctance.

"Sheryl Grantham."

"The radiologist?"

"Uh-huh."

Squinting in her direction, Morgan said, "I didn't recognize her. I guess I've never seen her in anything except scrubs. She looks great," Morgan added with a sigh, taking a serious second look at the Snickers bar.

"Sheryl and her husband are good friends with the Allenbys. She told me that their son was in a serious accident."

"Mike? At UF?" she asked.

"Yeah."

"Oh my God. When?'

"A few days ago."

"Is he okay?"

"He's in intensive care at Shands," Ben said. "He's got bilateral femur fractures and a busted pelvis. Evidently, he lost quite a bit of blood."

"What happened?"

"He was out jogging and got hit by a car. Sheryl said the driver took off."

"A hit-and-run?"

"It sounds that way."

"Did they catch the guy?"

"Not yet."

Morgan's mind began reeling like a spinnaker. "For a small college town, you'd think that would be pretty unusual."

"I guess even small towns have their share of unconscionable people," Ben said. He paused for a few seconds. Morgan could feel him studying her. "You have that look again," he told her.

"What look?"

"C'mon, Morgan. You know exactly what I'm talking about. What are you thinking about?"

"The whole thing just strikes me as a little strange—that's all."

"You already said that."

"We've recently had two bizarre Code Fifteens involving heart patients. If my theory's right, the person responsible has some irrational gripe with the hospital, specifically the Cardiac Care Center. The Center was Bob Allenby's baby right from the get-go. He was the one who breathed life into it and he was the one who supervised every brick of its construction. I just think it's a little strange that all of a sudden his son's the victim of some bizarre accident."

With no change in his expression, Ben nodded a few times and then put his arm around Morgan's shoulder.

"Do you remember that little talk we had before the play started—the one where you made me promise not to torture you about hospital stuff?"

"I remember," she said.

"Good," he said, pointing toward the theater. "Let's go back to our seats. We can talk about this some other time."

Morgan's stony look quickly faded into a cautious grin. "Good suggestion," she said. Ben took Morgan's arm and they headed back to their seats. As soon as they were seated, the lights dimmed.

Lost in thought, Morgan barely noticed the curtain go up on the second act.

CHAPTER
63

Walking down West Lake path between the groves of white mangrove and butternut trees, Gideon stopped from time to time to raise his binoculars and study the endless species of woodland birds that habituated Everglades National Park.

Of all the diversions he had tried, he found walking through the park the most conducive for peaceful, uninterrupted thinking. It was one of the few times he found relief from the infernal ringing in his ears, which seemed to be worsening with each passing day.

While peering among the tree branches, his thoughts moved from a nesting snowy egret to Morgan Connolly. After a considerable amount of deliberation, he had finally arrived at a plan to deal with her. Having prepared for any contingency, Gideon considered his plan infallible. All that remained was selecting the day. But at the moment, he had a more pressing problem.

Gideon replaced his binoculars in their case. He noted the time. Next, he slipped his cell phone from his back pocket and tapped in the number to Dade Presbyterian. When the operator answered he asked to be connected to the Cardiac Care Center.

"CCC. This is Mary. How can I help you?"

"This is Mike from patient transportation. We're going to be a little shorthanded tomorrow, so we're trying to get our schedule set up now. Do you have any patients scheduled for an MRI?"

"I'm sure we do," Mary answered. "Did you already call radiology scheduling?"

"I tried," he began with a moan, "but they have to be the most uncooperative and disorganized department in the hospital."

"I know what you mean. I'll check for you."

"I just need the names of the patients and the time of their MRIs. I'll make sure we have somebody up there to pick them up on time."

"No problem. The first one I see is Edward Hastings. He's scheduled for eight a.m. Christopher Verdugo is going down at nine, and Jerome Hazelton has a head MRI scheduled at three."

"I got it," Gideon said. "Thanks a lot. We'll be there."

"Thanks," Mary told him. "We usually don't get this kind of Ritz-Carlton treatment from the transportation department."

"In that case, tomorrow's going to be a very special day."

With nightfall approaching, Gideon turned around and headed back down the rustic path. Against the setting of a declining crimson sun, a large flock of noisy wild parrots swooped across the sky. Gideon stopped to watch. It wasn't until the last one had disappeared that he again started walking toward the parking lot.

His mind was riveted on Dade Presbyterian Hospital and how they had slipped away from him unscathed—an unfortunate turn of events he would not allow to happen again. This time, the catastrophic Code 15 he would deal the cardiac program would be a fatal blow. Not even the most forgiving AHCA bureaucrat would be able to turn a blind eye to such an egregious medical error. They would have no other choice but to close down the center. The media would not stand idle. The humiliation to Dade Presbyterian would be immeasurable, shaking public's confidence to the core.

Gideon harbored no doubt that tomorrow's disaster would be the death bell for Dade Presbyterian's Cardiac Care Center—a death bell that he'd waited a long time to toll. The only thing left to assure total retribution for the death of his sons would be the end of Morgan Connolly.

CHAPTER

64

Dressed in neatly pressed surgical scrubs, Gideon stood in the middle of the controlled chaos that defined Dade Presbyterian Hospital's emergency room.

For the third time since he had arrived, he checked to make sure his identification badge was firmly clipped to his shirt pocket. The credential, which was an excellent forgery, identified him as Mark Bellman, a respiratory therapist assigned to the department of pulmonary medicine.

Casually making his way over to a small desk, which was usually used by the nursing students, he took a measured look around. He then picked up the phone and dialed the Cardiac Care Center's extension.

"CCC. Naomi speaking."

"This is Stan from MRI. We're ready for Mr. Hazelton? Is he on his way?"

"Transportation just picked him up."

"Thanks a lot."

Feeling more confident with each passing moment, Gideon replaced the receiver and then strolled over to the clean utility room. Standing outside of the small storage room stood six time-beaten metal oxygen tanks. Gideon chose the tank closest to him. He reached for the handle of its metal dolly and wheeled it toward the exit. As he expected, none of the harried and preoccupied ER personnel took any interest in a respiratory therapist picking up a spare tank of oxygen.

If his calculations were correct, Mr. Hazelton would be starting his MRI in about ten minutes. Cautious to stay on schedule, Gideon walked straight past the MRI department. Continuing down the hall toward the main lobby, he stopped when he reached the On-Call Café.

The small bistro, located directly adjacent to the main lobby, specialized in salads and wraps. Since its opening it had been the preferred gathering place for many of the high school students who volunteered at Dade Presbyterian to accumulate community service hours.

Gideon's original plan was to go inside the café, but when he saw a gaggle of girls coming toward him, he changed his mind. All giggling and talking at the same time, they were dressed in the hospital's standard red pinstripe uniform. The young lady closest to him was taller and more spindly than the others. Taking note of her glowing complexion, Gideon motioned to her until he caught her eye. She pointed to herself and he acknowledged with a nod. He then gestured at her to come over.

Her nametag identified her as Amanda.

"Amanda," he began, purposely not introducing himself. "I wonder if you could do me a huge favor."

She looked back at her inquisitive friends, who were waiting for her. She motioned to them to go ahead without her.

"I guess so," she said with a coy smile.

"That's great. Do you know where the MRI department is?"

"Sure," she said, pointing past him. "It's just down the hall from the emergency room."

"You got it," he said, noticing that she hadn't once looked at his ID badge. "MRI just called me. They need an extra tank of oxygen. I was on my way over there but the operating room just paged me stat. That means they need me up there right away. Do you think you could wheel this tank over to MRI and deliver it for me?"

She looked at the dark green cylinder. From the look on her face and the way her friends kept eyeing her from inside the café, Gideon knew he had succeeded in making Amanda feel important.

"What should I do when I get there?" she asked.

"Just go straight into the MRI suite and leave the tank with the technicians. I'll call over there right now and tell them to expect you."

"Okay," she said with the same bashful smile, taking the handle of the oxygen tank.

"Thanks again."

Gideon was tempted to follow her to make sure everything proceeded just the way he had planned. But after a few moments, he decided it would be too risky. He watched Amanda make her way down the corridor toward the MRI department. The moment she disappeared, he marched off in the opposite direction.

CHAPTER

65

It took Amanda only a minute or two to reach the MRI department.

At the same time she was staring at the main door, Mel Kelalis, the chief technician, sat in the control room monitoring the images of Mr. Hazelton's brain. He looked up for a moment. Through a large window that separated the control room from the MRI machine he saw the door slowly opening. He assumed it was the other technician returning from her break with the diet soda she had promised to bring him. But when he saw Amanda's uniform, he stopped what he was doing and wondered why a volunteer would be coming into the MRI suite.

Keeping an eye on her, he noticed that her right arm was extended behind her. He was just about to get up, when he saw the perplexed-looking girl looking around the suite. Before he could say anything, she took a couple of cautious steps forward. With the door no longer blocking his vision, he saw the handle of the portable oxygen tank.

Wide-eyed from the panic clutching at his throat, he pounded on the window. Amanda immediately looked in his direction. Still hammering on the window with the palm of his hand, he jumped up, waved his arms, and shrieked, "Stop. Don't move."

Racing out from behind the control panel, he could see the fear and confusion sweep across her face. When she took another couple of steps forward he knew she hadn't heard him and that there was nothing he could do to prevent the cataclysmic disaster that she had already set in motion.

CHAPTER

66

Lying sedated in the MRI tube listening to piped-in music, Jerome Hazelton, a sixty-year-old accountant who had developed weakness in his right side while recovering uneventfully from coronary bypass surgery, had no clue that he would be spending the rest of the day fighting for his life.

As if it was nothing more than a cheap paperweight, the enormously powerful magnetic field created by the MRI snatched the oxygen tank from its carrier and sent it hurtling across the room. The metallic cylinder, now acting as a high-speed projectile, cut a path directly for the MRI tunnel. Although the tank was a blur, Mel could see it spinning through the air.

A millisecond later, the tank slammed into the outside of the MRI tube, where it remained stuck for a split second before being violently sucked into the tube. The horrible sound of the tank careening off the walls of the MRI resonated around the room like a gunshot in a box canyon.

Mel bolted back to the control console. He tapped the touch-screen command that moved the table holding Mister Hazelton out of the tube. He then grabbed a towel from the shelf above him and raced to the end of the MRI tube. Without consciously knowing why, he took a short step backward at the sight of the gaping wound the tank had sliced into Hazelton's head. Three jagged bone fragments protruded upward.

Together, they framed out a fountain of gushing blood that spewed into the air before raining down on the pillowcase and leaving an amorphous red blot around Hazelton's head.

Mel moved forward and pressed the towel hard against the wound.

"Can you hear me, Mr. Hazelton?"

There was no response. Not even a groan. Mel looked down to see if he was still breathing. His chest was definitely moving but its motion was shallow and sporadic. Trying desperately to stem the uncontrolled hemorrhage, he pressed the blood-soaked towel even harder against his skull.

Mel knew it was technically impossible to shut down the MRI's magnet. He also knew that if he called a code blue, personnel from all over the hospital would come running. There would be instant pandemonium and, no doubt, somebody would forget about the metal object precautions. The result would undoubtedly result in a second catastrophe. He looked over at Amanda, whose terrified eyes were locked on him.

Pointing to a phone on the wall, he spoke to her in a calm and clear voice. "Pick up the phone and dial three-four-oh-three. Tell the nurse who answers that Mel in MRI said we have an emergency and that they should call a code purple." When Amanda didn't move, Mel repeated. "Go ahead. The phone's right behind you on the wall. You can do it."

Amanda nodded, walked the few paces to the phone and picked it up.

"Now dial three-four-oh-three," he said, stealing another peek at Hazelton's face. "Go on."

She tapped in the numbers. "This is one of the volunteers," she began, looking back at him. "I'm in the MRI suite and Mel wants me to tell you to . . . to—"

"To call a code purple," he repeated slowly.

"He said to call a code purple." She listened for a moment and then hung up the phone. "They're coming."

"Good," he said, pointing to the control room. "Now I want you to go over to the control room over there and sit down."

Amanda started across the room. She hadn't been seated for more than a few seconds when the door flew open. Cara McCoy, the ER charge nurse, accompanied by two orderlies pushing a stretcher, raced in.

"Does anybody have any metal objects on them?" Mel yelled. They all shook their heads at the same time.

"What happened?" Cara asked, running over to the MRI.

"The patient was struck in the head by an oxygen tank," Mel answered. "He's bleeding like hell and he's barely breathing."

Cara slowly removed the towel to check the wound. "My God," she whispered. "Let's get him over to the ER."

The four of them worked together to slide Hazelton out of the tube and onto the stretcher. As soon as he was secured into place and an oxygen mask placed over his mouth and nose, the two orderlies and Cara raced him out of the room.

For the next minute or two, Mel could do nothing more than simply look around in disbelief. He then remembered that Amanda was still in the control room. He looked at her through the window, invented a smile, and walked across the room.

"Why don't you go back to the volunteer office? You did great, but I think you've had enough excitement for one day."

Amanda didn't say a word. She simply nodded and then slowly crossed the room and slipped out. Mel assumed she didn't have the first clue what had happened, but he was sure there would be several representatives from Dade Presbyterian's administrative and medical staff who would want to talk to her anyway.

After cleaning up the suite, Mel decided to go over to the emergency room to check on Mr. Hazelton's condition. He spotted Cara, who was charting at the core desk, and walked over.

"How's he doing?" he asked.

"Neurosurgery's in there now. They should be taking him up to the OR pretty soon."

"What are his chances?"

She shook her head slowly. "I don't know, but they can't be very good."

Mel massaged his temples for a few seconds. "I've read about these types of magnetic field disasters, but I never thought . . . I mean, you never think it will happen to you. This is the worst medical error I've ever seen."

Swapping an ominous look, Cara and Mel watched as Hazelton was whisked out of the trauma bay and taken to the back elevators on his way to the operating room.

CHAPTER
67

In recent years, the upscale area surrounding Fort Lauderdale's Las Olas Boulevard had developed into a preferred tourist destination.

Consisting of a wide array of eclectic boutiques, galleries, and multicultural restaurants, Morgan had always found the area intriguing but hardly a bargain hunter's paradise. When she spotted a vacant parking space she pulled in immediately. Grinning to herself, she wondered if the unexpected stroke of good luck marked the end of the worst run of misfortune she could remember.

Still smiling, she stepped out of her car and poured two dollars' worth of quarters into the meter. Satisfied that would give her enough time for her appointment, she walked east at a leisurely pace toward the *Sun-Sentinel* building, the home of Fort Lauderdale's largest daily newspaper.

When she was about a block away, her cell phone rang. She checked the caller ID and flipped the phone open.

"Hi, Ben."

"Are we still going flying this afternoon?"

"Absolutely."

"Have you heard anything more about Bob Allenby's son?" he asked.

"I spoke with Eileen Hale this morning. She told me he's doing a little better, but he's still in the ICU."

"That's something. Have you spoken to Bob?"

"We got a memo from the hospital board requesting we don't try to contact him as yet. I heard he's not doing too well."

"I'm sorry to hear that. Did Eileen know anything more about the details of the accident?"

"Only that it was definitely a hit-and-run," Morgan said.

"Hopefully, they'll catch the guy."

"Have you heard anything from that private investigator you contacted?" Morgan asked.

"Actually, she called me this morning. I forgot to mention it to you. She said Kaine's acting like somebody who's trying to disappear. All the easy things she routinely does to find people haven't worked. She said she needs more time."

"Okay. I'll see you at three out at the field."

Morgan entered the *Sun-Sentinel* building through a pair of glass doors that opened onto an octagonal-shaped lobby. Across the highly polished, inlaid marble floor stood the information desk.

"I'm here to see Jonathan Owens," she told the security guard. The elderly gentleman, who had been one-eyeing it until he realized she was standing in front of him, reluctantly reached for a clipboard.

"Do you have an appointment?" he asked in a crusty voice.

"Yes, I called earlier today."

"Name?"

"Morgan Connolly."

He picked up the phone but stopped and held it in midair. "Who'd you say you were here to see again?"

She smiled inwardly. "Jonathan Owens."

"Oh yeah," he said, tapping in the extension. "There's a Miss Connolly to see you," he said. "I'll tell her." He replaced the receiver. "Mr. Owens will be right down."

"Thank you."

Morgan moved to the side of the information desk, but

after a minute or so she walked over to the crowded café and peered inside. Out of impatience more than anything else, she began reading the huge menu displayed on the chalkboard behind the counter.

"Their food's pretty good," came a voice from behind her.

Morgan turned around, smiled, and shook Jonathan's hand. "Thanks for seeing me on such short notice," she told him.

"What's going on? You sounded on the phone like the wheels were coming off."

"It's not that bad."

"Do you want to go up to my office, or would you rather take a walk?"

"Let's walk."

Jamaican by birth, Jonathan was a confident and astute journalist who had the type of magnetism, good looks, and undying optimism that most politicians would trade their souls for. If asked, after a Johnnie Walker Black or two, he would claim to be one of the few reporters in south Florida who still believed in his profession.

Morgan had first met him five years earlier when he wrote a three-part story on Dade Presbyterian's emergency room. He quoted her several times in the piece. They also had served together on a charity board to raise money for Dade Presbyterian's new children's hospital that was scheduled to break ground in the coming months.

"Do you want to get some lunch?" he asked.

"I'm okay, but I'll sit with you."

He tapped on his abdomen a few times. "Actually, I'm trying to lose a few pounds. I've been skipping lunch lately."

They exited the building, walked past the lavish Riverside apartments, and then along a redbrick walkway that hugged the east bank of the New River. A procession of yachts moored to the massive concrete retaining wall rested quietly. Rising from beyond the other side of the river loomed the Broward County Jail, with its sandy brown exterior and pinpoint steel windows.

"What's going on?" Jonathan asked after they had spent a few minutes catching up.

"I want to talk to you about something, but it has to be off the record."

He chuckled. "Why does everybody tell me that?"

"Because you're a reporter."

"Okay, we're off the record—for now. Tell me what's on your mind."

"How well did you know Tony Wallace?"

"He was a colleague and a casual friend. We worked on a couple of stories together. What's your interest in Tony?"

"We still don't completely understand the exact circumstances of his death. I was the chairperson of the Patient Safety Committee and headed up the investigation."

Jonathan pulled out a cigarette and popped it between his lips. "I flunked out of premed, Morgan. Shouldn't you be talking to the medical examiner?"

"I'm talking to the right guy. Over the past couple of months, we've had an unusual number of serious patient errors. We've also had three mysterious Code Fifteens, all of which were catastrophic and medically inexplicable."

With a cautious tone, he said, "Define medically inexplicable."

"The point is I have looked at all three of these cases in minute detail . . ."

"And?"

"I have strong reasons to believe these Code Fifteens did not simply occur by chance."

Jonathan took a long drag, exhaled all of it, and without blinking an eye said, "I'm listening."

They continued along the path and then under the Third Street bridge. Morgan filled Jonathan in on the details of Tony Wallace's death, her predicament with the board of medicine and the other Code 15s. She was more than relieved he listened without any outward signs of skepticism.

"What's the administration's take on all this?" he asked.

"They think I'm a stressed-out physician with an overactive imagination, and that I'm looking for a quick way to explain away my incompetence."

They stopped in front of a small outdoor café that overlooked a park filled with soccer moms and strollers.

"I could use a cappuccino," Jonathan said, pointing the way. "How about you?"

"Sure."

"Grab a table. I'll be right back."

While she waited, Morgan watched a water taxi filled with camera-clicking tourists motor by. Jonathan returned carrying two cappuccinos and sat down.

"I'm still not sure how I can help," he said.

"I need to know more about Tony Wallace."

"Morgan, you're a doctor, not a cop. The best advice I can give you is to go back to the police and talk to them again."

"They're not going to help me."

"You have no way of knowing that for sure."

"Listen to me, Jonathan. My career and possibly my life are on the line here. Besides being stalked by a madman, I have AHCA and the board of medicine breathing down my neck. And, just to make things worse, my hospital's a hair away from suspending me. I can't waste what little time I have left trying to get the police to believe me."

"How do you know that Tony's death wasn't a legitimate medical mistake? Maybe he was just in the wrong place at the wrong time and this guy, Kaine, had nothing to do with any of this."

"At the moment, all I can tell you is that I have a strong suspicion that this wasn't some odd medical mishap."

"Do you have any proof at all that there's a connection between Tony Wallace and Kaine?"

"Not yet, but that's precisely what I'm trying to find out." Morgan waited while he slid another cigarette out of the pack and lit it. "What can you tell me about Tony?"

"He was a little rough around the edges and not the most sociable person I've ever worked with."

"Was he an ethical reporter?" she asked.

"Some people might call that an oxymoron," Jonathan said with a chuckle. "He may have moved the line from time to time, but I don't think he ever stepped across it."

"Did he have any kids?"

"That's kind of a strange question."

"I have my reasons for asking."

"He got divorced a few years ago. It got pretty ugly. The only saving grace was that they didn't have any kids."

"Would you say he was a good reporter?" she asked.

"I'd say he was an excellent reporter. He was a perfectionist when it came to research and accuracy."

"How aggressive was he?"

"I'm not sure I understand your question."

"Could he have antagonized the wrong person?" Morgan asked.

"Of course; he was a reporter. Tony wasn't one to be easily intimidated, if that's what you're asking. He wouldn't let go until he got to the truth. Reporters are usually pretty good at ferreting out the facts. We also know how to avoid pissing people off—doing both at the same time is the tricky part."

"Did you know anybody who might have wanted to . . . to—"

"To hurt him?" Morgan responded with a nod. Jonathan continued, "Not off the top of my head." He then paused for a few seconds. "Listen, Morgan. If I wanted to learn as much as I could about a reporter, I'd start by reading everything he or she had ever written."

Wondering why the same thing hadn't occurred to her, Morgan asked, "Is there some way I can get my hands on the articles he's written?"

"We have them all on file. I'll have one of the interns print them out and have them messengered over to you."

"Thanks."

"It's not that simple," he said, wagging his finger in her direction. "If this thing goes anywhere . . ."

"I know. You get the story."

"Exclusively," he clarified.

"Agreed."

They finished their cappuccinos and Jonathan walked Morgan back to her car. He waited as Morgan slid in behind the wheel.

"Keep me posted," he said.

"I'll call you as soon as I've read the articles."

"You should have them tomorrow."

Morgan had barely pulled out of her parking space when her phone rang. The number was unfamiliar to her.

"Hello."

"This is Emily at Chemalert Labs. Is this Dr. Connolly?"

"Yes."

"I have a note on the sample you left that you wanted to be called with the results. The sample contains a very high concentration of a benzodiazepine."

"Which one?" she asked the youthful-sounding woman.

"Versed."

Being one of the more commonly used preoperative medications, Morgan was quite familiar with the powerful sedative.

"I left a fax number on the request form. Would you please send me a copy of the report?"

"I'll send it this afternoon."

Her suspicions regarding her flight confirmed, Morgan felt lucky to be alive. There was no doubt in her mind that her coffee had been drugged by Mason Kaine. Her first impulse was to call Detective Wolfe. But as she reached for her phone, she was filled with second thoughts regarding the wisdom of her decision. Even if she showed him the report, what was to prevent him from assuming she had done it herself to prove to the authorities that she was correct regarding the Code 15s? With the stark realization that she'd have to find another way, Morgan never finished entering Wolfe's phone number.

CHAPTER

68

From her terrace, Morgan gazed out at the Atlantic.

It was usually a spectacular view, but today it was made dreary by an endless gray mist that lay static over the water. Sitting at a small rattan table, she leafed through the stack of articles that Jonathan had sent over. Owing to his prodigious nature and a career that had spanned almost thirty years, Tony Wallace had written an impressive number of articles.

Jonathan had also sent a biographical sketch of Wallace that the *Sun-Sentinel*'s public relations department had prepared. The brief bio mentioned that after graduating from Washington University with a degree in journalism, he had spent five years working as a reporter at the Jefferson City *News Tribune*. He then moved to California, but after two brief stints at small-town newspapers, he took a position with the Fort Lauderdale *Sun-Sentinel*. The bio was informative and fairly detailed, especially with respect to Tony's involvement in numerous community service projects.

Morgan picked up the pile of health-care articles and slipped off the oversized rubber band. Scanning the titles, she noted the first several stories addressed generic topics in health care. Non-contentious in nature, Morgan couldn't believe that any of them could offend anybody. Toward the end of the packet, she came upon two articles about Dade Presbyterian's Cardiac Care Center.

More than just slightly intrigued, she slipped them out of the stack, stood up, and walked over to the railing. She read the first article. Wallace had written it just after Dade Presbyterian officially announced it would be going ahead with its plans to build the most prestigious cardiac program in the southeastern United States. He was extremely complimentary of the hospital's leadership, praising their grit in making tough choices in a complex health-care environment. He even supported the board's decision to allow several other worthy programs to go unfunded so the Cardiac Care Center could be built.

Wallace had written the second article a month or so after the Cardiac Care Center's ribbon-cutting ceremony. It was more of the same, again extolling Dade Presbyterian for their perseverance and commitment to the community's health-care needs. Finding the articles repetitious, Morgan was barely paying attention when she began reading the last paragraph. But as she read on, her interest was suddenly piqued. When she finished it, she could hardly believe what she had just discovered.

She closed her eyes. The mysterious haze that shrouded how and why Mason Kaine had selected Tony Wallace to die was finally lifted. The strange irony was that Wallace himself had sealed his own fate by telling Kaine, along with two million other readers of the *Sun-Sentinel*'s Sunday edition, that during the second week of May he would be undergoing coronary artery bypass surgery at Dade Presbyterian Hospital's Cardiac Care Center.

CHAPTER

69

Morgan stood up and walked over to the railing.

When she noticed the temperature dropping and the wind picking up, she looked overhead. The sky had darkened. Morgan hoped it would be one of the last storms of the summer rainy season.

She walked back to the table, gathered up Tony's articles, and went back inside her apartment. Sitting at the kitchen table, she was, for the first time, starting to get an inkling of insight into Mason's Kaine's twisted mind.

Her cell phone rang. It was the security officer calling from the lobby.

"Dr. Docherty's here to see you."

"Send him up," she said.

Morgan checked the time. It was almost six. She stood up and headed for the foyer to let Ben in. When she opened the door, he was holding a white bakery box. The inviting aroma of its contents filled the entranceway. He handed her the box. She wasted no time in flipping open the top.

"Chocolate croissants? I thought we were going to an early dinner."

"We can eat later." He pointed to the box, still smiling like a proud child. "It wasn't easy finding those."

"How did you know that—?"

"You once told me you lived on them when you traveled through France."

Morgan closed her eyes and breathed in the aroma of the croissants. Ben could sense her ability to resist was toppling. After gently rocking her head from side to side, Morgan finally reached in, snatched one of the croissants, and took a small bite. The sheer delight on her face forced Ben to smile.

"C'mon into the kitchen," she told him. "Did you hear about the hospital's latest disaster?"

He shook his head. "I'm a little removed from the daily goings-on of Dade Presbyterian."

"A man recovering from a mitral valve replacement was having some memory problems so he was scheduled for a brain MRI. During the test, one of the candy stripers walked into the suite wheeling an oxygen tank."

"You're kidding."

"The guy died in surgery a couple of hours later of a massive head injury. The administration already reported it as a Code Fifteen. I told you this would happen."

"Maybe you should wait for the facts before assuming the worst."

"You're right. It's probably just another bizarre coincidence. But since I'm no longer the chairperson of the Patient Safety Committee, I guess figuring out what happened will be somebody's else's headache."

"Something tells me you'll find a way to get involved." Ben took a few steps closer and pointed to the folder. "What are you reading?"

"The articles written by Tony Wallace. I just finished going through them."

"And?"

"He wrote a couple of dozen stories about health care, but two were specifically about the Cardiac Care Center. He wrote the first one when it was still in the planning stages and the other right after it opened. He was extremely supportive of the project."

"As I recall, so were a lot of people."

"But not all of them were reporters with millions of readers. What do you want to drink?"

"Milk," he responded taking a seat at the table.

"Are you serious?"

"Don't I look serious? What's wrong with milk?"

"Nothing, assuming you're under the age of one or a baby cow. Read the last paragraph of the article on top." Morgan poured him a glass of milk while he read it. She said, "Now I know how Kaine knew when and why Tony Wallace would be in the hospital."

"You and a million other readers. That still doesn't give you a motive."

"The board was very concerned about the public's perception of the project. Right after the opening, Bob told me that they never would have approved the project unless they were sure public sentiment was behind it. Tony Wallace's articles may not have been the main factor that got the center approved, but I bet they sure helped."

"But as you said before. Bob was the one responsible for building the center. It seems more logical to me that Kaine would have gone after him."

"I think he did."

"By trying to kill his son."

"It's the only thing that makes sense," she insisted.

"Did Tony Wallace have any kids?"

"No," she answered. "It all kind of fits together nicely."

"I don't mean to burst your bubble, but you're still missing one small detail," Ben pointed out. "Kaine lost his sons to meningitis. He had no gripe with the Cardiac Care Center, so what's the connection?"

"I don't know yet," Morgan confessed, "But we're obviously dealing with somebody whose behavior to date has been somewhere between irrational and insane. Whatever happened that got him so enraged may make no sense to us."

"What do you do from here?" Ben asked.

"I'm going to go back and look at the Alison Greene case again."

"Alison Greene? Is she the one who died from the pacemaker problem?"

"Yeah."

"You never mentioned her full name before."

"So?"

"How old was she?" Ben asked.

"Twenty-seven."

"Did she go by Ali?"

"I think so. Why do you ask?"

"Do you know if she worked for one of the big department stores?"

Morgan stopped unloading her dishwasher and turned around.

"She was a buyer for Saks. How did you know that?"

"Because I met her once. I know her father pretty well. His name's Cam Greene. He's the CEO of SHS."

"What's SHS?"

"Strategic Healthcare Solutions. They're a large consulting firm. I retained them when I sold my business. Bob Allenby recommended them to me. The hospital has used them on several projects."

"Do you remember which ones?" Morgan asked.

A curious look covered Ben's face. "The most recent one was the physician compensation for emergency room coverage, but they were also involved in the feasibility study involving the Cardiac Care Center."

"How did you meet Alison Greene?"

"She was interested in learning to fly so her father had her call me. She came out to the school and took an introductory lesson. She got horribly airsick. I never heard from her again."

"What were her father's recommendations regarding the Cardiac Care Center?"

"His firm came out strongly in favor of it. They thought it would be a financial windfall for Dade Presby. The hospital used SHS's report to bolster both community and political support for the project."

Morgan's mind instantly shifted to her father and his long career at the hospital. He had always been very active politically. Not only had he served on numerous committees but he had risen through the medical staff leadership and was elected to the prestigious position of chief of staff, a position he held for two four-year terms.

Morgan now wondered if Kaine had two entirely different reasons for wanting her father dead.

"When Dade Presbyterian first proposed the construction of the CCC, my father was chief of staff. He was very much in favor of the project and came out for it publicly. I remember him being interviewed by both Channel Four and the *Miami Herald*. He told the reporters he would knock on every door of the twelve hundred physicians on staff to encourage them to support the new Cardiac Care Center. I also remember the hospital board making it clear that they would not proceed with the project without the support of the physicians."

"Of course that's what they said. The building of a state-of-the-art cardiac center was a no-brainer. As I recall, everybody supported the plan."

"But those people aren't in the public eye. My father, Bob Allenby, and Tony Wallace are notable exceptions. You have to agree it's also a little coincidental that both Bob Allenby and Cam Greene came out in the media in favor of the construction, and now, one of their kids is dead and the other one's lying in an intensive care unit."

Morgan walked over to a large central island. She leaned her back against it and slowly shook her head. Ben watched her carefully. The stress and frustration in her face was obvious. Rather than going any further with the conversation, he decided to change directions.

"I think we've talked enough hospital politics for a while. Why don't we go in the living room and watch an old movie or . . . or . . . something?"

"Something?"

"I thought maybe we could have a . . . a relationship talk," Ben told her as casually as he could.

"A relationship talk?" she said with an unavoidable grin.

"That's right. I thought it might make a nice change to talk about us instead of everybody else in south Florida."

She looked at him in silence for a few seconds. She then walked over to where he was standing, put her arms around his neck, and kissed him.

"Some things are obvious, Ben," she whispered. "They don't need to be discussed."

As she expected he would, he cleared his throat. "In that case, we can hold off on the relationship talk and just watch the movie."

Morgan pointed toward the living room. Ben nodded and followed her in.

CHAPTER

70

After an uneventful shift, Morgan arrived home at nine p.m.

Ben was teaching an instrument-rating class and for the first time in a couple of weeks, she ate dinner alone. When she was finished, she took her coffee out on the balcony. It turned out to be one of the nicest evenings in weeks and Morgan decided to take Limerick for a walk.

She had been out for about a half hour when she checked her watch. It was after ten. Morgan gave the preoccupied setter's leash a couple of quick, gentle tugs, hoping to coax him back toward her building. The distinctive aroma of ozone still clung to the air from an unexpected downpour that struck the Hollywood area just after nightfall.

As hard as she tried, she couldn't stop thinking about Mason Kaine. She had been over the Code 15s more times than she could count and she still had no clue what linked them to the deaths of Andrew and Jason Kaine and to the Cardiac Care Center. Finally, in a sea of frustration, she forced the problem from her mind.

Limerick ambled along, sniffing every patch of trampled grass with great interest. Morgan knew his routine and assumed he had figured out that if he moved at a glacial pace, his walk would last longer. Strolling past a chain-link fence that framed out the construction site of a new apartment building, Morgan glanced overhead at a starless sky. When they were halfway down the street, Limerick's head suddenly popped up. With a stiffened neck, he made a half turn and looked past Morgan. Expecting to see a fellow dog walker approaching, Morgan glanced back down the sidewalk. Unfortunately, the newly installed streetlights were more ornamental than practical, making it difficult for her to see anything coming toward her.

"C'mon, boy," she told him. "We're almost home."

It was when Limerick failed to respond to a few tugs on his leash that Morgan realized his eyes were trained on the opposite side of the street. His feathered tail was tucked up and under his hind legs and he growled softly. Feeling the first twinge of apprehension, Morgan looked across the street.

About a hundred feet away, standing on the opposite sidewalk, she could make out the silhouette of a man staring directly at her. She couldn't make out his facial features, but she could see he was wearing a bomber jacket and that his hands were shoved into the pockets. Her immediate fear was that the ape who had threatened her outside of the dry cleaners was following her. But after taking a hard look at his average physique, she dismissed the notion.

Morgan was just about to start back down the street when the man casually pulled his hands from his pockets and started down the sidewalk. Every cell of her body swelled with fear. Limerick stood his ground, but Morgan yanked on his leash and led him down the block. She was still a good five-minute walk to her building. She cursed herself for forgetting the pepper spray launcher she usually took with her on Limerick's evening walks.

Picking up the pace and listening intently for approaching footsteps, Morgan passed one small duplex after another. She heard nothing. Wrapping her hand around Limerick's leash, she prayed she would see another walker. But the small street remained empty. She was now only three blocks from her building, but they were long ones, and the knot of anxiety gripping the top of her stomach continued to tighten.

Finally, she saw the headlights of a car. She heaved a breath of relief, but as the two-seater rolled up to the stop sign, the driver signaled and turned. Just as the car disappeared down the small side street, Morgan heard the man's footsteps. Flushed with panic, she knew he was only a few steps away. Out of the corner of her eye, she caught sight of him diagonally crossing the street. Limerick stopped, but he didn't bark. The man, who had his cell phone pressed against his ear, smiled, tossed a polite wave at Morgan, but never broke stride.

Feeling more foolish than relieved, Morgan waved and then watched as the man continued toward the beach. Knowing she was safe worked wonders to slow her rapid breathing. She took the last two blocks at a slower pace. Happy to see her building and Hank Dire, the security guard, standing out front, she started up the circular entranceway.

It was just at that moment, when Hank smiled at her, that she felt the first jolt of piercing pain in her lower abdomen. Unable to take another step, Morgan bent forward and crossed her arms across her belly, trying to contain the agonizing spasm. A few seconds passed and the pain began to subside. She opened her eyes. Spotting a wrought-iron bench a few feet away, she took a few shallow breaths and made her way over to it and sat down.

Still doubled over at the waist, Morgan began counting backward from fifty, hoping for the pain to completely stop. Before she was halfway to zero, she felt a warm, wet sensation along her inner thighs, realizing the worst and most dreaded fear of any pregnant woman. She now shared that terror and anguish she had seen so many times in the pregnant women she had cared for in the emergency room. She tried pulling her knees close to her chest, but the pain began mounting again. She reached into her pocket, pulled out her cell phone, and tapped in Ben's number. He answered on the second ring.

"Ben, I need you to come get me. I'm outside of my building."

"Are you okay?"

"I'm having severe cramps and bleeding. I think I should go to the hospital."

"I'll be there in fifteen minutes. I'll call Jenny to meet us in the ER."

"Thanks," she said softly.

She then waved at Hank, summoning him for assistance. He came over immediately.

"Are you okay, Doc?" he asked.

"Actually, I'm not feeling too well. Dr. Docherty's on his way over to take me to the emergency room. Do you think you could take care of Limerick?"

Hank took the leash from Morgan but didn't move from her side. "Of course," he promised. "And if you're not back by the time my shift's over, I'll take him out again."

Morgan knew that if anybody loved dogs as much as she did, it was Hank.

"Thanks," she told him.

Between the spasmodic waves of pain, she glanced toward the building's circular entrance. She knew she was still bleeding. Frightened and unable to convince herself that everything would be okay, she spread her hands across her lower abdomen and gently pushed down.

Another few minutes passed. Finally, she saw Ben's car approaching.

Hank carefully helped her to her feet.

"Don't you worry about Limerick, Dr. Connolly. I'll take good care of him until you get home."

She managed a faint smile. "I know you will, Hank."

Ben pulled up and jumped out of the car. With Hank's help, he assisted Morgan into the front seat.

"How are you doing?" he asked.

"About the same. Were you able to reach Jenny?"

"She said she'd meet us in the emergency room."

Her eyes already starting to swell with tears, Morgan struggling to get each word out, she said, "I . . . I can't lose this baby, Ben. With everything that's going on, I don't think I'd be able to get through it."

"You're not going to lose the baby," he assured her, putting his hand on her shoulder. "Let's get to the hospital. We can talk on the way."

Hank waited until Ben had pulled away before walking Limerick back toward the building's entrance. Preoccupied with the setter, he never noticed the man across the street step out of his car.

Clutching a key in his hand, Kevin stared at the building. Feeling more desperate than he could ever remember, he prayed Morgan hadn't changed the lock.

chapter 71

It took Kevin three cigarettes to gather the courage to cross the street.

By the time he reached the front entrance, Hank had gone back inside and taken up his customary position behind the granite-topped information desk. Limerick, at home in his new surroundings, curled up at Hank's feet and went to sleep.

Displaying the biggest smile he could manufacture, Kevin strolled across the lobby.

"How's it going?" he asked Hank without slowing his pace.

"Can I help you?" he asked Kevin as if he'd never seen him before. Hank's military background had a predictable way of sneaking out when he was confronted with a potentially contentious situation.

Kevin stopped. "I was just heading upstairs," he said with a light shrug.

"Is Dr. Connolly expecting you?"

He chuckled and crossed his arms. "It's my apartment too, Hank. Just because we're separated doesn't mean I can't use the place."

"Go ahead," he said, pointing to the elevator.

"You're a good guy, Hank, but you might want to think about losing the attitude." When he reached the elevator, he cast a glance back at Hank before inserting his coded card. He waited for the red light to turn green and the doors to open, but it didn't happen. Having a pretty good idea why, he reinserted the card anyway. The result was the same. He slipped the card back into his pocket and walked back to the information desk.

"My key doesn't seem to work."

"The system's fine. It was just checked yesterday. I guess somebody changed the code."

"In that case, would you mind calling my wife and telling her I'm here?"

"I'm sorry. I have a written directive from Dr. Connolly not to do that."

Red-faced, Kevin took a few steps forward and raised his finger. Hank responded by standing up. With a frosty stare, he crossed his arms.

"Asshole," Kevin said, taking a step backward before starting for the exit.

"Yes, sir," Hank responded.

Hank waited a few seconds before coming out from behind the desk and walking over to the front door. Looking across the circular entranceway, he watched Kevin climb into his car and screech away from the curb. If he didn't know better, he would have guessed he was fleeing an armed robbery.

Hank had never liked Kevin, and the opportunity to watch him become unglued brought a self-satisfied smile to his face.

CHAPTER 72

Are you still having cramps?" Leslie Cardenas, one of the obstetrical nurses, asked Morgan as she helped her out of the wheelchair and then up on to the examination table.

"The last one was about five minutes ago, but it wasn't as bad as the first. I think they may be going away."

She slipped a blood pressure cuff on Morgan's arm. "What about the bleeding?"

"I think it's almost stopped. Have you heard from Dr. Silverman?"

"I'm right here," Jenny said, walking through the door pushing a portable ultrasound machine in front of her. Leaving the machine at the foot of the bed, Jenny walked over and gave Morgan's hand a quick squeeze. She then began her abdominal examination. "How are you feeling?"

"A little scared. I've seen a lot of women lose their babies this way."

"Try to relax. Tell me what happened."

"The whole thing was so stupid," Morgan said with a note of embarrassment. "I was walking my dog. I had just started heading home when I saw a man on the other side of the street. I thought . . . I thought he was following me and I . . . I guess I panicked."

"That would terrify any woman. What happened after you saw him?" Jenny asked.

"Nothing. It turned out to be nothing. When I got home a few minutes later, the cramps and bleeding started."

Ben coughed a couple of times and then in a quiet voice said, "I'll . . . I'll just wait outside."

"Why don't you go home?" Morgan suggested. "I'll be fine. I'll call you later."

"If Jenny says it's okay for you to go home, how were you planning on getting there?" he asked.

"I'll . . . I'll call a cab."

Ben nodded once. "Like I said, I'll be right outside."

Jenny waited for the door to close and then pulled ultrasound machine closer. "You really didn't think he was going to leave. He looks more worried than you."

"He's been a good friend."

"Blood pressure and pulse are fine," Leslie announced.

"Great," Jenny said, helping Morgan slide her shirt up. She then applied a generous amount of ultrasound jelly across Morgan's lower abdomen. "Start an IV of normal saline and send off some blood for a CBC and a type and screen."

"Type and screen? Do you really think I'll need a blood transfusion?" Morgan asked.

"I just want to be on the safe side," Jenny assured her.

Jenny lightly placed the ultrasound probe on Morgan's abdomen. Morgan averted her eyes from the monitor, concentrating instead on slowing her breathing and trying not to allow her terror of losing the baby get the better of her. She watched Jenny carefully, studying each expression on her face as she changed the angle and orientation of the probe.

After the fifteen-minute examination was over, Jenny looked up with a comforting smile and said, "The baby looks fine."

Overcome with relief and fighting back the urge to cry, Morgan thanked her. When Jenny had completed the rest of her examination and checked all of Morgan's blood tests, she pulled up a chair and sat down next to her.

"All of your lab tests look fine and the bleeding has stopped. How are the cramps?"

"Completely gone."

"Good."

"I'm sorry I dragged you in here," she told Jenny. "You've been great."

"If you really want to thank me, you'll go home and put your feet up for a couple of days." Jenny winked and pointed to the door. "I think I know somebody who wouldn't mind babysitting. Think about it. It might be fun."

Morgan smiled for the first time. "I told you, Jenny. Ben's just a good friend."

"I'd say he's a good friend who just happens to be in love with you. Is the relationship serious or not?"

"Ya know, Jenny, sometimes I think you've fallen out of the pages of a romance novel."

"I don't mind being known as a hopeless romantic . . . and I'm very happy for you and Ben, but you're in your second trimester. You have to take better care of yourself, and that includes keeping your stress level down."

"My stress level is no different than anybody else's."

"You're talking to me, Morgan. I'm not totally oblivious to what's been going on in your life. It's no secret what you're going through with the hospital and the medical board."

"I'll be fine, Jenny. I just need a little time to figure this thing out."

"Can't you put things on the back burner until the baby's born?"

"Unfortunately, I don't have that luxury."

"As a friend, do you mind if I ask why?"

"The board of medicine has their own agenda, and it doesn't include any consideration for the fact that I happen to be pregnant. These people go fishing with dynamite. If I don't defend myself, I could wind up losing everything."

There was a knock at the door. Jenny walked over and slid the glass door open. Ben poked his head in.

"Leslie said you guys were about finished in here."

Jenny motioned him the rest of the way in.

"Morgan's fine. But I've told her it's important for her to take it easy for the next couple of days. I volunteered you to babysit."

Ben walked over and helped Morgan off of the exam table.

After what seemed to be an uncomfortable silence, she said, "I'll try to take it easy."

Jenny gave her a hug. "Call my cell phone if you have any more cramps or bleeding. My twin sisters are in town this week. They're both in heavy-duty therapy. Have dinner with us. I don't know if I can get through the evening alone."

"As intriguing as that sounds, I'll have to get back to you," Morgan answered.

As she was heading for the door, Jenny tapped Ben's shoulder a couple of times. "Keep an eye on her for me. She really needs to slow down a little and take it easy."

"C'mon," he said to Morgan, picking up her purse from the end of the stretcher. "I'll take you home."

"I could use some dessert. Can we stop somewhere?"

His brow furrowed. "Jenny's only been gone for ten seconds. Did you forget what she said already?"

"I was just thinking that it would—"

"Don't think too much. It weakens the team."

"Fine," she said in a childlike pout.

Ben gave her a long hug and then kissed the top of her head. She hugged him back and they stayed that way for almost a minute. When she turned her head, he could feel her wet eyes against his neck.

CHAPTER
73

It had been two days since Morgan's unexpected trip to the emergency room.

She had experienced no further cramps or bleeding and was feeling the best she had since learning she was pregnant. It was a few minutes past twelve when she walked into the physician's dining room. She quickly scanned the room and spotted Mira Ramon making her way through the self-serve line. She walked over and joined her.

"I called your office. Your secretary said you might be here."

"How are you feeling?" Mira asked.

"Fine. I'd like to talk to you about something. Do you mind if I join you?"

"Grab a tray."

"I had a late breakfast. I'm going to skip lunch today."

"Both times I was pregnant, I couldn't even look at food for the first three months. Then one morning I woke up and didn't stop eating until I delivered." They shared a laugh. Mira pointed to a small table, led the way over, and then sat down.

"I was hoping you wouldn't mind answering a few more questions about that pacemaker case we talked about."

"Sure," Mira said, setting her a paper napkin on her lap and then taking her first spoonful of Italian wedding soup.

"How common is it for a young woman to develop complete heart block and require a pacemaker?"

"How young?"

"In her twenties."

"In two words: incredibly uncommon." Reaching for a packet of crackers, Mira paused for a few seconds. "Are you sure we're talking about the case, because I don't remember you mentioning she was so young."

"I may have overlooked it," Morgan confessed.

"So you're trying to find out how this young and otherwise healthy woman could have developed full-blown heart block that required insertion of a permanent pacemaker."

"I've checked every medication in the *PDR*. I've also looked at every infection we've ever seen in the hospital." Morgan lowered her voice. "I've even researched every poison known to mankind."

"Poison?"

"I don't know what else to think. I can't find a disease, drug, virus, bacteria, or toxin that would have destroyed her ability to pace her own heart. Is there anything you're aware of that could have caused the problem?"

Although she was silent, Morgan could sense Mira's level of discomfort rising.

"Look, Morgan. I've known you a long time, and I have some idea of what you've been going through lately."

"I'm not sure I understand what—"

"I just don't want to contribute to . . ."

"My paranoia and bizarre behavior?"

"I didn't say that. I just don't want to make things worse for you."

Morgan wasn't offended by Mira's concern. And, perhaps, under different circumstances, she might have been persuaded to let the matter drop. But she knew Gideon had somehow figured out how to murder Alison Greene and she desperately needed Mira's help.

"I'm well aware of what people are saying, but that doesn't make them right. I'm three months pregnant and in a matter of a few short weeks my whole life's been turned upside down. I'm running out of time, Mira. I need your help."

Mira put her spoon down and sat back in her chair. "There may be one thing, but it's a long shot."

Morgan pushed her chair closer. "At this point, I'm willing to listen to anything."

"About three years ago, the British were doing trial studies on a new antidepressant. The name of the drug was Axaptamine. The drug turned out to be an excellent antidepressant, but unfortunately it had one major side effect. In therapeutic doses it caused permanent heart block at a fairly predictable rate. After about ten people wound up with permanent pacemakers, they pulled the drug and stopped the studies."

Morgan looked perplexed. "But I did a complete literature search. Nothing came up."

"I'm not surprised. The drug never even came close to making the U.S. market. The only reason I know anything about it is because I attended a meeting in London where it was discussed."

"If somebody wanted to, could they get a hold of the drug?" Morgan asked.

"I guess if you passed yourself off as an independent lab wanting to do further studies, you could get it. Since they never finished the trials, there must be plenty of it around still."

"Do you remember who the manufacturer was?"

"No, but I'm sure any search engine would give it to you."

"How long after taking the drug did the symptoms of heart block begin?" Morgan asked.

"As I recall, it was pretty fast—within days, but not too many people know about Axaptamine. It's hard to believe somebody poisoned your patient."

"This guy's not exactly your average Joe," Morgan said, reaching across the table and taking Mira's hand in hers. She gave it a quick squeeze and added, "I'll let you finish your lunch in peace. Thanks for the help."

Walking out of the dining room, Morgan had no doubts that Mason Kaine was more than clever enough to have learned about Axaptamine. He also had the wherewithal to get his hands on the drug and figure out a way to poison Alison Greene with it.

CHAPTER

74

Having finally reassured an anxious mother that her three-year-old wheezing son would eventually outgrow his asthma, Morgan returned to the nursing station to finish charting her discharge instructions.

"You have a call on six, Dr. Connolly," the unit secretary told her, waving the phone in the air.

"Who is it?" Morgan asked, only half paying attention.

"She said her name was Adele Kaine and that it was personal."

Morgan looked up from writing the boy's antibiotic prescription.

"Adele Kaine? Are you sure?"

"Positive. Do you want to take it or should I tell her you're unavailable?"

"Tell her I'll be right with her," Morgan said, finishing up the prescription and putting it on the chart for the nurse to give to the boy's mother.

Wanting a little more privacy, Morgan made her way to the back of the nursing station to a small area shaped like an alcove. The space was made up of three partitioned cubicles, which were used by the physicians to dictate their reports.

With all of the cubicles unoccupied, Morgan selected the farthest one from the door, picked up the phone, and tapped line six.

"Hello."

"Morgan. It's Adele Kaine. I apologize for calling you at the hospital." Her voice was nasal.

"No need to apologize. It's nice to hear from you. You sound like you have a cold."

"I've been battling the flu all week but I'm finally starting to feel a little better. The reason I'm calling is to find out if you're still having that problem we talked about."

"I'm afraid so."

"In that case, I think we should talk. I've recently come across some information that I'm certain you'd be interested in seeing."

"What kind of information?" Morgan asked, taken back by the sudden urgency in Adele's voice.

"I'd prefer not discuss the specifics on the phone. I'm going out of town in the morning for four days. We can get together when I get back or, if you prefer, I can meet you tonight. I'll be working late at my office."

Morgan looked at her watch. It was five o'clock. The idea of driving to Coral Springs after a busy twelve-hour shift didn't thrill her, but with time running out, waiting almost a week to find out what Adele had on her mind seemed far less attractive.

"My shift's over at seven. Why don't we make it tonight?"

"Fine. Do you remember how to get to my office?"

"I think so."

"I'll meet you there at eight. I may be a few minutes late. I'll give you a call if I am."

"I'll be there . . . and thank you."

Adele said, "I'm doing this for both of us. I'll see you in a couple of hours."

For a minute or so after she hung up, Morgan sat in the cubicle staring blankly ahead. She then looked at her watch and realized that if she had any hope of being on time, she had to get back to the ER. She stood up. Heavy in thought, she wondered if Adele's information would be the answer to her prayer and incriminate Mason Kaine.

CHAPTER

75

It was seven p.m. when Morgan finished seeing her last patient.

She signed out to the physician relieving her, and by seven thirty she was heading north on the Florida Turnpike. The traffic was surprisingly forgiving, allaying any lingering fears she had about being late for her meeting with Adele.

By the time she pulled into the parking lot, the sun had completely faded. The lot was poorly lighted and the only car around was parked directly in front of the travel agency. Assuming it was Adele's, Morgan pulled in next to the late model sedan.

The four stores, including the front part of the travel agency, were dark. She checked the time. It was five to eight. Morgan turned off the engine, grabbed her purse, and stepped out of the Thunderbird. The only sound was that of a dog barking in the distance. Standing between the two cars, Morgan took a precautionary look around.

Even if she had never heard of Mason Kaine, her surroundings would have made her apprehensive. She was surprised that Adele would work late at such a secluded location. Instinctively, Morgan clutched her purse between her arm and chest, closed the car door, and started toward the store. The incessant barking of the dog abruptly stopped.

As she was making her way between the two cars, she

heard the sound of footsteps moving quickly across the pavement. She picked up her pace but before she could emerge from between the cars, the footsteps got louder. Her instinct was to lunge for the sidewalk, but before she could, she was seized from behind.

In an instant, the man's powerful arm encircled her waist and lifted her off of the ground. Before she could react, his other hand slammed against her mouth, smothering any attempts she made to cry out. Pulled tightly against him, she could feel his heavy breathing. In one swift jerk, he spun her away from him and then shoved her face hard against her car. The image of the hulking man who had confronted her outside of her dry cleaners about Kevin's whereabouts jumped into her mind.

He pushed his face against the back of her head. "All I want is your purse, lady," he said in a distorted whisper. "Don't try to turn around. I don't want to hurt you, but I will."

Morgan dropped her bag.

"I'm going to pick up your purse now. If you move, I'll strangle you."

Almost thankful she was only being mugged, Morgan nodded. As soon as she did, she felt the man's grip on her abdomen ease off. She expected him to lean over, pick up her purse, and take off running, but instead, she felt a sudden pin-prick along the side of her neck. There was no question in her mind she had been injected with something.

In a frenzied state of mind, she struggled to extricate herself, but the man's grasp on her only intensified. Pinning her against her car, Morgan could again feel the heavy weight of his chest heaving against her back. She knew he had no intention of letting her go, and whatever precious seconds she had to act were quickly evaporating. Every desperate attempt she made to squirm free met with even more resistance.

Gasping for air under his powerful hand, she looked across the parking lot, hoping somebody would come to her assis-

tance. Morgan's brain now whirled under the effect of the
drug. It was if she were clinging to a ghostlike carnival ride
that had spun off its tracks and was now hurtling her toward a
brilliantly lit tunnel. On the brink of unconsciousness, every
particle of strength and resolve she had vanished.

CHAPTER
76

Morgan awakened to the deafening whine of a powerful engine. She felt herself moving forward in a serpentine motion.

She had spent enough time on airboats to be familiar with the airplane engine's characteristic sound. Lying on her side on the bottom of the boat, her body quaked from the cold night air hammering against her. Although she had no idea where she was, she did have a clear recollection of everything that had happened to her.

After a few seconds, she forced open her eyes. Gazing toward the back of the boat, all she could make out among the dark night shadows was the airboat's huge fan and the vague silhouette of a man sitting high in the pilot's chair with his hand on the control lever. With a sudden surge of adrenaline pouring into her veins, Morgan struggled to come to her feet, but the duct tape binding her ankles and wrists wouldn't permit it. Squirming and twisting on the boat's cold bottom, she finally rolled onto her back. Breathless, she stared up at the cloud-covered sky. The boat suddenly decelerated. She heard a man's laughter.

"I know who you are," she screamed.

The laughter stopped. "Gideon. The name's Gideon," he said in an unnatural throaty voice.

From the rhythmic pelting of the thick reeds of saw grass

against the side of the boat, Morgan sensed they were winding slowly through the swamp.

"Take me back or—"

"Or what, Dr. Connolly? You'll scream?" He laughed again. "Be my guest. We're twenty miles from civilization. The only things out here that will hear you, you'd rather not attract."

"What do you want from me?" she demanded.

"Justice. Your incompetence was responsible for the death of my sons. It's time you took responsibility."

"There was nothing anybody could have done."

"I disagree," he said impassively.

Her body shuddered as if she were riddled with fever. "What's killing me going to solve?"

"I'm not looking to solve anything. I'm looking for justice," he told her, continuing to speak in a gruff voice.

"I'm begging you. Please don't do this. I'm pregnant."

He chuckled harder. "You're hardly in a position to preach to me about the loss of a child."

"You killed my father. Haven't you made me suffer enough?"

His voice suddenly filled with anger. "Don't talk to me about suffering. I had to stand next to my wife and watch her say good-bye to our sons. Can you, even for an instant, fathom her pain?"

Gideon throttled the engine all the way back. The airboat glided to a stop.

"We can still work this out. Let me prove to you that I didn't do anything wrong. We can go to the hospital administration and—"

"Shut up," he screamed. "Your pathetic begging insults both of us. I've been to your administration. They barely acknowledged me. I wasted hours begging them to talk to me. All I ever got was a poorly veiled courtesy call from some junior administrator whose marching orders were obviously to appease me with lies. I'm sorry, Doctor, but you'll have to forgive me if I have no interest in speaking to some condescending administrator."

Morgan struggled to keep calm. "Forget the hospital then—we can go to the state. I know a lot of people who would be willing to—"

"Stop lying to me. I'm not an idiot. I've been to every health-care agency in the state. Either they don't have the time or they don't care. Don't you understand? It's all a giant conspiracy between the hospitals, the government, and the doctors to conceal their guilt."

Morgan had dealt with enough paranoid patients to recognize the unshakeable conviction in Kaine's voice. Trying to convince him that he was wrong was like shouting at the rain.

Morgan lay motionless, prodding her mind to think of anything that would change Kaine's mind about killing her. Before she could come up with anything, she heard him climbing down from his chair. Her pulse quickened at the sound of his footsteps moving across the boat.

Without saying a word he straddled her body and placed his hand on her leg. The horrid fear of what might precede her death flashed in her mind. But his hand slid downward, to her ankles, where he unwrapped the duct tape. When he was finished he did the same thing to her wrists.

"Do you know how most people who become stranded in the Everglades at night die?" When she didn't answer, he said, "Hypothermia. The water temperature's about seventy-five degrees. The funny thing is that most people lost out here don't even think about hypothermia. They're too busy trying to avoid the gator holes. An angry mother alligator will shred you to pieces in a New York minute. The poisonous snakes will probably leave you alone, but I can't say the same for all the pythons and boas that live out here now. Did you know that a full-grown python can take down a panther?"

"I'm not the evil person you think I am. Please take me back," Morgan pleaded.

"It's not my responsibility to judge your sins. I'll leave that up to God. My job's to arrange the meeting."

"You're insane," she bellowed.

"Get up."

When she didn't move, he grabbed her arm and yanked her to her feet. Standing behind her, he pushed her toward the back of the boat.

"I can't see," she screamed.

A beam of light appeared at her feet. The force of his hand around her arm clamped down harder. She took one hesitant step after another until she reached the back of the boat. He made sure to stay behind her. He then turned off the flashlight.

"Step up on the side. I'll help you in."

"I'm begging you," she sobbed. Morgan could feel every stroke of her heart as she looked out into the endless black void beyond the end of the boat. For the first time, she viewed her death as a certainty, but her unspoken prayers were for her baby.

"I'll kill you," she whispered as she placed her foot up on the edge.

"Not in this lifetime. Now get off my boat." When she didn't move, he said, "I assure you, you'll last a lot longer if your clothes stay dry. It's your choice. You can either step off the boat or I'll throw you off."

Morgan considered lashing out at Kaine but knew he was right about the Everglades and hypothermia. She had taken care of several people who had gotten lost in the Glades who came into the emergency room with a very low body temperature. The last thing she wanted was to be thrown in.

"Why don't you just shoot me," she said.

"Because I want you to suffer as much as possible before you die. Don't complain. At least I'm giving you a chance. That's a lot more than you gave my boys."

Still frozen on the side of the boat, Morgan suddenly felt her arms and neck being sprayed with what seemed to be insect repellant. "I changed my mind," he said. "Keeping the mosquitoes off of you for a while will give you a chance to enjoy the ecosystem to its fullest."

And then, with his hands supporting her, Morgan stepped into the insect-infested swamp.

CHAPTER

77

Up to her waist in water, Morgan felt the slimy muck beneath her feet slither up between her toes.

She hadn't been in the swamp more than a minute when, above the raucous clamor of the wildlife and insects, she heard Kaine throttle up the airboat's engine.

"Don't leave me here," she whispered over and over again.

It wasn't until the boat moved away that the full terror of what was happening permeated every cell of her body. When the boat was about fifty yards away the front lights came on. She screamed out, begging him to return. But when she saw the lights rapidly fading across the grasslands, she knew her fate had been sealed.

Alone in the black abyss, she wept uncontrollably. Even though she didn't move, the dense saw grass that surrounded her stabbed at her neck and face. Leaping to her mind were accounts she had heard about people getting lost in the Everglades at night, and how they had walked aimlessly in circles for hours before they collapsed from hypothermia.

Morgan knew her one and only hope of surviving would be to last until daybreak. With the sunrise would come airboats and the chance of being rescued. Standing in the chilly water, playing a mind game with herself, she passed the time by plotting her revenge against Kaine. She slowly turned her wrist and noted the time. It was ten twenty-five.

The fear of attracting all sorts of predatory animals had prevented her from screaming for help. In spite of the repellant Kaine had sprayed on her, she found herself slapping away at the steady stream of insects landing on her face and neck. With her fear of not being rescued eclipsing her terror of what animals might be lurking nearby, she began to scream blindly into the night. Every few seconds she stopped, hoping beyond hope to hear a response or to see the approaching lights of an airboat. But there were no answers to her pleas, and there were no lights.

After a few minutes, she became so breathless from screaming that she was forced to stop. Between gasps of air, she noticed she was shivering. Without realizing it, she had allowed her arms to drop to her sides and into the water. She instantly yanked them out and folded them across her chest. She struggled not to think about the peril her baby faced. She rolled her wrist over and again checked the time. She had been in the water for forty minutes. The absence of any visual clues and her falling body temperature were making it more difficult for her to maintain her balance on the swamp's boggy floor.

She had just managed to steady herself when she suddenly heard a strange rustling of the saw grass. Before she had time to stop herself, she screamed out. Her eyes darted back and forth, trying to locate where it was coming from. She couldn't see a thing but had no illusions that the moonless night would offer her protection from the nocturnal predators that were all around her.

She heard the smooth crackling of the reeds again. She slammed her eyes shut and prayed that whatever was out there would leave her and her baby alone. With her eyes closed, Morgan never saw the thin track of light that suddenly appeared on the swamp's surface. It was no more than fifty feet from her and vanished as quickly as it had appeared.

Her only thought was to stay as still as possible. She clenched her hands. A minute or so passed and she heard nothing more. Only slightly relieved, she still didn't know if the animal had moved on or was, at this very moment, stalking her. Continuing to shiver, she felt as if her mental acuity was slipping. Fearing she was suffering from the early effects of hypothermia, she pulled her arms even harder against her body, struggling to preserve every precious degree of body heat possible.

"Only seven hours to go until sunrise," she joked out loud in a staccato voice. "I've stayed awake for forty-eight hours dozens of times. I can do this." She closed her eyes, telling herself over and over again that if she could make it through the night, the baby would too.

The first drone of the distant engine was so faint that Morgan almost missed it. When the engine became a little louder, her eyes popped open.

"Ignore it. You're hearing things," she whispered, likening the delusion to the sudden appearance of a desert oasis to a parched nomad.

But when the chopping reverberation became steadily louder, Morgan realized it was no invention of her imagination, and that the looming sound was that of a helicopter engine. Realizing it was behind her, she strung together a dozen or so baby steps to turn around. Momentarily wobbling in place, she extended her arms straight out to her sides and spread her stance to maintain her balance.

Her first thought was that the helicopter was passing over by pure chance. There was no chance the pilot would see her. She raised her eyes and stared at the sky. At first, what she saw was nothing more than a far-off speck of light. She locked her eyes on the dot and watched it become larger until it spread out into an ever-brightening beacon that painted the water's surface.

In near disbelief, Morgan watched as the helicopter descended, appearing as if it were coming straight toward her. The engine's roar filled the night as the chopper now hovered just above the water no more than fifty yards away from her.

Morgan waved her arms madly in the air. Above the deafening beating of the engine, she screamed in a voice already hoarse from yelling. "I'm here. I'm over here."

In the next moment, she found herself awash in a torrent of light from the helicopter's searchlight. Joyous to the point of tears, she continued to scream and gesture frantically at the helicopter, which descended the last few feet and came to rest on its two huge pontoons.

"We see you. Don't move," came a voice from a loudspeaker.

Morgan let her arms fall to her side. Her legs ached and it took every drop of strength in her body not to fall. It seemed like the longest two minutes of her life waiting for the officer from Fish and Wildlife to reach her. When he did, she began crying uncontrollably, shedding more tears of pure elation than she ever imagined she could.

"Are you all right, ma'am?" the officer asked, putting his arm around her shoulder.

"I . . . I think so . . . I'm just very cold."

"I've got you now. We're going to get you into the helicopter and then to a hospital."

"Please take me to Dade Presbyterian. I'm a physician there."

The officer helped Morgan over to the helicopter and then assisted her in. She was still shaking when he got her inside. He reached overhead, pulled two blankets down from a shelf, and wrapped them tightly around her.

He then rotated his microphone in front of his mouth and gestured to the pilot. "We're good to go."

"Thank you," she told the young man over and over again.

The powerful beating of the engine reached a crescendo, providing the helicopter with liftoff power. As it rose above the shadowy swamp below and then sliced across the night sky, Morgan said another prayer for her baby.

CHAPTER 78

No longer shuddering from the chill of the Everglades, Morgan lay in Dade Presbyterian's emergency room with an IV taped securely in the back of her hand.

"You're a lucky girl," Jenny Silverman said as she passed the ultrasound probe over Morgan's lower abdomen. "Everything looks fine. That's one tough kid you're cooking." Morgan's fear of what might have become of her if she hadn't been rescued paled in comparison to her relief that her baby had come through the ordeal unscathed.

Jenny asked, "Are you going home tonight or is Chuck going to admit you for observation?"

"I've been here for three hours. My temp's normal and I don't have any symptoms of hypothermia. I think I can go home."

"I guessed that. I was asking about the opinion of your doctor."

"I'm the one who hired him. I think he'll be reasonable."

Morgan took note that Jenny lacked her usual upbeat demeanor.

"Don't forget to call me tomorrow. I want to make sure you're okay."

"Tomorrow—I promise."

"Where's Ben?"

"He's on his way down from Orlando. He was supposed to

come back tomorrow morning but when I called him, he told me he wanted to fly back tonight."

"Is that safe?"

"Ben's an excellent pilot. It's a short flight. I'm sure he'll be fine."

"Call me if you have any problems."

After Jenny had turned off the ultrasound machine and left the room, Morgan laid back and stared up at the white tile ceiling, thinking about Mason Kaine. She assumed that his arrest would be immediate, and once the truth became apparent, she would be owed the largest apology ever tendered by Dade Presbyterian Hospital, the police, and the state medical board. Euphoric by the expectation of total vindication, Morgan couldn't help grinning.

The glass door to her examination bay rumbled open. Morgan raised her head from her pillow. Paula, one of the veteran ER nurses, closed the doors behind her and then walked over to her stretcher. After checking Morgan's vital signs on the flat-screen monitor, she took her temperature.

"Ninety-eight-point-four," she said. "Not too bad, considering how you spent your evening."

Just as Paula was finishing up her charting, there were three quick taps at the door. Morgan assumed it was Chuck coming back to discharge her. But when the door opened, a hefty man accompanied by a young, smartly dressed woman with pastel blue eyes stood in the doorway.

"Dr. Connolly?" he asked.

"Yes."

"My name's Vic Prieto. I'm a detective with the Broward County Sheriff's Office." His voice was gravelly and his sports coat was in desperate need of a pressing. "This is my partner, Detective Baxter." Morgan nodded and then with Paula's help propped herself higher up on the stretcher. The two officers moved to the middle of the room. Prieto spoke again, "The Fish and Wildlife officers filled us in on what happened, but if you don't mind, we'd like to ask you a few questions. The first thing is—"

"How are you feeling?" Jody Baxter interrupted, tossing her partner of ten years a disapproving glare for his usual insensitivity.

"I'm okay. Thank you for asking."

Jody had entered the police academy after completing a two-year associate's degree and had been on the force for a dozen years. Having maintained her humanity in an ever-increasing avalanche of violent crime, she showed up to work every day with an optimism that many of her fellow officers had long since lost.

"Are you sure you feel up to answering some questions?" she asked Morgan above her partner's incessant toe-tapping.

"I think so. Do you work with Detective Wolfe?"

"Actually, he was just promoted. He now heads up the Narcotics Division. Is he a friend?"

Hardly surprised she hadn't been notified that Wolfe was no longer involved in her father's case, she said, "My father was murdered a couple of months ago. He's in charge . . . or I guess I should say, was in charge of the investigation."

"I'm sure they reassigned the case," Jody said.

"The officer who rescued me told me a man saw me out there and called nine-one-one. I'd like to find out who it was so I can thank him."

"Unfortunately, it was an anonymous call," Jody answered. "The caller gave them your exact GPS coordinates. Fish and Wildlife's helicopters have infrared capability so it wasn't too hard for them to find you."

"I thought I heard something . . . but it was so black out there. I . . . I didn't see anybody."

"Were you screaming?" Prieto inquired.

"Until I was hoarse," she said, noticing his scuffed black penny loafers and mismatched. socks.

Jody said, "We suspect the man who made the call was an

alligator poacher who wanted to help, but for obvious reason, didn't want to get involved."

"I see."

Prieto said, "The officers told us that you were abducted in Coral Springs. They also said you claimed you were drugged and then taken out to the Everglades. Is that pretty much what happened?"

"It's not pretty much what happened, Detective. It's exactly what happened," Morgan answered, a little taken back by his offhanded manner. His skeptical tone was painfully reminiscent of Detective Wolfe's.

"Were you robbed?"

"No."

"Raped?"

"No."

"Assaulted?" he asked.

"Only if you count being dumped out in an alligator-infested swamp to die."

Prieto's expression never changed.

"You mentioned to the officers that you were contacted by a woman by the name of Adele Kaine earlier this evening who set up a meeting with you."

"That's correct."

"We called Ms. Kaine. It seems she's in Canada and won't be back until the weekend. She said she hasn't spoken to you since you showed up at her office a week or so ago. She told us about your meeting."

"I guess that makes perfect sense."

"I beg your pardon," he said.

Morgan wasn't sure if Prieto was obnoxious by nature or was purposelessly being obtuse.

"Obviously, it wasn't Adele Kaine who called me," she told him.

"When you spoke to her on the phone, you didn't realize it wasn't her voice?"

"No. If I had, I wouldn't have jumped headfirst into an obvious trap."

"An obvious trap," he repeated as he took notes. "Could you explain that to me please, Doctor?"

"I had only spoken to Adele Kaine that one time. Besides, whoever it was who called me spoke in a very nasal voice and told me she was getting over the flu." Morgan folded her arms. "I assume Ms. Kaine filled you in on what we talked about when we met."

"She gave us a general idea. She said you believed you were being harassed by her ex-husband."

"That's right. His name's Mason Kaine . . . and I think his intentions are a little more serious than simple harassment." Prieto looked up from his pad for a few seconds but said nothing. He looked at her as if he was less than convinced her story had any validity. Morgan tried again. "Mason Kaine tried to kill me tonight. He obviously got some woman to pose as his Miss Kaine to lure me to her office."

"Why?"

"To kidnap me," she answered one word at a time as if she were talking to a child.

"How would this guy know you were acquainted with his ex-wife?"

"Because he's been stalking me for weeks. He must have been following me the day I met with Adele."

After a faint roll of his eyes, Prieto asked, "I guess I still don't get it. Why would he want to harm you? What's his motive?"

"To get even," she said without taking a breath.

"For what?"

"For the death of his two sons. I was on call the night they came into the emergency room. They were both suffering from meningitis. They were already in critical condition and there was nothing we could do to save them. I spoke with Mr. Kaine afterward and he was irate. He accused me of incompetence and held me personally responsible for the unnecessary deaths of his sons."

"I assume you can positively identify the man who abducted you as Mason Kaine." Prieto continued to scribble on his pad, but when the room became deadly silent, he looked up. "Dr. Connolly, you can ID this guy, right?"

His question instantly upended her confidence. Her tone became uncertain and she spoke in a tentative monotone, "By the time I woke up I was already on the airboat. It was pitch-black. Kaine made sure to stay behind me the entire time. I couldn't see anything."

An awkward few seconds was brought to an end by Prieto's annoying sigh. "Dr. Connolly, I don't want to sound—"

Before she heard the inevitable, Morgan said, "I'm sorry, Detective. I've had kind of a rough night. Maybe it would be better if we finished this later this morning."

She turned away and allowed her head to fall back into the pillow. Prieto said nothing. He reached into his pocket and pulled out his card. He then walked over and handed it to Morgan.

"Just give us a call when you're feeling better. We'd like to wrap this up."

Acting as if Jody wasn't even in the room, he walked back to the door and slid it open. Before stepping out into the hall, he looked back at his partner with an impatient glare. But instead of following him, Jody walked over to a white vinyl chair, pushed it over toward Morgan's bed, and sat down.

"That looks like the same ultrasound machine my OB uses," she said with an easy smile. "Are you expecting?"

Morgan's eyes drifted to Jody's abdomen. She hadn't noticed at first, but the officer definitely had the early signs of a baby bump.

"I'm in my second trimester," Morgan said.

"Your first?"

"Yes."

"Mine too," Jody said with a sigh, rubbing her tummy. "I

don't know about you but I get ravenous and hypoglycemic every night about this time." Jody then looked over at her partner, who was still standing in the doorway with the same annoyed expression. "Vic, I'm feeling a little light-headed. I'm going to sit for a few minutes. Would you mind going over to the cafeteria and finding me something sweet to eat? A couple of doughnuts would be great."

Trying to hold back a giggle, Morgan pushed her lips together. Without saying a word, Vic exhaled audibly through puffed cheeks and stepped out of the room.

chapter 79

"He's really not a bad guy," Jody said, stretching her long legs out.

"Yeah. He seems like a real peach," Morgan answered. "You're obviously a very patient and tolerant woman."

"Don't be too hard on him. It's our nature as police officers to be cautious."

"Cautious is one thing; condescending and cynical are another. He didn't believe a word I told him. And that disbelieving scowl? Did he learn that at the police academy or was he born with it?"

"You sound like somebody who's been through the drill before."

"As I mentioned, my father was murdered a couple of months ago. I've had several conversations with Detective Wolfe. He and your partner share some of the same annoying mannerisms."

Jody swept a few stubborn strands of auburn hair from her forehead.

"I'm not going to tell you what to do, but you might want to reconsider your decision not to talk about this thing until later."

Feeling defeated, Morgan asked, "Why? What's the difference?"

"Because if you're right about this guy, he still thinks

you're wandering around out there in the Everglades; which means he assumes you'll be dead in a few hours. If he finds out you've been rescued, he might take off . . . or worse."

"I'm not opposed to talking about what happened out there. I'd just prefer to talk to somebody who will, at least, give me the benefit of the doubt. Am I reaching for the stars here?"

"No, and you are talking to somebody who wants to listen."

In spite of the harrowing events of the evening, Morgan had the presence of mind to realize that her best chance of being taken seriously by the authorities was sitting three feet away.

"Okay," Morgan said.

Jody pulled her own notepad from her purse. "Tell me what happened in the parking lot."

"I was supposed to meet Adele at eight o'clock. When I got there, the lot was pretty dark and there was only one other car. I pulled in next to it and then got out and started walking toward her office. Kaine came up from behind me. He was incredibly strong," she said shaking her head slowly. "I felt a pinch in my neck. I'm sure he injected me with something. The next thing I knew I was lying on the bottom of an airboat."

"Did they draw blood for a tox screen ?"

"Yes, but I don't think the results are back yet."

"You said before you spoke with this guy, Kaine, the night his sons died and that he was furious."

Morgan nodded.

"People get mad at their doctors," Jody said. "Most of the time, it wears off or they change doctors. They may even sue them or file a formal complaint with the medical board, but all of those things are a far cry from trying to kill them. So, my question is, how can you be so sure that's what's going on?"

After a protracted sigh, Morgan said, "It's a long story that involves a lot more than Kaine simply trying to kill me."

Stretching her legs out in front of her, Jody said, "I've got all night."

For the next half hour, Morgan summarized everything she knew about her father's death, Faith Russo, the Code 15s, and her present situation with the medical board. Jody took a lot of notes and asked several questions. Morgan's impression was that she was at least listening to her.

Just as they were finishing up, there was a quick knock at the door. Prieto stuck his head in, held up a doughnut, and waved it at Jody. She walked over and took it from him.

"I need a few more minutes," she told him. "Why don't you see if the paramedics have finished their report?"

"I'll get right on it," he said with a quick salute and a long smirk.

"What's going to happen next?" Morgan asked.

"I don't know. I'll have to discuss it with my captain and probably the state's attorney. It might take me a couple of days to get back to you."

"Why can't you just arrest Kaine? I can give you the name and phone number of one of his friends who knows where he lives."

Jody stood up from her chair. "Finding him won't be the problem."

"Then what is?"

Jody threw her purse over her shoulder and took a couple of steps toward the bed.

"Listen to me, Dr. Connolly. You never actually saw the man who kidnapped you. There's not a mark on you and you weren't robbed. From what you've told me, you're going through pretty tough times right now, especially from a professional standpoint. The people I answer to are going to ask the same question my partner's asking. Why didn't Kaine simply kill you and dump you in the swamp? And for that matter, why was he so theatrical about the whole thing? Most people who get tossed into a swamp as a part of her murder are already dead."

"Mason Kaine is insane. He wanted me to suffer. It's not as complicated as everybody thinks."

Morgan crossed her arms, gazing across the room blankly. Jody turned and headed toward the door.

"I'll call you in a few days. I promise."

For the first time in hours, Morgan found herself alone. Far from elated, she at least felt more encouraged than she had thirty minutes earlier. At a minimum, Jody Baxter had given her some hope that Gideon would ultimately be arrested. Morgan found herself wondering if Gideon already knew she'd made it out of the Everglades alive. When he did find out, contrary to Jody's opinion, Morgan doubted he would leave town. In fact, Morgan had no doubt he'd try to kill her again.

Her mind was lost in thought and she barely heard the few taps at the glass door. When she looked up Ben was standing there.

"Chuck said it was your call if you wanted to stay in the hospital overnight."

"I want to go home," Morgan said, sliding her legs off of the bed.

"I assumed that would be your answer. How are you feeling?"

"More discouraged than cold," she told him.

"I'll help you with your things," he said, assisting her off of the stretcher. "I'll stay with you tonight."

Morgan was happy he offered, because if he hadn't, she was going to ask him.

CHAPTER
80

With Morgan in tow, Limerick pranced north on A1A.

When he caught site of the small dog park that she took him to on a regular basis, his tail shot up, wagged madly, and he lurched forward. Morgan smiled and calmed the excited setter by holding tight on the leash and petting his neck. Once they were inside the park, Morgan walked over to a bench and sat down. To her surprise, there was only one other dog in the park, a springer spaniel, who in spite of Limerick's barking showed no interest in him. Morgan gazed around, enjoying a soft breeze from the west as Limerick walked about her legs.

Just as she finished untangling Limerick's lease from around her ankles, her phone rang. She pulled it out of her pocket and flipped it open. Will Johnson's name and number popped up in the display window.

"Hi, Will."

"How are you?"

"I'm okay," she answered.

"Eileen Hall called me and told me what happened to you. Are you sure you're all right?"

"Really, I'm doing fine. Once I found out the baby was okay, nothing else seemed to matter."

"Are the police involved?"

"They met me at the hospital. I was hoping they would arrest Mason Kaine, but they're still trying to determine if they have enough evidence."

"I'm glad you're okay."

"It's nice of you to call. I appreciate your concern."

"Listen. Do you feel up to getting together? Eileen has been bugging me for my final report and I'd like to get it to her. If you feel like you need some more time to recover from—"

"I'm fine, Will. I'd kind of like to get this thing wrapped up."

"Check your schedule. See if you can make it tomorrow at five."

"I don't have to check my schedule. I'm off until the end of the week so it shouldn't be a problem."

"Good. I'll see you then."

Morgan was taken back by the sense of urgency in Will's voice. It was a side of him she hadn't seen.

"You sound a little upset," she said. "Is there something else?"

After a few seconds of hesitation, he said, "I wasn't going to mention it until tomorrow, but I have some information about Mason Kaine I think you should be aware of. It may clear some things up for you and help you with the police."

"What kind of information?"

"Let's talk about everything tomorrow. I'll see you at five."

CHAPTER
81

DAY FORTY-THREE

"That was the worst Thai food I've ever eaten," Morgan told Ben. "Who recommended that place to you?"

Ben pointed to the walk sign and they started across the street. "My accountant. He swears by the place."

"Thank God he decided to concentrate on financial matters, because as a food critic he would have starved. The only good thing about the place is that it's only a block from the hospital."

Ben laughed and then shook his head. "Do you make all your lunch dates feel this good or is it just me?"

She took his hand. "The food may have been terrible but the company was four stars."

"Nice recovery," he said, as they approached the main entrance to Dade Presbyterian.

"What do you think Will's got on his mind?"

"I don't know, but I don't want to get too excited about things until I hear exactly what he has to say."

"Did you hear from Jody Baxter this morning?"

"No, but she told me it might be several days."

"You don't sound very encouraged."

"All I can do is hope that she will persuade her superiors to allow her to investigate Mason Kaine. If they do, I'll think they'll find out he's really Gideon, Stuart Artesian, and I. Ogden."

"I. Ogden?" Ben asked.

"The man who put the cross around Alison Greene's neck and probably killed her."

"I don't remember you mentioning his name," Ben said in a voice that was lost in thought. He took her arm, slowed his pace for a few steps, and then stopped. With a modest smile, he said, "You were right about this guy. He certainly likes to play games."

"What do you mean?"

"The name's an anagram. Unscramble I. Ogden and it spells Gideon."

Shaking her head, Morgan said, "That never occurred to me . . . How did you know that?"

"My mother loved word games. I spent most of my childhood playing Yahtzee, Jotto, and every other parlor game she could find. I even won the Scrabble championship at Northwestern."

"Just when you think you know somebody," Morgan said, with an impressed grin.

"So where do you go from here?" he asked.

"I've already told the police that I thought Gideon and I. Ogden were one and the same. I guess the anagram proves it. But I still need to find out one way or the other if Mason Kaine has a gap between his teeth."

"I know I've asked you this already, but are you absolutely sure that nobody who was in the emergency room that night would remember?"

"I doubt it. That was almost eighteen months ago. I spoke with him myself, face-to-face, and I don't remember. Any suggestions?" she asked.

"Unless you can come up with a time machine, I guess you're stuck for a while," he told her. "By the way, I got a call from Deborah Paniella this morning, the private eye I had called. She thinks she may have finally located Kaine. She said she needs a couple of more days."

"That's encouraging. It's nice to get some good news for a change."

Ben and Morgan arrived at the hospital and walked into the main lobby.

"Who are you going to visit?" she asked.

"One of my mechanics had his appendix out last night," he said as they walked past the security desk. Morgan waved at Pete Dennison, the security officer on duty.

"I'm sorry, sir," he said to Ben. "If you don't have a hospital ID, you'll need a visitor's pass."

"This is Dr. Docherty," Morgan said. "He used to be on staff here."

"I'm sorry, Dr. Connolly. It's the rule. We got a memo straight from Mr. Allenby. Nobody without a hospital ID gets in unless they have a visitor's pass. It only takes a minute."

"No problem," Ben said.

"Just stand on the yellow tape and look into the camera," Pete said.

Pete waited for the visitor ID to print out and then handed it to him. Ben held it up and looked at it. Peeling off the adhesive back, he said, "Not a bad likeness," he added, sticking the ID to his shirt pocket.

"I'm heading over to the ER," Morgan said.

"I thought you were off today."

"I'm just going over to say hi."

"Sure," Ben said. "Don't forget about tonight. We're eating at my place. I'm making dinner. I have a night lesson so let's make it at nine."

"I'll call you later."

Morgan headed across the lobby. When she reached the other side, she suddenly turned around, her eyes locked on the security desk. After a few moments, she looked toward the elevators, hoping that Ben hadn't gone upstairs yet. But he was gone.

"Oh my God," she whispered as she felt her heart doing cartwheels. "How could I have been so stupid?"

To the short line of people in front of Pete Dennison, the camera apparatus was nothing more than a fancy machine that popped out temporary identification passes, but to Morgan, it was a time machine.

CHAPTER

82

Detective Vic Prieto wedged his hefty frame into the front seat of the black Ford Taurus.

"How can you be so sure?" Jody asked him, sliding in behind the wheel.

A mystified look came to his face. "What are you talking about?"

"You know exactly what I'm taking about."

He grimaced. "Not Dr. Connolly, again? For God's sake, Jody, you're an experienced cop. The woman's certifiably nuts. I can't believe you're buying into her enchanted forest story."

Undeterred by Vic's condescending response, Jody put the key in the ignition and started the car.

"We're police officers. We're paid by the taxpayers not only to investigate crimes, but to look into possible crimes."

"Possible crimes, yes; wild-goose chases . . . no."

"Which brings me back to my original question. How can you be so sure?"

"Because the last time I checked, I didn't have the word gullible tattooed on my forehead."

"That's not an answer. What you're doing is relying on your instinct, which we both know has been wrong more times than a myopic handicapper at the dog track."

"This has nothing to do with instinct. It's about looking at the facts objectively. You should try it."

"I have."

"Then you'd realize that there's been no crime committed here. If you want to help Dr. Connolly, convince her to get more psychological help."

"Just tell me why you're so sure she's lying," Jody said.

Vic reached forward and lowered the radio.

"She's in trouble with the hospital and the state medical board, and she's still screwed up over her father's murder. She's also pregnant and in the middle of a divorce. I think even you would agree that's enough stress to screw somebody up."

"Are you trying to tell me that in order to clear her name, this woman drove herself out to the Everglades, jumped into a canoe, paddled out twenty miles, and then threw herself into the swamp hoping that some kindly poacher would come by and have her rescued?"

"Not exactly. I think she hired somebody to do it," Vic said.

"Are you kidding?"

"C'mon, Jody. We live in a city where you can have some-body killed for less than a hundred bucks. Dr. Connolly may be many things, but she's not a stupid woman. I'm sure she could have found somebody with an airboat to take her out to the middle of Lake Okeechobee and drop her off, wait an hour and then call nine-one-one."

"Were you aware that state medical boards and hospitals are notoriously lenient when it comes to physician discipline?"

"So? What's your point?" he asked.

"Dr. Connolly's not facing life imprisonment. There's no reason she would risk her life simply to vindicate herself. It wouldn't be rational."

"Who said anything about her being rational?"

"She may be stressed out and having some professional problems, but she's not irrational."

Vic snickered. "As I recall, there were a dozen or so cops who said the same thing about Ted Bundy. Am I crazy or weren't you standing next to me when we spoke to Wolfe? He's a good homicide cop. Didn't you hear what he said about her behavior in her father's murder investigation?"

"Of course I did."

"Then you obviously weren't listening very closely. He said she's become overly involved in the investigation and has nothing to base her theories on other than a desperate and illogical compulsion to find her father's murderer."

"Wolfe's a good cop, but he's not a psychiatrist and"—Jody paused, held up her hand to keep Vic silenced,—"he might be wrong."

"I don't think so."

"You heard what Adele Kaine said. She said this guy Kaine's capable of anything."

"So what? I have two ex-wives who would say the same thing about me."

Jody slowed down to let a mother duck and her ducklings cross in front of the car. "We're going out to Kaine's house later today."

"No way. I have a lot better things to do with my time."

A confident grin crossed Jody's face.

"How are things going with Nancy?" she asked. "Are you still thinking about getting engaged?"

Vic reached into his pocket, pulled out a stick of gum, peeled off the paper, and popped it in his mouth.

"I don't know," he answered with a measure of caution. "Why are we suddenly talking about my personal life?"

"I'm just making conversation. Did you ever buy that ring you talked my ear off about?"

"If you must know, I bought it last week. I'm just waiting for the right moment to give it to her."

"I wonder how Jana would feel about that?"

"Jana?"

"Jana, from Robbery—short hair, pretty face, big boobs. The one who laughs like a hyena."

"That's blackmail, Jody. I'm your partner, for God's sake. I'm in a serious long-term relationship now."

She laughed. "Long term? You're talking to me, Vic. I've watched the steady parade of women in and out of your life. Your relationships have about as much permanence as skywriting."

"You wouldn't do this."

"In a heartbeat," she assured him. "Just come with me to Kaine's house and I promise to take all of your disgusting little secrets to my grave."

Vic's chin fell. "You're supposed to be my partner. It's a sacred relationship. You could go to hell for this."

"I'm willing to take that chance," she said.

Crossing his arms in silence, he turned his head and looked out his window. Jody was quite familiar with Vic's proclivity for pouting. Certain he would be accompanying her to speak with Kaine, she contained her urge to laugh. In silence, she checked her side-view mirror and accelerated onto the interstate.

CHAPTER

83

Abandoning her plans to go to the emergency room, Morgan left the hospital and made the short walk across the hospital campus to Dade Presbyterian's main security office.

The small building was located between the two main parking garages. When Morgan walked in, she was relieved to see Al Bakersfield, the assistant director, sitting behind the information desk. Baby-faced, with a patch of sparse gray hair on his suntanned dome, Al made no effort to tame a waistline that betrayed his weakness for imported beer. Morgan had known him for years, and with one glaring exception, she regarded him as a reasonable man. For some irrational reason, he chose to ignore his chronically inflamed gallbladder, which had more stones in it than a gravel driveway.

In spite of her pleas, Al refused to have it removed. Every couple of months the pain became so unbearable that he wound up in the emergency room.

"How's it going, Al?" she asked.

His brow furrowed. "I'm okay. I hope you're not here to try and talk me into surgery." He patted his belly. "Me and the old gallbladder are doing just fine."

"That's not exactly the tune you were humming a few weeks ago. Why are you being such a baby? It's a routine operation. You'll be home the next morning."

"You mean if nothing goes wrong."

"Why should anything go wrong?"

"I work in a hospital. I hear all the gruesome stories of what goes on over there. I also read the papers and watch *20/20*. Hospitals are about as safe as hang gliding."

"It's not that bad."

He snickered, interlaced his fingers and set them down on the information counter. "A couple of years ago, a woman in an Ohio hospital was having some heartburn after a routine operation. Her doctor ordered an ounce of Maalox. The nurse, who was obviously not the sharpest knife in the drawer, got the Maalox and went into her room. And then, while this poor woman slept, this angel of mercy injected the antacid in her IV. Now, most children of ten would know that you're supposed to drink Maalox, not put it in an IV." Al raised his hands with his palms up. "Needless to say, the Maalox took care of both her heartburn and her heartbeat." Al scratched at his salt-and-pepper stubble and then added, "If it's all the same to you, I think I'll just hold on to my gallbladder for a while."

"Okay," Morgan conceded with a smile, "but don't come crying to me the next time you go overboard at Taco Bell."

"It's a promise," he told her, raising three fingers. "Now, since I doubt you came over here to discuss my health, what can I do for you?"

Morgan moved to the middle of the counter.

"I have a little problem that I need your help with."

He examined her over the top of his reading glasses. "What kind of a problem?"

"I have some questions about the Fast-Pass visitor identification system."

"Why would Dade Presbyterian's very busy chief of Emergency Medicine give a hoot about the Fast-Pass system?"

She tilted her head just slightly to one side. "It might be better if you didn't know. Do you think you can help me?"

"Fast-Pass isn't exactly a matter of national security, so I don't see why not. What do you want to know?"

"Basically, how it works."

"Well, we have one at every entrance and other strategic points in the hospital," he said pointing to end of the counter. "They're all identical to the one right there."

"Who gets photographed?"

"Anybody who enters the hospital who doesn't have a Dade Presbyterian ID has to go through the system. We photograph them, enter their intended area of visitation, and make a copy of their driver's license. The machine then spits out a paper ID about the size of a playing card that they stick on their shirt. The whole process only takes about thirty seconds."

"Can you show me how it works?" she asked.

"Sure. Move down to the end of the counter and we'll print out a pass for you."

Morgan took a few paces to her right and lined up in front of the small apparatus.

"Let me have your driver's license," Al said.

Morgan reached into her purse, pulled out her wallet, and handed it to him.

"I feel like I'm being arrested," she said.

"We have handcuffs for that, Doc." He pointed to the lens. "Look right into that little window."

Al rolled out the keyboard, slid Morgan's license into the Fast-Pass, and then tapped a single key. In a matter of moments, the machine spit out a black-and-white picture ID of Morgan. He peeled it off its adhesive back and handed it to her. She was surprised at how good the quality was.

"Does the computer store a copy of this?" Morgan inquired sticking the paper ID to her shirt.

"Sure."

"For how long?"

"Forever, I guess. The system has a huge memory."

Morgan cleared her throat and averted her eyes. "Supposing somebody wanted to retrieve copies of the passes issued on a particular day, at a particular station, for a specified period of time. Would it be possible?"

He placed his palms flat on the counter and smiled. "Why would somebody want to do that?"

"I didn't say they would. Think of it as a hypothetical question."

"I see," he said with a deliberate grin. "In that case, the answer to your hypothetical question would be that it's definitely possible."

Morgan took a step back. "Al, supposing I told you that I needed to see the Fast-Pass ID for everybody that came into the emergency room on March third of last year. Specifically, between the hours of nine and midnight."

"Are you serious?"

"There's more. I also need the passes of everybody who went into the Cardiac Care Center on May thirteenth of this year between the hours of seven and nine."

Looking as if somebody had just asked him to drive a getaway car in a bank heist, he crossed his husky arms in front of his chest.

"C'mon, Doc. What's this all about?"

"Al, if this wasn't incredibly important, I wouldn't be here asking you."

"It might help if I knew what you're trying to find out." Morgan stood silent. Al raised his hand. "Forget it," he said. "Don't tell me. I'm probably better off not knowing."

"If you can get me the pictures; I'll look through them and then destroy them." She put her hand to her heart and with a smile added, "I promise."

Al snuck a peek over his shoulder. Sitting on the other side of the office in front of a full wall of monitors, one of the officers manipulated a joystick. He appeared totally immersed in his surveillance.

"You realize, this may be an AHCA violation. I mean with respect to patient privacy issues. There are names on these IDs."

"Maybe," she said, "but technically, a person walking

into an ER hasn't been registered yet, so strictly speaking, they're not a patient and wouldn't be protected under AHCA regulations."

Al drummed the countertop and then rubbed his chin skeptically.

"Give me an hour. I'll have one of my guys drop them off in your office."

"Thanks, Al. You're a lifesaver."

"After you've had a look at these, you're going to destroy them—right?"

"I'll shred them into tiny strips and then incinerate them."

He smiled. "Okay, Doc. But this squares us for the free advice."

"I'd kiss you, but you're on duty."

He laughed. "My wife would shoot us both."

Morgan left the security office and was on her way back to her office when she realized she had completely lost track of the time.

"Shoot," she muttered, checking her watch. It was quarter to five. She reached into her purse and pulled out her cell phone.

Will answered on the second ring.

"Hi. It's Morgan Connolly. I'm so sorry but I got sidetracked and completely forgot about our appointment. Can we reschedule for tomorrow?"

She heard him chuckle. "I guess I've been guilty of the same thing myself more times than I care to admit. I'll check my calendar and give you a call."

"Thanks. I appreciate it."

"You sound a little frazzled. What's going on?"

"I think I may have finally figured out a way to find out if Mason Kaine was really the one responsible for my father's death and the Code Fifteens."

Morgan took a minute to explain her plan.

"Well, if it works, you may have found a way of eliminating a major conflict in your life," Will said.

"I'm sorry about our appointment," she told him again. "I know you wanted to get together."

"Tomorrow will be fine. By the way, if something comes

up tonight and you want to talk, just call me back. My family's out of town. I'll be here all night."

"I may do that," she told him with a genuine appreciation of his thoughtfulness.

Morgan started across the main road that traversed Presbyterian's campus. She was just about to step up on the opposite sidewalk when her phone rang. She checked the caller ID. It was the emergency room.

"This is Dr. Connolly."

"Hi, Morgan. It's Sherry. We have a little situation over here. I think we could use your help."

Morgan had known Sherry Chang for a long time. She was a competent charge nurse who wasn't prone to overreacting.

"What's going on?" Morgan asked.

"Kipplinger's on call today for internal medicine. We called him a little while ago to come see a patient in renal failure. I guess he forgot he was on call. Anyway, he had made plans to get out of the hospital early."

"So, he's been acting out a little."

"Ranting and raving would be a more accurate description. He's been on the warpath since he got here."

"Who's on for us?" Morgan asked.

"Patti. She's doing her best but . . ."

"Great," Morgan moaned under her breath.

Mild-mannered and accommodating, Patti Casoni was an excellent physician. But she was only one year out of residency, and on her best day, no match for the likes of Dr. Stephen Kipplinger.

"Tell Patti not to get into it with him. I'll be right over," Morgan said, turning around and heading back toward the emergency room.

CHAPTER

85

Above the rattling of its faulty air conditioner, Detective Vic Prieto guided the Ford Taurus down Mason Kaine's street.

"That's it," Jody said, gesturing at the two-story palatial brick colonial on the opposite side of the street.

Vic whistled. "Must be nice," he said, pulling up to the curb directly across from the house. "What do you figure? About three million bucks?"

"Four easy," Jody said.

They stepped out of the car into a warm afternoon and started across the street.

"Maybe we should ask the sheriff for a raise," he suggested.

They walked up the path to the front door. Jody rang the bell. A minute passed with no response. She rang it again. Finally, a disconcerted-appearing woman appeared at the door.

They each produced their identification.

"My name is Detective Baxter and this is Detective Prieto. We'd like to speak with Mr. Kaine."

The woman, who reminded Jody of her humorless and overbearing aunt, took a long look at their IDs. She then scanned them both, looking at them as if they were trying to sell her the latest miracle vacuum cleaner. The usual apprehension Jody was accustomed to seeing on the faces of the people she was about to question was absent. From

the entranceway, Jody noticed a tall, muscular man standing under an archway. He was dressed in a dark suit and
stood with his hands clasped in front of him. His gaze was
on them.

"Mr. Kaine has been ill," the woman said officiously. "He's
resting at the moment. If you would like to arrange a time
when—"

Vic wagged his finger and said, "We're police officers. We
don't arrange times. If Mr. Kaine's too sick to speak with us,
then we'll be happy to call nine-one-one and have him transported to the nearest emergency room. We'll let the doctor
decide if he's well enough to talk to us."

Trying to avert any further unpleasantness, Jody handed
the woman one of her cards. "Maybe you could inform Mr.
Kaine we're here and see if he'll agree to speak with us."

The woman folded the card in half, glared at Vic, and then
walked away. Jody watched as she slowly ascended the ornate
staircase.

"That worked," he said.

"The good cop/bad cop thing's getting kind of old. Anybody who watches TV is on to it."

"What do you think?" Vic asked. "Nurse, personal assistant, girlfriend, or all three?"

"I don't have the foggiest," Jody said with a half shrug as
she marveled at the flamboyant furnishings in the huge foyer.

A few minutes passed and Jody heard the clip-clop of footsteps coming down the staircase.

"Mr. Kaine will see you now," the woman said from the
bottom step." Vic winked at Jody and together they crossed
the entranceway. "I would ask that you conduct your business
as quickly as possible. Mr. Kaine needs his rest."

"We understand," Jody said, before Vic could make a re-
grettable wisecrack.

Once they reached the top of the stairs, the woman escorted them down a wide hallway and then past several bed-
rooms until they reached the end of the hall. She knocked

and then pushed the double doors, which opened onto an immense library with twenty-foot ceilings, silk drapes with French pleats, and floor-to-ceiling oak bookcases. Two cherry-stained ladders on brass runners faced each other across the room.

At first, Jody was so lost in the magnificence of the room that she didn't see the man on the other side of the library sitting next to a large bay window. When she finally did notice him, he was staring at her with his arms folded. As a police officer, Jody was used to surprising and unusual situations, but what lay before her left her speechless.

CHAPTER

86

It took Morgan over an hour to defuse the acrimonious situation in the ER.

With undying patience, she finally managed to convince Dr. Kipplinger that it wasn't the emergency room's fault that he had forgotten it was his day on call, nor were they trying, as he put it, to assassinate his patient. Forcing herself not to tell him what she thought of his bully-like antics took every drop of self-restraint she possessed.

When she arrived back at her office, it was well after seven. Kendra had long since left for the day. Morgan was anxious about the Fast-Pass IDs and prayed Al had dropped them off as he'd promised. She unlocked the door, walked straight past Kendra's outer office, and continued into her own. Sitting in the middle of her desk was a large manila envelope. After a brief sigh of relief, she picked it up and sat down. Sliding out its contents, Morgan tried to ignore the fine tremor in her hands.

Al had organized the Fast-Pass photo IDs into two piles: one for each of the dates she had requested. Beginning with the ones from the emergency room, she quickly separated out the women. This left her with approximately fifty photos to go through. Looking for Mason Kaine's Fast-Pass, she studied each ID in the same manner. First she looked at the photograph and then the name printed below it. When she was satisfied the ID was not his, she slid it to the back of the pile.

Morgan had gone through about half of the stack when she came upon a photo she recognized. Although time had partially eroded her recollection of his appearance, the ID was definitely Mason Kaine's. The name printed below the photo confirmed her suspicion. Even though the answer to her question was undeniable, Morgan stared at the photo for almost a minute. The picture of Kaine showed his front row of teeth to be normal. There wasn't even a hint of a gap.

After a soft sigh, she tossed the remainder of the passes back on her desk.

"I knew it," she whispered, putting the photo in the manila envelope.

With the disappointing realization that Mason Kaine was probably not the man responsible for her father's death or the Code 15s, Morgan stood up and walked over to the opposite side of her office. Taking a seat in a small armchair, she could feel the desperation building. Her eye was caught by a large framed photograph of her father at a black-tie reception that sat on the top shelf of her bookcase. The affair was put on by Presbyterian to honor him for his many years of commitment to the hospital. Even though it was another reminder of his death and how much she missed him, she still found herself smiling affectionately.

After a few minutes, Morgan stood up from her chair and walked back to the desk. She reached for the second pile of Fast-Passes, the ones that belonged to the individual who visited the Cardiac Care Center the night Alison Greene died. Based on what she had just learned about Mason Kaine, she had no expectation of finding his photo among them. But she was interested in seeing what I. Ogden looked like. More important, she wanted to compare his ID to those from the emergency room, hoping to find a match.

Morgan flipped through the CCC photos one at a time. She had only turned over a few when she came upon one that instantly made her breath catch. Even though there was a noticeable gap between the man's front teeth, she recognized his face immediately. Driven by a sudden rush of panic, her heart pounded out of her chest. Slowly, her gaze drifted down to the name on the pass. It read *I. Ogden*. Swallowing against a throat that felt as dry as cotton, Morgan grabbed for the original stack of emergency room IDs.

Her hands fumbled as she tossed each rejected ID back on her desk. Even while she frantically sorted through them, a part of her prayed she was wrong. When she was almost to the end of the pile, she came upon the ID she knew would be there. Morgan closed her eyes and forced herself to slow her breathing. After a few seconds, she slowly opened them again. She then held up the two photos, one next to the other. The names were different, but the man was the same.

Morgan reached for her cell phone, brought up the directory, and found the number for Jimmy's Place restaurant. She hit the call button.

"Jimmy's. Can I help you?"

"May I speak with Amelia please?"

"This is Amelia."

"This is Faith Russo's cousin," Morgan began, above the clattering of the restaurant commotion. "I'm sure you remember. We spoke at the restaurant a week or so ago."

"Of course, I remember," Amelia said. "Were you able to find anything out?"

"Actually, that's why I'm calling. I wonder if I could fax you a couple of photos. I'd like you to tell me if you think it's the guy who was interested in Faith."

"You mean Steve?"

"Yes."

"Sure," Amelia told her. She then gave Morgan the fax number. "By the way, he's never been back in the restaurant."

"I'm not surprised," Morgan responded. "Thank you. You can call me back on my cell."

"As soon as I have a look at them, I'll give you a call."

Morgan reached for the two photos and went out into Kendra's office. After running off the copies, she faxed them to Amelia and returned to her desk.

Waiting for her phone to ring, Morgan drummed her blotter. She then picked up the nearest pen and began doodling triangles and circles on a small pad. Every few seconds her eyes found the cell phone. She picked it up to make sure the ringer was set to its maximum volume. She was just about to put it down when it rang.

"Hello.'

"That's Steve," Amelia said. "There's no doubt about it. Where did you get those photos?"

"You wouldn't believe me if I told you," Morgan answered. "Thank you."

What was just a suspicion a few minutes ago was now an incontrovertible fact: the man who killed her father was the same one who murdered Faith Russo. He was also, almost certainly, the mastermind behind the other Code 15s. Morgan believed she now had the information the police couldn't turn a blind eye to. But in an abundance of caution, she decided to get Ben's advice before calling Jody Baxter.

She tapped in his number but after six rings, she got his voice mail.

"Ben. It's me. Please call me as soon as you pick up your messages. It's important."

Morgan checked the time and decided to give him an hour or so before making a final decision on her own regarding calling Jody Baxter. Confident for the first time the end of her nightmare was at hand, Morgan's mind drifted to the events of the day.

All of a sudden, she sat bolt upright in her chair. Her feeling of comfort and safety instantly evaporated. She could sense the color draining form her face, and without giving the matter any further thought, she knew the last place on earth she wanted to be at the moment was sitting alone in her office.

Struggling not to become unglued, she grabbed the two Fast-Pass IDs and pushed them deep into the manila envelope. She worked around her trembling fingers to fasten the envelope closed. She made no effort to gather up the others, leaving them scattered across her desk.

Jumping to her feet, she turned around and snatched her purse from her credenza. When she turned back around to head for the door, she gasped. Standing in her doorway with a friendly smile was the last person she wanted to see.

Openmouthed, Detective Jody Baxter watched as the man in the wheelchair pushed the joystick forward to rotate the chair around.

"I generally don't see people without an appointment but my nurse told me you're from the police."

His stubbly face, ragged gray T-shirt, and frayed flip-flops gave him the appearance more of an agoraphobic recluse than a cunning murderer of indescribable physical strength.

"You're Mason Kaine?" Vic inquired with some uncertainty in his voice.

"I am."

"Do you want to call for backup?" Vic whispered to Jody, who refused to look at her sardonic partner or acknowledge his dim-witted crack.

Kaine guided the wheelchair across the room, bringing it to a stop a few feet in front of them.

"Please excuse my inability to come downstairs," he offered, "but I'm still waiting for my elevator to be repaired."

Still tongue-tied, Jody realized she had to make a decision quickly. While making an apologetic withdrawal seemed attractive and maybe even the most politically correct, something told her to, at least, ask Kaine a few questions.

"We just have a couple of questions for you, Mr. Kaine. It shouldn't take too long."

Appearing annoyed, he exhaled loudly and said, "I suppose you're here about that lunatic, Morgan Connolly."

It was hardly the response Jody expected. Before Vic could say something they'd both regret, Jody jumped back in. "If you don't mind my asking, Mr. Kaine, what would make you think that's our reason for being here?"

"I'm paralyzed, Detective Baxter, not brain-dead. The woman thinks I'm trying to kill her. What I can't figure out is why. If anybody has a reason to be irate to the point of homicide, it's me. A lot of people would have filed a formal complaint of harassment."

"Why do you think she believes you're trying to kill her?" Jody asked.

"Oh, come now, Detective. Would you really have me believe you have no idea what happened to my sons? I think we both know if it weren't for Dr. Connolly's ineptitude, they'd still be alive."

"I'm not a physician, Mr. Kaine, so I'm not in a position to judge Dr. Connolly's competency as a doctor. What makes you think she's been harassing you?"

"For one, she showed up at the car dealership I do business with. She pretended to be somebody she isn't to grill my friend for information about me. Fortunately, he called to alert me to the problem. Obviously, she's lost her grip on reality. It's no secret that Dade Presbyterian and the Medical Board are finally catching up with her. Hopefully, they'll yank her license to practice medicine forever."

"You seem to have a great deal of information about Dr. Connolly. What makes you so sure she's having professional problems?" Jody asked.

Appearing as if his intelligence was being insulted, Kaine said, "I've lived in this area for a long time. I'm not without many close friends, some of whom are doctors at Dade Presbyterian."

Jody suspected that Kaine's flow of information was a lot more sophisticated than he'd have them believe.

Vic asked, "Besides this incident at the car dealership, are you aware of anything else Dr. Connolly's done that might be interpreted as harassment?"

"How about meeting with my ex-wife and pumping her for information? Why would she go to all that trouble of finding out where Adele works, setting up a meeting, and then hounding her for information if she didn't plan to use it for something?"

"Did your ex-wife tell you that?" Jody asked.

"No."

"Then how do you know about the meeting?"

"Adele has a big mouth. She loves to gossip. Suffice it to say, we still travel in some of the same circles."

Jody noticed his hands were wrapped tightly around the armrests of the chair and that they were quivering.

"Would you mind telling me how long have you been in a wheelchair?" she asked.

"About eight months."

"Were you injured?"

"No."

"I assume . . . I mean, are you completely unable—?"

"I am confined to this wheelchair, Detective. I'm paraplegic and completely reliant on this contraption to get around."

"Have you had any direct contact with Dr. Connolly in the past few months?"

He shook his head. "Absolutely not."

"And you're quite certain she hasn't tried to call you or contact you in any way?" Jody asked.

"No," he said, pushing himself up in his chair.

"You realize, Mr. Kaine, that even if you are correct about Dr. Connolly's actions, there's no law against an individual asking questions about somebody else."

"Unless that person has criminal intent . . . or so my attorney tells me." Kaine brought his chair a few feet closer. "If you don't believe Dr. Connolly's done anything wrong, why are you here?"

"She's concerned that you're holding her personally responsible for the deaths of your sons and that you have threatened her with bodily harm."

"I would say she's half right. Anyway, tell her I said to prove it," he said with a self-righteous scoff.

"That's not an answer, Mr. Kaine."

"Maybe I should be the one making that accusation." He paused for a few seconds and then asked, "Before you came over here today with these ridiculous allegations, did you know I was unable to walk?"

"No," Jody answered.

"Has it occurred to you that it would be a bit of a task to assault somebody from a wheelchair?"

"Under most circumstances. I would agree," Vic chimed in.

"Most circumstances?"

"With all due respect, you appear to be a man of means."

Kaine laughed. "Meaning I could hire somebody."

"It's hardly an original idea," Vic said.

"I guess if I were that hell-bent on revenge, I would want the pleasure myself. I wouldn't farm out the job."

"May I ask what happened to put you into a wheelchair?" Jody inquired.

"I have Guillain-Barré syndrome. It's a very rare disorder that otherwise healthy people can acquire after a viral illness. As you can see, I have a rather severe case."

"I assume you can substantiate the—"

"My neurologist's name is Myron Steddman. He practices in Fort Lauderdale. His phone number's in the book. I'll call him and give my permission to release all of my medical records to you." He maintained his silence for a few moments before saying, "Now, does that about do it?"

"Just one more question," Jody said, studying him intently to see his reaction. "Does the name Gideon mean anything to you?"

His expression never changed, nor did he demonstrate any outward signs of apprehension.

"I'm hardly a biblical scholar, but as I recall, Gideon was an angel."

Vic gave Jody's arm a light tug.

"Thank you for your time, Mr. Kaine," he said. "We apologize if we disturbed you."

"We may want to speak with you again," Jody added.

"Maybe next time you could extend me the courtesy of calling first."

Vic didn't say a word until they had left the house and were on their way back to the car. Jody had been his partner long enough to know that once his teasing started, it could be merciless.

"A superhuman killer with extraordinary strength," he said with an obnoxious chuckle.

"I may check out his story anyway."

"Now there's a brilliant idea. I mean, why not take a case that has already been a colossal waste of time and compound the lunacy by continuing to investigate it?"

"I said I *might*."

Vic opened the door for her. While she was getting in, he asked, "What was all that about Gideon?"

"It doesn't matter," she said dismissively. "Let's go."

Vic walked around to the driver's side and got in.

To her surprise, and absent any underpinning of cynicism or sarcasm, he said, "You know as well as I do that Mason Kaine didn't hire somebody to drag Dr. Connolly out into the Everglades and kill her. He's got nothing to do with any of this."

Without saying another word, he started the engine and slowly pulled away from the curb. "I know," Jody said.

At a complete loss for words, Morgan forced a smile. "I was just about to give you a call."

"You sounded pretty upset on the phone," Will said, taking a few steps forward. "I thought I'd take a chance and see if you were still in your office. I thought perhaps you'd like to talk about things."

"That was nice of you, but I'm fine . . . really."

His manner and voice were collected. "Are you sure? You seem very nervous."

"It's the ER. They just called. They're mobbed with patients. I was just on my way over to help out."

"Maybe we should talk for a few minutes before you go."

"I really appreciate the offer, but really, I don't have the time right now."

"Eileen called me again. Bob Allenby's really pressing her for my report."

"I'm a little surprised to hear that. I thought Bob would still be a little preoccupied. His son was seriously injured in a hit-and-run accident. The last I heard he was still up in Gainesville."

"He is. Eileen told me she's been in touch with him by phone and e-mail. It's a shame about Mike," he added. "I told her a little white lie and said my report was practically ready. I'm supposed to fax it to her first thing in the morning. I just want to make sure I'm comfortable telling them you're okay to continue your clinical practice. I'm sure the ER can get along without you for a few minutes," he said, walking over to the door and closing it.

Seeing no way out, she said, "Okay," then, looking at her watch, continued, "but I really don't have—"

"I'll have you out of here in a few minutes," he assured her again, walking over to the door and closing it.

"You can leave it open. There's nobody in my secretary's office."

He looked back at the door, ignored her suggestion, and then sat down. He removed a black leather computer case he was carrying over his shoulder and set it next to him.

"Did you find out anything from those ID pictures?"

Morgan's first impulse was to deny she'd been able to get them, but when she saw him staring at her desk, she chose a different approach. "I looked through them, but it turned out to be a dead end."

She felt his hard look on her. It was followed by a reserved but skeptical grin. "I'm not sure you're being truthful with me," he said.

"That's ridiculous, Will. I have no reason to lie."

"All evidence to the contrary," he said, pointing at the envelope in her hand. "I think you have all the reason in the world to lie." He moved forward in his chair. "I'm guessing you have Mason Kaine's photo right there in that envelope, which means you have mine as well." He interlaced his fingers behind his neck, leaned back, and sighed. "If I told you I was there that night in the emergency room seeing one of my patients, you probably wouldn't believe me."

Seeing no reason to continue the cat-and-mouse game, Morgan shook her head slowly.

"I think we both know you don't have privileges to practice at Presbyterian."

He grinned and then lightly slapped his thighs.

"This is good," he said. "We're definitely making progress. I assume the photo of Mason shows no space between his teeth."

Morgan said nothing.

"I'll take that as a yes," he said. "Knowing how compulsive you are, I'm going to assume you also have the photo IDs that were taken outside the Cardiac Care Center the night Alison Greene died." Will extended his legs, crossing them at the ankles. "When did you first suspect that Mason Kaine had nothing to do with your father's death or the Code Fifteens?"

Morgan was careful to listen to what Will was saying. Her only thought was to keep him calm.

Will renewed his question. "I asked you when did you know it wasn't Mason Kaine?"

"After I was rescued from the Everglades."

"And how did you arrive at that revelation?"

"The man who kidnapped me was quite talkative. He obviously wanted me to think he was Mason Kaine, but some of the things he said didn't hold together."

"For instance?"

"He talked about the night his sons died. He mentioned holding his wife and trying desperately to console her, but his wife was actually his ex-wife, and she was ten thousand miles away in Thailand."

"That would seem like a foolish blunder if he was trying to persuade you he was Mason Kaine."

"Maybe he's been walking around for a long time with more grief than any one person could bear. I'm guessing he just got caught up in the emotion of the moment and slipped."

Morgan watched the same supercilious smirk cross Will's face. "A very interesting observation. I think you mentioned there was more than one thing that made you suspicious."

"He spoke in a very hoarse voice. I've taken care of enough people with laryngitis to know the real thing when I hear it. He was obviously trying to disguise his voice. He also made sure I didn't see his face. Kaine would have no reason for doing that."

"Nor would anybody else who was planning on feeding you to the alligators."

"I think a part of him was subconsciously hoping I'd survive through the night. He hinted about it a couple of times and even sprayed me with insect repellant."

"Why would he go to all that trouble if he wanted you to survive?"

"Maybe making me suffer was more appealing to him than killing me."

Will applauded slowly. An arcane expression spread across his face.

"You keep saying he, Morgan. I think we both know who kidnapped you."

Seeing no reason to retreat now, she said, "Your dentist did an excellent job. How did you find out I was looking for a man with gapped teeth? That's one thing I never mentioned in any of our sessions."

"Your friend Dana provided me with the information. I called her in the ICU and told her I was from the legal department. She was quite willing to talk about Miss Greene's unfortunate death and I. Ogden."

"The anagram was a nice touch," Morgan said, her instinct telling her that Will wouldn't try anything violent in her office.

"I'll take that as a compliment."

"If you don't mind me asking, what's your connection to Andy and Jason Kaine?"

Will stood up and pointed to his watch. "It's getting late. We should be going. We can talk more on the way."

Morgan got up from her chair but remained behind her desk. Looking at him with a stony glare, she said, "I'm not going anywhere with you."

Will sighed and took a step closer to her. He placed his

hands on the edge of her desk. "That would be a bad decision for both you and your baby. My advice is to rethink it."

"There are people all over the place. If you touch me, you won't make it out of the building."

He shook his head slowly. "Don't try and con me, and don't think for an instant I won't kill you right here if you force me to."

"You're too smart for that."

Will paused for a few seconds before responding. His manner remained unruffled, his voice calm.

"This morning, I mailed a report to Eileen regarding your present mental status. It didn't paint a very encouraging picture. It says that in my opinion you're clinically depressed and that you are incapable of safely discharging your clinical responsibilities. It also said that I considered your behavior to be unpredictable and that a period of inpatient psychiatric care with suicide precautions should be considered."

"Nobody will . . ."

Will raised his finger to his lips and then reached inside his sports coat and removed a small black handgun. He raised the gun, leveling the barrel at her forehead. "If you refuse to go with me, I'm going to shoot you. Before you hit the floor, I'm going to call the police. It's a matter of complete indifference to me how long it will take for the first person to arrive. By that time the gun will be in your hand. Nobody will suspect I had anything to do with your death. All I did was witness your suicide. I even tried to stop you, but you wouldn't listen to me."

"Nobody's going to believe that."

"Based on your recent behavior, I think they will. Anyway, it's a moot point because you'll be dead. You should think about something else. When you die, so does your baby. The decision's yours. Refuse to go with me and I'll shoot you right here in your office. If you come, at least you'll prolong the inevitable. I guess if I were in your situation, I would take every precious second I could get. You're a bright woman. Maybe you'll even figure out some way out of this."

Morgan's fear paled in comparison to her rage. Every muscle in her body seemed to spasm at the same moment. With every drop of self-restraint she could summon, she clung to her composure. A few more seconds passed. Will remained silent, his hand holding the gun directly on her. It didn't take Morgan long to realize he was right.

"You're insane," she told him, coming out from behind her desk.

"Not really. At least I'm offering you a chance to live. That's more than you gave my sons." Seeing no good alternative, she started for the door. "Just one thing before we leave," he told her. "If you scream or try anything funny after we leave this office, I'll shoot you in the abdomen. The good news is that you'll have a reasonable chance of surviving. The bad news is—your baby won't. I'm not sure that's something you would ever be able to live with."

"There was no need to kill my father. He had nothing to do with any of this."

"Your father got off easy. He deserved to die a more horrible death."

"Why would you do all those horrible things? Is Mason Kaine blackmailing you?"

"I never met the man."

"Then why would the deaths of his sons fill you with such hatred and revenge? None of this makes any sense."

"To those you have to answer to, it makes perfect sense."

"Stop playing games, Will."

"You were right about one thing, Morgan. I want you to suffer. I want you to feel the same never-ending pain I've had to endure since the night you destroyed my family. Your crime against them was way beyond simple incompetence. It was cruel and depraved."

"Your family? What are you talking about?" she demanded in a voice that did nothing to disguise her frustration. "You just said you never met Mason Kaine. What were his sons to you?"

"Nothing."

"Then why are you so bent on—"

"Let's go," he said. "There'll be plenty of time for questions later."

Morgan made her way slowly out from behind her desk. "Where are we going?"

"North Perry Airport." Morgan stopped and looked at him as if he had misspoken. "Don't look so surprised," he said. "It's about time I took you up on your offer to go flying. And feel free to call me Gideon," he added with a chuckle. "I think you've earned the right."

CHAPTER
89

With his hand wrapped around her forearm, Will led Morgan down the hall to the back stairwell.

They exited the hospital at the far end of the cancer center, directly across the street from the parking garage. Without uncurling his grip, he escorted her across the street, where they took the elevator to the fourth floor. As soon as they stepped off, he gestured toward the opposite side of the parking deck. He said nothing. It was obvious to Morgan he knew precisely where she had parked.

Walking toward her car, Morgan's mind was reeling. For the moment she felt safe but Will was right about one thing; every minute she could steal increased her chances of getting away. She had no doubt there was a method to his madness, but his intent to have her fly him somewhere made no sense to her. Five thousand feet above the ground with her at the controls would be one of the few safe places left to her. She could only surmise that Will's fondness for playing mind games was responsible.

When they reached her car, he extended his hand. "Keys," he said. "And I'll take your cell phone too." Morgan reached into her purse, retrieved both of the items he requested, and handed them to him. Will opened the passenger side door. "Get in."

She complied and then watched him take a careful look

around before casually walking to the driver's side and climbing in. Morgan stared straight ahead in silence. She tried desperately, but she couldn't figure out why Will considered Mason Kaine's family his. She thought about their sessions at his guesthouse and what they had discussed. She flogged her memory to recall everything he had said about his family, hoping to find the clue that would explain his psychotic behavior.

They drove west in an early evening mist. Morgan could see the lights of the airport in the distance. Her mind's eye focused on Will's family portrait she had so admired. She could clearly she his wife and two sons, all of them dressed impeccably in white.

Morgan suddenly turned toward Will.

"My God," she muttered. Finally, after so many weeks, she understood what had driven him mad.

"Will, I'm . . . I'm sorry. I . . . I had no way of knowing."

He said nothing.

"Johnson," she whispered more to herself than him. "Will Johnson," she repeated in a louder tone. "It's such a common last name. I never stopped to . . . I mean it never occurred to me." Morgan stopped to gather herself. "I'm so sorry."

"I'm afraid it's a little late for apologies."

"I should have seen it sooner," Morgan said. "Your backyard was immaculate. Most of my friends with kids have yards that look as if they were hit by a toy tornado. I never saw a bike, a baseball bat, or anything that would suggest children live here. There was never another car in your driveway, and your garage was filled with boxes as if you were getting ready to move."

"Now do you understand why I have been chosen to right this injustice?"

"For weeks," she began slowly, "I've been reading and rereading the charts of every patient I saw that night. But I didn't look at the transcripts of the Fire-Rescue runs until a few days ago. Michael and Matthew Johnson, the boys in the car accident that night—the ones that North Miami Rescue called me about right after Andy Kaine died." She found herself forced to stop and take a deep breath. "Your sons were the two boys we sent to Ryder Trauma Center."

"Not we; you. It was your decision to have them transported all the way to Ryder. They both died because of your stupidity. When the police called to tell me about the accident, they told me to go to Dade Presbyterian. They didn't know you had instructed the paramedics to take them to Ryder."

"I was following protocol, Will. Dade Presbyterian is not a state-designated pediatric trauma center. I was doing what I thought would be best for them. Any emergency room physician would have done the same."

"I believe the state trauma protocol says that any seriously injured child should be transported to the nearest facility for stabilization. It doesn't matter if that hospital is a pediatric trauma center or not."

"That's true, but your sons weren't unstable."

"The paramedics disagreed. They told you they wanted to bring Michael and Matthew to Presbyterian, but you instructed them not to. They were only ten minutes away, for God's sake. There was an accident on I-95. The trip to Ryder took almost forty minutes."

"But, I . . . I had no way of knowing that."

"Maybe if you had had the decency to call and check on them, you would have. The pediatric trauma surgeon on call that night told us that Michael and Matthew would have survived if they had received more urgent medical attention. Did you even know they had died?"

"Ryder notified us a couple of days later. You're right. I should have called, but we were so busy that night."

"Too busy to take five minutes to come out and talk to me in person? Too busy to explain to me that my sons had been in a major car accident and were being transported to Ryder?"

"I don't recall if I came out or not but—"

"I'll save you the trouble of trying to remember. You didn't. You sent your first-year flunky resident instead."

"The call from the paramedics regarding your sons came in right after Andy Kaine died. I had already been informed that Jason was only minutes away. I spent the next two hours trying to save him. We stayed incredibly busy until five in the morning."

"Even if you were too busy to check on my sons, you could have called at the end of your shift or the next day to check on them."

"There were so many sick patients that night," Morgan tried to explain again.

"And you think because you were doing your job that exonerates you for your incompetent treatment of my children?"

"I don't think I was incompetent. That's what I'm trying to explain to you. I couldn't—"

"For months, I called the administration at Presbyterian. All I wanted was some answers. But all I got was lip service. Nobody would take ownership for the blunder. I was referred from one inept junior administrator to the next. Finally, I was pawned off on an administrative intern, six weeks out of college."

"I'm sure they tried to explain things to you. It was a terrible tragedy, but what else could they have done?"

"I wanted them to show me a little more compassion than was shown to my boys. I wanted them to promise me . . . to assure me that no child would ever be hurt again." With a fisted hand, Will slammed the steering wheel. His eyes exploded in rage. "You said a minute ago that you never saw my wife. Do you know why? It's because she's an emotional cripple bordering on catatonia. She can barely get out of bed."

"All I can say is that I'm sorry for what you've had to go through."

Will turned into the airport. His voice suddenly returned to an impassive tone, "I think you've already mentioned that."

He pulled up to her hangar and turned off the engine. Sliding his hands high on the steering wheel, he stared out of the windshield for a time. Finally he sat back in his seat. He turned to Morgan. He looked down at his watch.

"We're running out of time. Get out."

CHAPTER

90

Will led Morgan to the front of the hangar.

A single roof-mounted flood sprayed a sparse amount of light over the area.

"Open the lock," Will told her.

Morgan spun the combination until it popped open. Together they swung the metal door open. Five minutes later the Cirrus was out of the hangar and Morgan was preflighting the airplane.

While she checked the prop, she said, "I'll need to know where we're going. I have to file a flight plan."

He chuckled and shook his head. "That's bullshit and we both know it. Finish up and let's get going."

Morgan didn't see any reason to protest. She wasn't surprised Will knew she was lying. Having some idea of how his mind worked, she assumed he had done a little homework on basic flight procedures. Once Morgan had completed her preflight, she and Will climbed into the plane. Will threw the leather computer case on the backseat.

She was still sure that the safest place for her was in the air. After starting the engine, she radioed flight control, got clearance, and taxied out to the active runway. There were no other aircraft on final approach or waiting to take off. She was given immediate clearance.

Morgan pushed the throttles forward and started her take-off roll. When she attained enough speed, she pulled the controls back, easing the Cirrus into the air. With the centerline of the runway disappearing behind her, she retracted her landing gear and climbed out to the west.

"Where are we going?"

"Set a course for Freeport."

"In the Bahamas?"

"Yes."

"You want me to fly out over the Atlantic Ocean at night?"

"You're an instrument-rated pilot. Disorientation or vertigo shouldn't be a problem. Stop trying to con me."

Will waited until Morgan consulted her charts and then set a course for Freeport. The air was smooth and ten minutes later, they were over the east coast of Florida. Morgan watched as the lights of Broward County faded behind her. It was a cloudless evening with a brilliant full moon clinging to the night sky. Below, the running lights of dozens of freighters dotted the ocean like a distant galaxy.

"Tell me why," Will said.

"What are you talking about?"

"You said in the car that Dade Presbyterian's not a state-designated pediatric trauma center. I'm simply asking why."

Fighting to keep her tone subdued, Morgan said, "To become a pediatric trauma center is a very complicated process. It takes—"

Trampling on her words, he said, "Four years ago, the state informed you that Dade County desperately needed another pediatric trauma center. They had concluded that Presbyterian was the best staffed and in the best geographic area to assume that responsibility."

"That's true, but I—"

"You were the director of Emergency Medicine at the time.

The hospital relied heavily upon you and the other leaders of
the medical staff such as your father for guidance. But the two
of you came out strongly against it."

"Our children's hospital is still in its infancy. It was our
opinion that our emergency department hadn't yet developed the expertise to competently run a pediatric trauma
center."

"Then you should have seen to it that you got the staff,
equipment, and whatever else you needed to comply with the
state's request."

"I'm not disagreeing with you, but that's not the type of
thing you accomplish overnight. It wasn't that we abandoned
the idea. We just decided that we needed a few years to create
the appropriate infrastructure to support a pediatric trauma
center."

"That was crap for the customers then, and it still is. Do
you recall what Bob Allenby's official response to the state
was?"

"I'm sorry. I don't," Morgan answered.

"He told them that after careful deliberation, the hospital board had concluded that a pediatric trauma center would
be an economic burden that Dade Presbyterian couldn't
shoulder."

"That's the point of view of the hospital administration.
My decision to advise against a pediatric trauma center had
nothing to do with either business or politics."

"Bob and the board hid behind the lie of limited financial
resources, but less than six months later, they announced
their plan to pour millions into a new, state-of-the-art Cardiac Care Center. What they didn't mention was that the
county already had four such centers, all of which were cash
cows. I guess the projected return on investment justified
the expense in constructing a new cardiac program but not a
pediatric trauma center. If there was any hope of starting a
trauma center for children it died fast on the vine when Bob

and the medical staff leadership decided to support a new cardiac center."

After weeks of being plagued and tormented by the same question, Morgan finally understood why the focus of Will's obsession was the Cardiac Care Center.

Continuing her climb out over the Atlantic in gentle air, she said, "I'm not disputing your analysis of what happened. I'm saying it doesn't justify killing innocent doctors and patients."

"You act as if I had a choice in all this. I've already told you; I was chosen to correct this injustice you all perpetrated. You surprise me."

"In what way?"

"You're an emergency room physician, for God's sake. The number one killer of children in this country is trauma. Why is building another heart center more important than saving children's lives?"

"I'm not trying to say it is. I'm only—"

His voice filled with anger. "Many of those who championed the Cardiac Care Center—the ones responsible for this travesty—have to answer for the sins."

"Alison Greene did nothing to you."

"My sons are dead today because of her father's strong recommendation to the hospital to forge ahead with their plan to put up another heart center in Dade County."

Morgan could sense Will's grip on reality was becoming more brittle with each passing minute. Unfortunately, she had no way of knowing just how close to a complete psychotic breakdown he was. In the absence of a better plan, she decided the best thing to do was allow him to keep talking. She scanned her instruments. Noting her altitude was now three thousand feet, she dropped her nose a little to maintain her present altitude.

"Do you mind if I ask you a question?" she asked, still hoping his present state of mind might allow him to give her a rational answer.

"I don't mind."

"Killing innocent patients won't bring your sons back. Making Bob Allenby, Cam Greene, and myself suffer by hurting the people we love won't either. So, what do you gain by all this? Is this about nothing more than revenge?"

"Revenge? You continue to disappoint me, Morgan. I was hoping you'd be less obtuse. None of this has anything to do with revenge. It's about justice, and sometimes the only way to administer justice is by the most extreme measures." Morgan was stunned by the distinct absence of any remorse in his voice. "My one great disappointment is that you won't be around to be professionally humiliated by the state medical board."

"Was it worth Faith Russo's life?"

"She could have lived until she was a hundred and not have died for a more righteous purpose. The Cardiac Care Center is a scar on the face of decent health care. It has to be discredited to a point where AHCA has no choice but to close it down permanently. And those who created it in favor of a pediatric trauma center have to be held morally accountable. They have to answer to God. There's no other way."

"And you're the one responsible for the delivery of this justice?"

"I'm God's instrument on earth. He has entrusted me with this mission."

"I have to contact Freeport for landing instructions."

Will laughed. "It's a little early for that. Just stay on your present course and altitude." Out of the corner of her eye, she noticed Will was intently studying the instrument panel.

Morgan's sense of safety was suddenly shattered. A bolt of anxiety hit her and then spiraled down her spine.

"You're a pilot," she uttered.

He smiled. "I'm pretty new at it, but I do have my private pilot's license."

Flogging her self for her stupidity, she sat frozen in silence.

For the first time she felt that the finality of her predicament was undeniable.

"What are you going to do?" she asked.

"That's entirely up to you. You have choices."

"Still playing games, Will?" Morgan asked, noticing a mild cramp in her lower abdomen. Dreading what was likely to follow, she tightened her stomach muscles.

He laughed. "I assure you. This is no game. I'm going to slow this aircraft down to almost its stall speed. You will then open the door and get out. By the time I land you'll be winding your way through some shark's digestive system."

"You sick son of a bitch," she screamed. "You'll never get away with this."

He chuckled. "Of course I will. I have a nice, secluded airstrip all picked out. Within a day, your plane will be disassembled and its parts sent to South America. This time there won't be any helicopter to save you. The FAA will investigate, but they'll just assume you went up for an evening flight and never came back. It's happened before to a lot better pilots than you."

Having no doubt that Will was deadly serious in his intentions, she said flatly, "I won't jump."

"That's fine. As I told you, you have choices." He pointed to his computer case in the backseat. "I've brought something along that will help you."

Morgan looked over her shoulder. The case was right behind her seat. She watched him unbuckle his seat belt and turn in his chair. Hoping to distract him, she prayed he'd make the only mistake that might save her.

"The paramedics who were called to the scene of the accident told me your sons were stable. If you don't mind me asking, how did they die?"

"One had a brain injury and the other had a massively collapsed lung."

"A collapsed lung?" Morgan asked. "So, killing my father

by injecting air into his chest to create the same injury was some kind of sick poetic justice?"

Ignoring her question, he asked, "What's it going to be?"

"I'm not jumping," she told him again.

"A bullet to the head it is, then," he said with a relaxed shrug.

chapter 91

Unable to reach his case, Will stretched his upper body further into the backseat.

With her eyes glued on the flight instruments, Morgan quickly pulled her seatbelt as tight as she could. She then yanked the controls hard to the left. The high-powered aircraft responded instantly, snapping over into an inverted position. The force of gravity sent Will hurtling out of his seat. Even above the engine's deafening whine, Morgan could hear the thud of his head and neck slamming against the plane's ceiling.

Will's initial cry of pain faded into a series of disoriented moans. After a few seconds, Morgan rolled the plane back to its normal flight path. As she'd guessed, he was conscious but dazed. Holding his head with both hands, he rocked back and forth. His eyes looked as if he were a fighter on the verge of being counted out.

Fearing he would quickly come around, Morgan slapped and punched Will's head wildly with her right hand while her left struggled to keep control of the airplane. With each blow she summoned every particle of strength she could. After less than a minute, Morgan became exhausted. Her fist throbbed with pain and she could feel blood dripping between her knuckles.

Grunting and heaving one exhausted breath after another,

she let her hand fall to her side. She looked over at Will. He was still in a daze. She stole a few seconds to check her flight instruments. When she turned to look at him again, he had opened his eyes and was looking directly at her. The rage in his face sent a renewed wave of terror flashing through her.

To her surprise he didn't lunge in her direction. Instead, he struggled to push himself forward. Morgan's momentary confusion ended when she saw him stretch his arms for the controls. Fearing he'd get control of the plane, Morgan sent the Cirrus into a series of snap rolls. She was well accustomed to aerobatic maneuvers, and even in the presence of her pregnancy, she suffered no motion sickness with its usual incapacitation. With Will banging around the cabin like a wasp in a glass jar, she prayed he wouldn't be as fortunate.

The cabin was suddenly filled with the reverberating sound of metal. Before Morgan felt the spiral of cold air fill the cabin, she knew exactly what had happened. Will's door was no longer secure. Hearing nothing from him and hoping he was unconscious, Morgan decided to resume level flight. The maneuver only took a few seconds. Will was now upright in his chair with his head cocked to the right. He was breathing heavily. He had somehow managed to grab hold of one side of his seat belt. When she saw him reach for the other half, she again rolled the plane ninety degrees to the right. The new attitude sent Will crashing into his door. The force of his shoulders sprung the already tenuous lock and sent the door swinging open into the night.

With his weight and gravity working against him, Will's upper body slipped farther into the door frame. The only thing separating him from an uncontrolled freefall into the ocean was his death grip on his chair. Morgan's eyes flashed back and forth between Will and her flight instruments. To her astonishment, he pulled one of his hands from the seat, holding it out in front of himself, motionless. And then, out of complete stillness, his hand shot out at her. Finding her right forearm, his fingers slashed through her skin. The force of his grasp tightened, his fingernails plunging deeper into the soft tissues as if they were searching for bone. She struggled to free herself, but his grip was far too powerful.

Morgan knew the only thing saving her was to keep her right wingtip pointing toward the ocean and Will pinned in the doorframe. Her eyes flashed over at him long enough to see his face wild with rage. The thunderous blasts of air continued to fill the cabin. Morgan could see him struggling to pull himself back into the cabin. When those attempts failed, he managed to roll on his back. From that position, he began kicking madly at Morgan's right shoulder and chest. Dodging from side to side in her seat, she tried desperately to avoid his frantic blows.

Finally, she felt Will's grip on her arm weaken. Perhaps it was from exhaustion, but the reason made little difference to her. She amassed whatever strength was left to her and ripped her arm away. Once free from his grasp, she reached down to the left of her seat and pulled up a small fire extinguisher.

Will was clinging with both hands to fight the force of gravity wrenching him out of the plane. Without a shred of hesitation, Morgan wheeled the extinguisher across her lap and then slammed it into the back of his right hand. His guttural scream echoed above the howling wind. His bloodied fingers flattened out, quivered for a few seconds, and then slipped from the chair. With his grip now weakened, his right shoulder slipped outside the cabin.

For the first time she saw frenzy and desperation in his eyes. The only thing keeping him in the airplane was his opposite hand clutching the metal frame of his seat. His eyes locked on her, he made no pleas to save himself. Wrapping her fingers more firmly around the fire extinguisher, she elevated it over her shoulder. It would have been an easy enough matter to strike Will's other hand, but she couldn't.

Paralyzed with indecision, Morgan remained locked in a silent, icy stare with him. After a few more seconds passed, she realized he was successfully using his injured hand to pull himself back into his seat. She watched his heaving chest and could see the sweat pouring from his brow.

He stopped for a moment. Struggling to catch his breath, he screamed, "I'll kill you."

Filling her lungs to capacity, all she could think about was Will's sadistic murder of her father.

"You sick son of a bitch," she screamed, launching the fire extinguisher directly at his face.

The canister rotated a half turn before thumping him directly where Morgan had intended. His head snapped backward, tearing his grip loose. Morgan spun her head away and closed her eyes. His final scream was a piercing one that faded into the black abyss. When she looked back, she saw nothing except the open door.

Morgan didn't have time to consider what she had just lived through. Thinking for even an instant she was out of harm's way would probably prove to be a fatal error in judgment. She was now in a predicament that many a pilots considered a true nightmare. She was flying at a hundred twenty miles an hour with an open door. Her first move was to return the Cirrus to a normal flight configuration and begin a slow turn back to the west. Once she was on a course heading back to Florida, she picked up the radio, contacted flight control, and declared an emergency.

Following her emergency flight procedures to the letter, Morgan made a picture-perfect approach and touched down at the Hollywood–Fort Lauderdale airport thirty minutes later. Watching the emergency vehicles approach, she reached down, rubbed her abdomen, and began crying.

EPILOGUE

TWO WEEKS LATER

Ben and Morgan left her apartment and rode the elevator down to the lobby.

Ben had called ahead and had the doorman bring his car around to the front. After helping Morgan in, he got in on his side and started the engine.

"I heard from the medical board late yesterday afternoon," she said.

"You didn't say anything."

"We were having such a good time last night, I didn't want to talk about anything remotely related to the hospital."

"I assume the news was good."

"Their e-mail wasn't definite, but it seems like they've decided to drop the investigation."

"That's great news," Ben said, pulling out onto A1A.

With no enthusiasm in her voice, she said, "Unlike Bob Allenby and the hospital board, they probably won't feel compelled to apologize."

"Bob may surprise you. He's a little preoccupied right now. By the way, have you heard anything about his son?"

Morgan smiled. "He's actually doing better than anybody expected. He's already in rehab. Bob said his doctors expect a complete recovery." She paused for a few seconds. Her face became somber. "That's more than I can say for Will Johnson."

"You mean the man who ran him over? C'mon, Morgan. We've talked about this. You have to quit beating yourself up about what happened. You're lucky to be alive, for God's sake. Will Johnson was criminally insane. He murdered your father in cold blood and would have done the same to you. How can you feel any remorse for this guy?"

"He was sick, Ben."

"So what? The circumstances didn't exactly lend themselves to having him committed for long-term inpatient psychiatric treatment." Ben shook his head. "It's not as if you had some other option."

"I'm just saying that maybe with some help and medication he could have—"

Ben downshifted as he eased back down below the speed limit. "You need to let this go . . . at least for this morning. The only thing that really matters is that your baby's fine and that your professional life is back to normal."

She smiled. "What's the big surprise? Where are we going?

"I thought we could go down to South Beach. The Delano has a great brunch."

She whistled softly. "Very classy."

"It's an all-you-can-eat deal. It should be perfect for you." Morgan laughed. Ben cleared his throat in a way that betrayed he had something else on his mind.

"Ask me," she said.

"What do you say to taking a few days off?"

She grinned. "What did you have in mind?"

"I figured we could take the new jet down to St. Kitts. I've been looking for a reason to stretch her legs. There's a great Four Seasons down there."

"You're spoiling me," she told him as she leaned over and put her arm around his shoulders. "If I didn't know better, I'd say you have a little thing for me."

Ben slowed to a stop at a red light and looked over at Morgan. "Actually, it's a big thing."

"What makes you so sure?"

"My father once told me that he fell in love with my mother before they ever met. I didn't understand what he meant until I met you."

Ben's confession left Morgan speechless. Had it not been for the deafening blast of the SUV's horn from behind them, their kiss would have stopped traffic for a long time.

ABOUT THE AUTHOR

Gary Birken, M.D., is the author of the medical thrillers *Error in Judgement*, *Final Diagnosis*, *Plague*, *Embolus*, and *Code 15*. He presently lives in Hollywood, Florida, where he serves as the surgeon in chief of the Joe DiMaggio Children's Hospital. Please visit his website at http://garybirken.com.

Don't miss the page-turning suspense, intriguing characters, and unstoppable action that keep readers coming back for more from these bestselling authors...

Tom Clancy
Robin Cook
Patricia Cornwell
Clive Cussler
Dean Koontz
J.D. Robb
John Sandford

Your favorite thrillers and suspense novels come from Berkley.

penguin.com